I0589266

Praise for Final Fling

"I absolutely **love** the setting for this piece! You have **nailed it**."
Judge, Writers League of Texas, Manuscript Contest

For anybody who **loves a good mystery**, I HIGHLY recommend this series and this book in particular! The concept in this book is my favorite so far! BONUS FUN-There is an element in here that seems completely implausible but is based on a true story.
Mary H., Librarian and Writing Blogger

I loved it! Plot and characterization: **Masterful**. I did not see the end coming at all. [It] brought to mind a modern day, and much more accessible, Brigadoon. An **excellent and enjoyable** read! Where do I get the previous books?
Kim S., Editor and Educator

FIVE STAR REVIEW – Foster breathes new life into the cozy genre with a **suspenseful and clever** murder mystery that keeps you guessing until the end. Full of originality and unlike any cozy mystery you've read. Maggie Foster has created a world that will make you want to join the town of Loch Lonach and be part of the community. *Final Fling* is a **must-read** and a **must-have** for every mystery reader as it possesses true **originality** and an upbeat spirit with Scottish charm, a suspenseful murder mystery, and a unique world view.
Reviewed by Liz Konkel for Readers' Favorite

Would you risk losing everything for a chance at something better?

The Beverwyck Homestead inhabitants were used to harsh winter weather. Not so the visitors from Texas. When Jim Mackenzie and Ginny Forbes decide to take a Sunday afternoon stroll in the pristine wonderland outside their windows, they find their nerves and their wits tested. Lovely to look at, nature can't always be trusted and they find themselves literally out on limb, with death only an icy misstep away.

SIGN ME UP!

https://dl.bookfunnel.com/et9yw1y0qw

Click to join the Loch Lonach Community.

Get a **FREE** Short Story and access to insider news, Scottish lore, and entertaining details about life on the Loch Lonach Homestead.

FINAL FLING

DEDICATION

This work, the fourth in the series, is dedicated to the world's tinkerers, both amateur and professional, the scientists and engineers who solve problems in novel ways because they don't know it can't be done, so it doesn't stop them. Creativity, ingenuity, perseverance, and above all curiosity, with these, humans can conquer anything.

In addition, I wish to thank:
- John Orlando, who introduced me to Mama Dupree
- The Firewheel Fictionistas Writers' Group for their continued support and assistance
- Members of the Scottish community here and across the world who have given generously of their time and encouragement
- The tinkerers in my own life, particularly my father, who taught me how to learn
- My content experts, beta readers, and ARC team
- My long-suffering editor and brainstorming partner, Mary Foster Hutchinson, without whom none of these books would have been possible

ACKNOWLEDGMENTS

The Mackenzie Dress Clan Tartan is listed as WR1981 on the Scottish Tartans World Register.

The Anatole France quote is from *The Crime of Sylvestre Bonnard*

PR UNCIAL FONT

The Celtic font used on the covers, in the titles, and for the chapter headings in this series is PR Uncial, created by Peter Rempel. It has been a continuing source of delight throughout this endeavor and I am happy to have this opportunity to tell him so. It is free for personal use. You can download it here: https://www.dafont.com/pr-uncial.font

INSTALLING PR UNCIAL

Starting in 2018, Amazon released an update to its Kindle e-readers allowing the user to install custom fonts. Here is the link to the article with instructions on how to do that:

https://the-digital-reader.com/2019/01/02/how-to-use-kindles-new-custom-font-feature/

For Kobo e-readers, the instructions are here: https://goodereader.com/blog/e-book-news/how-to-add-custom-fonts-to-your-kobo-e-reader

DISCLAIMER:

Dear Readers:

This is a work of fiction. That means it is full of lies, half-truths, mistakes, and opinions. Any resemblance to any actual person, living or dead, is unintended and purely coincidental.

Similarly, the businesses, organizations, and political bodies are mere figments of the author's overactive imagination and are not in any way intended to represent any actual business, organization, group, etc.

Some of the locations mentioned actually exist, but the reader is warned that the author has re-shaped Heaven and Earth and all the mysteries of God to suit herself and begs the reader, for the sake of the story, to overlook any discrepancies in fact.

FINAL FLING

Loch Lonach Mysteries
Book Four

by Maggie Foster

“In any given moment we have two options: to step forward into growth or step back into safety.”

Abraham Maslow

“All changes, even the most longed for, have their melancholy; for what we leave behind us is a part of ourselves; we must die to one life before we can enter another.”

Anatole France

Cover design by M. Hollis Hutchinson

Foster, Maggie.
    Final fling: Loch Lonach mysteries, book four / Maggie Foster

ISBN (pbk)
    ISBN-13: 978-0-9989858-6-2

ISBN (epub)
    ISBN-13: 978-0-9989858-7-9

Fonts used by permission/license. For sources, please visit lochlonach.com

The Problem

with competition, of whatever kind,
is that someone must lose. And, more often than not,
after the judgment is handed down,
someone must pay.

CAST OF CHARACTERS

Ginny Forbes	An ICU nurse
Jim Mackenzie	An Emergency Room physician
Angus Mackenzie ("Himself")	The Laird of Loch Lonach, Jim's grandfather
Caroline Cameron	Ginny's Best Friend Forever
Alan Christie	Caroline's boyfriend
Hue Tran	A Dallas Police Crimes Against Persons Unit Detective
Blair Jamieson	A Highland Dance and Family Law Judge
Vanessa Ballantyne	The local haggis expert
Gary Feldman	A bereaved father
Wallace Hunter	A budding caber tosser
Josephine Dupree	An expert in Scottish witchcraft

Loch Lonach is a Scottish community established before Texas became a Republic in the geographic region that would become Dallas. It has retained its culture and identity. Loch Lonach boasts its own schools, police force, churches, and other civic institutions. The head of the community is the Laird, currently Angus Mackenzie.

Chapter 1

Friday Afternoon
Highland Games Athletic Field

There was a pause while the heavy-weight champion in the McLeod kilt grasped the narrow end of the chosen tree, lifted it, then waited for the stars to align. When he was ready, the massive load balanced, the space before him clear, he took a breath, and with a mighty bellow, tossed it into the air.

It rose and wheeled, slowing as it reached apogee, all eyes riveted on its flight. Even time slowed, in deference to the marvel.

The same force that brought the apple down on Newton's head altered the log's trajectory. It hung motionless for a moment, then fell, slamming into the dirt, sending shock waves into the stands. The air reverberated with the sound, mingled with the collective sigh of the watchers, and the return of speech, soft at first, then gaining strength. Another time, perhaps. He could try again, another time.

Ginny Forbes stood, rigid and silent, at the edge of the Heavy Athletics field. Her braid hung down her back, but the wind was behind her. It pulled the shorter strands of hair free, making a titian halo around her face. She had one hand up, to shade her eyes, the other on the talisman that hung from her neck. The angle of the light explained her furrowed brow, and narrowed eyes, but a sharp observer might have seen more in her bloodless cheeks, and the intensity with which she watched the demonstration. She flinched when the caber hit.

"Wow! I've never been this close before. Pretty impressive!"

Ginny glanced over at her best friend, forcing herself to relax. She let go of the talisman. "We're probably safe, as long as we stay on this side of the fence."

Caroline nodded. "That's my plan."

Three burly men in kilts, heavy gloves, and Highland Games tee shirts turned to face the stands, the tools of their athletic trade on the ground beside them. The corner of Ginny's mouth curved as she listened.

"Ye think ye can pick up heavy things and toss them aroond like toys, 'cause ye see the men do it. Yer big and yer brave and yer Scottish, sae how hard canna be?" This produced a round of laughter from the crowd.

"Harder than ye think." The instructor crossed his bulky arms and looked at the collection of well-formed young men from the community. It was tradition at the Games to invite any interested person to a free caber class. It was always well attended and often produced new recruits.

"The goal is tae *turn* th' caber end o'er end. Ye lift it, toss it in tae th' air, flip it and—if ye've done it right—it lands in a straight line in front o' ye, a perfect turn." He glanced over at the larger of the other two men. "Wee William, there, holds th' North American record for th' highest number o' perfect tosses." He addressed the record-holder. "Can ye tell the lads th' secret o' yer success?"

Wee William nodded. "When I was a bairn, I practiced tossing my cookies. By the time I was in high school, I could hit the bowl from across the room."

Ginny was still laughing when Caroline turned to face her,

one arm draped over the rail. "I'm going to miss this."

"What are you talking about?"

"Sharing things. Spending time together. Girl stuff."

"I'm not dying, just getting married."

Caroline nodded, a half-smile on her face. "I know, but Jim's going to expect you to spend your free time with him."

"Oh, Caroline!" Ginny crossed the space between them and pulled her friend into a tight hug. "He's not going to take your place! He can't. He's a man."

It was true, marriage would bring changes, *but not this one*, she thought to herself. "I won't let him come between us."

Caroline shoved Ginny away, a bright smile on her face. "We'll see how long that lasts. Here he comes."

Jim strode up to them, looking from one girl to the other, one eyebrow rising. "What are you two doing?"

"Just admiring the kilts," Ginny explained.

"The kilts, huh? Not the men in them?"

"Both—a kilt's no fun if it's not occupied."

Jim snorted, then sidled up beside Ginny and slipped an arm around her waist. The trio fell silent as the lesson took on a more serious note, the instructor outlining the physical danger of lifting, of failing to lift, of losing control of, and of getting in the way of a caber. A traditional caber measured nineteen and one-half feet in length and weighed one hundred and seventy-five pounds. Ginny looked up at Jim, his shoulders and biceps impressive, even in this company.

"Want to try?"

He shook his head. "No, thank you. I have no wish to injure myself just before our wedding." He smiled down at her, the expression on his face bringing a rush of color to her cheeks.

It was a bit inconvenient that the Games fell only three weeks before her wedding, but they could spare the two and a half days it took to help set-up on Friday, then work the Games on Saturday and Sunday, then help tear down on Sunday evening. It was only once a year.

"Come," Jim said. "I want to show you something." They took their leave of Caroline and headed for the vendor area.

Ginny lifted her face into the breeze. The day was glorious and the weatherman predicted the same for the following forty-eight hours. Perfect Texas weather for a perfect Texas Games. Her spirits soared as they passed tartan banners flapping from every stanchion and tent pole, and heard the pipers warming up in the middle distance.

Jim led her to the far corner of the Games grounds, to a booth tucked up against the outer fence, guarded by a heavy gate. He spoke to the vendor, who stopped what he was doing to wait on them, reached into a hidden stash, and brought out a tray of rings.

"He says he can resize them, if needed." Jim picked one out, and placed it in her hand. "Will these do?"

Ginny looked down and saw a narrow gold band decorated with a Celtic knot, the pattern weaving in and out, curving back on itself to form an infinite loop. She touched it with the tip of her finger, the silken metal soft and warm and heavy.

"Oh, Jim!"

He took the ring from her and slipped it on her finger. "And here is mine." It was a larger version of the same ring.

Ginny didn't think she had ever seen anything so exquisite in her entire life, but perhaps it was the meaning attached to those rings that took her breath away. "They're perfect!"

The vendor helped make sure they had the right sizes, and went over each with a jeweler's loupe to check for flaws before packing them into a small box and handing them to Jim. The purchase complete, he wished them joy and regretted that he would not be in town to dance at their wedding.

Ginny stepped from the shadow of the vendor tent into the

dazzling afternoon sun, its rays no match for the gold circlets now concealed in Jim's sporran—and tripped over the pavement. Jim caught her as she fell, and drew her into his arms.

"Three weeks, Ginny," he whispered. "Three more weeks."

* * *

The sun disappeared behind the trees leaving the sky streaked with rose and the grounds sinking into the half-light that precedes darkness. This was the gloaming and into it came the clans.

Ginny made her way to where the Forbes family was assembling. This would be the last year she would march with them. On May first, she would become a Mackenzie.

She looked around at the cheerful chaos. The Calling of the Clans had its roots in the muster of military-aged men, but today women and children and those past fighting age also participated. Each clan carried a banner with its badge and name upon it, to make sure the onlookers knew whom they were cheering. Most of those present were participants, but there were always some who came for the spectacle, and stayed for the ceilidh which followed.

Ginny heard the pipers approaching and felt her blood stir. She was sure bagpipes were encoded in Scottish DNA. You either loved them or you hated them. There was no middle ground.

In response to the Pipe Major's signal, a tall figure rose from his seat on the dais and stepped to the microphone. White headed, ramrod straight, in full dress kilt with two eagle feathers in his bonnet, Angus Mackenzie, the Laird of Loch Lonach, looked out over the crowd. The pipes would lead, followed by the clans. As they passed the reviewing stand,

Angus would call each clan and the clan would answer. It was an exciting beginning to a weekend full of promise.

A flash of something bright caught Ginny's eye and she turned to look. The woman making her way down into the bleachers stood out. Of African descent, she was wearing something long and sweeping, the multi-colored fabric almost obscured by strings of beads and silver bracelets. The woman's attire was unusual for the setting, but her ancestry was not. Anyone could be a Scot. The blood is strong and had been flung across the globe many times. Ginny's curiosity was not for the color of this woman's skin, but for the fact that she appeared to be an insider. Ginny had seen her earlier, setting up shop in the clan tent area, her offering to the public as yet a mystery. But there was no time to consider the puzzle further. The procession had started.

There were representatives of almost every clan here. The Scots had settled in most of early Texas and recruits to the Loch Lonach Homestead had been added throughout the intervening two hundred years. Visitors, too, came from all over the world for the Games and the Gatherings, and to march with their kith and kin. Ginny had seen Jim greeting the Douglases and recalled his mother was a Douglas. He had a half dozen well-grown cousins present, all with families.

The Forbes were positioned early in the parade, the Mackenzies closer to the tail. Ginny stopped in front of the reviewing stand, turned to face the Laird, and shouted with the rest of her people, "Grace Me Guide!" It was a shame her brother, Alex, could not be here, but his job had forced him to choose, and it was more important that he stood at Jim's side as best man at the wedding. There would be a family reunion then. Three weeks.

Her situation was about to change in more ways than just her position in the line-up. She surveyed the shifting mass of color, her eyes darting from bonnet to tartan to laughing face, each a memory, each a part of her soul, thinking about the fabric of their lives—then found herself poked in the ribs by the woman behind her. She turned and followed the Forbes banner to her place on the field.

* * *

As tradition demanded, the clans had vowed allegiance to the Laird, the pipes had led them into battle, and the party had begun on time. Ginny went up on her toes, looking around at the host crowding into the fiddle tent.

This was a premier event, a chance for the paid performers to come together with local talent for an impromptu jam session. In addition to the half-dozen fiddles, there were usually flutes and drums and at least one piper. Since many of the performers were world-class, it was always well attended.

It was impossible to sit still. Even the elderly and infirm could be seen tapping their toes in time to the music. Everyone else was on the floor. Tiny tots bounced up and down while their older siblings tried to imitate the adults. The Country Dancers reeled and whooped in the space in front of the stage. The Highland dancers and their Irish counterparts were off on the peripheries, dancing solo and unselfconsciously. No one cared. The music was too good to waste.

The party flowed on into the night, punctuated by fireworks and cheers. Ginny broke away from the dancing just long enough to get something to drink and admire a series of starbursts. She was hurrying back to her place in the set when she heard a cry. Falls were not unknown among the dancers, especially when a fast tempo was combined with volatile spirits and an imperfect floor. Ginny knelt beside her friend.

"I think I twisted my ankle," Caroline said.

Ginny looked around for Jim, but he was already beside them.

"Let's move her over there, under the light."

Alan Christie acted immediately, scooping Caroline into his arms, and carrying her over to the edge of the tent. He set her on a chair, then stepped back so Jim could reach the affected joint.

"I don't think it's serious, just a sprain." Jim looked up at Caroline. "No more dancing tonight. Ice first and elevate it, to reduce the swelling. Wrap it, if it makes you feel better, but stay off of it for at least a day."

"I can't do that!" Caroline protested. "I have to work the Cameron tent tomorrow."

Ginny smiled at her friend. "You'll just have to greet the public from a seated position. We'll put a chair out front for you to use."

Alan picked Caroline up again and addressed Ginny. "Will you please tell Mrs. Cameron I'll bring Caroline home tonight?"

Ginny nodded, smiling, then watched as Alan strode off into the night, his giggling burden clinging to his neck. She turned to find Jim watching her. He lifted an eyebrow.

"Looks like fun."

"Don't even consider it!" She grabbed his hand, and hauled him back into the dance. "We can't afford to lose *two* couples!"

An hour and a half later, the party was winding down, and Ginny was headed for the parking lot and home. The fireworks were over, the ranks of revelers thinning. The die-hards would be at it for another hour at least, but she needed sleep. This was going to be a short night and tomorrow would be a very long day.

* * *

CHAPTER 2

Friday Night
Loch Lonach Games grounds

Caroline had her head down on Alan's shoulder. Funny how she'd never noticed how broad his shoulders were. He'd been such a skinny kid.

"How about here?" Alan had chosen a spot behind the athletic grounds bleachers, in deep shadow.

"Looks good to me."

He set her gently on the ground and helped her undo the brooch that held her airsaid in place. The garment was no more than a large piece of tartan fabric, belted and pinned in place. It made a perfect blanket for star gazing.

It was a lovely night. The sky had been swept clean by the breeze and the ground was thick with new grass. With the big stadium lights extinguished (so as not to interfere with the fireworks), there was nothing between them and the sky.

"There's the Big Dipper," Caroline said, pointing.

"Ursa Major," Alan corrected.

"Okay, Ursa Major, and the North Star. That's all I know."

"You never snuck out at night to look up at the heavens?"

"I didn't say that. I just didn't have anyone to teach me the constellations."

"Everyone should know how to navigate by the stars. It's a

survival skill." Alan's tone of voice struck her as a bit– smug, was it? But deeper in timbre than she recalled. In the dark he sounded more like a man than the boy she had grown up with.

"Ummm." Caroline felt herself relaxing as the pain in her ankle eased. She searched her memory for another name. "Orion. You can find him by the three stars on his belt."

"He's not high enough in the sky yet. We'll have to stay up very late if we want to see him." Alan rolled up on his side, turning his back on the heavens. "What shall we do to kill the time while we wait?"

"You could teach me the names of the stars." Caroline heard him pull in a slow, deep breath.

"I can see the stars reflected in your eyes. No! Don't close them." His hand brushed her cheek, gently, softly. "Let me look at them, at you." She felt him lean down over her, a presence in the night air, visible as a shadow against the firmament. His lips touched hers and she found the warmth intoxicating.

When they came up for air, it was to find three children giggling at them. "Alan and Caroline, sitting in a tree . . . ."

Caroline sat up swiftly and addressed her nieces. "What are you doing here? It's way past your bedtimes!" The eldest, Elspeth, aged ten, answered her. "Daddy told us to find you."

"Why?"

"To tell you Grandmommy took your car, but she'll leave the light on for you."

"Oh. Okay." Caroline made a shooing motion with her hand. "Now scoot. You're going to be too tired to enjoy the Games tomorrow if you don't go to bed right now."

"I'm not tired!" This from the middle child, Lindsey, two years younger than her sister.

"Well maybe you're not, but Bridget is." The baby of the group, aged five, had settled down on a corner of Caroline's airsaid, curled up, and closed her eyes. "Take her home. I'll see you all tomorrow."

"Aye, Aunt Caroline." Elspeth gathered up her siblings and led them, protesting, away.

Caroline turned to find Alan shaking with suppressed laughter.

"Alan and Caroline . . ." He planted a kiss on her lips. "Sitting in a tree, or, in this case, on the ground." He kissed her again, pursuing her as she fell back onto the airsaid. "K . I . S . S . I . N . G." He planted a kiss with each letter.

Caroline threw her arms up to protect her head and neck, giggling. "This place is too public. We'd better go back."

"I know somewhere we can be alone," Alan said. "Come with me." He wrapped her in her airsaid, making an impromptu cocoon of the garment, then lifted her into his arms.

Caroline caught her breath. "Where are you taking me?"

"Up to the breezeway. There are a number of small rooms up there perfect for a quiet assignation." He was striding across the field as he spoke.

"And how do you know that?"

His laugh rumbled in his chest. "I have ears."

The breezeway was a tunnel, three-quarters of the way up the stadium, open on both ends to catch the prevailing wind. It provided access to bathrooms, water fountains, vendor stalls, the elevator that served the Skybox, and storage.

Alan skirted the end-most clan tent and turned up the ramp. Caroline pulled her arms loose from the airsaid, and wrapped them around his neck. "Should I be worried?"

He looked down at her, still climbing the ramp. "That depends. Do you trust me? Because you can."

She tucked her head down on his shoulder. "I know it."

"That's settled then. And it's about time. I've had something I wanted to ask you for ages."

"What is it?"

"Wait. I want privacy for this conversation."

Caroline lifted an eyebrow. Privacy! She was suddenly aware of how confidently he had stepped in and carried her off. He'd never done that before, taken charge like that. She found herself smiling.

* * *

Friday Night
Stadium Breezeway

"Who is that?" Caroline slid out of Alan's arms and onto the deck of the breezeway, balancing on her good leg.

"I don't know. Should we go?"

"Wait." Caroline's eye narrowed. "I know that voice. I know both of them. Let's get closer." She gingerly tried her sprained ankle, and found that it held her. She shuffled quietly forward, keeping to the shadows.

The male was angry. "You're a witch, that's what, and deserve to go to the devil!"

The female response was cool, self-assured. "You are violating the restraining order by accosting me. Shall I call the police?"

The glow of a cellphone in the woman's hand gave off enough light for Caroline to positively identify the speaker.

The man was pleading now. "All I want is a chance to hold my son, to see him on his birthday, and tell him I love him. That's not against the law."

"It is, actually. The decision from the bench was final."

He exploded. "Your decision! You decided I was a danger to my son. What do you know of it?" There was anguish and desperation in his voice.

"The testimony indicated the child was in danger. My duty

in such cases is clear."

The man took a step closer to the woman. Caroline could see his fists close. "You stupid fool! She lied. My wife lied. You heard the testimony. Chuck told you the truth, but you didn't believe him!"

The woman didn't move, but she held the phone like a weapon, ready to report the disturbance. "It has been my experience that young children do not understand what is happening to them."

Caroline pressed her lips together. She had been right. She knew both of them. Blair Jamieson was a local Family Court Judge, with a reputation for siding with the female parent in every case. Gary Feldman was one of Caroline's co-workers at Texas Instruments, someone she knew well.

"You wouldn't know the truth if it bit you on the ass!" Feldman started toward Jamieson, his fists rising.

She stepped back, into the archway that led out onto the stadium steps. "Stop! Do not come closer or I will issue a warrant for your arrest."

Caroline saw Feldman pause, then seem to crumple.

"It's my son!"

"You should have thought of that before you abandoned him at the mall."

"I didn't abandon him! He wandered off! That can happen to anyone."

"You left him there."

"I went for help!"

"I will not continue to debate this issue. The case is closed and the decision final. Take it up with your wife."

"I can't! You won't let me talk to her!"

The Judge shrugged. "Have your attorney contact hers. You know the rules. Now, do I call the police, or do you leave quietly?"

Caroline watched as Feldman wrestled with his decision. At length he drew in a deep breath and rose to his full height. He pointed a malevolent finger at the woman. "You had better watch your back. Anyone who destroys lives as carelessly as you do will come to a bad end."

Destroys lives! Caroline caught her breath.

Jamieson shrugged again. "Just doing my job."

For a moment Caroline was blinded by the rage that had seized her. Jamieson had destroyed her life, too, and never regretted it! When her vision cleared, Feldman had gone, faded into a shadow perhaps, hiding perhaps, waiting for the right moment to strike, perhaps.

Caroline surged forward, shaking off Alan's hand. "You bitch!" She spat the words out. "It isn't enough that you destroy whole generations of young dancers? You have to break up families, too?"

The woman turned to face her. "Caroline Cameron."

"I see I made an impression on you!"

"You made a foolish mistake and you, like Mr. Feldman, had best be careful not to run afoul of the law again."

Caroline drew closer. "All you did to me was to shatter my dreams, but that poor man has lost his family, because of you."

"My job is to protect those who cannot look out for themselves. It does not make me popular."

"It doesn't make you human!" Caroline took another step in Judge Jamieson's direction. They were almost nose to nose, in the archway that opened out onto the penultimate tier of seating. "Take care! I am no longer the girl you once had power over. Now I am your equal."

The older woman snorted. "Hardly."

"I am, in education and in professional accomplishments. And I've done some digging, ever since Gary told me his story. Do you have any idea how many people hate you? There are hundreds of followers on his social media site."

"Fools will follow fools."

"These are men whose hearts you have broken. You've cheated them of their children and their children of their fathers. Don't you feel any compassion, any sympathy?"

Jamieson shrugged. "Each of them got what he deserved."

"You cowardly, selfish, mean-spirited, old bitch!" Caroline put her hands out in front of her and shoved. The maneuver worked better than she had anticipated. The Judge lost her balance and tumbled down the concrete steps to the landing at the bottom of the mezzanine.

Caroline stared at her handiwork, satisfaction fighting with horror, then, to her genuine relief, Jamieson was rising, hauling herself to her feet, gripping the rail, and Alan's hands were on Caroline's arms, pulling her back from the edge.

"You shouldn't have touched her," he said.

Caroline sucked in a big breath, her eyes still on her nemesis, her whole body shaking with anger. Even in the dim light, she could see Jamieson was bleeding. There was a cut over her right eye.

Judge Jamieson looked up at her, her face twisted in fury. "I will see to it that you go to prison for this. You have attacked an officer of the court!"

"I shoved a bully."

"I'll have your job. Your license. Whatever it takes, I'll make sure you don't get away with this!"

Caroline's eyes narrowed. "I suggest you go see a doctor. You might need stitches."

Jamieson snarled. "You're going to need more than stitches before I'm through with you!"

"Come on, let's get out of here." Alan urged.

Caroline watched a moment longer, then allowed Alan to lead her away. He was right. She shouldn't have lost her temper like that. She was already regretting it.

She had known better, but the thought of all those people with no one to fight for them, to stand up to Jamieson for them, had overcome her reason. It was how she had been raised, to fight for the downtrodden.

They made their way onto the ramp, toward the clan tents and Alan's car. Caroline was struggling with her conscience, and her bad ankle, which was threatening to collapse under her. She could hear Alan's voice urging her to make haste, and heard again the threats Jamieson had made. Gary was right. A woman like that had enemies, a lot of them. It wouldn't be a matter of *if* with her, just *when* and *where* and *who*.

Caroline paused on the edge of the ramp. The problem was, Jamieson could do it, destroy Caroline's professional career, if she wanted to. Caroline frowned, thinking it through.

"What's wrong?"

"I'm sorry, Alan. I need to make a pit stop before we leave the stadium."

"I'll go with you."

She shook her head. "I'd rather you went across the field and got my bag out of the Cameron tent. Will you do that for me?"

He nodded. "Anything. All you have to do is ask."

Caroline smiled up at him in the starlight. "Thanks. I'll meet you back here and you can escort me safely home."

"With pleasure my lady!" He turned and hurried down the ramp to do her bidding while Caroline turned slowly and made her way back to the mezzanine and the public facilities.

* * *

Chapter 3

Saturday, Early Morning
Loch Lonach Games grounds

The sun was just clearing the fence line, the dew bending the stalks of grass, sparkling as the field emerged from shadow into the light. Ginny pulled her airsaid closer and picked up the pace. It was a glorious morning, a bit chilly for April, but that can happen, even in Texas. She was crossing the field from the exhibitor's entrance. If you arrived early enough, you could find good parking along the back fence, but there were restrictions. The gate was unlocked only in the early morning and late afternoon, for set-up and take down, and only available to those working the Games. Ginny and Jim had volunteered to man the First Aid tent for part of the day. That got them in. The rest of the day would be spent visiting friends and enjoying the sights.

She looked around at the still empty field. There were a few other early birds moving in the distance, a pop-up tent being raised, flags being unfurled, and a small knot of people off to her left, at the end of the heavy athletics area. That group had a Hieland Coo in it.

Ginny liked Highland cows. They looked like shaggy, red-headed longhorns, which wasn't really surprising since modern longhorns are descended in part from the Scottish breed. She veered off to say hello to this one, whom she knew, and her owner, whom she also knew. As she approached, he broke off from the group, leading the cow, and came to meet her.

"Morning John. Morning Annabelle!" Ginny rubbed her hand down the cow's nose and was rewarded with a wet snuffle.

"Morning, Miss Forbes. Good day for a Games, I think."

"Yes. What were you looking at?"

John looked back over his shoulder. Ginny followed his glance. Of the two remaining men, one was kneeling beside something on the ground. The other was on his phone.

"Annabelle got loose in the night. I found her o'er there."

Ginny smiled at the cow. "Something good to eat?" The field was kept trimmed, but in spring the wildflowers were always one step ahead of the mowers.

"A woman."

"Oh!" Ginny looked over at the scene, her smile fading. When she became the wife of the heir to Loch Lonach, she would have duties to perform, and they would include trouble-shooting at events such as this, but she had no official position yet, only her professional expertise to offer, and her curiosity to satisfy. "Is someone hurt?"

"Aye, ye could say that."

Ginny started to move toward the whatever-it-was, but John stepped in front of her. "Better not."

She looked at him in surprise. He knew she was a registered nurse. "I might be able to help."

John shook his head. "There's naught tae be done fer this one. She's deid."

"Dead! What happened?"

"Leave it, lass. That's no something ye should be seeing."

The last thing Ginny wanted was another corpse on her hands, but a quick glance in that direction showed one of the men motioning to her to approach. She sighed. "It's all right, John. I'll handle it."

He looked at her a moment longer, then shrugged. "Suit yerself. Come on Annabelle."

Ginny watched them move off in the direction of the livestock pens, then turned and made her way toward the trouble. There were more people gathering around the body, the gruesome discovery attracting attention as a matter of course.

As she got nearer she could see a pair of feet, one dark sock missing its shoe. The body was on its back and Ginny could see the woman had been wearing trousers, also dark, now damp from the morning dew. She was slim, skinny almost, with very narrow hips. The man kneeling beside the body was between Ginny and the woman's face so she couldn't see who it was. He heard her step on the grass and turned suddenly, rising, coming toward her. He was a stranger to her.

"You shouldn't be here, Miss. Go back."

The other man spoke to her as well. "Hae ye seen Dr. Mackenzie yet this mornin', Miss Ginny?"

"Not yet."

"We're trying tae reach him."

"He should be on the field somewhere." Ginny got out her phone and punched in Jim's number. "What shall I tell him?"

"Ask him tae come tae us."

"All right."

As she waited for Jim to answer, Ginny moved sideways, to get a better look at the corpse, her view partially obscured by the long shadows thrown from the rising sun, partly by the bodies of the living between her and the deceased.

The woman was wearing a credential around her neck, the kind that held a photo ID and allowed access to restricted areas at an event. So she was one of the officials. That was unfortunate.

Ginny's eye traveled up the woman's torso, noting that the front of the white blouse was marred by dirt and a spatter of blood. One leg lay crossed over the other, as if the body had been lying face down, and had turned over to face the dawn. There should have been a pale oval above the opening of the blouse. Ginny couldn't understand why she couldn't see the face. Then, suddenly, she did.

Ginny gasped, starting backward, tripping over the uneven ground and sitting down, hard. She dropped the phone, staring at the corpse.

No wonder John had said the woman was past help. Half her skull had been crushed, the contents spilled onto the ground. Splinters of white bone showed through the mangled flesh. The socket of one eye was broken and the eyeball hung from the optic nerve like some gruesome Hallowe'en decoration.

There was no question about the source of the injuries. The caber lay where it had fallen. At some time in the night, someone had hoisted that weight into the air, to the point where physics had taken over, bringing it back to earth with enough force to smash a human skull like an eggshell.

* * *

Ginny sat there, staring at the body. Rage came boiling up from some deep cesspool in her soul, spewing acid and fury. How could he have done something so stupid? Turned his back on a falling tree?

Medical terms like *cerebral artery disruption, meningeal tear,* and *orbital fracture* floated in and out of her consciousness as deduction fought with despair.

She didn't deserve this. No one deserved to have to see

this. She was struggling for breath, her heart pounding in her ears.

The corpse didn't deserve it either. Shouldn't she spare a thought for the victim? The dead woman was past caring, of course. Mercifully unaware of what she looked like. It was Ginny who would have to live with that image.

She tried to get control of herself. Her father's death had been an accident. He had been engaged in doing a favor for a friend, an act of kindness. But they had made a mistake and Ginny's life had been changed forever.

And here was another tree, and another death, and it just wasn't fair!

Someone knelt down in front of her, blocking her view, and Ginny looked up into Jim's face.

"Come with me." He took her hands and pulled her to her feet, then steered her over to a nearby golf cart. The officials used them for getting around on the grounds, and Ginny was glad to see it. Jim lifted her onto the seat, then climbed in beside her and drove off.

Ginny gripped the rail with both hands, holding tight—the uneasiness in her stomach not entirely the fault of the bumpy ride—and felt like a prize fool. Ten years of ICU nursing and she had behaved like a green girl. Rage blinded her again, this time directed at herself. Announcing she could handle it, whatever it was, then panicking like that. She'd seen bodies, mangled bodies, lots of them. It was just—

She couldn't think of the corpse's head without swaying. Jim put his arm around her waist and pulled her across the seat, holding her to him.

They didn't have far to go. The First Aid Tent was located at the edge of the clan tent area. He took her inside and insisted she lie down on the cot they had set up the afternoon before. He covered her with a blanket, then wrapped the blood pressure cuff around her arm and hit the button. "180 over 90, 140, 28. Slow it down, Ginny."

She knew what he wanted. She took a deep breath and held it for ten seconds then let it out slowly, then did it again. Five cycles in she could feel her pulse falling back to normal.

He triggered the blood pressure cuff again. "Much better!" He flicked his penlight in her eyes, checking her pupils. He looked calm, unfazed, very much the ER physician he was. Well, what did she expect? Hysterics from him? Not likely.

"Let's sit you up." He raised her head and Ginny felt a wave of dizziness, gone as fast as it appeared.

"I'm fine, Jim." She had a headache, but she knew that would last until the adrenaline cleared her system. "I'm sorry to cause trouble."

He shook his head. "No one who saw that could blame you. Robbie was almost as white as you were, and the other man had already lost his breakfast before you arrived."

"John tried to stop me."

Jim smiled. "I could have told him *that* wasn't going to work."

The tent was a bit more than a standard pop-up, as it was three times as big, had four walls, for privacy, and several sturdy chests containing medical supplies of various kinds. Jim pulled Ginny off the cot and settled them both on the largest of the chests, wrapping a blanket around her and his arms around the blanket. He planted a kiss on the top of her head. "So tell me. Why did you go look?"

Ginny swallowed. "Morbid curiosity. Officiousness. An instinct to meddle."

"Maybe you thought you could help?"

She drew in a shuddering breath. "I knew I couldn't do anything for her. John had already told me she was dead, but I felt I had an obligation. A duty to your grandfather.

Something."

"Quite right. You are his eyes and ears."

Ginny leaned into Jim's embrace. She was that. One set at least. Angus had spies everywhere.

"Who was it? The woman, I mean," she asked.

"Blair Jamieson." Jim dropped his voice to the pitch Ginny labeled as 'therapeutic'.

"Did you see him? Your father?" After the tree had landed on his skull, killing him instantly.

Ginny shook her head. "Mother wouldn't let us. She said we didn't need to know." She swallowed. "And now—" She buried her face in Jim's shoulder. "How am I supposed to forget that?"

"I don't know." He held her gently, rocking back and forth.

Eventually she got her voice back under control. "So what do we do now?"

"We're going to sit here and wait for instructions. The police will want to talk to you."

"To both of us, I expect."

"Yes, and while we wait you can tell me where we are in the wedding plans. I've been too busy to listen properly. Now's your chance to catch me up."

Ginny laughed. "What a bedside manner you have!"

"All part of the service." He bent down and kissed her.

She twined her arms around his neck. "I love you, Jim Mackenzie!" Her smile faltered. "But promise me something."

"What's that?"

"Promise you'll stay away from dead trees."

He caught his breath. "And cabers. I promise. And I want the same promise from you. Promise me you'll stay out of danger, as much as possible."

The corner of Ginny's mouth twisted. "Just being alive is dangerous."

"You know what I mean. Use your common sense. Don't put

yourself in harm's way." He cocked his head sideways. "You have me to think of now, not just yourself."

She nodded. "I'll do my best." She kissed him to seal the bargain. "All I plan to do for the next three weeks is get ready for the wedding. How dangerous can that be?" She smiled, but couldn't help feeling cold. The words of the burial service floated into her mind. *In the midst of life, we are in death.* She shivered and snuggled closer.

* * *

Chapter 4

Saturday Morning
First Aid Tent

Angus Mackenzie found them there half an hour later. He took one of the folding chairs, positioned it so he could face them, and sat down.

"Weel lad?"

"She'll do."

Himself looked directly at Ginny. "Is yer mither expected?"

"No, sir. She's coming tomorrow."

The Laird nodded. "Tis a good thing she wasna wi' ye."

"Tell us what's happening." Jim said.

"Th' police are here, and th' Medical Examiner is on her way."

"Will the gates open on time?"

"Aye. They've roped off a bit o' th' athletics field and posted guards. Th' public will no be allowed tae get close enough tae see. Wi' a bit o' luck, th' body will be gone afore nine."

"Which means we need to be ready." Ginny climbed to her feet, peeled off the blanket, and set about putting the First Aid tent back together. She turned to the Laird. "Can you get us an urn of coffee from the hospitality suite? I hadn't planned on it being quite so cold this morning."

He rose from his chair, lifting a skeptical eyebrow. "I'll see wha' I can do, lass, but nae promises. They hae their ain problems this morn."

"Oh?"

"Jim hae no told ye?"

Jim protested. "I haven't had a chance."

Ginny looked from one to the other, puzzled. "Told me what?"

The old man shook his head. "We've a dozen o' th' Games Patrons laid low. Th' haggis was tainted."

* * *

Saturday Morning
Athletic Field

Ginny was sitting quietly in the First Aid tent, sipping coffee. Jim had gone, first to get a cup of coffee for her, then to follow Angus up to the Hospitality Suite. He'd gotten several calls from the hospital during the course of the night, in his capacity as Infectious Disease specialist, and helped diagnose the source of the poisoning, and, from that, the recommended treatment. There had been no deaths—so far—for which everyone was thankful, but he had questions to ask of the Hospitality Suite staff. As a result, she was alone when the officer arrived.

"Excuse me, Miss. Are you Ginny Forbes?"

"I am." She rose and gestured to one of the chairs. "How may I help you?"

"I just need to get your statement."

Ginny nodded, taking her seat again. "Where do we start?"

"Your full name, please."

He asked a series of background questions, then instructed her to tell her story in her own words. Ginny did her best.

With the exception of the few moments between seeing the body and realizing Jim was there, she had a clear memory of the who, what, where, and when. She was less certain of the how and had no idea of the why, but someone else would undoubtedly have covered that.

"I understand you had a bit of a reaction to the body." The officer had his eyes on his pad, not looking directly at her. Ginny knew the police would be suspicious of anybody behaving in a way that seemed out-of-the-ordinary to them. "Yes."

"And why was that, Miss?"

Ginny took a deep breath, then looked the young officer in the face and told him.

He met her eyes, his own registering a flicker of compassion. "So you didn't know the victim."

"I did, casually. She was the head Highland Dance judge. We crossed paths at the Games and other Gatherings. I knew her name and knew her by sight, but that was all."

He nodded, making notes and asking for a few more details, then put his pad away. "Thank you, Miss. We'll be in touch if we need more."

The next visit was from Detective Tran. Ginny went through the same routine, rising, offering a chair and coffee, resuming her seat. The two of them eyed one another.

"Do you also want to hear how my father died?" Ginny asked.

She shook her head. "No. I looked it up last year." Tran Thi Hue had been the detective assigned to the case when Ginny began to suspect foul play in the death of one of her patients. Since then, they had collaborated on two additional cases. As a result, Tran was now the police department's official liaison to the Clan.

"Then how can I help you?"

"You can explain this death to me."

Ginny knew the caliber of the woman. She would use the tools at her disposal—tactfully, but ruthlessly. Ginny nodded.

"What would you like to know?"

Tran rose from her seat. "Come with me, please."

Ginny felt her throat close. "Is that necessary?"

Detective Tran eyed her. "I should be very grateful if you would give me the benefit of your expertise."

Ginny swallowed, trying to appear calm and professional. Not like earlier when she had disgraced herself in front of half a dozen witnesses.

"The Medical Examiner will likely be able to answer your questions better than I could."

Tran nodded. "When she is finished with the autopsy. In the meantime, I wish to pick your brain." She gave Ginny a sharp look. "You have a way of seeing things others miss."

Ginny rose and followed the detective out of the tent, smoldering. Not with rage, a whiney resentment this time. How much was she expected to put up with this morning? Hadn't she had enough? And, just to make her feel even more of a worm, why was she behaving liked a spoiled brat? What was wrong with her today? Okay. It had been a shock and a very nasty one, but was this what she expected of herself? Where was the courage she had been accused of having in such great quantity?

Jim had said she was the Laird's eyes and ears. Very well. She would look and listen and report back. She raised her chin, stiffened her spine, and prepared to face the nightmare. At least this time she would know what she was looking at.

Detective Tran lifted the police tape and held it up while Ginny ducked under, then led the way over to the body. Ginny rubbed sweaty palms down the sides of her skirt, breathing carefully, trying to be professional. It was a trauma patient.

One she couldn't hurt. One she might be able to help, if only posthumously.

"I am told this log is called a caber and it has something to do with the Highland Games. Could you explain, please?"

Ginny nodded, going through the basics of a caber toss.

"Could it be used as a weapon?"

Ginny considered the question. "It seems unlikely. There aren't many people who can lift one, and even fewer who could guarantee it would land where wanted."

"What about a team effort? Could it be used to kill someone who was already on the ground?"

"We often see two men lifting and carrying a caber. They could set it down here, but they would have trouble dropping it in precisely the right spot. The logs have a tendency to bounce—and roll." She glanced down at the caber itself, trying to ignore the crushed head beneath it. "You'd probably get a better answer from the Heavy Athletics coaches."

Detective Tran nodded. "They are on my list." She moved closer to the body, pointing to the corpse's arms. "These appear to be bruises."

Ginny looked at the purplish marks and nodded.

"What can you tell me about them?"

Ginny took a moment to collect her thoughts. "They're fresh. The blood hasn't had a chance to migrate to the lower areas of her body." She looked more closely. "The skin is torn as well. Abrasions." Broken nails. Silvery lines across her wrists. Jewelry still in place.

"Could these injuries be made by a caber?"

Ginny wrinkled her brow. "If she fell over the caber, sure, but not if the caber fell on her. They'd be massive, crush injuries. These look like something you'd see after a fight."

"Is there anything that surprises you, that appears out of place?"

Ginny frowned. "I'm surprised to find her here." She shook her head at the Detective. "Wait a minute, let me finish. What I mean is that the Highland dance contingent doesn't stay up late the night before a competition. From the condition of the blood, I guess she's been here overnight, which means she walked out onto the field during the night. That doesn't strike me as normal."

"An assignation, perhaps?"

Ginny nodded, then straightened up. "I'm sure the Medical Examiner can give you a more precise opinion." She looked over at the approaching official, dressed in a moon suit, followed by two assistants trying to roll a gurney over the grass and making heavy weather of it.

"Thank you, Miss Forbes." Tran was holding the tape up for her again. Ginny took the hint, ducked under it, and moved back, away from the investigation.

"Miss Ginny?" It was Robbie. She turned to face him. "I just wanted to return this." He handed her the phone she had dropped.

"Oh! Thank you."

He hesitated. "Did you know her?"

"I know who she is—was, but that's all."

"The scuttlebutt is she had a lot of enemies."

Ginny looked at Robbie, waiting for him to continue.

He shrugged. "My granddaughter dances. She and her mother both complain about the results, every time. Can't understand why some of the girls manage to win and others lose. You know how it goes."

Ginny nodded.

He shrugged again. "Just a thought."

They both watched as the M.E. inspected the body, spending almost no time doing so, then indicated to her two helpers that it was all right to move the corpse. The helpers took numerous photographs, then set their equipment aside and addressed the caber. Each man grabbed one end of the caber and tried to lift it. Neither could. Ginny suppressed a smile.

There was a stir among the spectators. Two men stepped forward and Ginny recognized them from the day before. They lifted the caber without difficulty, and set it down a little way off. Everyone now looked down at the wreckage of the dead woman's face. No one looked happy. The two helpers from the M.E.'s office collected more photographs, then put up the cameras and brought over the gurney.

Ginny'd had enough. She was too far back to tell if there were other things to be seen when the body was lifted. Besides, it was none of her business. Her job was to get through this weekend, then get ready for her wedding.

She turned, intending to go back to the First Aid tent, and caught sight of the African woman from the day before. She was dressed in an airsaid like Ginny's, but hung about with cups and small bags and heaven-knew-what. Ginny wondered again what brought her to a Highland Games.

The Games were a relatively modern invention, a result of the Scottish diaspora. Even before the Jacobite Rebellion, men and families were leaving Scotland for the Ulster Plantation and the Americas. After the Uprising, the English had tried to erase the Scots from their country and their memories. It didn't work.

Disarmed and scattered, their tartans, bagpipes, language, and way of life banned, somehow, they were stronger than ever. The Scots were everywhere.

They had settled and thrived. Scottish strength had won battles, tilled the ground, and manned the forge. Scottish minds had invented wonders, enriching civilization time and time again. And time and time again the exiled Scots gathered, from every corner of the globe, as the pipes sounded and the clans were called. The blood was strong in the children of Alba. But they were still human.

The African woman was standing with the others, staring at the spectacle of death. She looked half dead herself, her dark skin pasty, with a greenish cast to her lips. Ginny frowned. Shock and horror can do that, make a person ill, but was that enough to explain what Ginny was seeing? Or was there something else, something that would bring her to the First Aid tent before the day was over?

Ginny turned her back on death and headed across the field. The visitors coming through the gates would expect a cheerful reception, part of the price of admission. Ginny dragged her mouth into a smile, stiffened her spine, and reminded herself she was a Scot. The blood was strong in her, too.

* * *

Chapter 5

Saturday Noon
First Aid Tent

Ginny watched Jim inhale two BBQ sandwiches, chips, a pint of beer, and a quart of water, making mental notes about future grocery shopping and exercise regimens.

"No haggis in that, I hope?" she teased.

He shook his head. "I'm not a fan of liver."

"Duly noted."

He licked his fingers, then cleaned them with antiseptic wipes. "What?"

Her smile broke into a grin. "Do you always eat like that when my back is turned?"

He shook his head. "Festival food. One step short of a heart attack, but it sure does taste good!"

She laughed, then picked up the trash and deposited it in the garbage bag tied to the corner tent pole. She didn't have any room to criticize. She'd packed her favorite chocolates to help her get through this day.

He reached out a long arm as she came back and drew her into his embrace, giving her a kiss and a hug. "I'll have a salad for dinner."

"You won't have time," she replied. "We have to go home and change for the Ball."

The Grand March started promptly at seven with musicians flown in from Scotland so they were under orders not to be late.

"What time should I pick you up?"

"Six. I have the Bonniest Knees Contest to judge at four, so it's going to be tight."

"Bonniest Knees, huh? I'm not sure I like the idea of my wife fondling strange men's knees."

"Jealous? Already?" Ginny wrapped her arms around his neck and applied herself to putting his fears to rest.

"Ahem."

Ginny broke off, blushing. Jim, on the other hand, seemed completely unconcerned.

"May we help you?"

The older man stepped into the tent, pushing a teenager in front of him. The elder swapped a tiny smile with Jim before explaining their presence.

"Wally here has disappointed his clan and is in disgrace."

"Oh?" Ginny couldn't help feeling that this must be overstating the misbehavior, whatever it was. She approached the boy, taking note of his expression and posture. He was a strapping youth standing at least six feet tall (when not slouched over hanging his head in shame), with broad shoulders and evidence of many hours in the gym, pumping iron.

"Show the lady yer hands, boy."

He held out both hands, palms up, and Ginny saw the problem immediately. There were almost a dozen spots; inflamed, swollen, puffy, and undoubtedly sore. One seemed to be already infected and there was evidence he'd tried to pull the splinters out by himself.

"That looks painful." She looked up and found the boy's eyes peeking at her from behind dark curls, then sliding quickly away. "I think I know you," she said. "You're Ian's son." Ian Hunter was one of the notables among them, a state senator, rabid sports fan, and deadly with an edged weapon—in either hand.

The older man nodded, holding his own hand out. "Rory Hunter, Ian's brother and this scamp's uncle."

Ginny shook his hand, then turned to the patient. "Why don't you come over here and let Dr. Mackenzie take a look at those hands." She led the boy to a seat and turned him over to Jim, then went to get cleansers, topical anesthetics, and tweezers.

Jim was asking the boy questions and getting no answers. He looked up and exchanged a glance with Ginny who nodded very slightly, set down the supplies where Jim could reach them, then deftly steered the irate uncle out of the tent.

"It doesn't look too bad."

"It's kept him from the rope pull!"

Ginny listened sympathetically to the disappointment in Rory Hunter's voice. His nephew was *supposed to be* the anchor on his clan's team in the tug-o-war. He was *supposed to be* the reason they would win that competition. Then he had to go and tear up his hands so he couldn't grip the rope correctly, couldn't hold on. They'd lost. Not by much, mind, but lost nonetheless. Humiliating. To the *Campbells*, no less!

Ginny squashed the urge to laugh. The fierce Celtic temper was one of the reasons the clans had survived. One did not mock that, even at the Games.

Worse, the lad wouldn't say where he'd gotten those injuries. Boys will be boys, but he should have had more sense, the night before the competition, and what was he hiding, anyway?

Ginny nodded, offering sympathy and Scotch from the flask she always took with her to any Scottish gathering. Rory Hunter was winding down, his anger fading, but the confusion remained. Why was the lad refusing to say where he'd picked up the splinters? What had he been doing that he couldn't tell them about? And why had he hidden them, rather than asking for help? If those splinters had been removed last night, he'd probably have been able to use his hands today. He knew what was at stake. It didn't make sense.

Ginny found herself agreeing. What was the boy hiding, she wondered, and why? It wasn't that Scots teenagers didn't rebel like normal boys. They did. But they did it in ways that tended to be more productive. They tried to assume roles beyond their years and experience. Sometimes they got away with it. Sometimes they needed rescuing.

She suggested having a private talk with the boy, to see if she could find out what was going on, then sending him back to his family. Would that be all right with his parents?

Rory nodded. "Aye. I'll explain to Ian and thank you for it."

Ginny watched him trudge off toward the clan tents, thinking about the challenge of living up to a parent with a strong and very public persona, then slipped back inside the First Aid station. She got there in time to help Jim apply antiseptic ointment and wrap the hands in gauze.

"Keep them dry for twenty-four hours. After that you can wash with warm water, no soap, and reapply the ointment." Jim cleaned his hands, then sat down facing the boy and looked him in the eye. "Now, are you ready to tell us where you got those splinters?"

Wally shook his head, his eyes nearly starting out of their sockets.

Ginny examined one of the longer splinters, frowning down at it, then suddenly realized where she'd seen it before, or something very like it. "This is cedar."

Jim looked at her, waiting for her to explain. She turned to face him, then looked more closely at the boy.

"Wally, were you at the caber class yesterday?"

She watched as the blood drained from the boy's face. He slumped further in the chair, refusing to answer her. Surely it wasn't that bad? She came over and went down on her haunches in front of him. This brought her almost to eye level.

"What's wrong, Wally? What's happened?"

The boy put his bandaged hands in front of his face and started to cry.

"Talk to us, Wally. How can we help?"

"You can't help! No one can!"

"Tell me. What's wrong?"

The boy rubbed at his face with one of the bandaged hands, his expression nothing short of anguish. "I killed her. That's what's wrong!"

"Killed who?"

"That woman on the field. I killed her."

Ginny caught her breath, her eyes wide. She looked over at Jim, but he wasn't in better shape. His mouth was hanging open. Ginny softened her voice, coaxing the information from the man-child.

"You mean the woman they found this morning?"

Wally nodded, his eyes squeezed closed, tears leaking out from under the lids.

"Why do you think that?"

Wally threw out one of his hands in exasperation. "I don't think. I know!"

"What happened, Wally?"

It took them almost an hour to get the whole story out of him. Apparently he and some school buddies had decided to attend caber class yesterday. The evening had seen revelry and a certain amount of alcohol intake. After midnight, someone, he wasn't sure who, had challenged the group to a caber toss.

There had been the usual objections, but the cabers weren't locked up. They were just lying there, on the ground. The stadium lights had been put out, but there were still lights from the vendors, and moonlight. They could see to get on the grounds, over the fence, then onto the athletic field.

They carried one of the smaller cabers to a spot behind the stands. It took four of them to lift it, then position it so Wally could get his hands under it. That was when he got the splinters. He'd forgotten to bring gloves.

He was the only one who could have done it. He was the biggest in the group, strongest, too. He used the techniques he'd been taught earlier in the day, lifted the pole into the air, and heaved. It didn't go forward, though, it fell backward, knocking him to the ground, and slewing sideways. He hadn't heard it hit the ground, hadn't heard anything over the laughter.

Anyway, when they went to pick it up, he stumbled over a woman's body lying on the field, the caber on her head. He'd killed her! He'd dropped a caber on her head and smashed her head in and killed her and he wished he was dead and was sure he would be, when his father found out!

Ginny put her arms around the boy's shoulders and held him while he sobbed. She exchanged looks with Jim. It was an accident. Nothing more, but nothing less. The boys would probably be charged with criminal trespass and Wally might face manslaughter charges. In either case, the police would have to be told.

Ginny wanted to comfort the boy, but couldn't think of a single thing to say. The best she could do was help him face the music.

"Wally, listen to me. You will have to tell the police everything you know. That includes ratting out your friends. Do you understand?"

He nodded.

"Okay. Boys make mistakes, but so do men. I have a sneaking suspicion your father would rather see you in trouble for taking the initiative than for hanging back. Am I right?"

Wally looked up, still sniffing, and nodded. "He keeps telling me to be a man."

Ginny nodded. "That is exactly what you must do. Accept responsibility for your actions. Learn from your mistakes. Pay your debt to society, whatever that may turn out to be. Then forgive yourself and make sure you don't make the same mistake again. Can you do that?"

Wally sat up a little straighter and looked at her, then over at Jim, then back at Ginny. "Aye. I'll do what I have to. I'm not too proud to say I'm sorry."

Ginny exchanged glances with Jim, then stood up and held out her hand to the boy. "All right, then, Wally Hunter. Let's go face your father."

* * *

Saturday Afternoon
Games Grounds

Ginny was relieved when the next set of volunteers arrived and she could put the First Aid tent behind her. She'd seen enough mangled flesh for one day.

Jim led the way out onto the grounds, past a half dozen Homestead policemen stationed at the corner of the clan tent area. Ginny's forehead wrinkled at the police presence.

"Why so many of them?"

"They're canvassing, asking everyone if they saw anything last night."

Ginny silently thought it was an effort unlikely to yield results. The people who had been on the grounds last night were probably here today, and most of them would be able to name others, but it was more than three thousand people, the majority of whom had been drinking.

"Where to?" Jim asked.

It was a good question. Ginny toyed with the idea of skipping the remainder of the day, going home and taking a nap, but she'd made a promise, and she took that sort of thing seriously.

"Let's do the clan visits, then go listen to whoever is fiddling until it's time to set up for the Bonniest Knees."

Jim nodded. "Okay. Shall we start here?"

They moved slowly around the edge of the field, stopping at each of the clan tents and visiting with the inhabitants. As the Laird's grandson and his soon-to-be granddaughter-in-law, they had a social obligation to make themselves known and available. It was easy enough work. At each tent they were greeted cordially and offered food and fluid. Many of the clansmen and women knew Ginny, and Jim was coming to know a good percentage of them from the weekly ceilidhs.

When they got to the Camerons, Ginny found Caroline manning the information table. They exchanged hugs.

"I hear the most incredible rumors of you today," Caroline said. "Did you really trip over a body?"

"No. I never touched it and I didn't find it. I only fell down when I saw it."

"Tell me everything!"

Ginny promised to do so, later, when they had leisure for it. But as long as there were visitors on the field, they were all on duty and had to break off any conversation to smile at visitors and answer questions. She and Jim chatted for a bit with the Camerons, then moved on down the line.

Along the fourth wall of the field, the clans tents gave way to organizations. Among these were the military reenactors, the distilleries, the Celtic music associations, the heavy athletics, the Scottish genealogists, the Scottish Country Dance and Highland Dance associations, the Gaelic language school, and the Scottish history exhibits, including a newcomer, a booth dedicated to Scottish ghosts and witches.

It was here Ginny found the black woman. Ginny introduced herself. The other woman held out her hand. She looked better than when Ginny had seen her this morning, but still a bit peaked.

"This is all so interesting!" Ginny said. "What can you tell me about Scottish witches?"

She followed her hostess around the tent, examining the displays and listening to the explanations. She looked around for Jim at one point, but he seemed to have disappeared. She didn't blame him. He'd done his duty, and deserved to slip away for a bit. Besides, she'd catch up with him at the fiddle tent.

The woman's name turned out to be Dupree. "Josephine, though everyone calls me 'Mama'."

Ginny found out she was from New Orleans, that she was a toxicologist, and had gotten interested in medicinal plants early on. That had led to the historical uses and abuses of organic materials—especially the psychotropes—and an interest in black magic.

"There's good evidence that the so-called witches in each of the countries in which we find them were using mind-altering substances, some hallucinogens among them. That led to self-reports of flying through the air."

Ginny nodded. So far, the information jibed with what she knew. Outside the field of toxicology, the woman was a beginner, misunderstanding the Second Sight, for instance, but not saying enough to make it necessary to correct her.

"And how did you decide you wanted to share all this with the paying public?" Something about the hesitation that met this question gave Ginny pause. "I'm sorry. Am I being too nosey?"

"Not at all. Please forgive me. I'm still not myself."

Ginny looked sympathetic, and was rewarded with three pieces of information. Mama Dupree had eaten haggis in the Skybox last night, driven to Shreveport and back because of an appearance she had to give there so she hadn't gotten much sleep, and she was interested in the Highland Games because she had found a Scottish ancestor in her genealogy, a landowner in South Carolina. Not an unusual occurrence, but a touchy subject, nonetheless.

They chatted for a few minutes more, comparing notes on Shakespeare's famous trio of Scottish witches, then Ginny faded back to let Mama Dupree answer questions from the public. She watched as Dupree passed out business cards, was given one herself, then, her curiosity satisfied, she slipped out and headed for the fiddle tent.

Jim had saved a seat for her and presented her with a bottle of water, which tasted delicious. She whispered her thanks, and settled in to enjoy the music, one eye closed, the other on her watch. An hour later, the music behind her, she found herself seated on a folding chair, facing the Highland Dance stage, with a volunteer tying a bandana around her head.

"Can you see?"

All five of the woman chosen to judge the Bonniest Knees contest assured the organizers they couldn't see a thing.

"All right. The scoring works this way." It was secret ballot, using fingers behind the back to score the knees on their tactile attractiveness.

Ginny listened to the instructions. The men were not to speak. When each was in place, he was to tap the judge on her shoulder and she was to reach straight out and examine the knees with her hands. When she had reached her decision, she was to indicate her score and the judging would move on to the next contestant.

Ginny had a good understanding of healthy human anatomy. She followed the lines of the musculature, feeling the insertion points and edges of the ligaments, estimating the size of the patella, looking for deformities or misalignments, then adding points for a proper amount of hairiness. No grown man's knees should be smooth as a baby's bottom. Two were eliminated because of old injuries. One for a collection of growths Ginny sincerely hoped were not contagious. Another for violating the rule to be anonymous. One of the judges ran afoul of the process by reaching too high each time. In the end, they had their winner.

Ginny pulled off the blindfold and found a dozen men in kilts smiling at her. Not all were young, but all had the skin and bone structure of a typical Scottish male. To her surprise, Jim was among them. She wondered which set of knees had been his.

"And the winner is Geordie Hamilton!"

Ginny smiled and applauded with the rest, then rose to go.

"Wait! We have another trophy to award." The organizer handed something to Jim, who brought it over, knelt down and handed it to her. Ginny looked at the small plastic trophy. "Best Hands, Bonniest Knees Contest, Loch Lonach Highland Games," it said, with the year underneath.

The official was explaining to the crowd. "The Best Hands trophy is awarded to the judge the men decide did the best job of examining their knees. The winner this time is Ginny Forbes!"

Ginny flushed at the applause and at the sudden appearance of a microphone held to catch her remarks. "We got the most enthusiastic responses we've ever seen from the men. What were you looking for?"

"Health and hair."

The crowd roared with laughter and more applause, then finally let her go. Jim slipped an arm around her waist, then bent toward her, lowering his voice.

"Best hands, huh? Sounds like I won after all."

* * *

CHAPTER 6

Sunday Morning
Games Grounds

Sunday at the Highland Games started, as always, with a non-denominational church service on the grounds, followed by brunch. Hymns tended to be Presbyterian, but the congregation was enthusiastic, and the piping was a treat.

Not everyone attended. Angus did, of course. Jim would, as part of his duties. Ginny would, too, for the same reason. She sneaked a peek at the handsome man seated beside her, then reached over and took his hand. They were one day closer to being man and wife, and her heart fluttered every time she thought about it.

He smiled down at her, gave her hand a squeeze, then turned his attention to the service. Ginny tried to do the same, to remind herself that there would be eyes on her anytime she was in public, that she was a minor celebrity now, had been from the moment she agreed to marry Jim.

But her mind kept wandering, from the sights and sounds of the Tartan Ball the night before, to the lists of things yet to be done before May Day, to the dead woman on the field. She missed her entrance on the next prayer and had to really concentrate to get through the final hymn.

"What were you thinking about?" Jim asked, over coffee.

Ginny's smile spread across her face and reached her eyes. She had no problem answering that one.

"How much fun it is to see a man in a kilt dancing." She took a sip of her coffee, still looking at Jim over the edge of the cup. "Standing still is good, too, and so is marching, especially from behind, but dancing is better."

"Eat your breakfast." He pointed at the eggs and potatoes still on her plate, but she could see he was smiling.

She opened her eyes wide. "Don't you believe me? You can ask anyone!" This, by the way, was true.

"There is nothing more attractive to a woman than a man in a full dress kilt, unless it's a handsome man wearing just a kilt. A handsome, big, strong, broad-shouldered—" She broke off as a familiar face approached their table.

"Good morning, Detective Tran."

"Good morning, Miss Forbes, Dr. Mackenzie."

"Would you care to join us?" Ginny scooted over to make room on the bench.

"Thank you."

They chatted about the weather and the food and the Games in general for a few moments, then Ginny fell silent. There was no chance this was a purely social call.

"I have a question for you, Miss Forbes."

Ginny finished the last bite of eggs before picking up her coffee and turning to face the detective.

"Ummm?" She studied the older woman's face. Inscrutable she might be, but she was not without *some* facial expressions. She actually looked a bit uneasy this morning.

"I noticed the brooch you are wearing. Could you tell me about it, please?"

Alarm bells went off in Ginny's mind. This was not one woman admiring another's jewelry. The brooch would be part of the investigation. That was the way the detective's mind worked.

Ginny lifted both eyebrows. "This one?" She indicated the metal ring securing her tartan airsaid to her shoulder.

"Yes."

Ginny reached up and removed the brooch from the fabric, then handed it over.

"It's a penannular. Examples can be found throughout the world from the Iron Age forward, but the best known are Celtic. They work this way." Ginny demonstrated pulling the fabric up through the loop of bronze, piercing it with the pin, then tugging everything back into place.

"How did you come to possess this?"

"This one is a legacy. It was my father's."

The detective reached out and touched the ornament. "They are handmade?"

"Usually."

"Would you be able to recognize one as the possession of a specific person?"

Again alarm bells went off in Ginny's brain. "Probably not. You can buy them at Games or off the Internet these days. Do you have one to show me?"

Detective Tran reached into a pocket and withdrew an evidence bag containing a brooch very like the one Ginny was wearing. This one looked newer, shinier. Ginny recognized the effect of a different set of metal alloys used in the forging process. The metal had been twisted in the opposite direction from hers. The finials, too, were different, one being a dog's head, the other a bear's. Also, this one had blood on it.

Ginny studied the device, looking closely, and trying not to react. Against all odds, she did know the owner of this brooch. She'd complained to Ginny last night that she'd misplaced it, and had to wear something else to the Tartan Ball.

Ginny handed the bag back to Detective Tran. "I'm sorry. I

can't help you. Where did you find it?"

"On the ground, half buried in the mud, underneath Judge Jamieson's body. Could this have been hers?"

Ginny's brow furrowed. "It's possible. She wasn't wearing Highland costume, but it might have fallen out of her pocket. Was there a receipt with it? Maybe she had just purchased it. You could ask the vendors if they recognize it."

Detective Tran pulled out a notepad and pen, wrote something down, then looked back at Ginny.

"The bruises and abrasions on her arms—"

"Yes?"

"It is the Medical Examiner's opinion that she got them only hours before her death."

Ginny could almost feel Jim perking up his ears. Not that he hadn't been listening, but this was right up his alley.

"Judge Jamieson was seen at the event, Fiddle Faddle I believe it is called."

Ginny nodded.

"So she was alive at that time and dead when found the next morning."

Ginny nodded again.

"We have witnesses that place her in the Patrons' Hospitality Suite around midnight."

"Oh?"

"The Hospitality Suite is, I believe, located at the top of the stadium."

"Yes."

"In your opinion, could Judge Jamieson have sustained the injuries you saw by falling down the concrete stairs at the stadium?"

Ginny nodded. "Yes. The edges of the stairs could break the blood vessels and the rough texture of the concrete could tear the skin in just the way we saw."

"Do you know anyone who was on those stadium stairs on Friday night?"

Ginny's brow furrowed. "Jamieson was in the stands during the Calling of the Clans. Is that what you meant?"

"What about later?"

Ginny shook her head. "I went straight to the parking lot from Fiddle Faddle."

It was the truth, but it was clear Detective Tran did not believe her. She held Ginny's gaze for an uncomfortably long moment, then nodded. "Thank you, Miss Forbes. Please let me know if you think of anything else that could help us in our investigations."

Ginny nodded. She watched until the detective was out of sight, then turned and found Jim's eyes on her.

"You recognized it."

"Was it that obvious?"

"No, but I'm beginning to know how to read your face. Why did you lie to her?"

Ginny picked up the coffee, then set it down again. She looked up and met Jim's eyes.

"I didn't lie. I told her I couldn't help her. I need to talk to the owner before I know what to say—and to whom."

Jim moved the remains of the meal aside, then stretched his arms across the table. He closed his hands around hers and drew her to him, leaning toward her, making it easier to be heard above the babble of the crowd.

"I trust your judgment, Ginny. Lord knows, I should by now. Let me know if you need my help."

She smiled. "I will."

He hesitated. "I'm not going to ask you not to help Detective Tran. That was part of the bargain. But I want you to remember your promise to me. Don't take any chances. I want my bride at the altar on our wedding day."

Ginny nodded. "That goes for you, too! I don't want to be stood up."

He grinned. "What if I'm late?"

"Don't you dare!"

"Well, you know, I might get an emergency call from the hospital."

"Angus will *not* let that happen."

"Or cold feet."

Ginny felt her throat closing, all the joy draining out of her soul. Having decided to accept him, she now went in dread that he would change his mind about her.

He must have read her mind for he jumped up, came around to her side of the table and pulled her into his arms.

"It's all right, darling. I was just teasing. *Nothing* is going to keep me from that church on May the first."

Ginny turned her face into his shoulder and considered how fragile joy can be. Solid as a rock one moment, then vanishing into the mist.

He held her for a long time, murmuring reassurances into her ear and, very slowly, she recovered. But she had been shaken. And she really did *not* want to be left waiting at the church for a bridegroom that never came.

* * *

Later that same day Ginny was sitting in the stands, watching the sheep dog trials. It was soothing and entertaining to see how the dogs handled the sheep. Border Collies were reputed to be the most intelligent breed on the planet. They were working dogs, having been bred to herd livestock and sometimes small children. Innocents who took them home on the strength of their cheerful dispositions often had to get rid of them because they couldn't keep the animals occupied, resulting in the dogs finding other ways to amuse themselves.

"Miss Forbes? May I speak with you, please?"

Ginny gestured at the empty seat beside her, then turned to face the new arrival.

"I'm Wally's mother."

Ginny nodded. "What can I do for you, Mrs. Hunter?"

"You can speak to the police for me. Tell them Wally didn't kill that woman."

Ginny blinked. "Did Wally say that to you?"

The woman twisted her bag in her hands. "No. He says he tossed the caber that landed on her head, but there were no witnesses. It could have been someone else!"

"Mrs. Hunter, I'm sorry, but I only know what Wally told me. I wasn't there."

"You know that detective woman. You can tell her he wouldn't do something like that, get drunk and steal a caber. She won't listen to me, but she listens to you. You can tell her she's got it all wrong."

Mrs. Hunter was staring hard at Ginny, expecting her to side with the clan against the outsider. Ginny didn't even bother to glance around. There was no help for her and no avoiding this.

"Mrs. Hunter, I can't do that."

"They've brought charges! This will ruin his chance of getting into college! You have to help me!"

Ginny could sympathize with the anguish this poor woman must be feeling, but she could *not* set a precedent of that sort.

"Have you spoken to the Laird?"

Mrs. Hunter nodded.

"What did he say?"

"That the lad must face the consequences of his choices." She was crying now, tears rolling down her cheeks. "This will ruin him."

Ginny put her arm around the woman's shoulders and gave

her a hug. "We don't know that. The police haven't finished their investigation."

Mrs. Hunter removed a tissue from her bag and wiped her eyes. "Will you talk to her, at least?"

Ginny nodded. "I'll see what I can find out, but I won't be able to change her mind. Not if he's really guilty."

"Maybe they can be lenient, offer him a deal, like they do on TV."

"You should consider hiring a good lawyer. Do you have one?"

She nodded. "Himself took care of that."

God bless him! Of course he would.

Ginny gave her another hug. "Don't despair." She rose. "Shall I walk you back to your tent?" Mrs. Hunter nodded. "It's very kind of you. Thank you."

Ginny escorted Mrs. Hunter safely back to her husband, then went off to find Angus. Not that she thought she could do anything for the poor woman, but she needed to let him know she had been approached. After which, she needed to go find Caroline. It was time to see what she knew about that missing brooch.

* * *

CHAPTER 7

Sunday Early Afternoon
Games Grounds

Ginny smiled at Mrs. Cameron. "May I borrow Caroline, please?"

"Certainly, dear. Have a nice time."

Ginny pulled her friend across the grounds, noticing she still had a limp. She steered her into the substructure of the stadium, then down the hall, and into an unlocked storage room. She closed the door behind them then turned to Caroline.

"Sit!"

Caroline did so, her expression fading from amusement to something more like apprehension.

"What's up?"

Ginny grabbed a stool and sat, facing her friend.

"Where were you Friday night?"

"Here, of course. You saw me at Fiddle Faddle."

"After that."

"Oh." Caroline's eyes wandered off. "Here and there."

"Were you over by the athletics field?"

Her brow rose. "I might have been."

"Caroline, this is serious. Were you there?"

Her friend looked at her, eyes narrowing. "Why do you want

to know?"

"I have a reason. Please, just tell me. Yes or no?"

Caroline looked at her for a moment, then nodded. "Yes, but not for long."

"What were you doing?"

"What is this? An interrogation?"

"Yes! What were you doing on the field?"

Caroline was frowning now. "I don't see what business it is of yours."

"Please, please, PLEASE just answer the question."

"What's up, Ginny?"

"I can't tell you. Not yet. Focus! I need to know what you were doing out there."

Ginny watched the color rise in her friend's cheeks. "We were looking at the stars."

"You and Alan?"

"Yes."

"What else were you doing?"

"What makes you think we were doing anything else?"

"You took off your airsaid."

Caroline's face paled. "What if I did?"

"You lost your penannular brooch. You can't do that unless you take it out of the fabric and you only do that if you are taking the airsaid off."

Caroline nodded. "True. I must have put it down without noticing. Did you find it?"

Ginny shook her head. "No. The police did."

"The police!"

"Under the dead woman's body."

Caroline was gaping now.

"With blood on it."

"*What?*"

"Caroline! Do you know who the dead woman was?"

Caroline closed her mouth, licked her lips, swallowed, and nodded. "I heard it was Judge Jamieson."

"Yes. Did you see her on the athletic field?"

"No!"

"At any time?"

"No!"

"Was there anyone in the area who looked suspicious?"

"Not that I noticed."

"Tell me everything."

"We were looking at the stars, talking. But there were too many people coming and going across the field. So we left."

"When was that?"

Caroline screwed up her face. "Around eleven."

"How do you know?"

"Glen sent his girls to find me, and I checked my watch since it was way past their bedtime."

"Your nieces saw you on the field with Alan?"

"Yes."

"Well, that's something."

"What do you mean by that?"

Ginny brushed the question aside. "Where did you go from there?"

Caroline had her hands in her lap, her fingers intertwined. She dropped her gaze to them and left it there. "Alan said he knew a place where we could be alone."

"Where, Caroline?"

"The breezeway. There are alcoves on either side. Big enough for—" Her voice trailed off.

"Big enough for a man and a woman to do what comes naturally."

Caroline looked up quickly. "We didn't get a chance, but you might as well know. He proposed, Ginny! And I said yes! We're going to be married!"

Ginny felt her heart flip over, in sympathy and fear.

"That's wonderful, Caroline! I couldn't be happier for the two of you, but I wish you had gone home!"

"Why?"

Ginny almost laughed. Would have, if she hadn't been so distressed.

"Oh Caroline, darling! Don't you see?"

"See what?"

"Your brooch was found under Judge Jamieson's body. That puts you on the field in the same spot, and I'm sure the police will find someone who saw you on the breezeway."

Caroline was frowning. "Why should the police care?"

"Detective Tran was asking me about the bruises on the Judge's arms, if I thought she could have gotten them tumbling down the stadium steps. And now I find you and Alan were on the stadium steps at the same time the Judge left the Skybox. That puts you in the right place and at the right time—twice."

Caroline's face had paled. "Bruises?"

"Yes, there were bruises and abrasions on Jamieson's arms. The police want to know how they got there."

Caroline's brow furrowed. "I thought it was the caber that killed her."

"We have to wait for the autopsy to be sure. In the meantime, the police are trying to fill in the gaps. They're going to want to talk to you and Alan, to see if you heard or saw something."

"But we didn't! Why won't you believe me?"

Ginny took a moment to answer the question in her mind. Because the bruises implied another accident, and how likely was it that the Judge was in *two* unrelated accidents on the same night? Tran was suspicious.

"Because I don't see any way out of telling Detective Tran the truth." Ginny frowned. "She knows I was holding out on her. Either you or I will have to tell her the brooch is yours, but it would be better coming from you.”

Caroline's eyes had wandered during the explanation. She was staring, unblinking, at a spot on the storage room wall.

“Caroline?” Ginny had to try twice. “Caroline?”

Slowly Caroline looked back at Ginny. “The dead woman was Blair Jamieson. I knew her, from my Highland Dance days.” She stood up. “Do you think that detective will give me my brooch back?”

“I think you'd better go ask her.”

Caroline shook her head slowly, then limped across the room, and put her hand on the doorknob. “No. At least, not yet. I can get another if I have to.”

She let herself out, leaving Ginny staring after her. There had been an incident between Caroline and Jamieson, she remembered now. Acrimony, and accusations. Something Caroline had refused to talk about. Ginny rose and went off to see if she could find someone who remembered the details.

* * *

Sunday Afternoon
Games Grounds

Ginny stepped into the shade of the dance tent. International events, like the Highland Dance competitions, rated much larger stages and protection from the weather.

She looked around for someone to talk to, someone specific, and found him, a harassed man of about her own age, juggling clipboards, and directing traffic. The competitors were stretching or bouncing up and down to warm their muscles or securing bits of costume with safety pins. The youngest were running, in an excess of excitement and a dearth of parental supervision.

Ginny worked her way over to her friend.

"How are you holding up?"

Douglas Abernathy was something of a curiosity. Highland dance had its roots in battle tactics, fast reflexes, and an uncanny sense of balance. Over time it had devolved from a display of masculine strength to something young women did, but there were still a few male dancers, especially in the military. Doug was still competing, but he was also teaching and today, it was clear, he was trying to cope with the loss of the head judge.

"We managed to fly someone in from Canada, but we're behind schedule. It's been a nightmare!"

Ginny nodded sympathetically. "May I interrupt you? I have a question."

He gave her half a smile. "You can have three minutes, then I have to clear this stage and set up the next group."

"Do you remember Caroline Cameron?"

He nodded. "Nice dancer. I always thought she should have done better in the standings."

"Was there an incident about that, back when we were in high school?"

Doug wrinkled his forehead. "Yeah, there was. Jamieson disqualified her in the final round."

"Do you remember why?"

"It was a dress code violation." He made a face. "She was always a stickler."

"What happened?"

"Caroline filed a protest and we thought she was going to win, but—" He shrugged.

"Was that the end of it?"

Doug bit his lip. "I'm not sure I should tell you this. I'm not supposed to know."

Ginny waited. Gossip was often its own reward and there was no telling what was coming.

"There was an accusation of a bribe. The winner that year got a scholarship to Lyon College and *she* was Jamieson's student."

"Was it true?"

Douglas sighed. "We think so, but no one was willing to push it. There were other agendas behind the decision, so Caroline was just unlucky. Bad timing." He shrugged again. "I'm sorry. Got to go."

Ginny waved her thanks and found a seat among the spectators. She needed to think.

How would Tran interpret this? It was ancient history. Caroline had gotten over it. She'd chosen a different school, come home with a dual degree in physics and engineering from Wellesley and the Massachusetts Institute of Technology. Since then she'd added a master's degree and was talking about a doctorate. The loss of the scholarship to Lyon College hadn't hurt Caroline. It had helped her.

So, even if Tran was looking for something other than an accident, Caroline was in the clear. Whatever history she and Jamieson had, it was over and done with.

* * *

Sunday Late Afternoon
Games Grounds

Sunday was waning and the Games were winding down. Ginny sat in the stands, Jim beside her, enjoying the climax of the weekend. The competitions had reached the last stages, and each had been moved to this central location, so that all could attend, and cheer on the finalists.

These were world class competitors, some of the best Highland dancers, heavy athletes, and pipe bands Ginny would ever see. She cheered and clapped the performances, and again as Angus handed the winners their trophies.

Closing ceremonies followed on the heels of the awards, with the massed bands taking over the field and bringing the crowd to its feet. They cheered and whistled and shouted and clapped and laughed and danced and the sound of the pipes made her heart soar.

Ginny turned to Jim and put her arms around him, hugging him as tightly as she could. These were her people and this was her husband-to-be and it had been a glorious weekend, in spite of the tragedy. He seemed to understand, holding her close and smiling at her.

And then it was over. Not completely, of course. There would be farewell dinners after they finished striking the tents and hauling off the supplies.

Ginny and Jim climbed the stadium steps, up rather than down, toward the ramp that would take them to the clan tent area. As she reached the deck, she noticed a group of uniformed policemen waiting. They had their eyes on the crowd. She moved past them without problem, but when she looked back over her shoulder, she saw them start down the steps, in pairs, protective gloves on their hands and plastic bags at the ready.

Overseeing the activity was Detective Tran. Their eyes met for a moment, then Jim said something and Ginny answered him. When she looked back, Tran was gone.

* * *

CHAPTER 8

Monday Morning
Forbes Residence

On Monday morning Ginny sat in front of her computer scrolling through the images that had already come in. How she had let herself be talked into doing snapshot analysis she had no idea. Well, Himself had asked her to, but she was pretty sure the request had come from Tran.

The idea was an obvious one. Heaven only knew how many cameras had been on the field on Friday. The request had gone out on Saturday and Sunday and a dropbox set up. All she had to do was eliminate the ones outside the Window of Opportunity and look for Jamieson, to see who she had talked to on the night of her death. The police were undoubtedly dealing with the security cameras.

It took her an hour to sift through the first group, making sure the Judge did not appear in any of the pictures. She sighed, archived those and downloaded the next batch.

By lunchtime she had a grand total of three images showing the Judge talking to people at Fiddle Faddle. She forwarded them to the e-mail Tran had left with her, then pushed away from the desk, and headed for the kitchen. She found her mother making sandwiches.

"I thought you might be hungry."

"I am, thank you!"

"And Jim is here."

"He is? Where?"

"In the den, watching TV."

"Why didn't he come upstairs?"

"I told him you were working and he said he could wait."

Ginny grabbed a second sandwich and headed for the den. The TV was on and Jim was in there, but he wasn't watching the show. He was asleep.

She tiptoed over and looked down at him, her heart melting at the sight. She set the sandwich down, then bent down to kiss him, very, very gently. It was enough, though. He took a deep breath and stretched, then opened his eyes.

"Hi!"

"Hi, yourself."

He sat up, rubbing his head and neck. "Did I nod off?"

"Apparently. How long have you been here?"

He glanced at his watch. "Two hours."

She handed him the sandwich, then sat down facing him. "You look tired."

He nodded. "I was up late."

"After you dropped me off? I thought you were going home to bed."

"I did, too. Himself called."

Ginny's brow furrowed. "Where does that man get his energy?"

Jim laughed. "I don't know, but I need some of whatever he's using."

"What did he want?"

"He wanted to talk about the Games, what went right, what went wrong."

"Surely that could have waited?"

"He was upset about the haggis, and Jamieson."

Ginny nodded. "What's the news on the haggis?"

"The organism was *salmonella*, no surprise there. Not much of it in any one patient and a mysterious number of unaffected. All the ill ate early. There must have been a second batch and the theory is that whoever handled that first batch transferred the organism from his or her hands to the food."

"That makes sense."

"We're looking at the volunteers and anyone who was in the Skybox around six."

Ginny was suddenly reminded of Mama Dupree. "Did you talk to the Scottish witch woman?"

"No, should I have?"

"She told me she'd eaten haggis and been sick in the night, and she looked awful Saturday morning."

Jim nodded. "I'll follow up with her." He applied his attention to the sandwich and Ginny found herself watching him with interest. She decided he'd been well brought up. He chewed with his mouth closed, took reasonable-sized bites, and swallowed before he spoke again.

"He also wanted to talk about Detective Tran."

Ginny felt a small quiver in the pit of her stomach. "Oh?"

Jim nodded. "He seems to think she can be recruited."

"You mean corrupted."

Jim wiped his mouth with the napkin. "Well, 'aligned' might be a better word." He looked straight at Ginny. "He suggested, very carefully, that you might consider taking Detective Tran under your wing and teaching her how the clan system works."

"He hasn't forgotten we've got a wedding coming up, has he?"

Jim rose, pulling her to her feet and into his arms. "No, he hasn't forgotten and neither have I. There's no hurry. As a matter of fact, I came over to collect you so we could go work on the house. There's still a lot to do before we move in."

"Just let me get my purse." She broke out of his embrace and hurried upstairs, then back down to meet him in the front hall.

"Mother? We're off!"

"Okay, dear. See you at dinner."

Ginny winked at Jim. He never minded when her mother cooked for them. Probably a good thing. They might be eating here a lot.

* * *

Monday Afternoon
The New House

The house was a gift. Angus Mackenzie had located a suitable older five bedroom inside the perimeter, purchased it, then press-ganged a small army of roofers, electricians, plumbers, carpenters, painters, and engineers to make sure the fabric was sound. It had no termites, a stable foundation, new roof and insulation, and fresh paint, both inside and out.

The kitchen and bathrooms had been updated. New appliances had been delivered and hooked up and the electricity and water were both on. The air conditioning / heating unit had been replaced, the vents cleaned, the chimney swept, and the hot water system modernized. The locksmith had changed all the exterior access locks and had added an alarm system. Angus had also paid for a crew of professional cleaners to come. They had stripped everything and disinfected the (microscopic) life out of it.

The new carpet was still to be laid, and a section of parquet flooring, and quarry tiles in the laundry room. The yardmen were scheduled. Once the paint had dried, Jim and Ginny had added wallpaper borders and some detailing. That left three items of woodwork that needed repairing, all the interior handles to switch over to levers, and new electrical faceplates everywhere. Also, Ginny wanted to change some of the ceiling fixtures. They had asked the electrician to come back to hang fans and install light kits.

After the floors were in place, they could hang the curtains and move the big furniture in. And after *that*, they could start on the small items; dishes and silverware, clothes and cleaning supplies, books and pictures. Ginny stepped inside and looked around, despairing of hope.

"We're never going to be done in time!"

"Oh, yes, we are. Look!" Jim pointed at the van pulling up in front. "Here are the floors and here comes the carpenter." By dinnertime, there were six fewer items on their to-do list and the house smelled of floor wax.

Ginny paused on her way through the den to admire the fireplace again. Whoever had installed it had added a medieval stone arch as a decorative surround. She loved it and said so when Jim found her there.

"We need to do some shopping."

She nodded. They had already located furniture for the master suite. Jim had insisted on having Ginny's input on the selections, saying it was his responsibility to make a home for her, but she would have to use the items. One of the sofas was coming out of Jim's apartment, having been brought with him from Virginia. He also had his parents' dining room suite, china, silverware, and crystal, all in storage because his apartment was too small to house them. Ginny was supplying bookcases and a carved oak desk for the room which would become her office. Jim had permission to turn a sitting room off the kitchen area into a man cave. The remaining three bedrooms were set aside for future use.

They locked up the house and headed for the store.

"Can you come out with me tomorrow?" Jim asked.

"Yes, except that I have a fitting at one o'clock and we both have to work tomorrow night."

"I want to finish picking out the furniture this week so we can have it delivered on time."

Ginny sighed. "We're not going to be done by the thirtieth."

He reached over and took her hand. "We'll have the important stuff in place, a table to eat on, chairs to sit in, a bed to sleep upon. We can fill in the gaps as we go."

Ginny nodded. She was admitting to herself that a home was a work in progress, no matter how long one had lived there, when her phone went off. She pulled it out and looked at it.

"I missed three calls." She had left her purse locked up in the car while they worked.

"Who from?"

"Detective Tran." She scrolled down the list. "Oh, wait, here's a text message. And another from Caroline." She read them swiftly, then went back and read them again. Jim looked over at her.

"What do they say?"

When she didn't answer immediately, he asked again. "Ginny?"

She looked over at him, her mind still trying to surround the news.

"What's happened?" he asked.

"They've picked up Caroline."

"What?"

"The police. They've taken her in for questioning."

"About what?"

"The murder of Judge Blair Jamieson!"

* * *

CHAPTER 9

Ginny came storming back to where Jim sat, Mrs. Cameron on one side, an empty seat on the other, Alan across from him.

"They won't let me see her."

Jim shrugged. "You're not her lawyer."

"*You* got in, and Himself."

She knew, perfectly well, that Angus Mackenzie had entrée everywhere and that Jim, as laird-in-training, would be taken along. What she hadn't quite gotten used to was being excluded, now that she was no longer in the running for the position of laird. That would change after the first of May. In the meantime, she was relegated to consoling Mrs. Cameron. She sat down beside her and put her arm around the older woman's shoulders.

"I'm sure it's a mistake. Caroline couldn't kill anyone. I've known her all my life and she wouldn't hurt a flea." Ginny delivered the lines firmly, with conviction, but couldn't help remembering the sight of Caroline at their last meeting, evasive, argumentative, suddenly silent. She glanced across at Alan, wondering if they had made their plans public yet. He looked up and saw her.

Alan Christie had been a late bloomer. He'd been raised by

his grandparents after losing both of his parents to a home invasion. Somehow, the villains had overlooked him, asleep in his bed. He'd been four years old.

He'd had an unremarkable schooling and sports career, one of the less-steller athletes, fast, but clumsy. Eventually he had grown into his height, and in the last five years he'd filled out nicely. He'd also come back from college with a degree in architecture and a taste for theater.

He was, without question, the best swordsman they had, or had ever had. As tall as William Wallace, and with a natural grace that had come with self-confidence, he could lift the hand-and-a-half and make it look easy. He'd taken over the edged weapon lessons and proved an adept and sensitive teacher. Everyone liked him. Everyone admired him.

He'd had a crush on Caroline Cameron for as long as Ginny could remember, but Caroline had needed to do some growing up before she could see it. It was an imminently suitable match and Ginny prayed nothing would get in the way.

"I have already given the police my statement. They know she was with me," he said.

Ginny caught her breath. Caroline must have told him about their conversation. She nodded. A strong and virtuous man, supporting his fiancée in her hour of need.

"There, you see? Alan is her alibi. They can't hold her if she has an alibi."

They could, actually, if they suspected the source, and it was taken as a given that a man in love would lie for his lady. Still, that couldn't be all of it. They would never have picked her up if there weren't more to the story.

Ginny gave Mrs. Cameron another squeeze. "When is Mr. Cameron due back?" He was away on a business trip.

She stirred. "Tonight. Glen has gone to pick him up at the airport."

"Good." And that was that. They all fell silent. They would simply have to wait until the door opened and Caroline came out.

* * *

Monday Evening
Laird's Residence

Mrs. Cameron had wept and Caroline had looked terrified, but there had been no hitches. What's more, there had been a surprise appearance by the Hunter boy, also released to his family's custody, with an admonition.

"We won't hold you, either of you, but we would prefer that you stay where we can reach you in case we have more questions."

Detective Tran had explained. "It is, at this moment, impossible to tell the cause of death, though some form of head trauma is suspected. Experts have been called in and we hope to have a definitive answer in forty-eight hours. At that time, the prosecutor will decide what, if any, charges to bring against each of you."

Mr. Hunter signed for custody of his child, Caroline on her own behalf, and Himself counter-signed both, for the Loch Lonach community. There would be no flight from justice.

The Hunters went home, as did Mrs. Cameron, but Alan, Caroline, Ginny, Jim, and Himself reconvened at the Laird's house. He brought out the twenty-year-old Scotch and poured each a wee dram.

Himself took a pull on the drink, then set it down and looked across the table at Caroline.

"Are ye prepared tae tell us th' truth, lass?"

She swallowed hard, her hands on her glass, the contents

untouched. "Yes, sir."

"Let's ha'e it, then."

Ginny listened as Caroline recounted the dispute over the Highland Dance competition scoring, the connection to the scholarship, the written complaint, and its unsatisfactory outcome. No one interrupted her and Ginny found *that* more nerve-racking than a formal interrogation. Angus was giving her enough rope to hang herself. When Caroline stopped talking, he inserted a question.

"Th' police tell me there was an incident at school."

Caroline squirmed, her eyes darting from one to another, all except Alan. He sat beside her, not touching her, but facing the rest of them, clearly on her side.

"Aye, sir. There was."

What followed was not without its lighter side. In spite of landing on her feet, Caroline had nursed a grudge. When she'd found herself challenged at MIT to design a device no one had ever seen before, she'd had an inspiration. She'd looked up a law student friend, who helped her do the research, then another in the botany department, an expert in seed dispersal. She had then sat down and developed a miniaturized explosive delivery system that did not use any explosives, did not violate the U.S. mail laws, and did not do any actual damage to the container or the target. She had loaded her booby trap with a non-toxic, but persistent, dye, then mailed it to Judge Jamieson.

The Judge, having opened the envelope, found herself covered in dye and unable to remove it in time for either her court appearance that day or the reception that should have followed that evening. She had not been amused. Summoning her extensive network of insiders, she had the envelope traced and found not only DNA evidence that linked the device to Caroline, but that Caroline had been bragging about her success. Surreptitious images of the Judge, covered in dye, had found their way onto social media web sites. Proof that Caroline's design worked.

She was charged with assault and battery, but the charges were reduced to misdemeanor battery and, when no intent to actually injure the Judge could be proved, pled out. The fact that she had attacked an officer of the court made the situation worse. The fact that she could not have known whether the letter would arrive or be opened, and if so, when, made the allegation of intentional harm (public humiliation) null. The incident had left her with a criminal record, and job offers from three prestigious research facilities, one of them, Texas Instruments, in Dallas.

Ginny tried hard not to smile. Himself frowned hard, his bushy brows lowering, his hand turning his glass on the table.

"Is that how ye want yer children tae think o' ye, Caroline? As a prankster?"

Caroline hung her head. "No, sir."

"I'm no happy tae hear ye've abused yer gifts in this manner."

"I'm sorry."

He frowned a while longer, then lifted his drink to his lips and took a sip. Ginny did the same. There was more coming.

"They found yer brooch on th' field."

"Yes, sir." Caroline shot a quick glance at Ginny, then put her eyes back on the table.

"Ginny didna break yer confidence. Detective Tran figured it oot. She brought it tae me."

Caroline said nothing. Instead, it was Alan who answered him. He reached over and took Caroline's hand.

"The police showed me a picture of Caroline leaving the breezeway. I told them she was with me the whole time, at Fiddle Faddle, on the field, in the stadium, up until we parted for the night."

"And when was that, lad?"

"One thirty a.m."

"How do ye recall sae exactly?"

"We planned to meet again Saturday morning. The gates opened at seven for set-up. We decided we would meet for breakfast at six thirty, then go to the Games together. That left me exactly five hours to get home, cleaned up, slept, dressed again, and over to the restaurant. It seemed a long time to have to wait."

Himself looked at Caroline. "Fiddle Faddle started at seven p.m. If ye dinna separate 'til one thirty, ye were together six and a half hours. Were ye never apart in all that time?"

"Never!" Caroline voice was firm.

He lifted a skeptical eyebrow and Ginny saw Caroline blink.

"Oh! I know what you're getting at. Yes. I went to the bathroom twice and he went to go buy food once and Ginny pulled me into the dancing several times."

"We needn't concern ourselves wi' Fiddle Faddle. Just th' time on th' field and in th' stands."

Caroline and Alan looked at one another.

"We were together the whole time," Caroline said.

Alan nodded. "After she hurt her ankle."

"Except to go to the bathroom," Caroline added.

Himself nodded. "So, lass, if yer as innocent as all that, tell me. Why do th' police think ye pushed that woman down the stadium steps?"

Caroline took a deep breath, then sat up a little straighter and looked the Laird in the face.

"Because I did."

* * *

Monday, Late Evening
Forbes Residence

It had been an exhausting evening. Ginny sat on the Forbes' den sofa, curled up in Jim's arms, wishing she could stay there all night. Wishing he didn't have to leave. Wishing there hadn't been a body on the Highland Games field.

She admitted to a native curiosity—all right, an over-active curiosity—about the death. Who wouldn't wonder? But she was just too busy! She didn't have time to investigate a murder and she didn't want to. She wanted to get married. To Jim. Now.

She sighed heavily and felt Jim's arms tighten around her.

"What is it, darling?"

"She *cannot* be guilty. Not Caroline. Not my best friend!"

"You heard what she said."

"Yes, I did. She pushed that hateful woman down the stairs, but Jamieson got up again, vowing revenge. Caroline says she was alive and swearing when Alan pulled her away and I believe her."

Jim nodded. "Unfortunately, that part of the incident was *not* caught on camera, just the push and the fall."

Ginny frowned. "The autopsy will clear her."

"I hope you're right."

Ginny sat up suddenly and turned to face her fiancé.

"It has to! She's my Maid of Honor. I can't get married without her!"

Jim drew her back into his arms, cuddling her, holding her, and Ginny suddenly found herself weeping in frustration.

Her best friend could NOT be guilty of murder. She *had* to be cleared before the wedding and if the police didn't do it, Ginny would have to and she *didn't have time.*

They had made a mistake. That much was obvious. Caroline

could *not* be guilty. Not of murder. Not Caroline. *Not* someone she had known *all her life*, her sister in all but blood.

Jim said nothing, just held her gently, and let her cry.

* * *

CHAPTER 10

Tuesday Morning
East Dallas

It was Tuesday. Only nineteen days left. Ginny ignored the sudden breathlessness that followed the thought. It was excitement. Couldn't be anything else. It was a wedding. *Her* wedding.

She forced herself to focus on her shopping. She now had sheets, blankets, towels, and soap checked off her list.

"Just how addicted are you to making lists?" Jim asked.

Ginny ignored him and kept on walking. "We can't buy any perishables until the last week, but we can lay in coffee, tea, and peanut butter."

"Peanut butter?" Jim grabbed the list out of her hands and held it above his head, out of reach, while he read. "Hmmm. Looks like you're stocking up for a siege."

"May I have my list back, please?"

He grinned down at her. "What will you give me for it?"

She lifted an eyebrow. "What do you want?"

His grin expanded. He brought the list down and tucked it into her hand, then wrapped his arms around her and bent down to whisper in her ear. "I already have what I want!"

Ginny felt her mouth go dry. She was suddenly shaking, her palms damp with sweat.

"Ginny?" His smile faded, to be replaced by a look of concern.

She dropped her eyes, trying to think. What could possibly make her want to run from her heart's desire? She knew, of course, and so did he.

He pulled her closer, whispering in her ear. "It's all right, Ginny. It's going to be all right, I promise. Come on."

He guided her into a nearby coffee shop, bought her a hot tea heavily laced with caramel syrup, then sat down across from her and studied her face. "Talk to me."

She could see it in his eyes. This was one of the moments Dr. Gordon had warned her about. "Dinna offer him th' option tae back out," he had said. "Dinna shift the responsibility onto his shoulders. Ye must make yer own decisions."

She took a breath. "I hear so many tales of failed marriages, and—"

"And?"

One of the things Ginny admired most about Jim was his bedside manner. He didn't panic when faced with emotions. She would be able to talk to him, to use him as a sounding board to understand herself.

"We both know men are hardwired to procreate, then move on."

Jim's brow furrowed. "The ones who don't care whether their progeny live or die, yes. But that doesn't apply to me."

"We don't know—I don't know—whether this marriage is going to work." Ginny swallowed. "I want to fast forward to this time next year, after we've settled in and are used to each other."

She watched as his eyebrows drew together.

"It's scary, taking a chance on another human being, but we're not strangers. You know me well enough by now, to know there's no chance I will walk out on you." His expression softened. "I intend to love you, comfort you, honor and keep you, in sickness and in health and—"

"—forsaking all others, so long as we both shall live." Their eyes met and she smiled. "That's what I want, Jim! *You're* what I want, have always wanted!" She mouthed the words at him, suddenly shy, aware of the people around them. "I love you."

He smiled back. "I love you, too!"

And with that, the crisis was over, the two of them back to cheerful teasing, working on the new house, locating a toaster and a kettle and a bread knife. Ginny found her heart still beating a little fast, even as he slipped his arm around her, smiled down at her, pointed out something he wanted her opinion on. Trust was such a slippery thing. She took the paper out of her pocket and focused on the next item on the list.

* * *

Tuesday Afternoon
Bridal Shop

There would be three fittings in all. This was the first. On Tuesday afternoon Ginny stood in front of the mirror, following directions, watching the seamstress mark changes and adjustments to the gown she would wear on her wedding day. It was not the usual white satin seen in bridal magazines. That would never do.

Scottish brides had a serious challenge to overcome. It was almost impossible to match the splendor of a handsome man in full dress kilt. Period. What's more, Scottish brides, as part of the ceremony, were draped by their new husbands in a sash made of his tartan, the gown a mere backdrop for the decoration.

The Dress Mackenzie tartan was predominantly dark green

and blue, with the white background that distinguished the dress version from the daytime version, and a narrow red stripe, for a splash of color. That meant she could choose from among forest green, navy blue, dead white, and Christmas red – or she could choose something neutral, like gold.

The gown had a boat neck, high and straight across, both in front and back, with three-quarter length sleeves, princess lines, flared skirt, and godets. There was a detachable train, anchored at the shoulders and falling to the floor behind, in soft folds that let her braid hang down unimpeded. No veil. She would wear a crown made of her own hair, a few sparklers stuck into it, to match the diamond studs in her ears. Once the sash was in place, she would be adorned with a brooch, not the massive base metal she had worn to the games, but a finely wrought jewel, enough for anyone, even on a wedding day.

The brooch had been a Christmas gift from Himself, and represented the 'something old,' it being a reproduction of a very old Mackenzie piece. The earrings were from her mother and represented the 'something new.' She still needed something borrowed and something blue. A ribbon perhaps? Around the bouquet?

The florist was the next stop. She would need to take a piece of the fabric with her. And she would need shoes, something stable and comfortable. She would change into ghillies for the dancing, but she couldn't walk down the aisle in those.

"Done." For the moment. Ginny let them strip her carefully out of the gown, avoiding most of the straight pins and managing to get it over her head without losing an earring. Then the petticoat and chemise. The rest of the undergarments were already identified and laid out, set aside for use on the day.

There would be no trousseau—no time and no reason, since

they weren't going on a honeymoon, but—Ginny blinked at her reflection, watching the color rise in her cheeks. Why hadn't she thought of that before? She was Scots to the core and made a habit of wearing things out, especially things no one else saw. But he would see them.

She needed to go shopping, and not with her mother. She needed Caroline and they hadn't spoken since the conference at Brockaber. Ginny hoped Caroline wouldn't think she was being self-centered, or frivolous. It wasn't that. It was a gesture of her faith in her friend. And it would give them a chance to talk in private. She picked up the phone and found that her call went straight to voicemail.

Ginny blinked, then told herself it didn't mean anything. Caroline was busy, or her mailbox was full. Something like that. Because Caroline would want to talk to *her*, even if she was shutting out everyone else. Except Alan, of course. Maybe she could ask Alan to ask Caroline to call her. Ginny watched as her reflection slipped the phone into the pocket of her jeans. Odd. If rolling over to voicemail didn't mean anything, why was her reflection frowning?

* * *

Tuesday Afternoon
Flower Shop

They were able to squeeze choosing the flowers into the waning afternoon, but just barely. It took a lot longer than Ginny had anticipated. They had to decide on arrangements for the altar, for the rehearsal dinner table, for the reception, and for the two bouquets, hers and Caroline's. By the time she and her mother were done, it was time to go home and get ready for work. She had been delighted to find the bluebonnets were in season and in abundance. The state flower of Texas would be a light-hearted addition to the floral arrangements. "Something blue." Which just left the shoes. But that would have to wait, and the clock was ticking.

* * *

Chapter 11

Tuesday Afternoon
County Hospital

Jim pulled into a physician parking space at the big Dallas county hospital, slid out, and hurried across the sky bridge to keep his appointment with one of the epidemiologists who worked in the facility. He was anxious to see if his hunch was right. He found the man without trouble and strode over, hand extended.

"Nick! Great to see you. You're looking well."

The other physician had more than thirty years on Jim, and had been his mentor at one time, back in D.C. Jim noted with some regret that his friend looked older than a man of his years should.

"Jim, my boy! Good to see you, too. When did you move to Dallas?"

"It's been almost a year. If you've got the time, you can take me to lunch one day and I'll tell you all about it."

"Ha! I knew there had to be an ulterior motive for you wanting to see me. I can offer you Sonny Bryan's, but not much else. And I'll have to watch you eat." He patted his midsection. "They've got me on short hours and nothing that tastes good."

"Better than the stroke I heard you almost had."

The older man nodded. "Agreed." He gestured toward an

office just down the hall. "Come inside, where we can sit and talk."

When they were settled, Jim leaned forward. "You got my message?"

"I did, and he's here. I've seen him."

Jim stopped just short of rubbing his hands together. "Tell me."

"He presented on Saturday evening, about ten p.m., sick as a dog. Projectile vomiting, non-stop diarrhea, dehydration, delirium. It took us the better part of a day to get him to the point where he could tell us what happened."

"What did he say?"

The older man half-smiled. "A lot of foolishness, at first, but eventually we got the story out of him. He was taking a leak along a fence in your part of town and saw a woman in an apron put a bag in the dumpster on the edge of the parking lot. He said he'd found good eating in that dumpster in the past, so he investigated. There was a baking dish, still warm, with some kind of casserole in it, so he decided he'd help himself."

"What time was that?"

"Around eight p.m., but that's an estimate. He doesn't own a watch."

"Okay. What else?"

"He says it wasn't what he would have chosen, but it was heavy on meat and lots of spices so he ate until he was full, then curled up in a patch of tall weeds and went to sleep. When he woke, he didn't feel good."

"I'll bet! How much did he eat?"

"No way to know. The dish has disappeared. But it must have been substantial. By the time he crawled out of his nest, he was unable to stand. Someone drove by and called the cops, who called 9-1-1, who brought him here."

Jim did some quick calculations. "About twelve hours."

The older physician nodded. "When he got here, they lavaged his stomach, which was empty, and cultured his stool, which was full of salmonella. We put him in isolation, cleaned him up, rehydrated him, and waited for him to sleep off the worst of it. In the meantime, we had the lab run the DNA on that strain, which, as you know, got reported to the local health department. They went looking for a source."

"And found me."

"Right."

Jim had done something similar with his batch of salmonella victims at Hillcrest.

"As I understand it, you had identified a fancy dish of some kind being served at a party you were holding over the weekend."

Jim laughed. "The dish is a Scottish specialty called haggis." He leaned forward. "But, no, other than all the victims had haggis that night, we have not identified the source. All of the dishes and servers came up clean. No one saw a thing. I posted my query in the forlorn hope that someone could steer us in the right direction."

"And got lucky."

Jim smiled. "Yes! I feel especially lucky that he didn't die."

"You and me both. Do you want to see him?"

"I'd like to ask him some questions, if I may."

"Should be safe enough. Just stay away from his body fluids."

The two men rose and Jim followed his old friend through a maze of corridors to a room marked with caution signs and isolation garb. They both put on the gowns, gloves, and shoe covers.

"I recommend a mask as well. He has a bad habit of hocking. An old smoker, I think."

Jim followed the suggestion. He stepped into the room and

waited to be introduced.

"Mr. Jordan, this is Dr. Mackenzie, a colleague of mine. He's an Infectious Disease specialist and would like to ask you a few questions, if he may."

The cachexic man in the bed looked at Jim, then smiled and nodded. Only two natural teeth remaining, Jim noted. Sunken eyes, yellow sclera. Skin like tissue paper, lots of abrasions. He would probably bruise if you breathed on him.

"Thank you for your help, Mr. Jordan. Dr. Endicott has told me how you got here and that you ate something you shouldn't have."

"Thas right. Dam near kilt me, it did. Tasted funny, too."

Jim smiled. "It's an acquired taste." He pulled a set of pictures out of his pocket and showed them to the patient. "I was wondering if you could identify the woman you saw putting the dish in the trash."

"Well, I don't know as I can. It were dark an' she had 'er back turned away."

"I'd appreciate it if you'd take a look."

"Okay. Let me see them pictures."

Jim handed them over, making a mental note to disinfect them before he put them back in his pocket. Salmonella can be infectious for up to a year.

"Nope. Nope. Nope. This one." Mr. Jordan handed the photo to Jim.

"You're sure?"

"Yep. She were wearin a plaid skirt an I thought it kinda purty. Specially with th lace round her throat."

Jim took the photo over to the window and studied it in the daylight. He nodded. "This will do nicely! Thank you very much for your help Mr. Jordan." He held out his still gloved hand and shook the patient's withered paw.

"I hope she don't get inta trouble cause of me. She looked

kinda worritt already."

"We don't yet know what actually happened," Dr. Endicott said. "Perhaps it was an accident."

"Mighty purty woman. A man could do worse."

The two physicians took their leave, not forgetting to scrub the germs off the pictures and their hands, then Dr. Endicott walked Jim to the exit.

"Let me know how it comes out. You've got me curious."

"I'll do that."

Back in his car, Jim glanced at the clock. Time for one more stop. He put the car in gear and headed back to the Homestead, to his grandfather.

"Mr. Jordan identified this woman as the one who put the tainted haggis in the dumpster on Friday night." He placed the picture on the table in front of the Laird. Angus Mackenzie picked it up and studied it, then nodded.

"I ken her. She's been makin' haggis for th' Burns Nicht suppers for years." He set the picture down. "Will ye talk wi' her or ha'e th' police do it?"

Jim glanced at his watch. "I go on duty in just under two hours. No time tonight and none tomorrow." He met his grandfather's eye. "Is she a flight risk?"

The Laird shook his head. "I dinna think so."

"Then I'd rather talk to her myself, and take Ginny with me. She'll make it seem more of a social call and less of an interrogation."

The Laird's brow furrowed. "Surely 'twas just misfortune?"

Jim lifted an eyebrow. "If that's the case, why did she dispose of the evidence? I found nothing in the Skybox and nothing in any of the prep kitchens and I cultured everything in sight."

The Laird's brow descended. "'Tis a very bad business. Well, I'll see she disnna fly th' coop afore ye can talk wi' her, but dinna leave it too long, lad. We canna ha'e oor guests poisoned by th' cook."

* * *

Wednesday, Very Early Morning
Hillcrest Medical Center ICU

Just after midnight on Wednesday morning, Ginny looked up to see Jim crossing the Intensive Care Unit in her direction. He had taken to visiting her in the middle of the night when they were both on duty, to whisk her off for a midnight meal. Their behavior had resulted in a predictable amount of good natured teasing. Everyone knew about the upcoming wedding. Everyone knew the history of how they had met. Most considered it romantic in the extreme.

"Are you interruptible?" he asked.

"I am. What have you got there?"

He pulled up a chair. "I've been going over the reports on the incident of the haggis in the hospitality suite."

Ginny laughed. "That sounds like the title of a spy thriller."

He smiled. "So it does, but the truth is less exciting, thank goodness. No one has died, that we know of, and only one has been hospitalized, though a few ended up in the ER for rehydration." He set a sheet of paper down in front of her. Ginny picked it up and looked down the list of names.

"We've done our best," he said, "to identify everyone in the Skybox that night. Most are locals. The honored guests were enjoying a special dinner at the hotel, so none of them was affected. We cross-referenced the names on the patron passes issued by the committee, added in the identifiable interlopers, and came up with what we believe is a complete list of those who came in contact with that bad batch of haggis."

"Good job!" Ginny was only half-teasing. Epidemiology could be a challenge even under the best of circumstances.

Jim made a face at her. "I've talked with all the people on that list except for one." He pointed at the name.

"Mama Dupree!"

"Yes. She was there, around six p.m., and she told you she was sick the next day, but we don't have good contact information for her so we can't follow up."

Ginny looked up in surprise. "She bought a patron pass. She rented a tent. There must be some way to contact her."

"You'd think so. We've been leaving messages, but so far she hasn't responded. We're beginning to worry."

"Oh, Jim!" Ginny's brow furrowed. "She didn't look that sick to me. What's the incubation period on salmonella?"

"Twelve to seventy-two hours. Most of our cases said they woke up Saturday morning feeling queasy and got sicker as the day wore on. I know you spoke to her on Saturday afternoon. I also know she packed up and went home before the gates closed on Saturday, and didn't come back on Sunday. I was hoping she said something to you that will help us trace her."

Ginny screwed up her face, trying to remember what she and Mama Dupree had talked about during the half hour she'd been over at the booth. "She gave me a business card, but all I did was stick it in my bag. It will have the same information she gave the Games committee, won't it?"

"Probably."

"I assume you've asked the police to help?"

"Not yet, but we're about to. It might embarrass her to be visited by a patrol car, but we'd rather know she's safe."

Ginny nodded.

"And there's more."

Ginny smiled at his expression. "You look like the cat that caught the canary. What have you been up to?"

"We think we've identified the source."

Ginny listened in growing dismay to the story of the woman discarding an almost full dish of haggis, of the subsequent poisoning, and the eyewitness identification of the culprit.

"Vanessa Ballantyne! No! It can't be! I've been in her kitchen. I *helped* her make that haggis."

Jim's expression had settled into a watchful concern. "It's possible it was a mistake, but—"

Ginny's heart sank. "But she knows about the salmonella. If it was an accident, she should have come forward."

Jim nodded. "I want you there when I talk to her."

"It will have to be Thursday night."

"Or Friday, I know. I have Grandfather keeping an eye on her for us."

Ginny's brows drew together. "If you can't find Dupree—"

"Then we may have a death on our hands after all."

Ginny felt her throat tighten. "That would change things."

"Yes, it would. See you at two?"

She nodded. "I'll meet you at the cafeteria."

"Right." He rose, collected his paperwork, then addressed her formally, for the benefit of the passing staff. "Thank you for your help, Miss Forbes."

Ginny pulled herself together. "Delighted to be of service, Dr. Mackenzie."

He smiled at her, then hurried off, leaving Ginny to wonder what had happened to Mama Dupree and what was to become of the only woman in the Loch Lonach community who knew how to make authentic haggis.

* * *

CHAPTER 12

Thursday Evening
Ballantyne Residence

Between Tuesday night and Thursday afternoon both Jim and Ginny had been forced to concentrate on their jobs, leaving no room for confronting suspects. They were now on their way to meet with the haggis cook.

Jim glanced across at Ginny, thinking she looked both unhappy and tired. "Did I remember to tell you we heard from Dupree? She was sick and lying low, but she's mostly over it, and no serious repercussions."

"That's good." Ginny's reply sounded automatic, as if her mind was elsewhere.

"Aren't you pleased, that she's not dead?"

Ginny roused herself. "Yes, of course I am."

"But?"

She glanced over at him. "I was wondering if I contaminated that haggis."

Jim blinked. It was an angle he hadn't considered. He matched her frown. "Why?"

"Because I was there, along with her daughter. The three of us were washing and chopping and mixing and none of us was wearing gloves." She tugged at her seatbelt, pulling it away from her throat. "I assumed all the ingredients were fresh--

nothing smelled funny, or looked old. But there were aprons, countertops, bowls, chopping boards, knives. Any of those could have been infected. Even the water supply."

Jim shook his head. "I cultured her kitchen. It was an obvious place to look. Everything in it, including the dirty aprons, came back clean. Not a trace." He glanced over at her again. "So, unless you brought the organism in, failed to wash your hands—which I don't believe—and introduced it into that dish of haggis, you aren't the source."

Ginny twisted around to face him. "There was just the one, right?"

"Right."

"We made three recipes—traditional, beef, and vegetarian. It would have been impossible to taint just one of the dishes, the way we were working. So none of them could have been contaminated during preparation. The organism had to have gotten in later."

Jim's brow furrowed. He already knew about the three varieties of haggis, and he'd asked the afflicted which one they'd eaten. All of them had consumed at least some of the traditional recipe. He kept his voice matter-of-fact.

"I know you're trying to exonerate Mrs. Ballantyne, but it looks very much as if she did it herself."

"Then how do you account for all the people who ate the traditional haggis and *didn't* get sick?"

It was a good question. "I'm hoping she'll explain it to us." Jim parked the car in front of the house and got out.

They were met at the front door by a teenager, the competing Highland Dancer of the family. Jim watched as Ginny greeted the girl with a hug.

"Kirstie! How are you?"

"Okay, I guess."

"Douglas Abernathy tells me you are poised to win

Nationals."

Kirstie nodded, but said nothing, her eyes sliding away from the guests.

"May we see your mother?" Jim asked.

The girl nodded again and let them enter the house, closing the door behind them. "This way."

Jim couldn't help noticing evidence of a neglected household as they made their way through the common rooms. Unopened mail lay on the staircase. The kitchen looked as if it hadn't been cleaned in a week. Clothes were piled on the laundry room floor. And the lights were off.

The girl led the way through the house to a sunken room with huge windows looking out over a carefully tended garden. The house backed up on a creek and the vista sloped across the lawn, then down into the stream bed. On a good day, it would have been lovely.

"Mother, they're here." Kirstie stood aside, then disappeared without another word.

Vanessa Ballantyne, "Nessie" to her friends, sat with her back to the house, her face to the garden, a tumbler of suspiciously amber liquid in her hand. She did not greet them.

Jim frowned. The light was off in this room, too, though the sunlight filtered in through the picture windows. He watched as Ginny stepped into the room, then made her way to a point in front of Mrs. Ballantyne. She went down on one knee in front of the woman.

"Nessie? Are you all right?"

Jim followed Ginny, turning his back on the garden so he could see the woman. She looked almost derelict—filthy, uncombed hair, smeared makeup, black circles under her eyes. They were open, but dulled by the liquor.

"Mrs. Ballantyne?" He approached her, noticing the smell of neglect as he drew nearer. Ginny moved aside, giving him room to work. He did a quick assessment of her general condition, as much as he could without his medical bag, then turned his attention to her mental state. He pulled up a chair and sat down, facing her.

She blinked, then seemed to see him for the first time. She stirred, reaching for the table, trying to set the glass down and Jim had to intercept it to make sure she didn't spill it.

"Thank you." She sucked in a lungful of air, then lifted her face. "Do I know you?"

"I'm Dr. Mackenzie. You know Ginny Forbes." He indicated Ginny. Mrs. Ballantyne twisted around until she could see Ginny, then nodded and turned back to look at Jim. Inebriated, certainly. Possibly worse at this point. Jim wondered if she would be able to tell them anything.

As if she had read his thoughts, she sat up straighter and faced him.

"I'm the one you want. I'm the reason she's dead."

"Oh, Nessie!" Ginny sat down on the divan and put her arm around the woman's shoulders.

Jim's eyes flicked to Ginny, then back to Mrs. Ballantyne. "Why don't you tell me about it?"

Mrs. Ballantyne lifted a hand and rubbed the space between her eyebrows, then nodded. "I saw her around eleven, staggering into the elevator, as if she'd had too much scotch. But she hadn't drunk much, not where I could see. It was the toxins from the haggis. They must have made her woozy, unsteady on her feet. That's why she fell off the landing. I didn't mean to kill her. Just make her sick." Mrs. Ballantyne dropped her head into her hands.

Jim's eyes narrowed. "Why did you want to make her sick?"

"So she couldn't judge the competition." She looked up swiftly. "But I didn't want her dead!"

Once started, the words poured forth, as if a dam had burst.

Mrs. Ballantyne, along with a great many other dance mothers, had decided her darling daughter could not get a fair shake from Judge Jamieson, and Kirstie was up for a slot on the National competition stage, which would make all the difference, and Douglas said she was ready, that she should win, here, and at the National competition, she was that good. But, there was no way Kirstie could win if Jamieson was in charge.

Jamieson was a known cheat. She played favorites, took bribes, awarded trophies to the wrong dancers. Everyone knew it. And Kirstie deserved a fair shot. Not preferential treatment, you understand, but a fair and impartial judge who would do right by all the girls. It would be a good thing–for all of them–if Jamieson came down with a touch of the flu that weekend.

Blair Jamieson was known to be very fond of Mrs. Ballantyne's haggis recipe. Everyone knew it. That gave her the idea. She made two batches of traditional haggis, and introduced salmonella into one of them, then made sure she served the altered batch to Jamieson when she came up to the Skybox for dinner. As soon as Jamieson had gotten her "dose," Nessie swapped the tainted dish with the clean version.

The germs? Oh! That was easy. Fresh eggs from a local farm woman, with a warning to cook them thoroughly. Her chickens had tested positive last month. Fed some to the dogs and they got sick and the vet said it was salmonella.

She would rather not have had anyone other than Jamieson get sick, but it just wasn't possible to cook a special haggis just for Jamieson, then escape suspicion when she got sick from eating it. Also, she might have frozen it or not eaten it soon enough.

Mrs. Ballantyne's shoulders drooped. "But she wasn't supposed to kill herself. She was supposed to go home and sleep it off."

Jim interrupted. "Why do you think she killed herself?"

"That's what they told me Saturday. That her head was all smashed in. You know how hard it can be to get down those concrete steps safely. She must have fallen over the railing, and it's my fault."

She sat quite still for a moment, then lifted her eyes to the windows, focusing on something beyond the garden.

"I suppose I'll have to repeat all this to the police?"

Jim nodded. "I'll call Detective Tran. She'll know what to do."

Mrs. Ballantyne nodded, then shook her head. "You know what the worst of this whole thing is? Not the death. The bitch had it coming. The worst of it is, I missed Kirstie's win because I was too upset to watch the competition. I went home and got drunk and missed her big moment, her triumph. What kind of a mother does that?"

* * *

Thursday Evening
BBQ Joint

Jim waited while Detective Tran drove over, then watched as she questioned Mrs. Ballantyne. He had retreated to a positon oblique to the principals in this little drama, his back to the windows and the fading daylight. Something twisted, there, he decided, and it didn't help that Ginny was sitting beside the woman, her arm around her, supporting her.

Also, there was a discrepancy about symptom onset. The average was twelve hours. Mrs. Ballantyne reported that Jamieson had brought Dupree with her to the Skybox, around five p.m., and the two of them had indulged in generous helpings of the tainted haggis. The time of death had been estimated at between 2330 (when Caroline and Alan saw her alive and furious) and 0130 (when Wally and his friends dropped the caber on her head). That was only six hours after eating the haggis and too soon to expect wooziness from the exposure.

That fact *might* exonerate Mrs. Ballantyne. People varied, of course, and the large dose of the bug would have hastened the onset of symptoms. Still, Jim was inclined to assign the cause of death to something other than accident. He gestured discreetly to Ginny, then led her from the room.

"Detective Tran will let us know if we're needed, but it's going to be a while before she's done with Nessie Ballantyne. Why don't you let me buy you dinner? Somewhere quiet, so we can talk."

They settled on a little-used BBQ joint that featured corner booths and acoustic country and western music. Ginny said almost nothing as Jim ordered, then led her to a corner table. He watched as she pushed the food around on her plate, not speaking, not eating. He sighed, then set down his fork.

"I'm sorry."

Ginny looked up from her tray. "For what?"

"For the general cussedness of human beings."

Ginny's eyes clouded. "She knew what she was doing, knew she was putting people in danger, and did it any way!"

Jim nodded. "There was a lot at stake."

"But she knew better!" Ginny looked around the restaurant, then lowered her voice. "I'm very disappointed in her."

"As am I, and I didn't even know her."

Ginny met his eyes. "Still want to be Laird?"

He held her gaze. "Human nature is the same everywhere, even inside the Homesteads."

Ginny's eyes clouded. "I trusted her. I'll never do that again." She picked at her meal a few moments longer, then pushed it away. She crossed her arms on the table and looked at him. "Do you remember the story of Typhoid Mary?"

"Of course, she didn't believe in germs, so she ignored the health authorities."

"And ended her life alone on an island because she wouldn't stop working as a cook, even after she'd been told it was killing people. She couldn't adapt. Couldn't accept that she had to give up the job she loved to protect others." Ginny's frown deepened. She reached for her purse. "Take me home, please."

Jim drove to the Forbes residence in silence, waiting for Ginny to share her distress with him. He walked her to the front door, then slipped an arm around her waist and drew her toward him. She turned in his arms and buried her face on his shoulder, shivering in the light breeze.

"How could Nessie do that, taint food she knew she would be serving to her friends, maybe her family?"

Jim wrapped his arms around her and held her close. "Sometimes people make bad choices."

"You can almost excuse Typhoid Mary, if it weren't for the fact that she *knew* what she was doing was wrong. Everywhere she went, typhoid broke out. She kept changing jobs to stay ahead of the health authorities. She even changed her name." Ginny shook her head. "You'd think she'd feel guilty."

"She didn't though. She died insisting it wasn't her fault, in spite of all the evidence to the contrary."

Ginny looked up into his face. "Nessie knew what she was doing was wrong, and she did it anyway. Doesn't she realize how much damage she's done? Not just to herself, to the whole community."

Jim pulled Ginny closer. "From what I saw, she understands very well, and is suffering from her choice. She couldn't live with herself. You saw the state of the house. So when we showed up, she confessed. Unlike Mary Mallon, Vanessa Ballantyne is taking responsibility for her actions. Detective Tran will sort it out and there will be a penalty to pay, but we should all be able to recover, even from this."

Her eyes slid away from his. "It—It's difficult, to trust anyone, when someone you trusted implicitly does something like this."

Jim caught his breath, then slipped a finger under her chin, lifting her face to his.

"Each of us is capable of great wickedness. We have to be constantly on guard to make sure we don't do something unforgiveable in the name of a greater good. You already know this."

Ginny nodded.

"But the opposite is also true. Each of us is capable of great compassion, great courage, great sacrifice." He bent down and kissed her. "And, in my case, great love. It doesn't matter what lies ahead of us, my love for you will endure and persevere, and overcome whatever life throws at us." His eyes held hers. "Trust me on this."

Ginny nodded, then slid her arms around his neck.

"I am prepared to trust you with my life, husband-to-be. The question is, are you prepared to trust my cooking?"

* * *

Chapter 13

Friday Morning
New House

Ginny poured herself another cup of coffee and smiled across the table at her mother. The advantage to working twelve hour shifts back to back was that you got most of the work week knocked out in two days. Not this week, of course.

The trip to Nova Scotia had eaten up all of Ginny's vacation time, half her sick days, and two personal days (all she had coming). She hadn't dared to ask what kind of shift debt Jim had gone into to complete that trip. Himself had arranged it, of course. But it left them with no time off for a honeymoon. So both of them were working extras in the weeks leading up to the wedding, with the promise of an entire week off on the other side, including both weekends, to spend in their new home before they had to report back to work.

"What are your plans for today?" Sinia Forbes asked.

"I'm waiting for Jim to pick me up. The movers are coming today, and not a moment too soon."

Her mother smiled. "You'll get it done."

"We're on track, I think, as long as the caffeine holds out!"

Jim pulled up in front, declined coffee, scooped Ginny into the car, and headed for the new house. He led the way up the walk, unlocked the front door, and held it open. Ginny recoiled as the smell hit her.

"Whew! Is that the new carpet?" Ginny waved her hand in front of her nose, trying to dispel the odor.

"No. It's the new A/C." Jim headed for the thermostat and set the blower to full, then went around and opened all the windows. These, too, had been included in the upgrade. They were now double-paned and had new screens and blinds. Wide open, they let the April morning in, bathing the rooms in sunlight and a fresh breeze. Ginny leaned out the den window and breathed deeply, enjoying the cool air and the view out over the loch.

Today they were expecting delivery of the big furniture—all of it—from four different companies. And they had a two-page list of tasks to try to get through. Ginny pinned the list to the front of the refrigerator with a magnet, then threw herself at Jim, almost knocking him to the floor.

"Trapped! We're trapped here for the whole day!" She kissed him, then hunted for his ticklish spot.

"Hey! Stop!" He retaliated in kind and the two of them ended up on the floor, giggling. They were interrupted by the first of the delivery trucks.

By noon, three of the four trucks had come and gone and half the to-do list items had been scratched off. Ginny collapsed on Jim's sofa, now positioned in front of the fireplace, and took her phone out of her purse.

"Pizza!" She dialed the delivery number and ordered briskly, then found herself stumped by the question of where to send the food. Jim came to her rescue, holding a bill from the latest delivery under her nose so she could read the new address off of it.

"You don't have it memorized yet?" he teased.

"No, but I do have new return address labels on order. So there."

"Well, that's something, I suppose."

The dining room set was still *en route* so they had to picnic on the floor, sipping soda and water from bottles and using paper towels as napkins. Ginny didn't mind. As a matter of fact, she felt happier at the moment than she could ever remember being. Too happy. She was sure it couldn't last. She was right.

Her phone went off and she picked it up, glancing down at the caller ID. Her eyebrows rose. "It's Tran."

"What does she want?"

"Shhh. Hello?"

"Miss Forbes? This is Detective Tran."

"Good afternoon, Detective. To what do I owe the honor of this call?"

"The autopsy results are back."

"Oh! May I put you on speaker, Detective? Dr. Mackenzie is here and I'm sure he'll be interested."

"Certainly."

Ginny hit the button, then held the phone out in front of her. "Go ahead."

"The Hunter boy is in the clear. Judge Jamieson was already dead when the caber came down on her. The Cause of Death was brain stem herniation as a result of blunt force trauma to the skull and swelling of the soft tissues of the brain." Detective Tran had no trouble with the difficult medical terminology, and the bare facts were conveyed in the same soft voice she used for all conversations.

"The forensic evidence suggests she fell from the mezzanine level walkway to the seats immediately below. There was blood, hair, and skin on several of them, but no large pool of blood. She did not die on impact."

Ginny's brow furrowed. "She fell onto the stadium seats below where the fight took place?"

"Correct."

"But we found her on the field."

"The Medical Examiner is of the opinion that she must have regained consciousness at some point, gotten to her feet, and walked out onto the field, where she fell again, and lay until dead."

Ginny took a breath, trying to think. "Could she have fallen over the rail on her own?"

"It is possible, but that is not what happened."

Ginny felt her throat tighten. "How do you know?"

"There is evidence she fought her assailant."

Ginny grew very still. "You think she was thrown over the rail?"

"Yes."

"Well, that lets Caroline off the hook."

Detective Tran hesitated. "Unfortunately, it does not."

Ginny frowned, looking at Jim for support. "Alan took Caroline away while Jamieson was screaming at her."

"We have only their word for what happened."

Ginny's eyes widened. "You don't believe her? Or Alan?"

"We would prefer to have that detail corroborated by an impartial witness."

Ginny could feel a headache starting. "You think Caroline did it."

"At this point, she is the most likely suspect. She withheld evidence and lied to the police."

"Am I allowed to ask what evidence you found to support your theory?"

"In addition to the surveillance videos, we found epithelials from Miss Cameron on the victim."

"Of course you did! Caroline had to touch her to push her down the steps."

"You will recall the bruises on Judge Jamieson's arms."

"Yes."

"We believe they were made by someone's hands gripping her forcefully enough to control her. The marks appear to be hand-shaped and the same size as Miss Cameron's."

Ginny felt her stomach twist. "Wouldn't there have been marks on Caroline, too, if she fought with the Judge?"

"We found no evidence on Miss Cameron, but she was not examined until Sunday, by which time any DNA transfer that might have been present had been washed off."

Ginny sat quite still, trying to think of something to say that would prove Caroline could not have killed Jamieson, then realized the line was still open. "Is there anything else?"

"Not at this time."

Ginny swallowed. One more question. "Why are you telling me this?"

"She is your friend and I believed you would want to know."

"Yes. Thank you."

Ginny closed the connection then looked over at Jim, the joy completely gone. "What are we going to do?"

Jim rose from the floor and reached for his phone. "Call Grandfather, of course. If anyone can help, he can."

Ginny sat where she was, listening to the conversation, her heart tight in her chest. She refused to believe Caroline could have done anything like this. Not even in a fit of rage. She'd seen her friend mad, mad enough to spit nails. They'd even come to blows one day. It had consisted of Caroline picking up her stuffed rabbit and whacking Ginny on the shoulder with it. She had then burst into tears and fallen into Ginny's arms, begging for forgiveness. Best friends forever.

But there had been another time when Caroline had shoved someone, and that someone had fallen as a result. It had happened during high school. It had been more a matter of the two girls grappling with one another and both losing their footing on the slope. Neither died. Ginny wondered if the police already knew about that incident. She hadn't seen the alleged assault. Not that time, and not last Friday night. As a matter of fact, she'd never seen Caroline raise a hand to anyone, not after that stuffed rabbit incident.

Revenge by prank, that business with the letter bomb, now *that* rang true. Ginny could easily believe in a trap set to catch a rat, but this? Grabbing the Judge by the arms? Fighting with her? Deliberately shoving her over a railing? And Alan covering up for her? No. That she could not believe.

Jim slipped his phone back in his pocket. "She's not under arrest, not at the moment. She's under orders not to leave town, and Grandfather says Tran has placed a discreet tail on her."

Ginny jumped to her feet. "That's not fair! She's innocent!"

"Ginny, darling. You know that, and I know that, but the police don't have any other suspects."

"Well, that's no excuse! They ought to get out there and find the person who really did this!"

Jim nodded. "Grandfather says they're pursuing all leads, but that we should be prepared for a trial."

"A trial! Oh, Jim!" Ginny could feel the tears welling up. She hunted in her pockets for a tissue, couldn't find one, and had to resort to a paper towel. Jim led her over to the sofa, drew her down onto his lap, and wrapped his arms around her.

"It's going to be all right. We'll figure this out. There must be evidence somewhere that will point us in the right direction."

He held her until the tears subsided, then he pushed her to her feet. "We can't leave until the dining room set arrives, but we can be ready to go when it does. Let's get the rest of these chores done."

Ginny didn't feel like working on the house anymore, but Jim was right about having to wait for the delivery, and it gave her something to do. He was right, too, about the clues. There must be something they could do, something they could look for that would clear Caroline. They'd tracked down a murderer before. They could do it again. And as for the wedding, well, she could just let someone else worry about flowers and cake and shoes. She could go barefoot down the aisle and eat pizza at the reception, if necessary. This was more important. BFF.

* * *

Chapter 14

Friday Afternoon
New House

Ginny found it hard to wait for the dining room set to arrive. She had planned a good day, full of accomplishments. Hard work, yes, but peace and happiness and the sense of doing something worth doing, in preparation for a life worth living. Not this. When she ran out of tasks, she wandered from room to room, her focus on the trouble in her soul.

Jim caught up with her as she stood looking out an upstairs window, her hands braced on the frame, tensed to meet the onslaught she hadn't believed was coming. He slipped his arms around her and pulled her back against him, in silence, waiting for her to speak.

She drew in a breath, then leaned back into his embrace.

"What I don't understand is why she didn't confide in me. I took her into that storage room and gave her an opportunity to tell me her side of the story and she didn't. Have I lost her trust? If so, how? What did I do wrong?"

Jim shook his head. "I don't think it's you. I think she's ashamed of how she acted and just didn't want to admit it."

"Did she think she could hide the truth?"

"No, not with a witness."

Ginny was no stranger to disappointment, but this felt

different, as if the floor beneath her had betrayed her. Her eyes roamed the loch, searching for answers, for reassurance that the bulwarks of her childhood still existed. First her father; then Hal; now, this. She turned to look at her fiancé.

"What if she's guilty? What if they lock her up? I can't get married without my best friend!" A child's wail of grief and fear.

Jim held her close, kissing her hair, then her cheek. "Darling, listen to me. I hope Caroline will be at our wedding, but even if she can't, it's going to be all right."

Ginny sucked in a breath, then nodded. "We can postpone, if we have to."

Jim's brow furrowed. "I'm not sure we can. There are guests coming from Scotland and Canada, as well as all over the U.S."

Ginny took a moment before answering. "I hope you're not going to lecture me on being reasonable."

Jim slid a hand under her chin and lifted it until she could not avoid his eyes. "My beloved bride, the only woman whose presence is required at our wedding is you." He held up a hand to silence the protest on her lips. "Caroline might miss the ceremony, but it won't stop her from being your best friend. If she loves you, she'll understand."

Ginny pushed herself out of his arms, her cheeks growing hot. "You're the one who doesn't understand!"

Jim picked up the hand that had closed into a ball, and kissed the curved fingers, teasing them open, and intertwining his fingers with hers.

"I just wanted to put the situation in perspective. Your best friend needs your support right now—your love, and your compassion. But I need you, too."

Ginny felt her anger fading, to be replaced by something she couldn't put a name to, a shadow that settled on her heart. She looked back at Jim. He was right. They would weather this storm, but it might take some time. She focused on his words. "You don't mind if I try to help Caroline?"

"Anything you can safely do. Anything within reason."

Ginny nodded. "I'm going to tell her she needn't worry. We won't abandon her."

Jim smiled. "I'm sure she already knows. She's Homestead. But it won't hurt to remind her. Do you want to talk to her alone? I can distract Alan, if you like."

Ginny shook her head. "I have some shopping to do that I need her help with and Alan is not invited."

"Shopping? For the house?" Jim raised a quizzical eyebrow.

"No, girl stuff."

Jim studied her for a moment, the corner of his mouth twitching. "Secret girl stuff."

She met his gaze. "That's right."

He smiled. "You know I'm going to find out whatever it is after we're married, right? You won't be able to keep secrets from me then."

Ginny studied him for a moment, exploring the possible consequences of having no secrets from one's husband. She raised an eyebrow. "In that case, I'd better get all my sneaking around behind your back done in the next two weeks."

Jim's brow descended. "I don't like the sound of that!"

Ginny suddenly felt better. She smiled at him. Teasing him. "A final fling before I'm married. You wouldn't begrudge me that, would you?"

Jim scowled. "If I didn't know better, I'd think you meant another man."

Ginny's smile faded. "Oh, no!" she said. "I'm quite sure one man is going to be trouble enough!"

* * *

Friday Afternoon
East Dallas

"This one's nice."

Ginny glanced at the scarlet satin item Caroline was holding up then shook her head. "Not my color. Don't they have anything in blue?"

"Black, white, and red. What did you expect?"

Ginny's brow wrinkled. "Something for a grown woman, as opposed to an anorexic child."

"None of this stuff is supposed to be *worn*, at least, not for long. It doesn't have to live up to your high standards."

Ginny sniffed and went back to looking over the merchandise. She knew perfectly well what she would and would not be willing to pay for.

"Here's something." It was a silk camisole combo, in pale peach, and exceptionally soft to the touch.

"Let me see." Caroline nodded her approval. "You're still going to have to try it on."

An hour later, the saleswoman having taken her measure in more ways than one, Ginny and Caroline left the shop with a collection of high-end "skimpies." The only item that was likely to make a public appearance was the hosiery, chosen to complete Ginny's bridal outfit and go with the strenuous celebrating that would follow the ceremony.

"Shall we grab some dinner?" Ginny asked.

Caroline nodded. "Just let me stash these in the trunk." She had indulged in a few special items for herself as well. "Where do you want to eat?"

They chose a quiet café known to very few outsiders, slid into a corner booth screened by genuine ferns, and ordered the special. Once the drinks had arrived, Ginny opened the conversation.

"How are you doing?"

Caroline glanced up, then back down at her glass, and shrugged. "As well as can be expected."

Ginny studied her friend. "Talk to me."

Caroline lifted her eyes, and looked at Ginny, her brow furrowing. "What if it turns out I really did kill her? That she got a concussion and she looked fine for a while, but she bled into her brain, and it's all my fault?"

Ginny reached across the table and clasped her friend's hand. "If that's what happened, it was an accident. You didn't mean to kill her and we can prove it."

"How?"

"We have a witness. Alan."

"He will have to tell what he saw. I was mad. I pushed her. She fell and hit her head."

"But you didn't intend to *murder* her. They can't charge you with that."

"Manslaughter, then. It amounts to the same thing. My life ruined, by that woman. *Again*!" Caroline screwed up her face. "Why did I have to lash out like that? I knew better! I hated her and it showed and I knew I shouldn't touch her. Why couldn't I control myself?" She put her face in her hands and wept.

Ginny waited a decent interval, then, very carefully, asked the question.

"Why *did* you lash out at her?"

Caroline wiped her eyes, picked up her fork and addressed her salad. After a bite or two she said, "You mean, why did I respond with such strong emotions, after all this time?"

Ginny nodded. "What she did to you, thwarting your college plans, sent you in a much better direction, almost like it was divine intervention. You should be past it."

Caroline nodded. "I've been trying to figure that out ever since it happened."

"What have you come up with?"

Caroline sighed. "Arrogance, partly. 'Look at me! You couldn't destroy *me*.'"

Ginny nodded. "I can see you wanting to rub her nose in it, but there must have been more to it than that."

Caroline nodded. "It was Gary. He's been devastated ever since the verdict was handed down. I have to work with him and he hasn't been able to focus. I thought maybe I could help." She sighed. "I guess not. All I did was make things worse."

"Tell me about Gary."

Caroline finished her drink and ordered another. When it arrived, she took a sip, then set it down, took a breath, and began.

"At first, I didn't listen, just let him complain. You know—just to get him to do his job. Then, one day, he told me the name of the judge who had destroyed his world, and I recognized it. After that, I paid more attention. I started asking questions, then looking things up on the Internet.

"She has a track record that would do the Marquis de Sade proud. Hundreds of men denied the right to watch their children grow up. Dozens of suits filed with the State Bar, all alleging malpractice. Investigations in progress. Threats against her life—not by me, I might add. News articles, blog posts, petitions circulated. Even some boycotts and marches on the courthouse." Caroline shook her head.

"But what did you think *you* could do?" Ginny asked.

"Nothing, of course. Just be there for Gary. Let him cry on my shoulder while the authorities examined the records. I kept thinking, 'no smoke without fire.' You know."

Ginny nodded. "Okay, so she made enemies."

"Not just those. Don't forget the Highland Dancing scandals. I'll bet you could find a dozen candidates for prime suspect in that group. Disappointed dancers, frustrated mothers, ambitious instructors, even the sponsors."

This fit squarely with what Douglas had told her. "Do you suspect someone in particular?"

"Other than Nessie Ballantyne, you mean? No."

Ginny's brows drew together. "What do you know about that?"

"I know she poisoned the haggis in the hope Jamieson would be too sick to judge that weekend."

Ginny did a quick review of who had been present for those discussions with Jim about the haggis. Surely no one would have let that detail slip out. Not while the investigation was still fresh. Unless Nessie's daughter—

"Who told you that?"

Caroline waved the question aside. "A little bird." She looked straight at Ginny. "It's true, isn't it?"

"Yes."

Caroline sat up straighter and leaned toward Ginny, her finger tapping the table. "I'll bet that's it. One of them got pushed just a little too far. That's what happened."

Ginny screwed up her face. "Pushed? Caroline, there was no one else there. Who are you suggesting killed her?"

Caroline's brow furrowed. "I may not have been the only one to lose my temper at her. I'm sure lots of people would have been tempted to bash her skull in."

"By dropping a caber on her?"

Caroline shook her head. "No. Even if Wally could have controlled the caber—made it go where he wanted it to—that child had no motive for killing the judge. I'm looking for someone who hated her."

"Okay. Go on."

"How's this for an idea. What if someone else was in the neighborhood? Someone who overheard the fight. They lie in wait for Jamieson, who has to come down off the stadium steps at some point. They whack her on the head, really hard. Maybe we'll find a baseball bat, if we look for it."

Ginny nodded slowly. "Okay. It's plausible enough. I'll put it on the list."

"Oh! And here's another. Suppose she was feeling woozy from the concussion and fell over the railing, all by herself."

"Lost her balance, you mean?"

"Yes, something like that. In which case—" Caroline's face fell.

Ginny completed the thought. "In which case, the original injury is the cause of death."

"Yes." Caroline went back to poking at her salad. She was silent for a moment, then looked up again. "But not if there was another cause for her to be unsteady on her feet. That haggis, for instance, or too much alcohol."

"Well," Ginny smiled at her friend. "At least it gives us some ideas to follow up on."

Caroline nodded vigorously. "You mark my words. A woman with that many enemies was doomed. It wasn't a matter of whether, just when, and by whom!"

* * *

CHAPTER 15

Friday Evening
Cooperative Hall

Every Friday evening at the Cooperative Hall there was a gathering featuring food, drink, music, dancing, and gossip. On this particular Friday evening they were working on the set of dances chosen for Ginny and Jim's wedding reception.

Almost everyone was there. Not surprisingly, the Camerons were not, and neither was Alan.

Ginny had been thinking hard all afternoon. How could she possibly do what the police had not been able to, come up with another viable suspect in the killing of Judge Jamieson?

There was the vanishing Gary, of course. He might have found a baseball bat and used it. What about the idea that Jamieson could have tripped and fallen, all by herself. The railing was a problem, of course, since it was designed to prevent exactly that. But if she'd had enough alcohol, or something else got into her system, would that have been enough? In combination with a mild concussion?

There had been people on the field, preparing for the next morning, or coming back from Fiddle Faddle or the Hospitality Suite. The odds were good that someone had seen or heard something. The police would have interviewed everyone, of course, but they might not have known the right questions to ask. Maybe she could do better.

During one of the breaks Ginny got permission to address the crowd. She climbed up onto the stage, and picked up the microphone.

"Excuse me, please. May I have your attention?" When the talking died down she looked around the room. "You all know about the unfortunate incident at the Games last weekend." There were nods around the room and a few whispered comments.

"Before I go further, I'd like to ask for a moment of silence." As one, they rose to their feet and bowed their heads. Hated or not, Jamieson had been one of their own. No one moved, no one shifted weight from one foot to another, they closed their eyes in silent respect for death.

"Thank you."

They took their seats again, and Ginny found she now had their full attention. "As bad as losing Judge Jamieson was and is, the situation has gotten worse. The police think she was deliberately targeted, and they believe the killer is one of us."

That caused some startled reactions, and a few instinctive denials. She waited until the crowd settled down again.

"I've known Caroline Cameron my entire life." Ginny could hear the sharp intake of breath. Some had not known it was Caroline they were talking about. "I don't believe she's capable of something like this." That drew both audible agreement and some telling silences.

"The police have stopped looking for other suspects. They're satisfied they have the culprit. I'm not. I'm asking all of you to search your memories. I know you've spoken to the police. I know you've told them what you remember. I'm hoping there's more, some overlooked detail that will lead us to the truth."

Most still had their eyes on her. Some had dropped them to the floor, clearly unwilling to interfere in a police matter.

"I'm asking for your help. Call it a wedding present, if you like." There was scattered laughter.

"I'm hoping to clear my friend of this dreadful accusation. If I can't, then I will still thank you for your efforts, but if I can, then justice will have been served."

Dead silence.

"If you think of anything, anything at all, please let me know, or Himself, or Dr. Mackenzie." She took a deep breath and looked them in the eye, making contact with as many as she could.

"I would rather not start my married life with a cloud of suspicion hanging over us. Thank you all, in advance, for your patience, and your help, and may God bless us all, the living and the dead."

"Amen." The shout from the back of the hall broke the mood. Suddenly they were on their feet, surging toward her, eager to help clear the air, to do their bit for truth and justice. Ginny felt her eyes grow damp at the sight. And, just as suddenly, Jim was beside her, his arm around her waist, his support manifest. She leaned against him for a moment, then handed the microphone back to the musicians and headed for the stair.

* * *

Friday Evening
Cooperative Hall

Ginny was sitting at one of the Cooperative Hall tables, her back to the stage, her eyes on the notebook she had brought with her. Most of the people she'd spoken to had carefully explained they had nothing to offer, but they wanted to wish her well, and hoped Caroline would be free in time for the wedding. They liked Caroline. She was a good girl. Smart, too. Such a shame this had happened. Ginny made a note to ask Detective Tran if she could see what information the police had gathered from the same crowd.

"Miss Forbes?"

Ginny looked up to find Rory Hunter standing beside her. She smiled up at him and invited him to sit.

"I wanted to thank you for your help with Wally," he said.

"I'm so glad he's safely out of this!"

Wally's uncle shook his head. "Not completely. He's facing criminal mischief and trespassing charges, and deserves to. But he's sorry, and I hope he's learned his lesson."

Ginny watched the man fidget, then set her pen down, and leaned toward him, her arms resting on the table. "What can I do for you, Mr. Hunter?"

"Rory."

"All right. What can I do for you, Rory?"

He was looking acutely uncomfortable, and Ginny was not surprised at his next words.

"I have something I want to tell you. It may be nothing, of course, but then, it may be something. I just don't know. I may have heard something that night, Friday night, early Saturday morning, actually."

Ginny sat up straighter. "Oh?"

"I was sleeping on the field, with the tent. You know."

Ginny nodded. Sometimes the clansmen camped out on the field, if the weather was fine, or they were worried about vandals, or they weren't fit to drive themselves home.

"Something woke me, around midnight. I wasn't sure what it was, but I got up and looked around." He licked his lips, not making eye contact. Ginny waited.

"I didn't see anything, so I went over to the fence and, er, relieved myself, then went back to bed."

"You told the police?"

"No. Well, not this anyway."

"Why not?"

He hurried to explain. "I'm married."

Ginny's eyebrows rose.

He shook his head. "It's not what you think. It's just that, well, I'd been drinking. Heavily. She doesn't approve."

"Oh." Ginny tried not to laugh. "Just how drunk were you?"

"Enough so I couldn't see straight. Not quite double-vision, but not clear-sighted either."

Ginny's brow furrowed. "Did you see something?"

He shook his head. "Heard. At the time, I thought I was dreaming, or hallucinating, and chalked it up to the alcohol. But the more I thought about it, the more I was sure I'd heard a crash, and a woman cry out. By the time I was awake, of course, there was nothing. No sound at all."

Ginny had picked up her pen and was taking notes. "Where were you sleeping?"

"Under the ramp that comes down into the clan tent area, from the deck of the stadium."

"Ah!" Ginny chewed this over for a bit. "Something woke you, and you think it was a noise."

"Unless I dreamed it, yes."

"So you got up to investigate, but you couldn't see or hear anything out of the ordinary."

"Right."

"Is there more? Anything else you can tell me?"

Rory nodded. "I was just getting settled again, my head not working right, you understand."

Ginny nodded.

"When I heard voices, a man and a woman, just above me, on the ramp."

"Could you hear what they were saying?"

"I think she said, 'That stupid bitch,' – you'll pardon the expression – 'I hope they dis-something-or-other her.' Then he said, 'Never mind her. I have something much more important I want to do tonight.' Then she said, 'Maybe we should go back.' Then he said, 'She'll be fine. Come on.' Then I heard her squeal, then laugh. Then they moved off down the ramp into the clan tents, but it was none of my business, and I was asleep the next minute, and I didn't remember any of this until last night."

"Did you recognize the voices?"

"No."

"Would you, if you heard them again?"

"I don't know. Probably not."

Ginny studied the man across from her. There was no reason to doubt his story. It had the ring of truth. Was there anything else she should ask?

"What time was this?"

"The voices? Fifteen minutes after midnight."

"How can you be so sure?"

"I looked at my watch."

Ginny nodded, then smiled at her informant. "I take it you don't want Mrs. Hunter to hear about this?"

He nodded ruefully. "It would help a lot if she never did."

Ginny could sympathize. "Thank you for trusting me. I promise discretion."

He smiled and rose, taking his leave and merging back into the crowd. Ginny looked down at her notes. So there *had* been a witness!

The times would have to be checked against the date/time stamps on the surveillance camera, but the most likely explanation was that Rory Hunter had heard Jamieson falling down the steps after Caroline pushed her. That woke him. Then Alan and Caroline's voices coming down the ramp, just minutes later. It corroborated Caroline's statement about the time she and Alan left the stadium deck. Now they were getting somewhere!

Ginny felt her spirits lift, then plummet the next minute. This was not proof. This was the fuzzy recollection of a drunken man. It wouldn't clear Caroline with the police. She needed to find someone else who was in the stadium at the time in question. And, unless there was another with an equally damning secret, no such person existed.

* * *

Chapter 16

Saturday Morning
Forbes Residence

Saturday morning found Jim breakfasting at the Forbes' residence. He poured coffee into two mugs and set one down in front of Ginny, then settled into a chair across the kitchen table from her.

"Thank you, darling."

Jim couldn't help smiling. She hadn't even looked up. It was such a natural response, as if she'd been saying it all her life.

"You're welcome."

This time she did look up. Their eyes met, and Jim felt a surge of contentment. A good night's sleep. Sunshine warming the room. Ginny's smile warming his soul.

"What are you working on?" He didn't *need* to ask. He'd seen the same notebook out last night at the ceilidh. He just wanted to hear her voice.

"Two things. I've got a list of questions I'd like to have answered, somehow. And I've got a timeline of where Judge Jamieson was during the last few hours of her life."

"May I see it?"

She handed it over and Jim looked down at the page, tickled to find she had broken the hours into fifteen minute increments, starting with Fiddle Faddle, and ending with the discovery of the body the next morning. Lists and timetables. It was a good thing he approved of both.

"I understand the last entry, finding the body, but where did you get the first one, the starting point?"

"The security camera footage shows Jamieson tumbling down the steps at twenty-three forty-five. That's the last known picture of her—alive—so I started there. I'm hoping we can narrow it down as we go."

Jim nodded, studying the list. "We can eliminate anything after the caber fell on her."

"You're right. Would you please make that change?"

Jim reached behind him and grabbed a pencil out of the holder that sat on the counter. "We need to get one of these," he remarked.

"Yes, dear."

Jim grinned. He was going to like hearing that! At least, he *thought* he was. He went to work revising the timeline.

"Wally and his gang came over the fence around one a.m. That's according to what Wally says and the witnesses who saw the boys leave the bar. The lights were out on the field, but not in the vendor area. I'm not sure they ever turn those out. Do they?"

"I don't know. Does it matter?"

Jim shook his head. "I don't think so. It was dark on the field in any case. How long would it take to steal a caber?"

Ginny shrugged. "Ten minutes? If you knew where they were and didn't have to hunt for them."

"Okay. Say ten minutes to locate the cabers, ten to find one you can lift, than another ten to get your hands under it, lift it, run with it, heave it into the air, and watch it fall."

"Did they do that more than once?"

"Good question. Add it to your list."

Ginny did so.

Jim continued. "That would make it around one-thirty when the hammer fell."

"Caber."

"You know what I meant."

"I do."

Jim looked up swiftly and caught her eye. "Say that again!"

She grinned at him. "Aye, Mackenzie. I do."

"I love the sound of that."

"Back to work!"

He did as instructed, still smiling. "As I was saying, that would make it around one-thirty a.m., at which point, as we now know, she was already dead, but we don't know for how long. When the caber fell, it would have torn blood vessels and smashed open the ventricles, splashing cerebrospinal fluid and blood everywhere."

Ginny made a small sound and Jim looked up to find her staring at him, the color draining from her cheeks. He sprang to his feet and went to her, going down on one knee, taking both of her hands in his.

"Ginny! I'm sorry!" He saw her swallow, then take a breath.

"I'm all right, Jim. This is evidence. Go on."

He studied her for a moment longer, then nodded, and returned to his chair. "The average time needed for blood to coagulate, once it hits the air, is five to fifteen minutes. But her blood was mixed with the cerebrospinal fluid, which diluted it. Also, she'd been drinking so she was mildly anticoagulated. So the blood evidence is not as helpful as it might have been."

"The lab said she was dead before Wally got there," Ginny said. "Is it safe to say she died before one-fifteen?"

Jim nodded. "Yes, I think we can use that as a pretty accurate guestimate."

"Okay. So she must have died somewhere between twenty-three forty-five and one-fifteen. That gives us a one-and-a-half hour window."

"True, oh Queen!" Jim looked at her across the table. Her color was back, her expression composed. If he hadn't known her history, he wouldn't have suspected anything was wrong. Brave and strong and clever.

She lifted an eyebrow at him, then continued. "Caroline and Alan report that Jamieson was on her feet and swearing at them five minutes after the push."

"Ten minutes to midnight."

Ginny nodded. "If Rory Hunter's testimony is reliable, Caroline and Alan were headed down the ramp at a quarter past midnight, looking for somewhere private to talk."

"That leaves twenty-five minutes unaccounted for. What were Caroline and Alan doing during that twenty-five minutes?"

"Their testimony says they started down the ramp, then Caroline decided she had to pee, limped back up the ramp by herself, went to the bathroom, then limped halfway down the ramp to meet Alan who had gone to get her bag from the Cameron tent."

Jim's brow furrowed. "I know it takes women an unconscionable amount of time to empty their bladders, but would it take twenty-five minutes? Really? That's enough time to hustle back up the ramp, tip Jamieson over the rail, then scoot back down in time to meet Alan coming up, using the bathroom as a plausible excuse."

Ginny frowned at him. "You cannot mean that."

Jim shrugged. "If I were the police, I'd be wondering about it."

Ginny frowned harder. "But Rory said Caroline wanted to go back to check on Jamieson, and Alan said not to worry, that she'd be fine. That sounds like they both believed she was still alive. The police can use that as evidence that neither of them knew she was dead—if she was, which we don't know, yet."

Jim shook his head. "Unfortunately, all we have is hearsay, and an unreliable source at that. What we need is something solid. Something that can be checked."

Ginny nodded. "Okay. Caroline's brooch was found under the dead woman, and no matter what you say, I refuse to believe Caroline and Alan planted evidence under a corpse."

Jim gazed at his intended, thinking how green her eyes were in the morning light, and how fierce her expression. "It does seem a bit far-fetched."

"If we could *prove* when she lost that brooch, it might help corroborate *part* of her story."

Jim nodded. "So what we're looking for is the time she took it off."

"Caroline's nieces, all three of them, agree that she and Alan were lying on the field on her airsaid at ten forty-five."

Jim made a note.

"They left Fiddle Faddle at ten. It would take ten minutes to get from the fiddle tent to the athletics field. Factor in fifteen to twenty minutes for canoodling before they were interrupted, that puts the airsaid shedding at between ten-fifteen and ten-twenty."

Jim grinned. "Canoodling?"

"You know what I mean."

"I do!" Jim smiled into her eyes, then picked up the pencil, and made a note. "Brooch dropped on the field at approximately ten-fifteen. Judge still alive at that point, per security camera."

"And, if either Caroline or Alan had missed it, they wouldn't have left it lying on the ground. They would have taken it with them."

"Okay, that makes sense."

Ginny took a breath, her worry for her friend evident on her face. "You're right, though. The police will want something more than Alan's word to exonerate Caroline. It wasn't just those twenty-five minutes, either. What about the time between the conversation on the ramp and the time Wally and company arrived? Can we account for any of that?"

Jim's eyes narrowed. "Maybe. Let's look at what the corpse does. She was alive when the camera evidence says Caroline pushed her, right?"

"Right—at eleven forty-five."

"Okay. Both Caroline and Alan described Jamieson's threats to ruin Caroline's career."

Ginny nodded. "Too bad the camera didn't have audio."

Jim sighed. "Too bad Rory slept through that."

"He was very drunk."

Jim snorted. "Too bad we don't have solid proof of *that*."

"It might hurt more than help. And it can't be helped."

"True." Jim nodded. "Okay. Jamieson screams at Caroline, but does not follow her."

Ginny cocked her head sideways, her hair catching the sunlight and exploding in a flash of red and gold. "How do you know?"

Jim caught his breath, lost in the memory of her scent and the feel of her hair against his cheek, then forced his mind back to the puzzle. "Jamieson doesn't appear on the breezeway camera again."

"Okay."

"Which means she left the stadium some other way."

"Down the steps you mean."

He nodded. "Right, and after Caroline and Alan were gone, assuming they're telling the truth."

"I'd stake my life on it."

Jim gave her a hard look. "Let's hope you don't have to."

Ginny nodded. "Go on."

Jim rose and helped himself to another cup of coffee, to give himself a moment, then returned to his seat. "Jamieson may have been alone or she may have had company. There's no evidence either way."

"If the irate father, Caroline's co-worker, hung around instead of going home, he might have seen something."

Jim nodded. "Or tried to approach her again."

Ginny's brow furrowed. "That seems risky. According to Alan, Jamieson looked strong enough to get herself home, and angry enough to punch anyone who got in her way."

"But Alan may have been mistaken. Most people who suffer a blow to the head, even a mild one, are a bit unsteady on their feet for a bit. Caroline's friend might have taken advantage of that."

"Yes." Ginny added it to her list, then picked up her coffee, sat back in her chair, and stared off into space.

Jim watched her closely. She had one of those faces that reflect the thoughts going on behind it. He could see the wheels turning, could tell when a new idea occurred to her, and when she discarded it and moved on to another.

"We don't know when the bruises were made. Just that they were less than two days old," she said.

"Right."

"Okay," Ginny said, "Try this on for size. What if the angry father, who has a history of violence and a restraining order against him, didn't leave the grounds? What if he followed Jamieson and bashed her on the head, then dumped her over the railing?"

Jim considered the possibility. "There's a problem with that theory. Blunt force trauma with something heavy enough to kill a grown woman—a baseball bat or an iron pipe—also requires muscle to wield it."

"Or rage."

"Yes, or rage. That's my point. The person attacked is either felled with a single blow or whacked to an unrecognizable bloody mess. In either case, she dies where she is attacked, and we know Jamieson didn't do that because there was no pool of blood either on the mezzanine or on the seats below. She walked to the spot where she died."

"How do we know she walked?"

"No drag marks no heavily-indented footsteps to indicate she was carried, and no cart or other wheels tracks to imply she was rolled to that spot. The police found a pool of vomit at the base of the stadium stairs. The DNA is Jamieson's—more evidence that she was mobile when she started out across the field. Also, they found her missing shoe between the steps and the spot on the field where she came to rest."

"So she was whacked out on the field."

Jim shook his head. "The police don't think so. The scene, messed up as it was by caber-tossers and Hieland Coo, didn't support a killing blow to the back of the head. The livor mortis indicates she died face up."

Ginny was slow to respond. "You've been busy."

Jim nodded. "After I dropped you off yesterday, I went over to the precinct and talked to Detective Tran."

Ginny looked at him. "She told you all this?"

"I asked her to go over the medical evidence with me and she did."

"What else do you know, and when were you going to share it?"

Jim sighed. "There was no time to talk at the ceilidh and you were about to drop afterwards. I decided it could wait until today." He crossed his arms on the table. "Are you going to be mad at me for waiting until after you'd had some sleep before I dumped this in your lap?"

She blinked, her expression softening. "No, Jim. I can handle a little paternalism, as long as it doesn't go too far."

He nodded, his brow furrowing. "I wish I could sweep it all away. You shouldn't have to deal with any of this." He stretched his arm across the table and took her hand. "I want to make your life perfect. Please don't hold that against me."

She rose, came around the table, and sat down on his lap, wrapping her arms around his neck. "When you fall asleep on the couch and those curls get loose, you look like an over-grown cherub and I want to take you in my arms and carry you to bed and tuck you in."

Jim found himself laughing at the image.

She continued. "I understand wanting to protect the ones you love. But I need transparency from you. I need to be able to trust you."

He wrapped his arms around her and hugged her tightly, then kissed her. "You can trust me in the same way you can trust yourself. Once we are married we'll be one flesh, two halves of a single whole."

She smiled. "My better half."

He kissed her again, several times in fact. "Two weeks, my darling. We're down to two weeks."

"And the house isn't finished!"

He brushed her face with his hand, smiling into her eyes. "It doesn't have to be. The minute I carry you across the threshold, it will be our home."

She laid her head on his shoulder and snuggled close. "Home and hearth and husband. Oh!" She suddenly sat bolt upright.

"What is it?"

"I've just remembered something!" She climbed off his lap and headed for the notepad. "Something else Caroline said."

Jim sighed to himself. Two more adjectives drifted into his mind. Tenacious, and single-minded. She could concentrate on whatever she was doing to the exclusion of all others. It was something he would have to get used to.

"What did she say?"

Ginny was studying her notes. "She said I should look among the dance community for a motive."

Jim nodded.

"And Detective Tran said those marks on Jamieson's arms indicate she'd been gripped hard by someone."

"Right."

"Here it is." Ginny read swiftly, then set her notes down and looked at him.

"Okay. We've got two possibilities. One, she got dizzy and fell over the railing on her own, and two, someone threw her off the mezzanine."

Jim lifted an eyebrow. "The police believe the latter."

Ginny nodded. "Because she was able to walk out onto the field."

"Which implies another person on the scene, ready, willing, and able to push her over the railing."

"Right, but there's at least one more possibility."

Jim drew in a breath. "Oh?"

"What if she got dizzy and someone tried to catch her as she was falling? That might explain those marks on her arms."

Jim's brow contracted. "If someone was trying to help her, why didn't they call an ambulance?"

"Because, when faced with the apparently dead body on the stadium seats below, he or she chickened out. Maybe whoever it was saw an opportunity to be rid of her. Just walk away and pretend they hadn't been there. That would fit our angry father profile. And might fit a number of Highland dancers."

"Including Caroline."

"Other than Caroline."

Jim nodded slowly. "It's possible. But how do you explain her accidentally falling over a waist-high railing, especially with someone there trying to prevent it?"

Ginny shook her head. "I can't. And I don't believe it was an accident. I believe she let someone get close enough to lay hands on her. Which lets out the angry father. But—someone she knew well, someone she trusted? Maybe one of the other judges, or an organizer. Someone like that?"

Jim nodded. After confronting two enemies, if Jamieson had been approached by a friend, the human instinct would have been to feel relief.

"That still doesn't explain how she got tipped over the railing. If she was alive enough to struggle, why didn't she grab one of the bars and hang on?"

"Maybe she tried. Maybe she was drugged."

Jim screwed up his face. "How?"

"I have no idea, but listen." Ginny counted off the points on her fingers. "One. She was a dancer, which means nimble with a good sense of balance. Two. She was seen drinking Scotch. Someone might have doctored it behind her back. Three – and I know this doesn't fit the usual timeline for onset of symptoms, but we both know patients are infinitely variable. If she ate the haggis, she *might* have been feeling the effects of the salmonella. Four. Caroline said she had a cut on her forehead. Suppose someone was there, pretending to help and put something on that cut that dropped her blood pressure. It would have made it easier to push her off balance."

She leaned toward Jim, her eyes kindling. "And Five, I've been wondering how Caroline could have pushed her in the first place. Jamieson was already on her guard. She'd been arguing with that man, someone who had a history of violence. Then she's faced with a known enemy from her past. Why did she let Caroline get so close? Why didn't she back away? Why didn't her self-preservation instincts kick in?"

Jim blinked, then nodded. "Good question."

Ginny jumped to her feet. "I need to see the toxicology screen. Want to come?'

Jim rose, nodding. "Where are we going?"

"To the source. I need to talk to Andy."

* * *

Chapter 17

Saturday Noon
Dallas County Morgue

"So my question is, was she drugged with anything that would make her unsteady on her feet?" They were seated in one of the conference rooms at the county morgue, talking to Andrea Goddard, one of the medical investigators and a long-time friend of Ginny's.

Andy flipped through the autopsy report. "Detective Tran asked me to remind you this is protected information. There are details in here the police don't want to get loose before the investigation is complete."

Ginny nodded. She hadn't been sure Tran would agree to the request, after that business with the brooch. She must think Ginny had something to offer the investigation.

"Okay. Here it is." Andy read carefully, then put the paper down on the table and looked straight at Ginny. "How did you know?"

"May I?" Jim reached for the file. "Cyclobenzaprine."

Andy nodded. "Her blood alcohol was just under the legal limit and we found traces of a compound in the cut over her eye. Topical lidocaine, like you get at the store to treat sunburn, and a botanical we think is hibiscus. The lab is working on that." Andy turned back to Ginny and asked her question again. "How did you know we'd found something?"

"I didn't. It's just that I expected a woman like her to have better reflexes."

"I don't follow."

"According to Caroline, Jamieson had been arguing with a man who had threatened her. She turned her back on him, which, under the circumstances, seems ill-advised. That's when Caroline—er—reproached her, for her callous inhumanity."

Andy was leaning back in her chair, listening. She nodded. "We found evidence of Caroline's DNA on the victim's clothing."

Ginny nodded. "In Jamieson's place, I would have stepped back. Put some distance between myself and Caroline's wrath, and made sure I was a good distance away from that angry father, too."

Andy's brow furrowed. "Slow to respond, huh? Do you have a theory?"

Jim set the toxicology report down and joined the conversation. "Self-preservation is a pretty strong instinct. You have to do a lot to suppress it. If Jamieson thought she was in control of the situation, she might not have responded as quickly as if she had been on high alert." He reached out and tapped the report. "Or she might have been impaired."

Andy's eyebrows rose. "Couldn't hold her liquor?"

Ginny laughed and Jim shook his head. "Cyclobenzaprine is a skeletal muscle relaxer. Combine it with alcohol and the effect is enhanced. Add lidocaine, even in small doses, and you get a hypotensive effect, which could cause dizziness. And—I think I read this somewhere not too long ago—hibiscus tea is under investigation as an alternative treatment for high blood pressure, and is showing promise. So maybe she tried to move and her legs just didn't work as well as usual."

Andy nodded. "Cyclobenzaprine requires a prescription.

We'll see if we can trace the physician and find out why she was taking it." She gathered up the papers, rose and smiled at the pair of them. "Thanks for your help. Y'all take care."

* * *

Saturday Afternoon
Forbes Residence

Jim leaned back in his chair and stretched. "You realize we have to work tonight?"

Ginny nodded. This was their regular weekend. "So concentrate!" They had taken a half hour for lunch and were now focusing on the victim, trying to get some idea of who else might have wanted her dead.

The woman had an online presence, but it wasn't one Ginny envied. She'd been able to find the usual job information; current position, education, professional organizations, and so forth. Everyone posted a resume online. Also photos.

"I've got some articles she wrote. Just the credits, though, not the content. You have to pay for that."

Jim nodded. "According to this, she was a Republican and a member in good standing of the state bar, the Dallas Bar, and the Family Law section of the American Bar Association."

Ginny moved to the next page. "Here's something. It seems she wasn't popular with either the public or her peers."

"Now we're getting somewhere!" Jim moved around so he could see over her shoulder. "What am I looking at?"

"It's one of those sites where anybody can post a review, this time about judges. It's called *The Robing Room* and it appears to be national."

"Whew! Some of these comments are nasty."

Ginny nodded. On a scale of one to ten, Judge Jamieson

ranked near the bottom. And it wasn't just disappointed clients. Many of the comments were from people who worked with her. "Is this evidence?" Ginny asked.

"Of her poor people skills, yes."

"Just like with the Highland dancers."

"This one says she didn't know the law." Jim pointed at a scathing review.

"But this one refutes that, saying she's too quick to use the law as a weapon. I wonder which one is right?"

"Doesn't matter. This tells us she made enemies. Lots of them. Which opens up the field considerably."

Ginny looked up at him. "Do the police know that?"

"They might not think it relevant. They're used to being the target of dissatisfied customers. Besides, how many of those people were on the Games grounds between eleven and midnight? It still has to be someone who had access to her."

Ginny nodded, but wasn't willing to give up on the idea completely. She copied the web page address, launched her e-mail program, composed a note to Detective Tran, explaining her concern, sent it off, and made a note to follow up with Tran later.

"You make a good point. Let's see if there were any of Jamieson's colleagues at the Games." Ginny copied the list of Dallas County Family Law judges into a file, then plugged the names into the database for all the known attendees of the Games. Normally, this would not be possible, but Himself had made the master files available to expedite the search. It didn't help, though. There were no matches.

"Okay, no co-workers. What about clients?"

"That's going to be a long list and you may come up against lawyer-client privilege."

Ginny made a face. "True." She thought for a moment. "Caroline said her coworker, Gary-what's-his-name, was there and making threats against Jamieson. Surely I'm allowed to see if he put any of them in writing?"

Jim nodded. "Angry people do some very stupid things."

Twenty minutes' work had the answer. Gary Feldman (last name supplied by Caroline) was among the more active participants in a series of protests against Judge Jamieson. There were static images, video clips, petitions, news coverage, and a number of opinion pieces on the subject of Judge Jamieson's long history of favoritism toward the female parent in custody decisions.

"Wow!" Ginny looked up from her reading, her faith shaken. "This isn't real, is it? I mean, you can't trust what you find on the Internet, can you?"

Jim moved his chair so he could face her. "I see a lot of family tension in the Emergency Room, stuff you're spared in the ICU. I'm sorry to have to say what you're seeing in those articles is probably genuine. They have the ring of truth." He reached out and took her hands. "Are you worried, about us not being able to work out our differences without resorting to the courts?"

Ginny met his eyes. Both Jim and Angus had asked what her plans were for after she was married, since night shifts (although her favorite) were not conducive to raising children. Ginny had balked when Himself raised the issue, but he had made it very clear that her first responsibility as wife to the heir, was to produce another heir.

Since the beginning of the year, she'd been swapping one night shift per week for a pair of floating six-hour shifts designed to cover the new-hire preceptor training. They had set up a schedule of classroom materials, supplemented with online study, followed by working with experienced preceptors, with Ginny supervising the whole thing.

Himself had suggested expanding the training and

supervisory work to cover more areas of the hospital and moving her to day shift. Ginny had returned a non-committal answer and passed the question on to Jim.

"Does he have that kind of power? I mean, I know he runs that place with an iron fist, and I know the new ICU Head Nurse has to answer to him, but can he force her to change the schedules this way?"

Jim had nodded. "He can and he will." He had taken her in his arms and looked down into her face, his expression troubled. "It's a big change, I know."

She had leaned against him. "Nursing is a young woman's job, but I'm not old, yet, and lots of nurses work through their pregnancies."

She had taken it for granted they would have some adjusting to do, but not once had it crossed her mind she and Jim might disagree on how to raise children. She felt her heart flutter.

"We haven't talked about children. Neither of us has any already so we're both going to be first-timers. That is, assuming we *can* have children. How does one manage the responsibility? Is it fifty-fifty, or does the father take the lion's share with a boy and vice-versa for the mother with a girl?"

Jim shrugged. "I don't know. I was an only child."

Ginny's stomach clenched. "What if we don't see eye-to-eye? Are we going to fight over our children? Divorce because of them? Like these people?"

Jim shook his head, his expression firm. "No, we are not. Whatever comes up, whatever happens, we're not going to let our children tear us apart. You and I will work it out, behind closed doors, then present a united front to the little monsters."

Ginny felt the corner of her mouth rise. "Monsters?"

"Yes, monsters. All children are born monsters. You have to

civilize them, and you only get eighteen years to do it in." He pulled her out of her chair and into his arms.

"Ginny, darling, my love, don't worry. You have the excellent example of your mother and father, and I have mine, and we both have Grandfather. There will be disagreements, I'm sure. But I'm equally sure we can work them out without ending up in Family Court."

Ginny wrapped her arms around him and held on tight. So many things to worry about! So many changes in her life. She mumbled into his shirt. "I'm sorry. I don't expect trouble, not trouble on that level. It's just—" She looked up into his face.

He nodded, then bent down and kissed her. "Don't worry, my love. We can handle children." He smiled at her. "How about we give it a break? There's just enough time to take a load over to the new house."

Ginny felt a twinge of irritation. Why wasn't *he* worried about the coming changes? Why was *she* the only one having panic attacks? She frowned to herself, but nodded, closed the computer, and followed him to the car. The sun was out and there was a fresh breeze, a delightful April day. Ginny closed her eyes, filled her lungs with the cool air, and let herself relax. She had mastered one career. She could master another. Surely. Probably. No pressure.

* * *

CHAPTER 18

Saturday Night
Hillcrest ER

Jim was bent over almost double so he could reach his small patient, one of his regulars, his stethoscope pressed to the child's chest. Not as bad as it could be, but he might need to call the child's pulmonologist and suggest a few changes. This was the fourth visit in as many weeks.

"Let's give him a breathing treatment."

"Right doc." The respiratory therapist was ready, having anticipated the need. He lost no time assembling the nebulizer and adding the medication to the reservoir.

Jim turned to the caregiver. "Did you bring his meds with you?" She nodded and handed over a paper bag with the prescriptions in it. Jim took them out and looked them over.

"Where's his rescue inhaler?"

The woman looked apologetic. "We ran out."

Jim's brow furrowed. "Well, we can't have that." He strode down the hall to his office and dug around in his stash of freebies the drug reps always left for him. He found what he was looking for and hurried back, to find an argument in progress.

The child was not the son of the caregiver. She was a foster parent and only one of a series Jim had dealt with. She was on her feet, facing the admissions clerk, a worried look in her eye.

"We can't accept this in payment." The clerk was sorry, it showed in her face, but her hands were tied. "You'll have to pay up front and be reimbursed."

"Haven't I just told you I haven't got the money? The authorization is there, right there." She stabbed at the papers in the clerk's hand.

"Yes, I know, but this one is outdated. You need to get the judge to sign the new one."

"The judge? You mean Judge Jamieson?"

"Yes, ma'am. I'm sure she'll be happy to authorize emergency medical care. But until she does, you'll have to pay. According to these records, it's part of the deal you signed."

The woman was growing more agitated, frantic, the panic just below the surface. "I can't do that."

"Can't do what?"

"Can't go back to Judge Jamieson."

"I'm sure it will be all right. She's worked with us on many children like this one."

"You stupid girl! Haven't you heard? Judge Jamieson is dead! Murdered!"

Jim hastened to intervene.

"Let's take this outside, shall we?" He herded the two women out the door before either could say another word. "I don't think Richard needs to hear this discussion."

The caregiver took a deep breath, then nodded. Jim turned to the clerk.

"Paula, will you please call the house supervisor and ask her to intervene for you?"

"Yes, sir." She hurried off. Jim turned back to the caregiver.

"Mrs.?"

"Corey."

"Mrs. Corey. I'm sorry you're having this trouble. Don't

worry about Richard. We'll take care of him, either way."

"Thank you, doctor!"

"May I ask a question?"

"Sure. Anything."

Jim chose his words carefully. He was trying to avoid committing a HIPAA violation. "Without breaking any confidences, can you tell me what role Judge Jamieson plays in getting emergency room visits paid for?"

Mrs. Corey didn't hesitate. "She has to approve everything. Richard has a trust fund and the court appointed ad litem has to get everything signed off on before money can be spent. We were trying to get that resolved. Now she's dead, heaven knows what will happen. We may have to give Richard back."

"I'm sure the court has a procedure for something like this. It can't be the first time a signature was unobtainable."

"No, I suppose you're right."

"Don't worry. It will all get worked out. In the meantime, let's go check on Richard." Jim held the door for her as she reentered the exam room. He found the respiratory therapist just finishing up and Richard looking a lot better. A few more minutes with the stethoscope, some discharge instructions, the rescue inhaler in place in the paper bag, and he was ready to move on to the next patient.

* * *

Sunday, Very Early Morning
Hillcrest Cafeteria

Ginny took a sip of her coffee, then set the cup down. "I hadn't thought of that angle."

"Neither had I."

They were at lunch, what the night shift called lunch, anyway. It was two a.m. and the cafeteria was closing for its daily cleaning. The food had been put away and the security gates had been lowered and secured in place. They would be asked to leave, soon, and to put their dishes on the conveyer belt that would carry them to the washers. All in order and as it should be, unlike the mess the family law courts must be facing with one of their judges gone.

"Money is a really good motive for murder."

Jim nodded.

"Do you think there can be a connection?"

"It's always a possibility, but I'm finding it hard to imagine a hard-as-nails, already-under-the-microscope family law judge being able to fiddle the books."

Ginny nodded. There might be another motive for murder buried in the Judge's finances, but Ginny wasn't going to be able to dig it out. She didn't have access. "Maybe all she was doing was saying, 'No,' a lot."

Jim emptied his cup and started to gather the trash, his brow still furrowed. "I never worked with the woman, but our admin downstairs says she was very much pro-child. If the kid needed something, all the guardian had to do was ask."

Ginny rose, sighing. That didn't sound like the Jamieson she knew. "I'll hand the idea on to Tran. The police might find something we never could."

"True." Jim picked up her tray and his own and headed for the conveyor belt.

"So, who benefits if the judge is removed from power?" Ginny asked, following him out.

"Anyone who disagreed with her, I suppose, and the person who will get her job."

"Her entire staff, maybe, if they get a better-tempered woman in her place."

Jim nodded. "But none of that seems like a motive for murder. Do you want to go up to the roof for a bit? We've got twenty minutes left."

"Yes." Ginny followed him into the elevator and out onto the top level of the parking garage. The landing pad reserved for the helicopter ambulance was empty so they had the deck to themselves. She looked out over the retaining wall.

"We still don't know that it *was* murder," she said. "Maybe someone lashed out in a fit of fury, then stormed off without waiting to see what happened."

"You mean like Caroline?"

"Someone else."

"Maybe, but whoever it was must know by now that she's dead."

"Maybe he or she is too frightened to come forward."

Jim nodded. "In which case, we may never know what happened."

Ginny frowned. "That won't do. We need to clear Caroline's name and that means finding the real killer."

He wrapped his arms around her, drawing her back against him. Ginny tipped her face up to the stars and breathed in the night air. Jim must have interpreted this as an invitation for he bent down and began nuzzling the space under her right ear. She giggled, then twisted in his arms to face him.

"This is serious. Pay attention!"

He grinned. "Yes, ma'am. Okay, what's the next step, Sherlock?"

"You tell me. *You're* the epidemiologist."

Jim blinked.

"What?" She teased him. "You'd forgotten?"

"No. I just never thought of that as being the same thing."

"You investigate leads. You eliminate suspects. You test hypotheses."

He nodded. "So I do. All right, the next step should be a neighborhood canvas."

"What's that?

"You find out everything you can about the known case; where they work, live, shop. Who they hang out with, routines, preferences. Then you go ask each of the people in those same areas all the same questions. Door to door, if necessary."

"Whew!" Ginny shook her head. "I don't have time for anything of the sort. I've got a wedding to prepare for. You'll have to do it."

"Me? You think I've got nothing to do but cool my heels until the big day?"

She smiled up at him. "You don't have a bridal shower and fittings and formal portraits and no shoes and a mother hounding you every step of the way."

Jim laughed out loud. "For your information, my little bride-to-be, I have a very full schedule. I owe the Journal another article and the deadline is Thursday. I have to spend all day Tuesday at the new house waiting for the installers to hook us up to the Net, and the inspectors to come sign off on the work already done. I'm planning to take my article with me and see if I can finish it while I'm waiting.

"I'm going to have to take the car into the shop. It's making a wheezing noise when I ask it to accelerate and I don't want it conking out on me. I've got paperwork to fill out at the Dallas County Health and Human Services offices, to finish up the salmonella scare. That will take half a day at least. The emergency room physician who was going to cover for me during our week off is MIA and has to be replaced with a Rent-A-Doc, which means extra paperwork to make sure he's properly credentialed. I got a request from no fewer than six local news media outlets, all of whom want to interview me about lairdship and the bigwigs who will be in town for the wedding. *And* my Prince Charlie jacket hasn't arrived. Which means I *do* have a fitting to go to and I hope to heaven they got the measurements right. We won't have time for more than a few small adjustments."

Ginny had started laughing about half way through this recital. "Oh, you poor baby! I withdraw my suggestion. You're going to be too busy to investigate anything!"

"Quite right. Speaking of too busy, we'd better be getting back. This has been a typical Saturday night for me. I hope yours has been quieter."

"Not much. It's been nice to get away for a bit."

They turned, arms still around each other, and made their way back to the elevator.

"I have an idea about the neighborhood canvas though," Ginny said, "if you think it's really necessary. Himself can ask for volunteers. Lots of people are curious about what happened and would probably leap at the chance to be nosey in a good cause."

Jim nodded. "That's a good idea. We'll ask him first chance we get."

The elevator arrived and they stepped inside. Their work stations were on different floors so they would be parting when the doors opened. Jim bent down and kissed her, then sighed. "Let's take the rest of the night off."

She smiled at him. "Two weeks, Jim. Two more weeks. Then we can take a night off."

* * *

<h1 style="text-align:center">CHAPTER 19</h1>

Monday, Late Afternoon
Police Substation

Two busy shifts prevented Ginny from returning to her investigation until late on Monday afternoon, at which time Detective Tran presented her with a present, and a physical impossibility.

"Thank you for coming in. I know this is a busy time for you."

Ginny nodded. "I'm always happy to help the police."

Detective Tran met her gaze and held it until Ginny began to blush. "I mean, if I can."

Detective Tran continued to look at her in silence. Ginny began to sweat, then fidget, then could contain herself no longer. "Is this about the brooch?"

"You were not entirely truthful with me about what you knew."

"I was, actually. I *suspected* it was Caroline's, but I didn't *know* it was."

"What did you do after I left you that morning?"

"I found her and asked her about it. She didn't tell me anything."

Tran nodded. "That conforms to her testimony." She continued to gaze at Ginny. "I would be most grateful if you would trust me in the future."

Ginny swallowed and nodded.

Detective Tran slid a piece of paper across the desk toward Ginny. "It is my wish to have a productive working relationship with the Loch Lonach community. To that end, I am sharing some of the information I received this morning. We found fingerprints on the railing over which we believe Judge Jamieson fell."

Ginny picked up the paper and read the report. "Gary Feldman."

Tran nodded. "Following up on your research into the Judge's detractors, I had the lab expedite that set. There are some interesting features. First, it is a full set, no partials, which is unusual. Second, it is both hands, not just one, and includes the palms. The positioning implies Mr. Feldman wrapped both hands around the rail while standing on the mezzanine. This is a common behavior for persons who are holding onto the rail while looking for something or someone."

Ginny nodded. So she had been right! Gary had hung around and waited until Jamieson was alone again!

"Third, this pair of prints is not smudged in any way. That implies Mr. Feldman was the last person to touch that rail before it was examined by the forensic technicians."

"So he could have tipped her over the rail, then leaned over to see where she landed."

"Correct." Tran took the report back, tucked it in a file, then clasped her hands in front of her. "We had Mr. Feldman picked up and brought in for questioning. He categorically denies he played any part in Judge Jamieson's death. After some considerable time and thought, he admitted he was present and heard what he believes to be her scream as she went over."

Ginny had unconsciously leaned forward, her eyes

widening. A witness!

"He says the sound occurred around midnight, which corroborates Mr. Hunter's testimony. Mr. Feldman reported he had been sitting in a small closet on the breezeway at the time."

Ginny stared. "A closet? What was he doing in a closet?"

"Smoking." Detective Tran's eyes flickered. It took Ginny a minute, but she managed to work it out.

"Smoking a joint."

"Cannabis. Correct. We found the residue in the corner of the enclosure. He says he dropped it when he was startled by the sound. He exited the closet and looked around, but saw no one." Tran caught Ginny's eye again. "Following the timeline, Miss Cameron's testimony is that she was in the bathroom at the time. We are unable to confirm that. We were able to find Mr. Feldman's prints in the closet, but the Ladies restroom had been cleaned too thoroughly and too recently for any evidence of Miss Cameron's presence to remain."

Ginny nodded. She would have to find another way to prove Caroline's alibi.

"Mr. Feldman states he made his way down to the mezzanine and looked over the rail. Judge Jamieson's body lay draped over the stadium seating, apparently dead. He describes studying her for several moments, then deciding he had no obligation to call an ambulance. He exited the stadium and went home."

"How did he get onto the field in the first place? I mean, did he have a ticket?"

"Yes. He discarded it at some point between that night and when we spoke to him this morning, but says he bought it online and he has a credit card record of the purchase."

Ginny nodded. It might not matter, but it was helpful to know he would be in the database if they needed to look.

"As near as we can tell, Mr. Feldman has abided by his restraining order and has not posted any information on social media about the death. He will, of course, be charged with stalking and approaching Judge Jamieson earlier that evening." Detective Tran leaned forward. "In confessing this much, he has demonstrated a motive for and the opportunity to end Judge Jamieson's life."

"And the means," Ginny added.

Detective Tran shook her head. "His DNA has not been found on the dead woman and biometrics of his hand prints do not match the marks on the victim's arms."

"Oh." Ginny felt her shoulders sag. She had been so hoping Gary Feldman would replace Caroline as Prime Suspect. Not gonna happen.

"We will continue to investigate his statements, however, to assure ourselves there are no discrepancies."

"Thank you."

"I have something else to show you." Detective Tran took another sheet of paper out of her file, and handed it to Ginny. "You are already aware we matched DNA samples from Miss Cameron to those found on the clothing of the deceased."

Ginny nodded, then pulled herself together and focused on the report in her hand.

"As you also know, collecting fingernail scrapings is routine in any death where there is any suspicion of foul play. What you may *not* know, is that someone beat us to it."

Ginny's head jerked up. "What?"

Detective Tran nodded. "We believe someone well-versed in forensics investigations attempted to remove this evidence before leaving the scene. She did not succeed."

"She. A woman." But not Caroline. If Jamieson had scratched Caroline, they'd know about it by now.

"Yes."

Ginny sucked in a deep breath. "Do we have something to compare it to?"

"Yes." Detective Tran removed an image from the file and laid it down in front of Ginny. "The DNA matches this woman."

Ginny looked at the trim dark woman in military uniform and wondered if she'd seen her somewhere before. "Who is it?"

"Her name is Marguerite Costas. She lives in Redmond, Washington. She is ex-army, a communications specialist, now working for an information technology firm. She is married, with one child, a boy. Her husband is also employed by the same firm."

"What was she doing in Dallas last weekend?"

"She was not here."

"*What*?"

"Mrs. Costas has an alibi. She was in Redmond, at a fund-raising dinner last Friday night. She was one of the speakers. The entire thing was filmed and she appears at regular intervals in the video, easily identifiable. The airlines have no record of her flying to Dallas. Witnesses and a system of electronic tracking they use on the books at the library place her in the local stacks with her child on Saturday, and she was seen by a dozen or more persons at church with her husband and child on Sunday."

Ginny's head was spinning. She was silent for several minutes, trying to process the information. Eventually she looked up at Detective Tran. "If she wasn't here, how did her DNA end up under the fingernails of our dead woman?"

"That is what I was hoping you could tell me."

* * *

Monday Evening
Brochaber

On Monday evening, the four of them were seated around the Laird's dining room table. Sinia Forbes had produced an especially delectable casserole on short notice and brought it over. Himself had supplied the side dishes. Jim had brought the wine, Ginny the bread and dessert. They were discussing Detective Tran's bombshell.

"Why was there a DNA sample on file for this woman?" Mrs. Forbes asked.

"She was in the army. They do routine swabs in case they need to identify body parts."

"Well, that's fairly gruesome."

Ginny nodded. "But rational."

"So, how did skin tissue from this woman in Redmond end up under the nails of our victim?" Jim asked.

"*That* is what Detective Tran would like to know." Ginny frowned. "So would I."

"A ruse, perhaps? Someone who dinna like tha' Redmond woman?" Himself lifted an expressive eyebrow.

"Trying to frame her, you mean," Jim said. He looked dubious. "I don't know. It wouldn't be hard to get your hands on donated skin tissue. We use it as a wound dressing. But the lab would be able to tell if that were the case."

"Tran said it was fresh skin and fresh blood. No evidence of any source other than another human being."

"Lab error, then."

Ginny looked at him. "Andy has always sworn by the accuracy of the crime lab in Dallas. She tells me it's one of the best in the world."

"That doesn't mean they never make mistakes. Human error, you know."

Ginny nodded. Human error was in the front of every mind in the health care industry, hers included. "I can ask, but I *assume* they re-ran the test after the results came back." She jotted down a note to call Andy and ask her to follow up on that.

Jim nodded. "Okay. You make sure they double-checked and I'll do some research on tissue transfer. They would have to collect the skin from the donor, clean it, get it to Dallas, then get it under Jamieson's fingernails somehow." He looked at Ginny. "That implies the Redmond woman was in on it somehow."

"Not necessarily. She might have been attacked and scratched by a stranger."

"If she's being set up to take the fall for a murder, it's not going to be random."

"She's not going to take the fall for *this* murder. She wasn't here. She can't have done it."

Mrs. Forbes interjected. "If someone wanted the Redmond woman's tissue to be found under Jamieson's fingernails, why did someone try to dig it out after it had been planted there?"

"Good question." Jim screwed up his face, then shook his head. "There's an explanation somewhere and that woman is part of it. I'll stake my reputation on it." He looked over at Himself. "And speaking of reputations, what about the Judge? Have you had a chance to ask anyone about that?"

"I've set hounds on th' trail, but naught, yet."

"What about her cell phone?" Mrs. Forbes asked. "Did they find it?"

"Yes," Jim answered. "The police found it on the field. They think maybe she tried to pull it out to call someone, but dropped it and couldn't find it again. They looked at all the calls, and text messages, and pictures, and so forth." The other three nodded. "There was a message on it asking her to meet someone in the Skybox at eleven p.m."

Ginny nodded. "Detective Tran knew all about it. They followed him off the grounds before midnight. Not a possible suspect. I'll see if I can find out more."

Sinia shrugged. "If someone planted evidence on the body, it's proof of premeditation."

Jim nodded. "Yes, and if it was Caroline, trying to throw the police off the track, there will be a trail from Redmond to her. It doesn't rule her either in or out."

Ginny tapped her pencil on the pad of paper. "Well, it's still progress. At least we have a working theory to present to Tran. What else can we do?"

"You, young lady," her mother answered, "have duties to perform elsewhere. Tomorrow you have a bridal shower and a fitting and we need to find you some shoes. That will take up most of the day."

Ginny sighed, then nodded. "I also have an appointment to talk to Jean." Jean Pollack, the Loch Lonach Matron, had been in charge of the Skybox on Friday.

"I've already talked to her," Jim pointed out.

"Yes, about the haggis. I'd like to see if she noticed anything else." Ginny dimpled. "She won't mind. She prides herself on being on top of everything that happens in the Homestead. If she didn't see anything herself, she'll know who did."

* * *

Chapter 20

Tuesday Morning
Ginny's Car

"Where are we on the checklist?" Ginny was addressing her mother, who sat in the passenger seat of the little Volkswagen, her pen out and poised over her clipboard.

The morning had gone well. There were only a few more things to do to finish the dress—the petticoat seemed to have a mind of its own and Ginny was not about to let a mutinous undergarment ruin her wedding—so everything should be ready on time.

"Two fittings down, one to go."

"Would you please make a note that Caroline will need to practice removing the train? And can we set that for next Wednesday?"

"Assuming she's available, of course, dear."

Ginny let the comment go. Jim was scheduled to work the night before so he would be asleep and no danger to their plans.

"The photographer will meet us at the dress shop on Tuesday and get the formal portraits out of the way. Do we need to confirm that appointment?"

"Already done, dear."

She had scheduled her last shift before the wedding for

Sunday night, which meant she would be asleep on Monday, but free to do whatever was still needed between Tuesday and Saturday. Eleven days left, twelve counting today, of which four were not available and the last one, Saturday, was booked solid. That left seven days. One week to get ready for her wedding and clear Caroline of the charge of murder, and she still needed to find shoes.

"Shall I read the list?"

"Yes, please."

"Jean tells me she's got three-quarters of the out-of-towners who have RSVPed booked into rooms at the Homestead. The laggards will have to go into commercial hotels." Jean Pollack was in charge of finding lodging for the guests. Also for coordinating the food for the reception.

The cakes (plural) needed to be picked up from the baker on Saturday, but Jean would do that. The rehearsal dinner would be held at the Hall and catered.

"The church and Father Amos are both reserved, as is the Cooperative Hall for the rehearsal dinner and the reception. We finished the flowers last week and I sent the final check yesterday. The band for the reception sent a note saying they were going to be coming in on the day, so we've arranged to have them picked up at the airport and brought straight over."

Ginny nodded. They would need time to set up the sound system and warm up the instruments. The dances had been chosen more than a month ago and their usual RSCDS instructor, Alasdair Gorrie, would be Master of Ceremonies.

Sinia Forbes put her clipboard down. "Have I forgotten anything?"

"Your dress?"

"All taken care of. No need to worry about that."

Ginny smiled at her mother. "I wasn't worried. I know you'll look lovely."

"We're all going to look lovely! It's a good thing we have a party planned for after the ceremony. I'd hate to be all dressed up and nowhere to go."

Ginny's mind leaped forward. Nowhere to go! When the reception was over, Jim would take her home, to their new home, and they would begin their married life together.

One of the first things that had happened when she and Jim announced their intention was that Himself had arranged prenuptial counseling with the parish priest. Father Amos had required them to answer a lot of very hard questions, mostly about how they planned to handle trouble. They had answered the questions and signed the paperwork and been given permission to wed with the church's blessing. One more facet of the very public life they were undertaking.

She sighed. At least they would have a few days alone before they had to show themselves again. Which reminded her, she needed to do some shopping.

"Would you please start a grocery list?" And a wish list of problems Ginny would like to see disappear, the dark cloud hanging over Caroline first. One week!

* * *

Tuesday Midmorning
Cameron Residence

Ginny rang the doorbell with some trepidation. She hadn't seen Caroline for more than a week and felt a bit guilty about spending time on the wedding when she should be investigating. Caroline met her at the door and the two friends hugged each other long and hard.

"Do *not* worry," Ginny told her. "We're working on this." She'd come early so she and Caroline would have time to catch up. She shared all the evidence they'd uncovered, and the progress of the investigation. "And if you can think of anything I've overlooked, please tell me."

Caroline shook her head. "I've been thinking about it nonstop. All I could come up with is that Alan was with me the whole time, except for the bathroom, of course."

Ginny nodded. "They'll have to drop it. There isn't enough evidence to convict anyone."

"But that would leave suspicion hanging over my head. I don't want that!"

"We're not going to let that happen. And it won't be much longer in any case. I need you by my side on May Day. That's our deadline!"

Caroline smiled. "I believe you. If anyone can do it, you can." She rose and led the way into the library. "And now, before the others get here, come see what I got you." She handed over a cheerfully wrapped box.

Ginny tore the wrapping off and pried the lid open. Inside lay a dozen plain white cotton underpants, new, and exactly what she would have purchased for herself. Also a pair of new bras to match.

"Caroline! They're perfect! How did you know?"

"I talked to your mother. She seems to have read your mind, or maybe you let something slip, but she told me what you needed was practical, everyday wear, since that's what he'll see every day. And it's the everyday things that matter in the long run."

"Thank you!" Ginny tucked her gifts away in the box and set them aside, following Caroline into the living room, and joining their mothers in a glass of champagne.

The older women were discussing Alan, and Ginny listened with delight to the universal approval. He'd been marvelous, sticking to Caroline without fail, in no doubt of her innocence and his role in her defense.

"Why didn't I see how wonderful he is sooner?" Caroline asked.

Ginny grinned. "I have no idea."

"You were right. You were right about everything! We haven't talked about a date, yet. He's afraid of jinxing us, but it won't be long. You'll be my Maid of Honor."

"Matron!"

Caroline laughed. "Yes! You beat me to the altar and I never thought *that* would happen."

Ginny didn't begrudge the jibe. She'd thought the same. Caroline was the cheerful, bubbly one, with lots of social activities, and much attention everywhere she went. They had both thought she would be married first.

"If you wait long enough, I can supply small children to destroy your wedding reception."

"No, thank you! And none in the ceremony either. Just you, me, Alan, and his best man, whoever that might be. Which reminds me, I want to know how many people are coming for your wedding."

Ginny squirmed. This was one of the things that had been taken out of her hands.

"I would rather have had a small ceremony. You know that, right?"

"I know, but you're marrying the heir. There's no way it won't be an event."

Ginny nodded ruefully. "Every Homestead has been invited to send a representative. It seems like everyone Angus has ever known is coming. Jim's invited friends from school, and his ex-girlfriend."

"Really?!"

"She rescued us from the snowstorm and we became friends so it should be all right."

"Well, that's very magnanimous of you. Who else?"

"Well, everyone in Loch Lonach is invited and most will come."

"The church isn't going to be big enough."

"No, but that won't stop them."

"No." Caroline grinned. "It's a good thing I'm in the wedding party, otherwise I wouldn't be important enough to get in the door."

"Don't be ridiculous! I'd squeeze you in next to Mother, if I had to."

"Oh, Ginny! I'm so afraid I won't be able to come!"

"Now don't start that! You're going to be there. You have to be. You remember what I told you about the train?"

Caroline nodded. "I have to unhook it at the shoulders so Jim can put the sash around you, then carry it out of the church when I recess. I remember."

"We have to rehearse that away from Jim. He can't see the gown before the day."

"You know where to find me."

The doorbell interrupted them.

"Here they come!" Ginny downed the champagne and allowed Caroline to pour her another.

* * *

Tuesday Afternoon
Pollack Residence

Jean Pollack was an older woman, somewhere between Angus Mackenzie and her mother's age. She had stepped into the duties of Matron when Mrs. Mackenzie died. She was small-boned and big-hearted, with the rapid movements of a restless bird. Her eyes were bright as a bird's, too. They missed nothing. She and Ginny were seated in the "parlor," a comfortable room with windows that looked out onto the street.

"Yes, I've told your mother not to worry about a thing. She needs to focus on you. We'll take care of the rest."

"But there are so many people coming!" Caroline's question had stirred up all sorts of misgivings in Ginny's breast.

"Getting stage fright, deary?"

Ginny wrung her hands. "Maybe. It's more people than I anticipated."

"Not more than a typical Gathering."

"No, I suppose not."

"And the only people you have to pay attention to are Angus, Jim, and Father Amos."

Ginny nodded, then sucked in a deep breath and changed the subject. "What can you tell me about the Friday night of the Games?"

Jean nodded several times. "I've been thinking about it ever since your call. Most of what happened is standard fare, same old people saying the same old things. But." She rose and hurried into the kitchen, then back again, handing a photograph to Ginny. "I found this and thought you might be interested."

Ginny studied the image. "Who is this with Jamieson?" They were seated, with their faces close together and tipped toward one another, as if in private conversation.

"I don't know him. He came up just before eleven, went straight to her and sat down. All they did was talk. No eating, no drinking, no laughing. A very serious conversation. Then they both rose and left together. I didn't see him again."

"And you have no idea who he was?"

"He had a patron's ribbon so I got the lists out and looked at them. You know we check the names of who comes and goes, so we can estimate the amount of food and drink to supply."

Ginny nodded. She had suspected something of the sort.

"There wasn't any name on the list that could have been him."

Ginny blinked in surprise. "Where did his ribbon come from, then?"

"He was a 'guest' attached to the Highland Dance contingent."

"Oh!" Well, that made sense.

"So, I've been thinking you should take that picture and show it to the Highland dancers. One of them may know who he is."

"That's a very good idea. Is there anything else you can share with me?"

Jean laughed. "You know I would, willingly, if I had anything else. And if I hear anything, I'll call you."

Ginny rose and took her leave. "Thank you!"

"See you soon, and don't you worry. It'll all turn out right."

* * *

Tuesday Afternoon
Forbes Residence

Douglas Abernathy, when applied to, had no trouble identifying the man in the photograph.

"His name is Augustus Fellows and he's the Regional Judging Coordinator for the Federation of United States Highland Dancing Teachers and Adjudicators, Southwest region."

"Wow. Did you see him, at the Games?"

Doug nodded. "He introduced himself to all of us and stayed to help on Saturday. And I, for one, was glad he was there.

With Jamieson dead, and without his help, we might have had to cancel."

"Serendipity."

Doug nodded. "Very much so."

Ginny had thanked Doug for his help, then asked one more question. "Did he say why he was in Dallas?"

"Something about networking. He had planned to visit us in the morning, then go on his way."

Doug had also provided contact information for the organization. Ginny now sat facing the telephone, composing what she wanted to say to the man. She dialed the number Doug had given her, explained who she was, and was connected with Mr. Fellows.

"Yes, I was there. I wanted to talk to her, face to face. We're so short-handed. I was hoping she'd agree to emeritus status. Not so much responsibility, and not so much travel."

"Forgive me if I seem a little slow, but did you say she was leaving?"

"Yes. She had turned in her resignation. That's what we were meeting about. I was trying to talk her out of it."

"Did she give a reason?"

Mr. Fellows hesitated. "Medical reasons, I believe, though she didn't say so directly."

"Can you recall what she *did* say?"

"Not in her words. Something to the effect that she was past it. Which didn't make sense to me. She was only in her fifties. Most of our judges are tough. They tend to last into their seventies."

"You helped out on Saturday, I believe?"

"Yes. I had planned to visit, you understand, just to observe, but I was pressed into service when we learned Jamieson wouldn't be available."

"Did you notice anything else, anything out of the ordinary?"

"Well, now that you mention it, yes. She was a bit wobbly. As if she'd had too much to drink, but she didn't seem drunk to me. And I didn't smell liquor on her breath. I wondered if that—the balance problem—had anything to do with her resignation. I gave her my arm to get into the elevator, but by the time we got to the mezzanine, she was over it, whatever it was. She was very firm. Said she didn't need any help getting home. I remember thinking that all ex-champions are in denial about getting older. They teach and it keeps them fit and young, most of them. But it doesn't last forever. Growing old is something that happens to all of us and no one wants to admit it."

"Thank you Mr. Fellows. You've been very helpful."

"Let me know if there's anything else I can do."

Ginny hung up the phone thinking about what she'd heard. A Highland dance champion whose legs wouldn't work correctly any more. That fit with what she knew so far. But what could have caused the deterioration? And did it have anything to do with the muscle relaxant they found in her system?

* * *

Chapter 21

Wednesday Morning
East Dallas

Ginny fidgeted a bit, as she always did when seeing her gynecologist. The exams had been done weeks ago, but the test results were now back and she was in the physician's office, facing her across the desk, waiting to hear the verdict.

Dr. Berry smiled at her, then picked up a yellow folder, opened it and spread several sheets of paper out on the desk, inverted so they faced Ginny.

"First, you're healthy as a horse. I see no reason why you shouldn't have healthy babies in spite of getting a late start."

Ginny made a face. In the obstetric world, any woman approaching her first pregnancy after thirty-five years of age was considered high risk. Ginny had been twenty-eight last October and would be twenty-nine in six months, easily into her thirtieth year by the time the first child appeared.

"I assume Jim has seen his urologist?"

"He told me he had, and they found no problems."

"Good." The physician went over some of the specifics included in the assessment.

"You don't smoke, which is good. I recommend giving up alcohol until you're done with childbearing."

"Ouch!"

Dr. Berry nodded. "I know, but scotch is a known factor in fetal injury and it's just not worth the risk."

Ginny nodded.

"In the same vein, I recommend all my patients take no dietary supplements. We'll monitor your bloodwork, and I'll add a vitamin if you aren't getting everything you need. Okay?"

Again Ginny nodded.

"You already know how to eat a healthy, well-balanced diet, get enough exercise, and plenty of sleep. What are you doing about stress-reduction?"

Ginny squirmed. It was a good question. "There are changes coming and all of them are stressful. I'm probably moving to day-shift at the hospital and, also probably, not going to be actually taking patients in the ICU. Himself wants me to focus on my new role."

Dr. Berry looked sympathetic. "I can imagine. How do you feel about that?"

Ginny paused for a moment to gather her thoughts. "I am one-hundred percent committed to my new life as Jim's wife and the Matron of the Homestead, when he becomes Laird."

"But?"

Ginny met the older woman's gaze. They had become friends over the years and Ginny knew the doctor had married a man as intelligent, well-educated, and influential as herself. She would understand Ginny's misgivings.

"But I can't seem to find the right balance between the woman I have been and the one I am supposed to become." She gestured toward her own breast. "How much of me do I get to keep? I'm not cut out for the role of lackey."

Dr. Berry sat back in her chair and sighed. "No, you're not." She studied Ginny for a moment, then spoke. "I suppose you're asking me how I managed the transition in my own life."

Ginny nodded.

Dr. Berry smiled. "I will do you the courtesy of telling you the truth, but I would rather you didn't discuss it with anyone else, including Jim—especially Jim."

Ginny took a breath. "Oh? I mean, of course I will keep it to myself."

Dr. Berry nodded. "The first three years were hard. I kept thinking I could be honest with Peter. I wanted no secrets and to be able to be open with him. He said he wanted the same." Her eyes strayed to the far wall and the certificates of achievement that covered it. "He agreed to everything. The continual schooling, the conferences, the residencies that meant months away from home. He was wonderful. He supported me, encouraged me, took over most of the household jobs, never complained. But there came a day when I realized there was something wrong."

Ginny held her breath.

"I had gotten close to where I wanted to be, and done well. I was getting offers from all over the country for positions I would have given my eye-teeth for, before I was married. I still wanted them, but I found I wanted something else more. I wanted my husband to be happy.

"It took four months of difficult conversations. He didn't want to level with me and I had to bully him into it. Eventually he told me the truth. He didn't want to play second fiddle to my career. He liked his job and the house we had bought together. He wanted to stay where he was—and he wanted children."

Dr. Berry took a breath, fixed her gaze on Ginny, and shrugged. "I had to choose between having a family and having an illustrious career. I chose family."

Ginny nodded. She wasn't in quite the same positon. Jim would not be playing house-husband to her career. Instead, she would be moving into his shadow.

Dr. Berry continued, her eyebrows expressing her discomfort. "I had some back-peddling to do, and relationship repair. He had bought into my success as a reflection of his own. We had to—both of us—redefine ourselves. I chose to set up a private practice. He chose to apply for tenure at the University. We both chose to settle down."

Dr. Berry leaned forward, resting her forearms on the desk and speaking directly to Ginny. "I can't make those choices for you. I can only tell you they're out there. Each time we make a big decision—getting married, having babies—we shut off other opportunities. Examine how you feel about those lost chances, then choose, with your eyes wide open. And don't forget that we grow and change over time. What matters passionately to us when we're young may seem silly later." She smiled at Ginny. "I have one more thing to add, because I know you. It's perfectly acceptable to be the power behind the throne. Exercise your influence in private and trust Jim to listen. I have a good feeling about him."

Ginny nodded, smiling. "Thank you. This has been a big help."

"Good, now there are a few more things we need to go over. I've got your genetic profile here and there are some specifics we should discuss." She tapped one of the documents on the desk with a forefinger.

"You will not be surprised to find you have the MCR1 mutation, the one that accounts for your red hair. I believe you also know this means you require higher levels of anesthetics, and that you are at greater risk for skin cancer, specifically malignant melanoma. That same gene gives you a thirty percent higher risk of endometriosis, and a fifty percent higher risk of developing Parkinson's.

"This middle column shows you have seven variants of the genes that control high blood pressure. This does not mean you'll necessarily develop essential hypertension, but we need to keep an eye on it, and on you during any pregnancy that may ensue.

"No known cancer variants. There are a couple of suspicious markers for diabetes and insulin resistance, but we don't know enough about them to make a prediction. What I will say is that your health is in your hands. Stay away from empty calories. You know how."

Ginny nodded.

"The last set refer to the pre-conception genetic screening we routinely do for inherited diseases. I'm happy to say you carry none of the lethal genes."

Ginny found herself relaxing. She hadn't wanted to specifically bring up the possibility, but she had hoped there were no dreadful surprises lurking in her DNA.

"We need to do Jim, too, of course." Dr. Berry folded her arms on the desk. "Is there any chance you wouldn't go through with the wedding if he turned out to be carrying one of these?"

Ginny felt her eyes widen. She stammered. "I don't know. I hadn't thought about it."

"Then the sooner he comes in, the better. I can expedite that set of analyses."

Ginny swallowed hard. "What would be our options? I mean, if we marry and he has something awful and the child inherits it?"

Dr. Berry's eyes softened. "It's up to the parents, of course. We offer medical abortions if the child has no chance of a normal, or even acceptable quality of life. We do that, too, with accidents that occur in utero. Sterilization is an option. There are various ways to combine gametes from screened donors with the unaffected parent's contribution. There are people looking at gene therapy, but nothing that can be counted on, yet. The final option is to do nothing."

Ginny blinked. She couldn't wrap her head around such a weighty choice, not on short notice. Obviously, the thing to do was get Jim tested—immediately.

"How long does it take? I mean, for Jim to be tested?"

"If you get him in here today, I can make sure you have the results in five working days."

"Count on it." Ginny's brow wrinkled as a new thought struck her. "I suppose this sort of information is confidential."

"Of course."

"But you could get access to it with a court order?"

Dr. Berry looked at her for a moment before replying. "There would need to be a very good reason and only a very small number of people would be authorized to receive the data. Do you have something specific in mind?"

Ginny nodded. "There was some unidentified DNA under—uh—someone's fingernails. The police had it analyzed and the results are impossible, so I was wondering where else to look."

"Impossible?" Dr. Berry smiled. "That sounds intriguing. Is it an ongoing police investigation?"

"Yes."

Dr. Berry's eyes grew round. "Oh." She thought for a moment, then shrugged. "People leave DNA everywhere. Have you considered another way to get a sample?"

"If I knew who I was supposed to be sampling, I could probably come up with a plan, but I don't. Not yet." Ginny's mind wandered back to the lethal genetic diseases. She had studied them in school and knew there were some appalling possibilities. Did anyone in the Loch Lonach community carry such a burden? She'd never heard.

"Dana, this is going to sound intrusive and don't answer me, if it's none of my business, but I'm thinking ahead to my future responsibilities. Does Himself know of anyone in the community who has or has had this sort of genetic challenge? Would the Laird be one of the authorized persons?"

Dr. Berry hesitated. "Yes. He is one of the authorized persons. When Jim takes over, he will be, too."

Ginny nodded slowly. "And mental illness? Would he know about those sorts of secrets, too?"

"He might. That's not my field. Why do you ask?"

"Jamieson had scars on her wrists. I saw them on Saturday, when Detective Tran was showing me the bruises on her arms. They were long healed, but, at some point, either she was cutting herself or attempting suicide."

"There might be another explanation, but I agree that old scars across both wrists is suspicious for suicide attempts. Do you think it might be relevant to the murder investigation?"

Ginny shook her head. "I don't know. And maybe not, but I'm trying to find out all I can about her. You have to be pretty miserable to want to take your own life."

Dr. Berry nodded, her eyes growing sad. "I've seen that level of misery in some of my patients, but we try to help them cope. No one wants more deaths in the family."

Ginny gave her a small smile, then rose from her chair. "You're a good woman, Dana Berry."

Dr. Berry rose, came around from behind the desk, and took both of Ginny's hands in hers. "You get Jim over here so we can put those fears to rest. And let me know how your investigations are going. I've got a sneaking suspicion I'm going to enjoy hearing the rest of the story."

* * *

Chapter 22

Wednesday Noon
East Dallas

Jim looked up from his article, then glanced at the clock. She was early. They had arranged to go to lunch, with her picking him up because his car was in the shop.

"Sorry for barging in like this." Ginny slipped his spare key back into her pocket as she crossed the room. She came up behind his chair and twined her arms around his neck. "I know you're busy."

He reached up and pulled her arms loose, then swiveled his chair around and drew her down onto his lap. "But you have something to say that can't wait."

She nodded. "I'm under orders to haul you over to my gynecologist's office today, this very minute."

Jim's smile faded. "Is there something wrong?"

She shook her head. "No. We just need your DNA. I asked if I could sample you for them and was told—politely—not this time. So I have to make sure you keep my promise, after which we can go to lunch."

Jim nodded. He was at a good stopping place in his work. "Just give me a minute to close down the machine." Ginny slid off his lap and let him attend to his writing. "There." He rose, then put his arms around her and pulled her into a hug. "I'm guessing this has something to do with Grandfather's mandate to reproduce as expeditiously as possible."

Ginny nodded. "We also talked about the possibility of something going wrong."

"Ah." Jim pulled her tighter, planting a kiss on the top of her head. "Nothing is going to go wrong, my love. I won't let it."

Ginny tipped her face up to his. "She says I can't have any more alcohol until after we have all the children we want. That's going to be a very long dry spell."

Jim started laughing. "How many children do you plan on having?"

She raised both eyebrows. "If you look at my genealogy, the average was thirteen per family."

Jim caught his breath. "This is something we haven't talked about! I was expecting two or three, not a baker's dozen!"

"Well, not all of them survived to adulthood back then, so they went on having them until the woman either died in childbirth or reached menopause."

Jim drew her close again. "I repeat. I am *not* going to let anything happen to you! Even if it means no children at all."

"Your grandfather will have something to say about that."

"Nope. That's between you and me and your obstetrician."

Ginny pushed herself out of his arms. "Speaking of which, let's go."

Jim let himself be herded out the door, into her car, and over to the medical plaza. He felt a little silly among the all-female clientele, in spite of his medical training, but they didn't keep him waiting long. When they were done collecting and clocking in the sample, they smiled, promised fast results, and let the two of them go.

"What would you like to eat?" Jim had examined his fiancée's face, then settled into the passenger side seat without suggesting he take over the driving. She was a good driver and he had said he was willing to put his life in her hands. He snugged the seatbelt down.

"Salad, with meat."

"Okay."

They drove to the restaurant in silence, Jim alternating watching the road and watching Ginny. She seemed preoccupied. When he had her seated and the lunch orders placed, he reached across the table and took her hand.

"Talk to me."

Ginny's eyes focused on his. "She says I'm healthy as a horse and there's no reason why I shouldn't have plenty bonnie bairns, as long as you do your part."

Jim smiled at her. "Which I am willing to do."

She raised one eyebrow at him, then let it fall. "But she is a conscientious professional. In addition to covering all the things that can go wrong with a pregnancy, both mother and child, she presented me with my DNA results."

Jim took a careful breath. "And?"

Ginny frowned. "I hadn't realized my risk of Parkinson's was so high."

"Because of the MCR1?"

"Yes. Also endometriosis."

Jim nodded. "Both of which have a familial component and no one in your family has had either."

"That we know of."

"That we know of. What else?"

"High blood pressure markers, which mean she's a bit worried about pregnancy-induced hypertension."

Jim nodded. That was a possibility, and he would have to pay close attention to make sure it didn't kill her and the baby. "What else?"

"No cancer genes."

"That's good."

"Some useless non-markers for insulin resistance and diabetes. Those came with a lecture on healthy lifestyle choices."

Jim smiled. "So we eat at home. I can get used to that." Without suffering. The woman could cook.

Ginny's brow descended. "She then raised the specter of stress-related illness and asked me what I planned to do about it."

"Which is?" Jim had to wait for his answer while the lunch arrived and the waitress made sure they had everything they wanted.

"Caffeine and sugar have to go."

Jim expressed mock horror. "No! How will you survive the night shift?"

"The night shift will have to go as well." She looked across the top of her salad. "But you knew that."

Jim nodded. His grandfather had outlined the plans already in place and those he was hoping to implement within the next month. His brow wrinkled. "But that means I won't have anyone to visit in the ICU anymore."

Ginny gave him a hard look. "I should hope not."

Jim winked at her across his salmon and lemon butter. Both of them would have fond memories of those night shift visits.

"So," she continued, "when will *you* be moving to day shift?"

"At the end of my first year, which is in three months, give or take a week or two."

She nodded. "That will make a lot of things easier. In the meantime, we'll be ships that pass in the night."

Jim sighed to himself. He was looking forward to holding her in his arms as they slept. Well, it wouldn't be *every* night, just the ones he had to work.

"Anything else I should know about?"

Ginny nodded. "Something occurred to me while Dr. Berry was talking about genetic diseases."

"Oh?" Jim paused with his fork halfway to his lips. He refused to believe they were going to lose the genetic lottery, but it was hard to know as much as he did and not be afraid.

"Jamieson had old scars on her wrists. The kind you see on someone who has attempted suicide more than once."

Jim frowned, but went back to his meal. "What's the connection?"

"I don't know if there is one. We see so many teenaged girls with depression. But Dr. Berry said suicide is one of the responses to lethal gene combinations." Her eyes grew sad. "I can understand that. Such a devastating thing to have to live with. Either you're going to die horribly, or you gave the gene to your child, who is going to die horribly. The guilt must be enormous."

Jim nodded, sobered by the thought. "It's not my field, but I've heard some of the physicians talking about the challenges, and the experimental gene therapy they're working on. No cures, yet, but hope for the future." Funding the research was a problem. Funding was always a problem.

"Anyway, I was wondering if we could get a look at Jamieson's medical records."

Jim looked up from his plate. "I can't afford a HIPAA violation." Medical records were carefully protected from prying eyes. The statutes made it clear that curiosity would be punished.

She shook her head. "The woman is dead and the police will have authorized access. I was just wondering if Angus would, too."

Jim blinked. He was still getting used to the idea that the Laird of Loch Lonach had extraordinary powers as well as extraordinary responsibilities. "You think Grandfather should ask Detective Tran for access?"

"Yes."

Jim turned the idea over in his head while he finished his meal. If his grandfather could get the actual records, Jim could interpret them. Probably. It would be interesting to find out why she'd been on cyclobenzaprine. Ginny hadn't given up the idea that Jamieson fell over the rail without anyone's help. Medical records might be able to rule that out.

"Won't Detective Tran have talked to the Medical Examiner? They routinely order records if there are any."

"You're thinking about someone who dies in a hospital," Ginny pointed out. "We send the current admission records along as a matter of course."

"And sometimes they ask for more." Jim nodded. "That's my point. They found prescription drugs in her system. Wouldn't the M.E. have been curious?"

"I would have." Ginny put down her fork and looked across the table at him. "Are you busy this afternoon?"

"Yes. I've got to go pick up the car then go to the Health Department."

"Can't you do that over the Internet?"

"Apparently not. What did you have in mind?"

"The medical school library."

He smiled at her, thinking back to the last time they had gone to the library together. "I wish I could, but when the Health Department is done with me, I have to go home and finish that article. You'll just have to manage alone."

She sighed. "Well, all right. If I have to."

He laughed. "You can drop me off at the car agency on your way over."

* * *

Wednesday Afternoon
Medical School Library

Ginny glanced at the clock as she entered the library. Two hours—tops—after which she would have to go home to get ready for work. Tonight, tomorrow night, then the weekend. Four more twelve-hour shifts to get through. She had better hustle.

"Excuse me." Ginny presented her credentials and smiled at the librarian. "I'm hoping you can help me find something that isn't already on the Internet."

The librarian laughed. "That's getting harder, but we still have private collections. What are you interested in?"

"I've got a very tentative connection between suicide attempts and a genetic anomaly. Is anyone researching that?"

"As a matter of fact, yes." The librarian led Ginny to a study room, then spent fifteen minutes ferrying dissertations, journals, and non-circulating books from the depths of the collections to Ginny's desk.

Ginny went through the material as quickly as she could, finding a clear correlation between a devastating diagnosis and deep depression. With one exception. One of the genetic disorders *presented* with depression, before physical symptoms began, and long before a diagnosis was made.

"That can't be it," she told herself. "No one can have Huntington's Chorea and win every Highland Dance competition she ever entered."

But it seemed one could. The age of onset was variable. Some showed motor symptoms in their twenties, but the majority didn't begin to deteriorate until the mid-forties or fifties.

Ginny found references to interpersonal difficulties, to isolation, to the Kubler-Ross stages of grief, hideously elongated to cover years of suffering.

"Which would explain why she was so hard to get along with."

She also found an epidemiology report.

It seemed there was a region in Scotland where there was a high rate of incidence of Huntington's, the Grampian Mountains. People in that region, and people descended from those who had come from that region, were at risk. Two clan names, in particular, were associated with this high rate of carrying the Huntington's gene, Menzies and Robertson.

Blair Jamieson's mother had been a Robertson.

* * *

CHAPTER 23

Thursday Wee Small Hours
Hillcrest Medical Center ICU

It was three-thirty a.m. on Ginny's Intensive Care Unit and she was (temporarily) caught up. Her patients were sleeping. All medications had been administered and treatments done. The charting was up to the minute. Even the drawers had been restocked.

She had shared her library discoveries with Jim during their break, and he had been suitably impressed, even saying he would very much like to confirm her hypothesis with Jamieson's medical records and personal physician.

Ginny had smiled happily. "It makes the chance of its being an accident much greater."

Jim had shaken his head. "If it weren't for those skin cells under her fingernails, I'd be inclined to agree with you, but she was struggling with someone."

Ginny had slumped over her meatloaf, and Jim had taken pity on her.

"I'll tell you what I think it means. I think it means that whoever touched her—and that includes Caroline—got a bigger response than they expected. If I shoved you hard enough to make you take a step back, I would not expect you to fall to the floor."

Ginny had considered this, then nodded. It might be a mitigating factor in Caroline's case. "And it might have made it easier for someone to push her over the railing," she offered.

Jim had finished his bite, his eyes on her face, then responded. "Not, I think, over the rail. Push her up against it, yes. Then whoever it was slid an arm under her knees, lifted her, and tipped her backward, like a see-saw, using mechanics and the laws of physics. That's how I would have done it."

Ginny had stared at him in sudden, acute dismay. She had a vivid, uncomfortable sensation in the small of her back, of a bar digging into it, of her feet flying up towards the sky (as they used to do when she was a child on a swing), and the black terror of falling, falling, falling. She had dropped her eyes, staring at her plate, unable to eat, unable to speak. He wouldn't. He *couldn't* do that to her. He could, of course. He outweighed and out-muscled her by thirty percent. He could, if he wanted to. Her hand crept instinctively to her talisman.

"Ginny?"

She had to fight for control of her fear. Fear. The natural, automatic fear that resulted in self-preservation. But also the learned fear.

"Ginny? Are you all right?"

Not really. How do you tell your fiancé you're afraid he will kill you the first time you put a foot wrong? The answer was, you don't.

Ginny dragged her mind back to her job. She rose, walked through her assigned rooms, making sure everything was still all right, then went back to her desk.

She could do nothing further for Blair Jamieson until they had access to her personal life. Angus had promised to pull strings and Detective Tran had promised to get a release for the medical records. The timeline was essentially complete. They knew where she had been and to whom she had spoken during the last night of her life.

They were beginning to build a profile of the dead woman. Missing were friends and family. No parents living, no siblings found. No husband or lover or even high school boyfriend. A very lonely woman, and very private. Her online presence was entirely work-related.

Ginny found images of Jamieson as a girl on the Highland Dance podium, wearing blue ribbons and holding sterling cups, and one showing her as a woman judging an event, but they had all been posted by other people. She didn't talk about herself, not online. Also, she never smiled. Not even while holding her trophies up for inspection.

Ginny turned her computer around and started a new search. Marguerite Costas, the owner of the DNA found under Jamieson's fingernails. The police had already covered the time frame for the murder. Ginny swiftly confirmed what Detective Tran had told her about the weekend of the Games. Marguerite's alibi seemed water-tight.

Ginny drummed her fingers on the table, thinking hard. She read murder mysteries, a lot of them, and—somewhere— someone had said no alibi was unbreakable. Of course, they were only talking about the ones they *had* broken, so maybe it wasn't really true.

Most of this alibi relied on images. Ginny pulled up the public images of the fund raiser and located Mrs. Costas. She checked the date/time stamps, then the name tags (both on the attendees and the digital ones assigned after the image was uploaded), then the spelling of all the names. Couldn't find a loophole.

Plugging Marguerite's face into the image search brought up a lot of possibilities, though. Ginny examined each one carefully. Marguerite in the Army. Marguerite speaking at a professional convention, Marguerite smiling for the camera at numerous receptions. A formal portrait. A formal family portrait. Informal family snapshots; some still images, some video. Marguerite on vacation (apparently), attending a voodoo celebration in New Orleans.

Ginny stopped. New Orleans? It wasn't impossible, of course. People did visit New Orleans, even from Washington state. She hunted for more. Fifteen minutes later she had some very interesting theories forming in her mind, but no more time to devote to the search. Her patients needed her attention. She put the computer away and went back to work.

* * *

Friday Afternoon
Forbes Residence

Normally Ginny liked her job and looked forward to the feeling of satisfaction she got from it. Right now, though, she could have used the time. She had hoped to do more research while on duty, but whatever gods were in charge of such things were having fun at her expense. She'd been too busy to sit down. She fell into bed both mornings and had to be roused on Friday afternoon to eat.

Having consumed a well-balanced meal and a caffeine-free beverage, Ginny got out her files and checked them carefully, to assure herself she had not been hallucinating. The idea was still there, waiting to be examined. But suspicions were not proof. She was looking for facts.

Ginny opened her image manipulation software and laid out the clips in a grid, rejecting any that were too oblique to make facial features recognizable. She had a tool that let her copy a selected piece of an image, then empty it, leaving just the outline. She used this to compare the two faces, adjusting for resolution and image size.

The women in the images weren't identical. Marguerite was thin, fit, in good shape for a woman her age, as befitted an Army officer. Josephine was heavier, with full cheeks and jowls. But the noses matched. So did the ears. So did—and Ginny found this interesting—the shape of the eyes, the eyebrows, and the mouths. In spite of the makeup.

The image search utility used an algorithm that was a watered-down version of the same one used by facial recognition software. It measured features and made a best-guess estimate of what other images might fit the criteria.

Ginny did a quick search on biometrics and found that ears were being suggested as the best way to identify individual humans, with the caveats that twins' ears matched and that there was insufficient research to prove ears did not change over time. Also the usual comment that injury, deliberate mutilation, and gravity can change the shape of the ear. But the majority of the data supported the ear (the whole ear) as an excellent way to identify individuals, especially as they walked past a surveillance camera.

Ginny sat back in her chair and thought for several minutes. It could be coincidence, of course. But she'd already met one doppelgänger. She was reluctant to believe there might be another. It was more likely that these two women were twins who had grown apart.

Different names, of course. Josephine Dupree and Marguerite Costas. Costas was Marguerite's married name. Her maiden name was Warburton. Josephine's records indicated she had never married and Dupree was the name she had been given at birth. Ginny blinked slowly. At birth.

She felt a small "click" in her brain. Siblings separated at birth were usually adopted. Those records were sealed, except by court order, and there was no reason to think the police would be granted the right to explore Marguerite's childhood. Or Dupree's either, for that matter. Neither was charged with a crime and there were no compelling arguments she could make.

The differences between them would argue against the genetic tie, but genes did not control appetite or a predilection for vigorous exercise. Lifestyle did that. Could she persuade Detective Tran to look into the possibility? Maybe Tran could come up with a reason, some excuse she could use for opening those records.

Ginny launched a blank document and laid out her theory. When she was satisfied, she picked up the phone, called the police substation, and was connected with Detective Tran.

"Yes Miss Forbes. How may I help you?"

"I may have a theory about how Marguerite Costa's DNA came to be under Blair Jamieson's fingernails."

Ginny could almost hear the smile on the other end of the line. "Please continue."

"The obvious explanation is that the evidence was planted, but there are problems to be overcome with that theory. How to obtain the skin cells, how to transport them to Dallas, and how to get them under the dead woman's fingernails."

"True."

Ginny nodded into the phone. "On the plus side, that theory would explain what you found—that it looked as if someone had been digging under Jamieson's nails. That would be true if someone was scraping skin into the spaces, trying to simulate an attack."

"I agree. You have an alternative theory?"

"Yes. I suspect Costas has a twin." Ginny explained her research findings and her analysis.

"You think her twin was present in Dallas and did the actual killing?"

"I do."

"And you think that twin was Josephine Dupree?"

"Yes."

Ginny heard a sigh.

"I wish I could confirm your theory, but I cannot. Ms. Dupree has provided a sample of her DNA and there is no chance she and Mrs. Costas are related."

Ginny felt as if someone had sucked all the air out of the room. She was silent for a full minute, then shook herself firmly. It was a mistake to fall in love with one's own hypotheses. It resulted in bad data.

"That is disappointing." She took a breath. "May I ask why you had a sample to use for comparison?"

"Ms. Dupree to Mrs. Costas, you mean?"

"Yes."

"For exclusion purposes. As you know, DNA transfer from person to person is very common, and our collection techniques have gotten so sensitive that very small amounts on a victim's hands can be sequenced. It takes only 0.5 nanograms of DNA to produce a usable sample. The technique is reserved most often for family members and coworkers, those who share living space with the victim. In this case, Ms. Dupree was seen with the victim at dinner. It was possible that some of the unidentified DNA found on Judge Jamieson's hands might have been acquired there. We sampled everyone known to have been in the Skybox that night."

"I see. Thank you for explaining that to me."

"Miss Forbes."

"Yes?"

"I want you to know that I value your input and I am grateful for your help. Please do not think I am dismissing your theory on any grounds other than hard evidence."

"I understand." Ginny hung up the phone. Damn! Such a good theory, too! It explained all the facts. Well, she'd just have to keep digging. At least she hadn't been laughed at.

* * *

Chapter 24

Friday Evening
Forbes Residence

On Friday evening, they gathered around the Forbes' dining room table to eat and talk. Three of the four—Ginny, Jim, and Angus—had news to impart. Sinia Forbes took notes.

Ginny had never paid enough attention to her mother's role in the clan. Only recently, since Jim's arrival, had she begun to realize Sinia Stewart Forbes was the official secretary and the unofficial historian of the community. She watched her mother's swift, efficient record keeping and marveled that she had never done so before.

"How did you come up with a theory like that?" Jim wanted to know.

Ginny looked back at him. "When I did the image search, I found someone who looked like Marguerite Costas visiting New Orleans, sans husband and child. I checked the date and found the real Marguerite accounted for, in Redmond. So I looked further and found 'Marguerite', in voodoo costume, performing in New Orleans, Baton Rouge, Shreveport, and Alexandria. That led to finding flyers, advertising those events, which—apparently—are not taken seriously. The voodoo they practice is just for fun, for the tourists."

"She was wearing a costume?"

Ginny shook her head. "The woman in costume was Dupree. It took me a while to sort it all out, because they don't look that much alike. Dupree has at least sixty pounds on Costas and I had a mistaken belief that identical twins looked, well, identical. But there were the biometrics and it was plausible."

"But their DNA isn't a match?" Her mother looked sympathetic.

Ginny smiled ruefully. "Apparently not."

"Sae we need tae find anither wha could hae done th' deed."

"My favorite is still that angry father," Jim volunteered. "He had a history of violence against Jamieson and he was on the scene,"

The other three nodded.

"Aye, but how tae prove it?" Angus asked.

Ginny shook her head. "I don't know. I'll have to think about it."

Angus nodded. "Ye do that, lass. Jim?"

"I looked at Jamieson's medical records today."

Ginny frowned. "Today? But you worked last night."

"And got off late, as you know, because you had to wait for me. But I'd made an appointment, so I kept it. Dr. Mayfield was her primary and he confirmed what we suspected. Jamieson had the Huntington gene and she was beginning to deteriorate."

"Oh, the poor woman!" Sinia echoed Ginny's sentiments.

"Dr. Mayfield had prescribed the cyclobenzaprine to help with the onset of spasticity. He was also arranging psychiatric counseling. Jamieson was just entering the mild phase, but she knew what was coming. Her mother had died of it and she, Jamieson, had been diagnosed in her early twenties. Dr. Mayfield said she'd been in a support group since the diagnosis was made. He also said he'd never worked with a more determined patient. She wanted to be independent, as long as it was possible."

Jim turned to his grandfather. "And you knew all about it."

The Laird nodded. "In my official capacity and w' th' strict requirement tae keep it under my hat fer as along as possible."

"Were you going to tell me, ever?" Jim asked.

Angus nodded. "Once th' woman was deid, 'twere no longer necessary tae keep her secrets. And tha' leads me tae this." He pulled over a notepad and examined it before continuing. "As she's gone, and murdered inta th' bargain, th' bank hae let me tak' care o' her affairs. I held her Power o' Attorney for just tha' purpose, because she had nae family. Th' disposition o' her estate is in keeping wi' wha' we ken o' her. She's left th' entire thing tae the Huntington Disease Foundation, tae be used tae further research inta this condition."

"Is it much money?" Sinia asked.

Angus nodded. "A bit. A fine legacy, and 'tis hoped 'twill do some good."

Jim glanced swiftly at Ginny, then just as swiftly away, and Ginny thought she caught a shade of guilt in his expression. She blinked. What was that about?

"And that's it?" Jim asked, his attention focused again on Judge Jamieson's affairs.

Angus shrugged. "Th' accountants are going o'er the files. If there's a problem we'll hear o' it. In th' meantime, 'tis up tae th' Homestead tae make funeral arrangements, as soon as th' police release th' body. I've a small ceremony planned fer this evening. I'll ask ye tae join me in it, when th' time comes."

The weekly Friday night ceilidhs were more than just dances, they were a time and place for the clan to come together to talk and support one another. With the wedding coming up and the death of a prominent member of their community to discuss, there was little chance anyone not actually in the hospital would miss it.

Dinner over, Angus went home to change, Sinia disappeared into the kitchen, and Jim took Ginny into the living room, settling down in a corner of the sofa and tucking her up against him.

"Now," he said. "Tell me what's troubling you."

Ginny sighed, snuggling closer. "Nothing, I guess. It was just such a good theory."

"I liked it, too. What else have you got up your sleeve?"

"Nothing, at the moment. I guess I'll have to find someone else."

"The woman had so many enemies. There has to be someone other than Caroline who wanted her dead."

Ginny baulked. "Caroline did NOT want her dead. Caroline just barely touched that woman and she fell down the steps and now we know it was because of her disease, not because Caroline pushed too hard."

Jim backpedaled. "I'm sorry. I didn't mean that the way it sounded."

Ginny relented. "I know you didn't. I just wish I had some way to help. Even if the police can't prove it was her—because it wasn't—this could ruin her life. If we can't find the real culprit, some will whisper, and that can do just as much damage."

"True. Well, I haven't given up and I know you haven't. Let's hope Grandfather's neighborhood canvas did some good."

Ginny nodded, then pushed herself out of Jim's arms and onto her feet. "They won't tell us."

Jim followed her to the front door. "Why not?"

Ginny sighed. "Because she was universally hated and they're glad she's dead. And, though they love to gossip in private, they don't want to be called tattle-tales."

"Even if it means they can help clear Caroline's name?"

Ginny shook her head helplessly. "They don't care who did it. They'll leave that to the police. Most of them, anyway." Alan would care. So would the Camerons.

Jim folded her into his arms and held her close. "Maybe you're wrong. Maybe they care about justice as much as you do."

She looked up into his face. "Why should they?"

"Because, my love, without justice there can be no mercy, and without mercy, there can be no humanity, and the Scots have always wanted to think well of themselves."

She smiled, then nodded. "Well, if it takes playing one ego against another to uncover the truth, I'll do it, but I'd feel better if all I had to do was ask."

* * *

Friday Evening
Cooperative Hall

There were only two more opportunities to practice the dances that would be on the program for Jim and Ginny's wedding reception. Everyone was eager to get past the business and on to the music, but Angus had called them to attention and they were required to listen.

"Yer all aware tha' Blair Jamieson was killed th' first nicht o' the Games this month." There were nods all over the room. "What ye may not ken is tha' th' woman was suffering fra a brutal, terminal disease." He had their attention now. "She inherited a gene fra her mither tha' caused her t' lose control o'er her muscles."

Ginny watched as the listeners silently consulted one another, their expressions puzzled.

"This disease robs th' sufferers o' their ability tae walk, tae talk, tae care o' themselves." He paused and looked around the room.

"Livin' w' such a curse takes a toll. She wanted nae pity frae us, and showed nane tae herself. She was a hard woman who fought fer every grain o' respect. She earned her way tae th' top o' th' Hieland Dance podium. Her peers respected, though they dinna like her."

There was some foot shuffling at that point.

"She dinna let tha' stop her. She had seen wha' happened tae her mither. She knew her fate. She dinna let tha' keep her frae college, law school, passin' th' State Bar, and bein' elected Judge in the Family Law Courts o' Dallas County.

"Her frustration at being unable tae make a lasting career o' the dancin' she loved did no' keep her frae teachin', then volunteering tae judge, tae do wha' she could fer th' art, tae keep th' Scottish way o' life alive."

Ginny felt, rather than saw, their attitudes shifting. Angus knew his audience.

"Her courage, in th' face o' a devastating fate shows all o' us wha' the best o' us can do, in time o' need. Lest ye think her less than human, there were times she tried tae kill herself. And there were those she chose tae trust with the horror o' her illness. But tae us she showed th' bravery, th' integrity, th' strength o' William Wallace. I ask ye now tae lift yer glass tae a woman few o' us knew, but all o' us should honor. Clansmen, I gi'e ye Blair Jamieson."

Ginny lifted her glass and downed the wee dram, her eyes damp. How many times had she dismissed an unhappy patient, a troublesome one, as someone who was incorrigible, unforgiveable? She must remember not to do it again.

Angus turned the stage over to the musicians, who took their sweet time settling in and warming up. A natural response to Angus' speech. There wasn't a man or woman in the room untouched by the thought of what they had not realized they were witnessing.

She was standing by the punch table, waiting for the dancing to begin when she was approached by a woman who lived in the same neighborhood as Jamieson, Mrs. Harris, one of the dance mothers Ginny had seen around the Games tents over the years.

"Miss Forbes—Ginny—I heard you were asking for information about Jamieson. Are you still?"

Ginny nodded. "We're hoping to find something that will lead us to her killer."

"Not Caroline Cameron?"

Ginny shook her head. "They found DNA under Jamieson's fingernails, but no scratches on Caroline. So we're working under the supposition there was someone else present. Someone we don't know about, yet. And we're asking for help. Do you have anything for me?"

The woman shook her head. "I was home early that night. We had the competition to prepare for. I heard nothing, saw nothing. Neither did Shelly."

Ginny nodded, wondering why Mrs. Harris had come over, then.

"I just wanted to tell you I'm so sorry I didn't come forward before. I hated Jamieson. But I didn't know her, didn't try to get to know her. We'll put our heads together, all of us, and see if we can find anything. Anything to help Caroline."

"Thank you."

"Will there be a funeral?"

Ginny nodded. "Himself will let us know when and where."

Mrs. Harris nodded. "I'll be there." She moved off.

Over the course of the rest of the evening this scene was repeated, with apologies to her and to Himself and promises of better effort to try to find the real killer. By the end of the night Ginny found her spirits rising. They were good people. They just needed a reminder.

Ginny managed to get through the dances, supported by fellowship and caffeine. She had to fight to keep her mind on what she was doing, and Jim was definitely drooping. They were both glad to finish the rehearsal, say goodnight, and make their way home to their beds.

Tomorrow was Saturday. They had plans to spend the day at the new house, moving their smaller possessions onto shelves and into closets. There would be time during the day to revisit the evidence. In the meantime, the best thing to do was sleep, and let her subconscious chew on the problem.

At least now she had the community on her side, and that was a big step forward.

* * *

Chapter 25

Saturday Morning
Caverns

Jim tossed his list onto the table and went in search of Ginny. He found her on her knees, her head in a cupboard, applying adhesive shelf liner.

"Ahem."

Ginny backed out of the cupboard, smoothing the liner down as she came, sat back on her haunches, wiped her hands with a rag, and smiled at him. "You're timing is perfect. I need a break."

"I have come to tell you we have an appointment."

"We do?"

"Well, *I* do, but I've decided you should come with me."

She rose to her feet. "Okay. Where are we going?"

"The caverns. I'm instructed to present myself to Reggie. He is to give me an assignment."

Ginny lifted one eyebrow. "This has all the earmarks of an edict from your grandfather."

Jim nodded. "Come on. It wouldn't do to be late." He herded her toward the door, letting her grab her purse on the way out.

They swung around the lake and drove to the Loch Lonach Homestead grounds. The weather was fine so there was a good crowd of tourists wandering over the site, gawking at the demonstrations and displays. Jim drove around to the employee entrance, parked, and escorted Ginny inside the main complex. They both knew the way to the elevators, and they were both known, so there was no delay in getting the necessary clearance to descend.

Once inside the elevator, Ginny turned to him. "Any idea what this is about?"

Jim shook his head. "I've stopped asking. Half the time Grandfather expects me to already know and the other half he expects me to figure it out on my own."

Ginny grinned at him. "Poor baby! Well, that's what you get for wanting to be laird. He'll do his best to make sure you're ready."

"As you have reason to know."

"As I have reason to know." The elevator door opened and they stepped out. "Shall I drive?"

Jim hesitated for a split second then nodded. She knew her way around the caverns better than he did.

They climbed into one of the waiting golf carts and took off, Ginny expertly navigating the twisting, turning paths that led into the bowels of the complex. Ten minutes brought them to the electronic heart of the stronghold. Reggie met them at the door.

"Right on time. Himself will be pleased when I tell him since he has the idea that the two of you should have your feet held to the fire in the matter of courtesy and we've got over five hundred people coming from out of town for your wedding, and I'm surprised it's not more, but some of the guest list had to be cut because we couldn't squeeze any more into the church and he wouldn't like to offend anyone. Did he tell you what I have in mind?"

Jim shook his head.

"Well, it was that little contretemps on the Games grounds that gave me the idea, you know, because someone said they wondered why the body hadn't been found earlier, and I started to wonder the same thing, but, of course it's crowd control that's the issue, and no one likes to interfere with the fun and that includes any restrictions on movement even though we still have to have *some* rules but you understand that."

Jim nodded, then stole a look at Ginny. It was hard to keep a straight face when listening to Reggie. He was originally from New York and could carry on a conversation—both sides—without help, and without benefit of oxygen.

"The obvious solution, of course, was real-time GPS, but we wanted to do away with issuing devices, even wearable ones, since they can be lost or damaged or traded and those will only work well when you're out in the open and the equipment needed to track a shipping container at sea using the satellites is way too big to be used on a person, so I asked around and the new guy, Fleming, took a look at the problem then came up with a few suggestions, and the two of us spent some time building a prototype and it looks good so Angus said he'd send you down as a guinea pig to see whether the idea will work well enough to launch full-scale human trials."

Jim made a face. "Is this going to hurt?"

Reggie laughed. "Shouldn't. It's just paint. Well it's paint we've made some improvements on, but still just paint. Unless you're allergic to it which is one of the things we wanted to see. We've done the animal testing, but at some point we needed a human volunteer." He turned to face Ginny. "Two would be better than one and you've got the MC1R mutation so if anyone is going to have an inflammatory reaction to the compound it should be you."

"I'm not sure I like the sound of that," Ginny said. "Why don't you tell us what you have in mind?"

"Oh! Didn't I say? Well it's a tracking system. The idea is that you put something that can be picked up by external sensors into a neutral carrier, in this case the face paint, and apply it to the person you want to keep an eye on but it's face paint so it doesn't look weird, just like a decoration, but the whole thing gets hooked into the computer which means the person who's been tagged—we're calling them paint tags for the moment—the person who's been tagged can go anywhere he or she wants and the system will track them, but not interfere, though it's possible to set up alarms, of course. It would be a combination of portal control like the anti-theft devices you walk through at the store and cell tower pings. If we'd had this in play for Jamieson she would have been found hours earlier because one of the parameters is movement and is it happening and if it should be and isn't the subject can be checked up on. So when she decided to lie down on the field and die, the computer would have flagged it and might have flagged her erratic movements getting out there. I haven't gone that far into the possibilities yet."

"How does it work?" Jim asked.

"We're using RFID which stands for Radio Frequency ID--identification, you know—and there are three versions, passive, semi-passive, and active, depending on whether there's a power source attached to the tag or just to the reader. The upside to RFID is it can see through walls. The downside is that the active and semi-passive tags, which have a power source built into them, have been too expensive to be much use in a mass market, and the range on the passive tags is really short, only about twenty feet. So the challenge was to make one that was small, inexpensive, and had a much wider range, which meant either covering the subject with paint or goosing up the power in the readers. We decided to start with making the tags smaller. We had access to the raw materials and it's essentially just nanotech kicked up another notch. Jon is a real wizard at making those things do what he wants them to. You'd almost think it was magic if you didn't know better. Anyway—"

"Wait!" Jim interrupted him. "Fleming? Jonathan Fleming? The guy who just won two Nobels for his medical nanotechnology breakthroughs?"

Reggie nodded. "That's the one."

"When did he join Loch Lonach?"

"Three months ago. We've been recruiting him for years and he was dragging his feet but he came around to it in the end. Seems nice and he's happy as a kid in a candy store with the new toys Angus gave him. Anyway, so we were thinking of all the ways we could use the technology to get some safety nets in place without getting in the way since the Games grounds are a lot bigger than twenty feet across and we didn't want to force people to walk through gateways every time they turned around. We were focusing on the Highland Games because of the corpse, so that's where we started." He took a breath.

"We could tag wanderers of course and that was the first thing Jon suggested, Alzheimer's patients, but we don't get many of those at the Games, so we jumped to kids. If a mom tagged her kids as they entered the Games grounds she could let them go without worrying about losing one of them though they could still get into trouble because they're kids but I have in mind a cellphone app that would let her track the little darlings so she could see if they tried to enter the Scotch tasting tent or spent too much time hanging out with the edged weapons but if there was any real concern like the kid trying to enter a restricted area or leave the grounds entirely the computer could pinpoint the child and the Loch Lonach police could go pick him up and those we *could* use gateways for, since nobody would be surprised to see a door blocking the entry to a restricted area."

Both Jim and Ginny nodded. Kid control was always a challenge at the Games.

"Then Jon suggested tagging everyone at the Games using the hand stamps. We could build scanners for admission—which would mean we wouldn't have to buy those plastic wrist bands—and to allow access to the parking garage or the Sky Box, and if someone—one of the adults—goes down we can have the system linked to basic medical information like does he have a heart condition or is she a diabetic which will help with the first aid which the two of you should appreciate."

Jim nodded. There would need to be some way to control access to the protected health information, but that could be handled.

"Right, so we've got emergencies and access covered and were thinking what else and it occurred to me that the big boon for us is the marketing data we'd get from just watching where people go and what they spend their time doing. We could collect real-time tallies—find out which events were popular and whether there was a better layout that took advantage of the traffic pattern and which bathroom needed servicing first and with a bit of tinkering the paint designs could be used to identify where they bought their tickets and we could tweak that to make it easier and more attractive and we could tie visits to specific vendors to rewards and do you remember the kids and the clan tent passports?"

Ginny nodded. "Sure. The kids got a small book made to look like a passport, and when they visited the clan tents, or one of the educational displays, they got it stamped. If they filled up their passports, they got a prize."

"Right. Well the problem has always been participation on the part of the adults at the clan tents. They want to be nice but they're talking to someone and don't see the kid arrive, hang around for a bit, then move on. This way the kid will get credit for the visit without adult help."

Ginny laughed. "They won't learn much that way."

"We'll set it up so they have to interact with the material to get the reward. We can figure something out. Each tag could have a unique identifier and when the tag is queried, that information would be personalized so if a guest wants to be added to a mailing list, he just has to get scanned and it's all automatic. I draw the line at targeted marketing after the Games are over, though. That's just plain evil, but we could set the system up to flag someone who's had one too many to be safe behind the wheel or put a spending limit on purchases so parents can control the cost of the Games. The point is, the tags can be used to do lots of good things if we can figure out how to extend the range to cover the entire complex and not just the designated areas that require access points and we need to do some field testing to answer some of the questions like how long will the tags last, how much paint is needed, and what side effects should we expect, if any, though if the tag-ee is allergic and that can happen we can put the tag on a piece of paper or cardboard like a luggage tag and hang it around his neck. So does that sound like something you'd be willing to do?"

Ginny had settled down on a chair, listening as Reggie came to his conclusion. She nodded. "I'm game. How big do these tags have to be? Quarter sized? Half dollar?"

Reggie shrugged. "We don't know, but the tests so far indicate a bit larger. Jon says he can miniaturize further if we get the go-ahead." He walked over to his work station, took out several pieces of paper, and brought them over. "Here are some proposed designs." He handed them to her. "What do you think?"

Ginny looked at the designs one by one, with Jim peering over her shoulder. They were all Celtic knots of some sort: mythic animals impossibly contorted, twining vines heavy with leaves, abstract rivers of color that flowed back on themselves. All drew a smile to her lips. "It's going to be hard to pick just one."

Jim reached over her shoulder and pointed to a design laden with interweavings and suggesting a bronze shield. "I'd like this one, please."

Reggie nodded, located the template and began setting out his colors. "And for the soon-to-be Lady of Loch Lonach?"

Ginny smiled and pointed to a Tree of Life in shifting blues. "This one. It reminds me of my talisman, and I like the colors."

Reggie smiled. "All right, then. The next question is, where do you want them to be placed on your bodies?"

"Oh!" Ginny spread her hand across the design she had chosen. It was eight inches in diameter. "I guess I was thinking the back of my hand, but this won't fit."

"How about your shoulder?" Jim suggested.

Reggie held the design up, inspected it, then shook his head. "I'm going to suggest her back and you, too, although yours would fit on your thigh, if you like."

The next forty minutes were spent cleaning the selected canvases and applying the technology-enhanced paint, using the stencils. Jim had the satisfaction of seeing Ginny's tag applied just below the nape of her neck, the blues overlying a base of black that made them seem to shimmer. His own tag ended up looking even more like a metal shield when the several layers of color and the sealant had been added.

"These are works of art!"

"Small ones, yes. No sense wasting talent and we've got some here." Reggie put the finishing touches on the shield and stepped back. "The paint dries almost instantly. It won't wash off and we'll need to use a special solvent to remove it when we're done testing. I'll put the two of you in the database and you'll just have to remember to behave yourselves for the duration. Any questions?"

Ginny nodded. "What's the range on the reader?"

"The prototype we're working on will read the paint tags from just under a mile away, but it has to be looking in the right direction since these tags don't transmit information, they only reflect it. Well, that's not quite accurate. It's closer to say the tags get activated by the energy coming from the reader, then they glow in the dark, but not the sort of glow a human eye can see. It's not the right wavelength, so we need the reader. Have you ever been out at night and seen an animal's eyes catch the headlight and suddenly appear out of the darkness even though you can't see the animal, just the eyes? That's how it works. You point the reader at the tag and it lights up. When we get the go-ahead we'll add readers to the cell towers and patch the database into the system so we can write an app anyone can download and use. Eventually we'll want full coverage of the Games grounds, including the fields and parking lots, which means five miles in any direction."

"What about the caverns?" Jim asked. "Will it tell you if someone is down here?"

Reggie lifted an eyebrow. "That's a very good question. We know it will pinpoint a tag in the SkyBox, but we haven't tested the ground penetration capabilities yet." He turned around and made a note. "We'll have to see. Okay. Thank you both for your help. You don't need to do a thing until it's time to remove the paint. Just go about your usual life. Let me know if the tags give you any trouble."

Ginny nodded. "Oh, we will, and we'll want them off before the wedding. I have no intention of walking down the aisle wearing a tattoo, however temporary."

Both of the men laughed.

Reggie waved goodbye as they climbed back into the golf cart and headed topside, Jim driving this time. He glanced over and saw Ginny grinning at him. "What?"

"I was just thinking about the history of body art, especially woad."

"That blue stuff our Pictish ancestors used to use?"

"Yes, the plant-based dye they used to decorate their bodies before they went into battle."

Jim looked over at his bride-to-be and grinned. He had heard the rumors. "I'm not the one wearing blue."

* * *

CHAPTER 26

Saturday Afternoon
New House

Jim had dropped Ginny back at the house and gone off to get his formal jacket fitted, leaving her to finish lining the cupboards and move the dishes into place. The bathroom still had to be done. And every time she turned around, she found something else to put on the shopping list.

The house still smelled of various upgrades (paint, carpet, wood polish) so she had all the windows open. A late April breeze ushered the scent of budding fruit trees and wildflowers and sunshine into her work space. She breathed deeply and rejoiced in the absence of allergies.

Also on her list for today was testing the various faucets and electrical outlets and mechanical connections. The water pressure was strong. So was the Internet signal. She was moving from outlet to outlet, methodically plugging in a lamp, turning it on and off. Ginny sang to herself as she worked.

One week from tomorrow was her wedding day. She stood for a moment, lamp in hand, looking at the front door, imagining Jim opening it, carrying her across that threshold, and then—

The door opened and Jim came in. He caught sight of her and smiled, and Ginny blushed to her hairline.

He stood where he was for a moment, studying her, then set his keys on the little table in the front hall, walked over, took the lamp from her hand, and put it on the floor. He slid his fingers under her chin, and lifted her lips to his. Ginny shook at his touch. She put both hands on his shirt, her fingers noting the slightly uneven texture and the warmth where it lay against his skin. He, too, smelled of sunshine.

"Ginny—" he started.

His phone went off, followed promptly by hers. It broke the spell.

Ginny pulled her phone out of her pocket and looked at the number. Her mother. Her mother? Now?

"Hello?"

"Ginny! Is Jim there? Himself is looking for both of you."

Ginny turned to face Jim, her eyes widening in alarm. "What's wrong?" Jim was looking grim.

"They've arrested Caroline," her mother answered. "Himself will meet you at the police station."

"We're on our way." Ginny put her phone up and stared at Jim. "This can't be happening."

He put an arm around her waist, and turned her toward the door. "Let's go see what's changed. We'll deal with it, whatever it is."

They drove in silence to the police substation, were checked in, then left to cool their heels in Detective Tran's office. Both had been there before. It hadn't changed.

"They should paint those walls," Ginny said, by way of an irrelevance.

Jim nodded. "Maybe we can make a project of it, one day." They lapsed into silence.

When Detective Tran appeared, she wasted no time on pleasantries. "Miss Cameron is being questioned, and will most likely be released on bail, but not anytime soon. I advise you to go home."

"We were told to meet my Grandfather here," Jim said.
Tran nodded. "He is here."

"May we see her, Caroline?" Ginny already knew the answer to that one, but asked it anyway.

"Not at this time."

"Can you tell us what triggered this arrest?" That was Jim.

Detective Tran hesitated, then answered his question. "Some new evidence has come to light."

"What evidence?" Jim again.

Detective Tran looked at both of them. "You know I am unable to discuss an ongoing investigation with you."

"But—" Ginny began. Detective Tran held up her hand.

"Ask me nothing I cannot answer. Go home. I will let you know when there is news."

Jim nodded. "All right, but we have to check in with Grandfather before we leave."

"This way." Detective Tran rose and led them down the hall and around a corner to a series of private offices. Even with the door closed, they could hear Angus Mackenzie's voice. He rarely raised it, rarely needed to. He must be very upset at the moment.

Detective Tran knocked and was invited in. Through the opening Ginny could see a harried man behind a desk and Angus leaning toward him, hands planted on the blotter. They both looked at the newcomers. Detective Tran did not bother to introduce them, just left them facing the double set of authorities.

Angus glanced at them, then went back to his quarry. "I'll no ha'e ye harassing th' lass without counsel. Ye'll wait 'til he arrives."

The man behind the desk nodded. "She's a *person of interest* in this investigation. We'll wait, but she stays where she is."

"Aye, and sae will I." Angus dropped into the chair facing the desk, then looked over at them. "Jim, I'll thank ye tae tak' my place wi' th' counsel this afternoon. Tell them wha's in th' wind and ask fer a postponement. If they will no', tak' notes. I'll catch up wi' ye this evening."

Jim nodded.

"Ginny. Yer tae go tae th' Camerons. Do wha' ye can wi' them. Tell them I'll come when I can."

Ginny nodded. When the Laird turned back to the man behind the desk, both Jim and Ginny left, retracing their steps out the building and to the car.

"Drop me at my house, please," Ginny instructed. "I want my car."

Jim nodded. "Don't wait dinner for me. I'll grab a bite to eat on the way over."

"We both have to work tonight!"

"I know. So does Grandfather." He pulled up in front of her house and let her out. "I'll pick you up at six."

Ginny nodded, then hurried through the house to the garage, explaining to her mother as she went. "I'll call you as soon as I know anything."

She backed out of the garage and turned toward the Cameron's house. There was a very good chance they would know less than she did, and Angus had sent her as his representative, not as an investigator. But she would have to ask, and they would just have to forgive her.

* * *

Saturday Afternoon
Cameron Residence

Ginny rang the doorbell and was admitted promptly. Mrs. Cameron looked past her, as if expecting someone else.

"Isn't Himself with you?"

"No, ma'am. He asked me to tell you he'll be with you as soon as he can, but he's making sure Caroline is treated properly. May I come in?"

"Of course." Mrs. Cameron led her into the front room and offered her iced tea, which Ginny accepted as a way to normalize the situation.

"Now, tell me what happened."

Mrs. Cameron nodded. "The first we knew about it was when Alan called. He said he and Caroline had been at her apartment. The police came to her door. Lots of them, Alan said. And they put Caroline in a squad car and asked Alan to wait outside and they searched her apartment. They took things out in bags, but the only thing Alan could identify was her computer. Then they asked him for his DNA, and he told them he'd already given a sample to the police and they checked and it was true. So then they called someone on the phone and talked for a bit, then they asked him to accompany them to the police station for further questioning and he went, because they were taking Caroline and he wanted to be close, but they wouldn't let him talk to her."

Ginny nodded again. The police wouldn't want their suspects comparing notes until *after* they'd been questioned.

"He repeated what he'd already told them about Jamieson and what happened that night, then they asked him a whole bunch of new questions."

"About what?"

"About her work and about a package she got from

Washington."

Ginny's brow furrowed. "Washington, D.C.?"

"No, Washington state. Redmond, he said. And I guess it meant something to him because he seemed agitated about it."

Ginny's eyes widened. "Caroline got a package from someone in Redmond, Washington?"

Mrs. Cameron nodded. "They wanted to know if it had been delivered to the TI campus or to Caroline at home, or somewhere else. Alan told them he knew nothing about a package, but they seemed skeptical. He said they almost accused him of covering up for her and I wouldn't put it past them to think he'd lie for her."

Ginny silently agreed. "What was in the package?"

Mrs. Cameron shook her head. "He didn't know. He said he didn't know much about her work, either. Everyone who works there has to sign a non-disclosure agreement."

Ginny nodded. Industrial espionage was big business. "Go on."

Mrs. Cameron shrugged her shoulders. "I called David and he called Himself and the two of them went to the police station to see what they could do. Then David called to say he was meeting Ken Muir downtown to fill him in.

Kenneth MacAlpine Muir was a criminal defense attorney of some note in the Dallas area. Although Ginny had a basic distrust of lawyers, especially those who defend the guilty, she was glad to hear Ken was on the case. No one doubted his brain, or his brass.

"Can you tell me anything else?" Ginny asked.

"I don't think so. That's all I know." Mrs. Cameron turned her head sharply and listened for a moment. "That's David's car!" She rose and went to meet her husband. Ginny rose, too. She stayed only long enough to hear what Mr. Cameron had to report, then made her excuses and hurried away.

The problem, she told herself, is the police only have one viable suspect. Not surprising if they had tunnel vision. If she could point them in another direction, she could take some of the heat off Caroline. Gary had been cleared, at least in so far as the body was concerned. He hadn't gotten close enough for his DNA to get on her. Just on the railing above where she landed. Well, she would get back to Gary later.

No other people had been found on camera in the area at the time. No other witnesses had come forth to say they saw something.

Her favorite suspect was still the person who left skin cells underneath Jamieson's fingernails. Not Marguerite Costas, of course. Her twin, Josephine Dupree. Because, from a scientific stand point, that was the explanation that made the most sense.

Dupree had an alibi, of course. She had told the police, when asked, that she was performing on stage in Shreveport that same evening, had driven back to make the show. With the DNA sample ruling her out, no one had examined that alibi closely.

Ginny felt a sudden qualm. If that package from Redmond had contained Marguerite's skin cells—

She shook the thought off. She couldn't examine the idea until she'd had a talk with Caroline, or Himself, or the lawyer— someone who knew what the police thought they knew.

In the meantime, she would try to break Dupree's alibi. She would do what Dr. Berry had suggested, get a DNA sample from some other source. It wouldn't be admissible in court, of course. The police would have to obtain the same evidence legally. But it might provide another *person of interest* and that might be just enough to shake their faith.

The first thing she needed was an alternate sample of

Dupree's DNA, and she thought she knew where to get it. She hurried back to her house, rummaged in her bags, found Dupree's business card, and made a beeline for Reggie and his lab.

"If there is any DNA on that card, can you pull it off and run a sample?"

Reggie spent a minute examining the card, dusting it for prints, then adding solvents designed to separate soil from the surface. He shook his head at last.

"There's nothing here. I'm sorry." He handed the card back to her. "It looks like it's been cleaned with privacy spray—that stuff they use in the labs to remove all traces of the DNA you've just finished with, to make sure there's no cross-contamination with the next specimen in line, which you can understand if the outcome of a paternity case is hanging in the balance. No one would want the lab sued for pointing the finger at the wrong man. It's not that hard to make, really. All you need is some bleach, but the commercial version is cheap, about four dollars an ounce, just spray and rinse, and it's guaranteed to degrade and remove any DNA you might have left on the test surface so you can use it again without worrying about it." He gave her a half smile. "Sorry I couldn't be more help."

Ginny drove home trying to control her disappointment. She had seen Dupree touch that card, had taken it from her hand, had dropped it in her bag, and not touched it since. At the bare minimum, it should have had Ginny's DNA on it. Surely that was suspicious in itself?

But it left Ginny with a very sticky problem. If Dupree had been that careful, had gone to that much trouble to prevent genetic snooping, what were they going to have to do to get their hands on a clean sample of her DNA?

Because, the more she thought about it, the more

convinced Ginny became that Marguerite Costa, that package from Redmond, and Josephine Dupree were connected. And, since the police were satisfied they already had the culprit in custody, it was up to Ginny to prove them wrong.

* * *

Chapter 27

Saturday Late Evening
Hillcrest ICU

Ginny had never been less motivated to go to work. She forced herself to pay attention to shift report, to assess her patients carefully, to triple check the medications and other orders, taking no shortcuts, aware that any mistake on her part could have dire consequences. But all the while, the problem of Caroline was niggling at the back of her brain.

It was ten-thirty before she could draw her first breath. She glanced at the clock, then decided Caroline would still be awake.

"June, can you watch my patients for ten minutes? I need to make a phone call."

"Sure." The nurses set up coverage for breaks as part of the routine for each shift. June already knew Ginny's patients almost as well as her own, just as Ginny knew June's. The timing had to be negotiated, though.

Ginny grabbed her phone from her pocket and headed for the break room, dialing as she went. Caroline picked up on the second ring.

"Ginny! Where are you?"

"At work. I'm calling from the break room so let me know if there's something you don't want overheard."

"You talked to my mother?"

"Yes. What did she mean, about a package from Redmond?"

"It's true! I'd forgotten all about it and recycled the box, of course, so I couldn't prove anything."

"What was in it?"

"Something for work." Caroline hedged.

Ginny's brow furrowed. "Is it something you can tell me about?"

"Well, I'm not supposed to, of course. But I can tell you in very general terms. And you have to promise not to pass the information on to anyone else."

"I can do that."

"Okay. What I'm working on is part of a master plan to send people into outer space."

"The Mars project?"

"I didn't say that and I don't know."

"Okay. What you're working on is theoretical."

"Right. So there's a company in Redmond that TI has a contract with. A big one."

"Microsoft."

"No. They're a competitor. It's the one that's building rocket ships. I should say *one* of the ones. You understand."

"I do. Go on."

"Well, the designers want a skin-tight suit of neural interfaces for the astronauts to wear. In addition to the usual, collecting data from the person, they want the suit to be able to send instructions to the neurons in the person's body."

"Wearable tech. We've had that for a while."

"Not like this. My job is finding a way to make the two-way communication system between an external controller, like a computer, and the internal controllers, neurons mostly, flow seamlessly, no interruptions, no matter what."

"Wow."

"Yes. Well, I'm not in biotech. I'm working strictly on the communication two-way street: materials, signals, and stability. The tech side, rather than the bio side."

"Okay. So what was in that package?"

"Specs and a tissue sample."

Ginny caught her breath and Caroline hurried to explain.

"Not a real one. Well, it's real skin, but it's created in one of the labs. They've been cloning it for years, to use in tests. They use the same tissue to eliminate one of the possible confounding variables. Comparing oranges to oranges, you see."

"Yes. And you needed more."

"Yes."

"Wow."

"So what the police found was that this company in Redmond sent me a tissue sample."

Ginny thought for a moment. "How did they know where to look?"

"I asked the same question. They didn't answer me directly, but some of the questions led me to think they followed up on the skin cells under Jamieson's nails, and the investigation led them to that company."

Ginny steeled herself for bad news. "Caroline, whose tissue was it?"

"No one alive today. Not Costas."

Ginny breathed again. "You were able to turn the sample over to them?"

"No. My boss is handling all of that. They came in with a search warrant and seized what they could find, which was just the tissue on hand."

Ginny didn't miss the implication. "So the police are thinking where you can get one tissue sample, you can get another."

"Right. It proves it's possible to ship skin cells through the mail. They think I could have had Costas' skin cells shipped to my apartment, or a post office drop box. Something like that."

"But you didn't."

"Of course I didn't!"

"Sorry. I was just confirming the truth."

"Well, here's something else you can stick in your analysis. I've had some time to think. Why would I go to the Games with Costas' DNA in my pocket? Assuming I knew Jamieson would be there, how would I know I'd get a chance to toss her off the mezzanine?"

"With Alan glued to your side? And the twisted ankle?"

"The police aren't letting either of those arguments stop them. But listen. Suppose I made an appointment to meet with Jamieson and she was willing to come to that spot at that time. How could I control who else might be in the neighborhood? I couldn't. We already know Gary was stalking her and he wouldn't have told me about it."

"The police might argue you two were in it together."

Caroline paused. "All right, they might, but what about the traffic to and from the bathrooms, or the elevator? I also couldn't control whether or not the lights would still be on, though the police are arguing they were on a timer and I might know that and also that I might know how the security cameras worked." She took a breath.

"But here's the thing. I didn't have time to shake off Alan, meet with Jamieson, get close enough to grab her, drop her on her head, go down to the next level of the stadium, scrape my skin samples under her nails, climb back up to the breezeway, and be coming down the ramp when Alan met me and Rory Hunter overheard us talking. There just isn't enough time for all of that. I've got two witnesses that say I was somewhere else within minutes of the scream. I might be guilty of throwing her overboard, but not of trying to frame someone else for the deed."

Ginny nodded. The argument made sense.

"Okay. I have to go back to work, but I'll add your comments to the list. You take care and try not to worry. We'll find the proof somewhere."

Ginny heard her friend's voice on the other end of the line, still roused, but with a note of fear edging the denial. "I'll do my best."

"Keep thinking. And I'll keep digging. I promise."

Ginny hung up and hurried back to her desk. She jotted down the major points Caroline had made, added some question marks, folded the paper in quarters and tucked it into an inside pocket of her scrubs. She really could *not* think about it anymore tonight, but this way the ideas would still be there when she got the chance to look at them again, even if it wasn't until Monday afternoon. And, in the meantime, her subconscious could be chewing on them. Which, in Ginny's experience, tended to be a very good thing. With that comforting thought she went back to work.

* * *

Monday Afternoon
Forbes Residence

When Ginny woke on Monday afternoon, her last pair of ICU shifts behind her until after the wedding, she tackled the problem of identical twins that didn't look like identical twins.

Ginny had always been fascinated by science, especially the kind relating to the human body. She collected articles and papers and dissertations on discoveries and the evolving research they triggered. Her inventory covered all the biological sciences, also anthropology, archeology, zoology, theology, and anything else that sparked her imagination. She turned now to her folder on human growth and development.

The embryology material was the stuff of nightmares. There were so many things that could go wrong. Add a second embryo and you could see identical twins, fraternal twins, conjoined twins, parasitic twins, vanishing twins, fetus in fetu, dermoid cysts, and chimeras. Ginny skipped over the pictures, grateful that twins didn't run in her family. Jim's either.

She located the folder she was looking for and opened it to the studies done on twins separated at birth.

The environment in which a set of twins grew up could alter their DNA in two ways. The first was by triggering a mutation, an actual change in the DNA code caused by exposure to radiation, a chemical, or other environmental toxin.

The second was through epigenetics, the instructions that tell the organism how to use the information encoded in the DNA strand.

Epigenetics, Ginny read, *is the study of heritable phenotype changes that do not involve alterations in the DNA sequence.* Heritable translated to 'capable of being inherited'—passed on to the next generation, which meant the change had to affect the germ cells, egg or sperm. Phenotype meant observable characteristics or traits, like hair color.

On the assumption that the women had been identical at birth, the change must have been applied after birth. But Ginny had no way of knowing whether there had been a fundamental change in the DNA itself, a mutation, or a change in an instruction to the gene, either applied or withheld.

Under environmental pressure, a section of the genetic code (usually a gene) can be either turned on or switched off by adding or removing small chemical tags to one of the DNA letters. This change leaves a mark that can be located and identified.

Many of the separated-twins studies had been conducted, with varying levels of support, on the possibility of a genetic component to behavior. Because of the implications, the majority of the studies focused on crime.

All the studies agreed that removing the opportunity for crime, or training the child not to engage in that behavior, exerted more influence than genes. When the environmental factors were controlled for, however, the genetic link surfaced.

Even more startling was the demonstration that identical twins separated at birth and raised in dissimilar environments, by strangers, still showed a tendency to engage in criminal behavior without in any way being aware of the other twin's actions.

Further study showed that the similarities were not limited to antisocial behavior. Separated twins often chose matching life styles, names, hobbies, and occupations.

Among the articles was one dealing with stress. The author suggested that stress could alter the expression of the genes that controlled eating behavior.

Weight control was a complex problem, with many facets other than an oral response to perceived stressors. What made this proposal significant was that, if true, it meant the stressful environment of one twin, which manifested itself in the subject being overweight, might result in differences *which would show on the DNA analysis*.

So, the environment in which Costas and Dupree grew up could have resulted in either a mutation in the genetic code or an eventual mismatch in the epigenetic markers on the DNA strand. Which meant that the two DNA samples could be compared.

If she was right, it would prove Costas had not been in Dallas and Dupree had. The only problem was that, before Ginny could test her theory, she had to get her hands on Dupree's DNA. And that, as she had already found out, was not going to be easy.

* * *

Chapter 28

Monday Evening
Hotel Conference Room

"Tell me why we're doing this," Ginny demanded. "I thought we were supposed to keep a low profile."

Her mother answered her. "It's no longer possible to live completely apart from the rest of Dallas. We need to have cordial working relationships with our neighbors and one of the ways to do that is to be open with the press."

"Are you saying we've been sacrificed on the altar of politics?"

"Yes, darling. You're doing this for Jim, so he can be seen as a red-blooded, American male just like themselves."

"Ugh!"

"We can't control the media and they have a tendency to write cruel things about people they don't understand. It's better to show them a controlled version of the truth than spark suspicion and end up with the most aggressive of the lot breaking down our doors."

"But Angus has been handling them for as long as I can remember."

"Yes, and one day it will be Jim's turn, with you at his side."

Ginny peeked around the corner into the banquet room and marveled at the extent of Angus' preparations. He had arranged this face-to-face at a local hotel and provided a buffet, complete with open bar, to put the reporters in a mellow mood. They chatted with one another, old hands at the news game, expanded now to cover every possible type of media. Ginny hadn't met any of them, but technology can be put to work to help in situations like this.

Angus had required semi-formal attire for the two of them, specifying kilt and tartan sashes, and warned them they would be photographed. He had supplied the guests with specific questions, but they were free to ask anything they wanted. Ginny hoped they would be sympathetic.

"Are you nervous?" Jim had come up behind her and was peering over her shoulder at the assemblage.

"Terrified! Why did they come, other than for the free food?"

"Grandfather has business holdings throughout Texas. He's always news."

"So why isn't he here?"

"Because, this time, we're the news. Ready?" He tucked her hand under his arm and led her into the room without waiting for an answer.

Ginny stood beside him as the photographers took thousands of images, then allowed herself to be handed up onto the dais and seated at the table, facing the room. Jim took his own seat beside her.

The hotel had provided a very low riser, just enough elevation so the two of them could be seen above the heads of the seated press. The table had a white skirt, with ruffles, which went well with the tartan. There were microphones in front of each position. They would be recorded.

"Good evening," Jim began. "Thank you all for coming. If you haven't already done so, please help yourselves to the refreshments."

The reporters now found seats, hastily finishing whatever they had put in their mouths.

"Who would like to begin?" Jim asked. Several hands went up. Jim smiled and pointed at one of them. "Yes, Mr. Morales?"

Ginny would have been astonished to find Jim using the reporter's name if it hadn't been for a voice in her ear whispering the same. It had been Reggie's idea to wire the pair of them, and Sinia's to make sure everyone had to check in with her and present press credentials, with pictures, before being admitted. The reporter looked gratified.

"I understand you two are getting married."

Jim nodded. "In five days, seventeen hours, and twenty-four minutes."

Everyone in the room laughed, including Ginny.

"Looking forward to it, are you?"

"I am." He spotted another hand in the air. "Ms. Cole?"

The young woman who stood up, the better to be heard and seen, looked as if she would like to bring the pair behind the table down a peg or two.

"We were told your grandfather is Angus Mackenzie, is that true?"

"It is."

"How is it that we haven't seen you in Dallas before?"

"I was born in Dallas, but raised in Virginia."

She pursed her lips. "I find it hard to believe that Mr. Mackenzie has managed to hide you from the press all these years."

Ginny didn't take her eyes off the woman reporter, but the corner of her mouth twitched. "Public property," Himself had said. "Public figures. Be prepared." Well, someone as good-looking as Jim would probably be of interest to all the women reporters in the DFW area.

Jim nodded at the woman. "After my parents were killed in

a car accident, my grandfather invited me to come home to Texas." He reached over and took Ginny's hand, then looked back at the reporter. "And I'm very glad I did."

The reporter looked at Ginny. "You're Ginny Forbes, I believe."

Ginny nodded. "That's right."

"Is it true that someone tried to kill you last October?"

Ginny felt her cheeks pale, but didn't break eye contact. "That is correct."

"Tell us about that."

"Not at this time."

Jim pointed to another reporter and Ms. Cole was forced to sit down. "Yes, Mr. Vogel."

"What exactly is a laird?"

Jim relaxed. "It's a job description, like being a CEO of a company."

"But we're talking about a community, not a company, right?"

"The community is incorporated, and is run under the same rules as any other incorporated town, under the jurisdiction of the state and federal governments."

"I thought an incorporated municipality had elected officials. You sound like the heir to a throne."

"All our officials are elected, including myself. The titles differ, but the roles are similar."

"So the laird is like the mayor?"

Jim nodded. "And the council is exactly what it sounds like."

"Well, that's not very romantic."

Jim smiled, "You were expecting castles, with knights in shining armor?"

"Well, you have to admit it's a little out of the ordinary to set up a press briefing like this, no matter how illustrious the couple."

Jim nodded. "My grandfather is well known to you. He wanted you to get the chance to know us as well."

Another man spoke up and Ginny heard, "Edward Wolf," in her ear.

"I've been out to your place, the Homestead, I think they call it."

Jim nodded.

"It's living history, isn't it?"

"Yes. All of the buildings are authentic and the reenactors are held to strict standards of scholarship."

"So what is it, a form of school?"

Jim shook his head. "It's a museum. The site shows anyone who's interested what it was like to live on the north Texas frontier in the early days, but we are not an accredited educational institution."

"Do you dress up? I mean, other than your kilt." Ginny smiled at the speaker. At least he'd done his homework. He knew what to call what Jim was wearing.

"We all do. It's one of the responsibilities we share."

Another woman rose. "You said you share responsibilities. So does a laird have any power? Or is he just a figurehead?"

"That's a loaded question, Mrs. Russo. The answer is, it depends on the person. Each of the homesteads—"

She interrupted. "There are more?"

"Yes, there are Scottish Homesteads all over the north American continent. Each of the Homesteads functions with all three branches of government; executive, legislative, and judicial, but on a very small scale and only locally, within the community. The point is that no one person has much power. We share that. But the executive—the laird—does have responsibilities and is authorized to use his power if needed to get things done."

Another man rose, his face full of curiosity. "Okay. Help me out here. I've lived in Dallas my whole life and I've never heard of you or this place before, not until we got this call and my editor told me to come find out what was going on."

"Island communities are actually pretty common. The city has grown up around existing townships over and over again."

"DFW is pretty cosmopolitan. Why haven't you been absorbed, like all the rest?"

Ginny knew the answer to that one and wondered if Angus had made sure Jim knew it as well.

"When the Loch Lonach community was founded, there was no one here. All the frontier pioneers were farmers and they needed land. When Dallas started expanding eastward, it flowed around the private holdings."

"But why haven't I heard a whisper of this Scottish stuff before?"

"You have, though you may not realize it. The name 'Dallas' comes from a place in Scotland. John Neely Bryan, the founder of Dallas, came from Tennessee, as did thousands of other Ulster Scots. Lots of the early settlers in Texas had Scottish roots. Some scholars estimate the percentage was as high as sixty-five percent. Some say more."

"But this Scottish stuff, the kilts and so forth. That's not something you see roaming around Dallas, unless there's a parade."

Jim paused for a moment and Ginny thought she saw him take a slow breath, but his smile never wavered.

"I think what you're asking is why the Scots haven't made an issue of being Scottish. You don't think of us as an ethnic subgroup, right?"

"Right."

"The answer is because we don't think of ourselves that way either. We're just like all the other people in the area, immigrants from another land, Scotland in this case. We have normal lives, normal jobs." He turned to Ginny. "My soon-to-be-wife is an ICU nurse. I'm an Emergency room physician."

"Now *that's* romantic," someone called out, and the room laughed.

"Your grandfather isn't typical."

Ginny almost snorted. The man must know Angus Mackenzie from *somewhere*.

Jim looked at the speaker, an older man, seated in the first row. "Because he doesn't own a pair of trousers?" Ginny had trouble controlling her face.

"Well, that, too. No, because he's one of the richest men in North America."

Ginny held her breath. Reporters liked money. They liked to admire the rich—and to hate them.

Jim shook his head. "I expect what you found when you did the research was the balance sheets on the Homestead, which is in his name because it has to be assigned to someone. But he doesn't actually own it. He's a trustee and he shares that responsibility with others."

Jim recognized the next questioner. "Ms. Jordan."

"I don't care whose name is on the papers. I get it. He's rich enough and powerful enough to get us out here tonight. What I want to know is will there be any bigwigs at the wedding?"

Jim glanced at Ginny, then back at the reporter. He nodded. "A few."

"Can you give us details?"

"My grandfather has prepared a short list of names you might recognize." He pulled a folded piece of paper out of his sporran and read from it.

"Illinois Senator, Maury Patterson. Captain Wilhelmina Scott of the National Space Force. Rear Admiral Benjamin Maxwell, Retired. Dr. Jonathan Fleming, double Nobel Laureate in biomedical engineering. Dr. Robert Edward Lee, President of

Washington and Lee University, Lexington, Virginia. Dulce Wiseman, CEO of Texas Instruments. And the Honorable Karen Hoffman, currently serving on the Supreme Court.

"In addition to these are a retired British actor, the Canadian ambassador, the head of the Forbes clan in Scotland, and someone who goes nowhere without a security detail." He folded the paper and put it back in his pocket, then folded his hands on the table.

"But do you want to know the truth?" he asked. They nodded. "I don't care who's coming." He reached over and took Ginny's hand, his eyes on her face, smiling into her eyes. "I'm marrying the most beautiful woman in the world. That's all that matters to me."

Ginny smiled back at him, the cameras going off in volleys around them. She was pretty sure she heard an "aww" from someone in the crowd before it broke out into multiple conversations and headed for the bar.

"Miss Forbes?"

Ginny looked up to find one of the women addressing her. "Yes?"

"Forgive me, but could you tell me what this thing is?" She pointed to the tartan sash draped over Ginny's shoulder.

"Of course." Ginny rose to the occasion, literally, rising from her chair and showing the reporter the way the fabric was folded, then pinned in place, and explaining the role of tartan in Scottish history. Jim was doing the same with his kilt.

The two of them drifted down onto the floor of the room, surrounded by eager questioners with innocuous, easy to answer questions about bagpipes, and the Homestead schedule, and how the two of them had met. Someone thrust a drink into her hand and Ginny smiled her thanks, then continued answering questions for another hour.

She asked a few, too, expressing interest in the reporters'

jobs, and using their names, and getting full credit for being so prepared. She turned on the charm and it wasn't long before she had the whole collection of them eating out of her hand.

Jim freed her from her admirers at last, said farewell, then steered her out the back door and into the waiting arms of her support crew.

"Well!" Sinia was smiling broadly. "That went well."

Jim nodded, then caught Ginny's hand, pulling her into a few impromptu waltz steps, followed by a less impromptu kiss.

"You were wonderful, sweetheart!"

Ginny returned the salute. "You handled them perfectly! I was so afraid they would hate us."

"Not a chance. Not after they got to talk to you."

Sinia intervened. "Come on, you two. We have to vacate the room and get the sound equipment back to Reggie." She held out her hand for the earpieces.

They stripped the room and got everything loaded up, then Jim pulled Ginny aside.

"I have a question for you. A private one."

"Oh?"

"That's the first time you've had to face an audience and let me take the lead. It won't be the last. Can you bear it?"

Ginny looked up at him and nodded. "But don't be surprised if I end up passing you notes."

"I won't mind, as long as you're discreet about it."

"You can ask my mother to vouch for me. I learned the basics in elementary school, but it takes a master to pass notes in a class your own mother is teaching, right under her nose."

* * *

Monday Evening
Forbes Residence

Ginny stripped off her party clothes, got into sweats, and went back downstairs to fix herself a bite of dinner. She'd been too keyed up to eat at the hotel. She made herself a sandwich, poured milk into a glass, then took both into the living room, stretching out on the sofa. She could hear Jim moving around in the dining room, and the clink of glasses. He followed her into the living room, set her drink down on the table, and watched as she surrounded the rest of the sandwich.

"Hungry?" he asked.

"Better now." She wiped her fingers and reached for the scotch. She took a sip, her eyes on him. He had turned and was pacing the floor.

"Something on your mind, Jim?"

He started, then looked over at her and Ginny was sure she had seen guilt in his eyes. She sat up and watched him struggle with something. He looked at her, looked away, downed his drink, set the glass aside, then sat down on the edge of the chair, facing her. She watched him suck in a deep breath.

"I have a confession to make to you."

"Oh?" What on earth was coming?

"I've been keeping a secret from you and I think I'd better tell you, before the wedding."

Ginny sat very still. "Is it that bad?"

His brow contracted. "Probably not. It was just all this talk about money, first Jamieson, then Grandfather."

"Go on."

He hesitated. "It's about Hal."

Ginny blinked. What was left that they hadn't said to one another about that dead and gone relationship?

"I didn't want to upset you, and, at the time, I thought this was for the best. But now I think I'd better come clean, and let you make your own decision."

"About what?"

Jim sucked in a deep breath. "There's a trust fund. For you. From his mother. He talked me into taking over the role of trustee. Until you were able to consider what to do about it."

Ginny felt cold. Stiff and cold. Less than a week before her wedding, Jim was telling her that her old boyfriend had made her a gift of money. A gift she couldn't accept. But he, Jim, had done so, in her name. Without asking her.

"It's rather a lot of money." Jim sounded nervous. "And he made it clear it wasn't his money. The gift is from her, because she liked you so much. And I know you liked her."

Mrs. Williams had been a good friend, a mentor, and had hoped Ginny and her son would marry one day. But, money?

"You hid this from me?"

He squirmed. "I took the burden on my own shoulders, temporarily. Until the time was right to tell you about it."

"The right time was at the time the gift was offered." Ginny's eyes widened. "You told me you wanted no secrets between us. And all the time you were sitting on this one."

"And I have now honorably bared my soul and humbly ask for your forgiveness."

Ginny stared at him. "Since October!"

Jim nodded, his expression unhappy. "You don't have to keep it. You can give it away. That much, in an endowment, could do a lot of good."

Ginny took a careful breath. "You're missing the point. I don't want his money. I don't want *anything* from him."

Jim nodded, then stood up. "I understand." He hesitated, then started for the front door, then turned back to address her. "We'll do whatever you want."

Ginny sat without moving. She heard him let himself out

and the door close behind him.

It was a breach of etiquette to accept such a gift from a man you had decided not to marry, but the greater sin was Jim's. He had made a decision for her, without consulting her. Taking care of her and her affairs. Which was what a husband had a right to do, was *supposed* to do. Except, he wasn't her husband at the time.

Ginny found herself torn between reason and rage. How dare he? This was the man she was going to marry. And he had known she would disapprove. And still kept it from her. He was still making unilateral decisions about her, about her life. And in five days he would have the legal right to do so. After which, she would have to fight him for control of her own business, her own life.

She dragged herself to her feet, made sure the house was locked up, said goodnight to her mother, then climbed the stairs, her feet heavy on the treads. Five days left of freedom. Five days left to be a whole woman, a person in her own right.

She got ready for bed and crawled between the sheets, hoping to understand her own heart better in the morning, but she didn't get much in the way of sleep. There were too many things to think about.

* * *

CHAPTER 29

Tuesday Morning
East Dallas

Ginny stood very still, waiting for permission to move. This was the final fitting of her wedding gown. She stared at her reflection in the mirror and fought down nausea.

From the very beginning, the problem had been his ego, his paternalism toward her. He was the doctor, she was the nurse, a lesser human being at best. Not to be listened to, but instructed, and dictated to, and ordered about.

Then came the anxious hovering, treating her like a patient, rather than a companion. There had been trust issues, too. Natural enough, considering, but she had told him, in so many words, if he wanted her to trust him, he would have to be trustworthy.

On the trip to Nova Scotia, he was the leader of the expedition and she was along as camouflage. She'd been useful, if you considered saving him from the wolf to be helpful, but he still hadn't thought her capable of matching his wits or determination.

And now? Now he tells her he has been sitting on a lie for the better part of a year. Preaching to her about honesty and openness, and telling her she should expect to keep no secrets from him. And all the while he had been hiding this from her.

"There. Done. Let's get started on the pictures."

The bridal portraits were traditionally done by the shop. Ginny let them lead her to the stage, noting it was mercifully free of flowers, hearts, and cupids, just a plain backdrop that would not detract from the subject. Someone added a bit more makeup, then handed her a bouquet. Another positioned her carefully: arms, hands, head.

"Ginny, darling, smile for me, please."

She did her best, trying to remember what it felt like to be happy.

He had confessed. Surely that counted for something. And he'd done it before the wedding, not springing it on her after it was too late. Not hiding it from her until his hand was forced. What's more, he'd been sorry about it.

"Look this way, please."

"What a lovely bride!" She had collected an audience. Weren't all brides lovely? Cynical thought.

"Ginny smile!" She took a deep breath and concentrated on her mother. *She* was happy. Maybe she was remembering her own wedding. In any case, Ginny could smile at her happiness. It was enough to satisfy the photographer.

"None of these do her justice," she heard him say. "We'll have to see if we can do better on the day."

After the photos, she was stripped and the gown and all its parts carefully packaged for transport to her home. The whole process took more than three hours and was followed by a *tête-à-tête* with her mother over coffee.

"Now. Tell me what's wrong."

Ginny looked across the table and found nothing but compassion.

"It's Jim."

"I already knew *that*. What about Jim?"

Ginny took a breath, then told her, explaining carefully about the trust fund and Jim's decision not to tell her until now.

Her mother sighed. "Well you can't keep it, even if the money did come from Mrs. Williams."

"I know. That's not the problem. I want to think—I wanted to think that he respected me, trusted me. That he didn't think I couldn't cope with the truth."

Mrs. Forbes took another sip of her coffee, her eyes on Ginny. "How do you intend to handle this?" she asked. "Because, in five days you will have a husband to manage and you should have a plan in place."

Ginny gave her a crooked smiled. "That's what Charlie said, that Mandy managed him and he loved it, and it was up to me to make a marriage with Jim work." Her smile faded. "It sounds so coldblooded. Unromantic. As if Jim is just another job of work I have to do."

"Darling, marriage is hard work. It takes effort every single day to build a satisfying life with another human being. Where Jim is concerned, that means being willing to see him as a fallible human being, not a paragon."

Ginny squirmed for a moment, then met her mother's eye. "Am I looking for a father figure? A replacement for Daddy?"

She shook her head. "I don't think so. I think what you're looking for is something that doesn't exist, a life without misunderstandings, or hard feelings, or compromise." She leaned forward. "You and Jim have known each other for less than a year. You both still have some growing up to do and you both will change over time. That's normal. What you have to figure out is how you're going to manage disappointments, yours as well as his."

Ginny reached across the table and took her mother's hand. "So tell me, what's the secret to a happy marriage? Because *you* had one."

Her mother smiled and squeezed her hand. "You have to be brave enough to be honest and loving enough to forgive. Both of you. And, of the two, love is the more important. The truth can be spread out over time. Kindness needs to be front and center every minute."

Ginny smiled at her mother. "I have a feeling I'm going to need more of these little pep talks. Are you willing to coach me through this transition?"

"Anytime darling. Just don't be surprised if I'm honest with you."

Ginny's smiled widened. "As long as you're also kind, I can handle honest."

* * *

Tuesday Afternoon
Forbes Residence

Jim sat on the front stoop of the Forbes residence in the cool April breeze and sweated. He was here, waiting for them to come back from the dressmakers, ostensibly to tell Ginny what he and his grandfather had been able to find out about Jamieson's banking arrangements. But there was that other little matter.

Jim was wise enough to know that pleading with Ginny would not restore him in her eyes. He would have to wait until she brought it up, then follow her lead. He shifted uncomfortably. He hadn't wanted to be in this position. When Hal had made the suggestion, his first instinct had been to refuse. He should have followed it. But he'd been asked to help give her time. And he could not deny that she needed it. Not then.

But that was then and this was now and they were five days away from their wedding. Which was why he had decided it was time to tell her.

She was absolutely right, of course. Any reminder of that relationship would act like a pall over their happiness. Not like Sarah. His own near-brush with matrimony hadn't left bitterness in its wake. Sarah was coming to the wedding, at Ginny's invitation. Instead of being mortal enemies, she and Sarah had bonded over him. Jim shook his head. Women were strange creatures.

Jim, like most of his sex, had approached this change in marital status with the mindset that it wouldn't change anything in his life. He would go on with his job, eat the same things he had always enjoyed, indulge in sports and outdoor activities to the same extent, watch what he wanted to watch on TV, and let her do the same. Friends, with benefits.

He was beginning to get a glimmer of the depth of the shared life they would lead. They hadn't specifically talked about finances, except for the counseling sessions with Father Amos, but they would keep separate bank accounts as a matter of course, and set up a third for the household expenses. One or both would have to take over paying the communal bills. Maybe they should alternate months, so neither felt shut out of the money handling decisions. His meals were likely to improve (one could only hope). His outdoor activities would change when he moved to day shift (but probably stay unchanged until then), at which point he wanted to go back to sailing.

Ginny had said she'd like to learn. He should set a goal. By next fall he should have located and purchased a small sailboat, to replace the one he'd left in Virginia. It was something they could do together.

Together. Jim rubbed his hands over his face, then hair. Assuming she still wanted to be together.

He watched as the car rolled to a stop in front of the house. The passenger side door opened and Ginny got out, almost invisible under the dress bag. The wind made it hard for her to close the door, but she managed. She was starting up the walk, struggling to keep the bag from escaping her arms, and Jim was on his feet and three-quarters of the way down the sidewalk before she could take two steps.

"Let me help with that." He took the bag from her and slung it over his shoulder. It was heavier than he had expected. "Is there anything else?"

Ginny shook her head. "I can get the rest out of the car later."

Jim nodded. Mrs. Forbes had already driven off, to go around the back and pull the car into the garage.

Ginny led the way up the walk, opened the door, and ushered him inside.

"I'll take that," she said, reaching for the bag.

Jim let her go, watching as she hauled the thing up the stairs and into her bedroom. Her wedding gown, and she'd neither smiled nor made any attempt to kiss him.

"Jim! How lovely to see you!" Mrs. Forbes had come through the house and now approached, both of her hands outstretched. "Will you let me feed you?"

Jim felt a rush of warmth toward this woman who would soon be his mother-in-law.

"I'd love that. I have to work tonight." And if she didn't feed him, he'd have to leave early so he could feed himself. And he wanted to spend this time with Ginny.

He kept Mrs. Forbes company as she prepared the meal, setting the table and following instructions without rancor. He could do that with Ginny, too. He should. He should make a point of helping around the house. It wasn't as if he didn't know how.

Over the meal, Jim shared what his grandfather had been able to find out so far.

"It appears she was clearing the decks."

"What do you mean?" Mrs. Forbes asked.

"All of her routine bills were on autopay of some description, so she didn't have to do much with the bank. That included her groceries, which were delivered and paid for using a credit card. She was down to only one, by the way. She had closed all her other accounts within the last two years."

Ginny nodded. "Because of her disease progression."

"That's the assumption. All of her affairs were being transferred into other people's hands. She had been looking for a place to live, too, one with assistance available."

"Ugh!" Ginny said. "I would hate that."

Jim gave her half a smile. "No one likes losing their autonomy. It's indicative of the woman's character that she faced it so squarely."

"Yes." Ginny addressed her plate, her eyes avoiding his.

"Grandfather has seen her Will. Everything she dies possessed of is to be liquidated and given to the Huntington Disease Research Foundation. And there's a life insurance policy."

Ginny looked up. "Why would a life insurance company issue a policy on someone with a death sentence hanging over her head?"

"Turns out there's a special pool for people like her. Very compassionate of the insurance industry, if you ask me, but they get their share. The insured has to live for at least two years after taking out the policy. The payout is lower, and the cost is higher than standard policies. And the company gets to use the money invested until the death of the policyholder."

Mrs. Forbes nodded. "It will be enough to cover the funeral costs, I expect."

Jim shook his head. "Her funeral arrangements were prepaid. The beneficiary of this policy is the Foundation and the face amount is ten million dollars."

Both women stared at him. Mrs. Forbes recovered first. "What kind of premium does a policy like that carry?"

"More than I'd be willing to pay, but the return on investment was high. Besides, it was her money. If she preferred an insurance policy to simply handing over the money each month to the Foundation, that's her choice."

Mrs. Forbes nodded. "Of course." She eyed his plate. "More pot roast or would you prefer dessert?"

"Neither, thank you, though I wouldn't turn down a cup of coffee."

"I'll get it started."

Jim turned to Ginny. "I'd like a word with you, please."

She nodded, then rose and cleared the table. When they both had coffee prepared the way they liked, she led him into the living room, gestured to a chair, and sat down facing him, her coffee in hand.

"What can I do for you, Jim?"

"It's the other way round. With me working the next two nights and sleeping the following days, I want to make sure there's nothing I need to get done before Friday. I'm hoping one of your lists was devoted to me and my responsibilities."

She shook her head. "I wouldn't dream of presuming."

Jim frowned. "You won't help me?"

"I've been told part of my job as a wife is to manage my husband, but I don't like the sound of that. I don't think one adult should be in control of another, not in a marriage."

And there it was, his opening. He took a moment to make sure his voice didn't shake. "Ginny, please forgive me. I made what I thought was the best decision possible at the time."

She sighed. "I know. What worries me is that you might take the same attitude if something like that comes up in the future."

Jim proceeded carefully. "I might have to." He saw her stiffen and hurried to explain. "If you are unconscious, for instance."

Her brow furrowed. "All right, I'll make an exception for comas, but I don't want to be left out of decisions that affect me, just because you think you know better."

Jim shook his head. "If there's one thing I've learned from you, it's that I don't always know better." In spite of himself, it had come out sounding resentful.

Her eyes grew cold. "Let me be clear," she said. "If we marry—"

Jim caught his breath, but bit his tongue, letting her continue without interruption.

"I know there will be times when decisions will have to be made quickly or when one of us isn't available to be consulted. That's part of life. What I don't want is for decisions that affect *me* to become routinely *your* province. That's how abusers control their victims."

Jim wasn't even surprised to hear her use the term. It hurt, but she was a professional. She'd seen what could happen.

He set his coffee down, then hers, then sat down next to her on the sofa, trying to pull her into his arms. She stood up and moved across to the chair he had just vacated.

He sucked in a deep breath.

"My mother told me something one day that I've never forgotten. She said, in any successful relationship both people have to be willing to let the other win. Sometimes the outcome will be right and sometimes wrong. That's not the point. Sharing a life together means sharing the responsibility. Compromise and compassion. Love and life." He smiled at the memory. "She also said, a wise man knows when to let go and let his wife take care of him."

"Sound advice." Ginny rose. "She sounds like a wise woman."

Jim rose, too. "You would have liked her, I think."

She ushered him to the front door. "I'm sorry I never got the chance to know her. Have a good shift."

He put his hand out to stop the door from closing on him. "Wait."

"What is it?"

"I need to know if we're still engaged."

She was silent for a moment, her face showing neither grief nor anger, just fatigue. "I'll think about it. Goodnight."

* * *

CHAPTER 30

Tuesday Evening
Forbes Residence

When Jim had gone, Ginny retired to her office. She sat in her chair, staring at the computer screen, trying to understand herself. She was still mad, but she was also frightened.

He'd lectured her on not keeping secrets, knowing all along he was keeping this one from her. Where there was one secret, there might be another. There *had been* another, the one Lisa had hinted at. How was she supposed to trust him? With her happiness, her safety, her life?

There were degrees of guilt, of course. He hadn't hidden a previous marriage or scattered bastards up and down the east coast.

Himself had called her in one day last month and asked her what Jim had told her about himself. It had been a pleasant enough chat, but it hadn't fooled Ginny. Jim was still on trial and would be for some time. Angus had asked a number of questions, then nodded, apparently satisfied with her answers.

But Jim kept taking it for granted she would fall in with his plans, accommodate him, as he was accommodating his grandfather. All very rational, very cerebral.

Her phone went off and she looked at the caller ID. Jim. Ginny flipped the phone over to silence the ringer and let it go to voice mail.

She knew what he wanted. They had parted civilly, but not cordially. He wanted her forgiveness for keeping the secret, for being paternalistic in her direction, for waiting so long to tell her. She wanted assurance that it would never happen again. He hadn't been willing to go that far. That would have to change, but not tonight.

She set the problem of Jim aside and opened a blank document on her computer. She wasn't willing to give up her pet theory about the murder, yet, either, and would love to give the police enough for reasonable suspicion to go investigate Dupree, but there were difficulties to get past.

So, instead of following the evidence, she needed to look at the problem from Dupree's point of view. Means, motive, opportunity. And an alibi.

The means was blunt force trauma to the back of the head applied by dropping the victim approximately thirty feet to the stadium seating below the mezzanine. *If I were planning a murder*, Ginny thought to herself, *I'd want something more reliable*. And if I were Dupree, I'd use a drug. Wasn't she a toxicologist? Wasn't that what she'd said at the Games on Saturday, when they were chatting about Scottish witches?

Okay, so why use something as chancy as pushing someone over a rail? And the same question would apply no matter who did the pushing. Target of opportunity perhaps? Jamieson was standing there and looked ripe for the fall? What if the murderer knew about the disease, that Jamieson was already unsteady on her feet? Wouldn't it just make her more likely to crumple to the concrete floor, rather than fly over the rail? Were her hands as weak as her legs? So she couldn't get a proper grip on the rail? And did the murderer know it?

What's more, the fall didn't actually kill her outright. Jamieson woke up, stumbled out onto the athletic field, fell on her face, rolled over, then died. So if someone had pushed her over the rail, why hadn't that someone come back to finish the job? *Had* someone come back to finish the job?

Ginny paused, her eyes narrowing. Gary had come back. He'd leaned over the rail and seen Jamieson on the seats below and told the police she looked dead. So dead it didn't even occur to him to call for an ambulance. All he'd decided to do was slip away and let someone else find the body. She wondered, for a moment how he had taken the news that Jamieson had not been dead. That she had regained consciousness and walked and fallen and died elsewhere? That, had he called for help, she might have lived? She must ask him that one. Ginny made a note.

Moving on.

Motive. Not a clue. Why should Dupree kill Jamieson? They had been seen talking in the Skybox over dinner, but everyone said they were apparently strangers before then. They might have a history, of course. Had Tran checked? Was there anything Ginny could look up that might establish they knew one another before that night? Schools? Jobs? Military service? She made herself another note.

Opportunity. Dupree was in Shreveport when Jamieson died. She had told Ginny that much when they met on Saturday afternoon.

There was no problem proving Dupree was on the Games grounds on Friday afternoon and early evening. They had photographs, eye witness testimony, and the salmonella poisoning evidence. Dupree could try arguing that she got some other kind of bug, or that she picked up the food poisoning somewhere else, but that wouldn't fly. People who've had salmonella can be infectious for up to a year. The lab could compare the bug in her system to the strain Nessie had used, and prove it was the haggis she ate that night that made her sick. Ginny should see if the police asked the people at Fiddle Faddle and in the Skybox what Dupree had said, if anything, about her plans for the night. She made another note.

But Dupree hadn't argued that she wasn't at the Games on Friday afternoon. She'd said she drove to Shreveport and back on Friday evening. Why?

Ginny opened her search engine and plugged in the city and the date, looking for any events Dupree might have attended. It took only fifteen minutes to find six possibilities. Examination of five of them showed no record of Dupree in attendance at a toxicology-related convention, a fund-raiser for a political candidate, an awards dinner for authors of scientific tomes, a reception for donors to a children's hospital, or a televised panel dealing with a hypothetical terrorist attack centered around a chemical bioweapon. She might, of course, have attended something that didn't require her to register or be on anyone's guest list. No way to tell without more resources.

The sixth event looked more promising, a voodoo festival.

Ginny knew less than nothing about voodoo, but the advertising images reminded her forcibly of Dupree's costume. Even at the Scottish Games, she had hung mysterious bags around her neck, and had unexplained ornaments pinned to her tartan sash. Ginny clicked through the website, looking carefully at the contents.

As was often true, the website posted images of past years' events, and many of them were images taken by visitors. Lots of people waving at the camera. Among them was a picture of four women, all in African costume. Ginny recognized Mama Dupree immediately. Third from the left. She'd been wearing the same outfit on Friday, at the Games. The tag said the image had been taken two years ago. Ginny looked further.

What she needed was another picture of Dupree at that

festival, this year's festival and Friday night specifically. Or, rather, what she wanted was to NOT find Dupree, though that wouldn't prove she hadn't been there. The advertisement said she was expected, that she was one of the entertainers, and gave times she would appear on stage. Ginny followed the prompts and found her, on stage with a snake, surrounded by an admiring public.

Ginny enlarged the images as much as she could, then printed the best of them, then did the same with the picture of Dupree. She put them down side by side, and studied them carefully, but was unable to draw any conclusions. The woman on stage was wearing makeup, handling a large boa constrictor, and had been moving. The image wasn't good enough to tell.

But moving pictures also made it onto social media. Ginny flipped over to the video hosting service and searched for the Shreveport voodoo festival, Friday night, this year. She watched in fascination as the woman on the stage went through a series of stylized motions. It meant nothing to her, but the audience seemed to appreciate it.

All she could say for sure was that the woman on stage wasn't Costas. She wasn't rail thin and didn't carry herself the way someone with a military background would. So it might have been Dupree, or it might not have been Dupree. Might have been someone else. Not proof, either way.

Ginny sat back in her chair and thought for a moment. She'd seen Dupree in the stands during the Calling of the Clans. Others had seen her go up the ramp to the elevator and then at dinner with Jamieson in the Skybox. Then nothing until the next day.

She'd been there, in the crowd, when Tran had taken Ginny back to the scene of the crime to look at bruises. She had stayed long enough to talk to most of the visitors on Saturday, but packed up early and not returned on Sunday. Not that either day mattered. What mattered was Friday night.

Jim had contacted Dupree and she had reported eating haggis and feeling ill on Saturday and Sunday. Was she lying? Ginny wrinkled her nose. Probably not. She'd looked genuinely ill on Saturday morning. If it had to be proved, Jim could ask for a stool sample. So, no holes in her story so far.

Was there an alternative explanation for why she looked so bad on Saturday morning? Because she drove to Shreveport and back the same night and didn't get any sleep, for instance?

Ginny checked the mileage and the time stamp on the video. If Dupree ate haggis at five p.m., then jumped in her car and drove three hours, non-stop, to Shreveport, she would get there in time to appear on stage at nine p.m. Say two hours to do the show, get out of costume, then jump in the car again and drive back to Dallas. That put her back in Dallas around two-thirty or three a.m.

She might have spent the night in Shreveport, of course, and risen early, to get back to Dallas in time to see the corpse at eight-thirty. That would mean getting up around five. Doable either way, if the show was over around eleven.

Ginny sighed to herself. The alibi stood. Dupree'd had time to do what she said she'd done, get to Shreveport, do the show, then get back to Dallas. And, if that was what she had really done, she could not have been on the stands killing Jamieson at midnight.

* * *

Chapter 31

Wednesday Morning
Forbes Residence

Ginny rose the following morning and went down to breakfast to find her mother had placed a to-do list on the table, with her name on it.

"What's this?"

"Just what it looks like. You have four days to make sure everything is done before the wedding and some of that time is already spoken for."

Ginny poured herself a cup of coffee, then settled down to read her mother's list. "Hair and make-up will have to be done on the day. The manicure can be done the day before."

Her mother nodded. "Do you want me to make the appointments for you?"

"No, I'll call and set them up." Ginny continued down the list. Shoes. "Where do I go for shoes?"

"I have an idea. Are you free to do a bit of shopping this afternoon?"

"What's wrong with this morning?"

"This morning, young lady, you are going to sit down at the dining room table and write thank you notes for every gift that has arrived so far."

Ginny threw her mother a startled look. "Gifts?"

"Wedding presents."

"I thought I was supposed to do that after the wedding."

"The ones that are hand carried to the reception will need your attention in the two or three days after the wedding. Anything you can get done before will give you that much more time after the ceremony."

"Okay." Ginny shrugged. It shouldn't take much effort to knock out a dozen thank you notes. "I'll do that first thing."

She finished her breakfast, collected her computer, her stationery, and a pen, and retired to the dining room.

"What—?" She stared in astonishment, then dismay at the stacks of brightly wrapped presents. They covered all the surfaces in the room and spilled onto the floor. They climbed in pyramids toward the ceiling in every corner. They cut off the light from the windows and filled the spaces beneath the chairs. They looked like an invasion force, ready to take over the city.

Ginny turned and fled back to the kitchen, to find her mother laughing at her. "I warned you not to let it get too far ahead of you."

"Where did they all come from? Why are there so many?"

Mrs. Forbes rose from her chair, plucked a pencil from the cup on the counter, then came over to embrace her daughter. "You are marrying the heir. Every Homestead in the country has sent at least a token. What's more, you will be expected to establish good working relationships with each of them. I recommend you keep careful records."

"How?" Ginny was stammering at the thought.

"I will help. Now, let's get cracking, shall we?"

Ginny loved her mother very much and trusted her implicitly, but at that moment she would cheerfully have strangled her. "You knew this was going to happen. You've been collecting all of these, behind my back, to spring it on me like this!"

Sinia smiled that sweet, serene smile that, up until now, Ginny had always admired, and nodded. "Some lessons are best learned by example. I've had the official correspondence of the Homestead on my plate ever since Katy Mackenzie died. You will do well to hire someone to act as your secretary when Jim becomes laird. It's a formidable task and won't be your only responsibility."

She cleared a space at the table, sat down with the pencil and a pad of paper, and looked at Ginny. "You open and I will record, then we'll tackle the thank you notes."

It took them two hours just to open the packages. In some cases, Ginny had to hunt for the name and address of the giver. In others, she had to ask her mother to explain the item that emerged from the tissue paper. Apparently she was expected to do a lot of hosting, and would need esoteric pieces of silver and hollowware to be able to pull it off.

At the end of that phase of the task, Ginny paused long enough to haul the colorful refuse out to the trash bin, several bags of it, then resolutely took up her pen.

"Hand written, right?"

Her mother nodded. "Some things a lady cannot get out of, even a busy one."

Ginny did her best, writing half of them out with genuine cordiality, before her hand started to cramp and the gratitude became forced. Her mother proofread each before stuffing them in envelopes and adding the addresses. It was well past lunchtime when they finished. The gifts themselves, sans boxes, were now piled high in the dining room.

"We'll drop these off at the new house on our way out to shop," Sinia said.

Ginny nodded soundlessly, rubbing her aching wrist and hoping there wasn't too much more of the same ahead of her.

"But before we go," her mother smiled at her, "we reward ourselves. Come with me."

Ginny followed her into the kitchen, sat where indicated, accepted the wee dram, and waited for her mother to join her.

"This, my darling daughter, is for you." Sinia opened the refrigerator, took out a dish, and placed it in front of Ginny.

"Oh!" Ginny felt her eyes widen. "You remembered!"

"Of course." Sinia brought over plates and spoons and handed a serving piece to Ginny.

After her husband's death, in an effort to ease the pain, Sinia Forbes had allowed each of her children to experiment in the kitchen, with whatever they wanted to make. Over the course of the next year there were a number of disasters, some of which proved inedible. But out of the experiment had come two desserts, one Ginny's, one Sandy's. They had been named in honor of their father, and ceremoniously created on the anniversary of his death until the two of them went off to college.

Ginny smiled across the table, finding her mother's eyes as moist as her own.

"I know," Sinia said, "that you wish your father was here to give you away. I do, too. But I want you to know that he's never far from us, and always available if you need to talk to him. And I know he'll be by my side on Sunday, whether I can see him or not. Never doubt how much he loves you. And so do I."

Ginny rose from her chair and swept around the table, pulling her mother into her arms and letting the tears fall without restraint. Here was something else to think about. If she married Jim, she would have to leave her mother alone in the house that once had held a happy family.

* * *

Wednesday Afternoon
Forbes Residence

Ginny dropped her purse on the bed, kicked her shoes off, and breathed a sigh of relief. They had managed to fit all the gifts into the two cars, deliver them to the new house, lock them inside (with the drapes drawn and a list on top of the haul), and, leaving her mother's car on the street, gone off to shop for shoes. Three hard hours later, she had a pair that would do.

On the way home they'd had to retrieve the second car, then swing by a to-go restaurant (because there had been no time to cook), and pick up dinner. Which left them just enough time to get back before Angus arrived. He had called to say he had news.

She tucked the wedding slippers into the closet, pulled on fuzzy booties and went downstairs, only to find that five more packages had arrived while they were out.

"How long will this go on?" she asked.

Her mother smiled. "No more than two weeks, I should think. The bulk will arrive before, or be delivered by hand on the day, with a few stragglers coming in late. There's Angus."

Ginny met him at the door and ushered him in. Over coffee, Ginny shared her attempt to break Dupree's alibi and her failure to do so, then turned the floor over to the Laird. "What do you have for me?"

"Ane verry suspicious bank account entry."

"Oh?"

"Aye. Jamieson had an offshore account."

Ginny blinked. "I thought those were reserved for criminals."

"Aye, criminals and the verry rich."

"Was she that rich?"

"No. 'Twere set up fer a single purpose, then closed agin."

Ginny closed her mouth and waited for Himself tell the story in his own way. When he merely went back to sipping his coffee, she tried prompting him.

"And what was that purpose?"

He met her eye, a small smile playing at the corner of his mouth. "I wasnae able tae find oot."

He was teasing her, but this wasn't Ginny's first rodeo. She put on her sweetest smile and simpered. "I would so like to hear all about it. Please?"

Angus burst out laughing. "Aye, lass. I thought ye would." He set his cup down and looked at her. "'Twas buried in th' final accounting. A single payment o' fifty thousand dollars, paid last December."

Ginny caught her breath. "To whom?"

Himself shook his head. "Tha' th' bank wasnae willing tae say."

Ginny's eyes narrowed. "She set up an account, put money in it, made one payment, then closed the account, right?"

"Aye."

"And the bank has the information about what account the money was paid into, right?"

"Aye."

"But they won't tell her executor?"

"Th' account is closed. I've nae standing tae demand th' information."

Ginny sat back in her chair, thinking hard. "The police do. This is an ongoing murder investigation."

He nodded. "I've informed Detective Tran o' wha' I found."

"And?"

"And she's lookin' inta it, but those banks are known for their discretion."

Ginny sucked in her cheeks. A Dallas County Court judge with a secret offshore bank account. A payment to an unknown recipient. The judge subsequently murdered. She metaphorically rubbed her hands.

"You're right. That *is* news!"

"Dinna get yer hopes up, lass. It may turn oot tae be innocent."

Ginny shook her head, her eyes glowing at the implications. "If it was innocent, why use a secret bank account? No. I have high hopes of that clandestine transaction!"

Himself smiled at her across the table. "Let me ken how I can help, lass."

"Oh, don't worry," Ginny grinned at him. "I will!"

* * *

Chapter 32

Wednesday Evening
Forbes Residence

As soon as it was polite to do so, Ginny closed the door on the Laird and retired to her office. She had some serious thinking to do.

Her mother's warning about the work associated with the Homestead had shaken her. Ginny hadn't trained as a secretary and didn't know anything about protocol. What's more, she wasn't interested in learning. And there was that press conference as further evidence. She was out of her league and she ought to admit it. She needed space and she needed time and she needed to clear her head to consider both of those things. Starting with some fresh air.

She grabbed her keys, told her mother she was headed for the park, and fled. Twenty minutes later she was striding along the path that circled the loch. The sun was down, but the sky still glowed with dying light, fading to soft shadow amid the trees, then darkness in the thick underbrush.

The evening was perfect, a shifting breeze keeping the early insects at bay. The water rolled a bit, sighing against the shore. Fish slapped the surface, showing sudden silver before disappearing beneath the swells. The path was dry underfoot and cloudless above, with the moon already rising, almost full and huge on the horizon. Blue and pale green, and bird song eased into night.

Ginny climbed to the highest point on the trail and stood looking at the scene. Years and years she had spent here, in this park, on this rock. The place was home. She felt something twist inside her.

She wasn't being asked to leave this place. That wasn't the problem. It was the suffocating weight of her new life that dragged at her heart. When was she going to be allowed to be herself again? Ever?

She had worked nights all these years because she liked to stay up late and sleep late. No more. From now on, she would be forced to rise early. Everyone said you got used to it, but she knew better.

She had been responsible for herself and for her patients, and to a much lesser extent, her mother, while she was single. Once married, she would be responsible for Jim as well, and not just while on duty at the hospital, all day, every day. And after that, she would be responsible for his children. She corrected herself. *Their* children. She wanted children. But she already knew they would take every minute of every day, for years.

She didn't want to resent Jim, or their children. She didn't want to hate her new job and long for the carefree days of her youth, or pin all her hopes on a future that might never materialize. How did one find peace amid sweeping changes? She'd been happy as she was.

She turned and made her way down the rock to the path, walking away from the lights, avoiding people who had come out to enjoy the evening. She didn't want to talk to anyone. So it was with extreme irritation that she found herself hailed by Caroline and Alan, out for a stroll along the edge of the loch.

"Ginny!"

She stopped and waited for her friends, trying to stuff her emotions back into the dark hole in her breast.

Caroline and Alan settled one on either side of her, taking an arm apiece and smiling at her.

"Where's Jim?" Caroline asked.

Ginny felt a stab of irritation. As if she couldn't be seen in public without that man. "He has to work."

"And you came out alone?"

This time, instead of irritation, Ginny felt fear. Was she already so changed that even her best friend was surprised to see her acting alone? "I had to clear my head."

"Well, we're glad we ran into you," Alan said. "Because Caroline has had an idea."

"Yes! I tried to call you, but I guess your phone is off."

Ginny pulled her phone out of her pocket and looked at the messages. "Here it is. What did you want to tell me?"

"You know Detective Tran won't tell either of us a thing, right?"

Ginny nodded.

"But everyone else is talking and we've been picking up details that way."

"What detail are we talking about?"

"Dupree's DNA."

"What about Dupree's DNA?"

"Well, it's the problem," Alan said. "It didn't match any of the samples the police found on Jamieson's body."

"How do you know that?" Ginny asked.

"Er. Well. I was talking to Reggie, you see. And he suggested we look around."

"He did, huh?" Ginny didn't bother to keep the skepticism out of her voice.

"Okay, so I asked him if he could access Caroline's police file."

Ginny stopped dead on the path and stared at the other two. "He could?"

"Yes."

"And he did?"

"You mustn't give him away! He just does it for the challenge, because he enjoys working with computers. And Angus likes that he can help out in a crisis."

Ginny nodded. Having a tame hacker on the staff was a definite benefit. What's more, if she asked, she was sure she would find Reggie never did a thing that could be considered outside the law. He was both smart and careful.

"Okay, where is this going?"

"Well, the sample Dupree submitted didn't come from the Dallas police. It was mailed to them by the New Orleans police, on a card. The Dallas lab did the analysis, but it occurred to us, to Caroline, that we didn't know for sure if the sample actually belonged to Dupree. It might have gotten mixed up with someone else's."

"Or swapped," Caroline added.

Ginny looked from one to the other. Mistakes had been known to happen, even in the best police departments. "Is there more?"

"No," Caroline shook her head. "We just wanted to share that idea and see if you thought it might explain the evidence."

Ginny nodded slowly. "Yes. If there was a mix-up, that would explain two women with very similar biometrics having such dissimilar DNA."

"Which means, we need another sample of Dupree's DNA. If you still think she's our best bet, of course."

Ginny sighed heavily and took off walking again, the other two hurrying to keep abreast of her.

"Personally, I think she's our only chance to clear your name, but there isn't a single piece of evidence that gives the police, Dallas or New Orleans, the right to bring her in for questioning, much less demand a DNA sample, or search her house for clues. She's bulletproof."

"Well," said Alan, "that means either she's innocent, or she's learned to cover her tracks really well."

Ginny nodded, then changed the subject. "You and I," she said to Caroline, "need to practice with that train."

Caroline nodded. "I've been thinking about that. There isn't room enough in my apartment to swing a cat, so I asked Mom if we could practice at home and she said yes. Alan can run interference for us, if Jim happens to show up on the doorstep."

"He won't. He's working tonight and tomorrow night. He'll have to sleep between."

"Good. Nine o'clock suit you?"

"Perfect."

Ginny took leave of them, drove home, and sequestered herself in her office. She sat down in her chair and stared at the computer screen. Alan was right.

What sort of a person had a water-tight alibi? Not the innocent. They hadn't expected to need one. So they spent the night at home, alone, or drove to some secluded corner where it was still possible to look up and see the stars, or enjoyed a public entertainment at which they knew no one and couldn't say who might have seen them and they'd lost the admission ticket which they'd paid cash for anyway.

Not so Dupree. She had told people her plans for the evening. She had made a very public appearance, performing on stage, doing something sure to be recorded. Proof positive that she was where she had said she would be, doing what she had said she would be doing.

Ginny opened her computer and located the video feed for Shreveport, Voodoo Festival, Friday night, and looked at the clip again. The date and time matched. Ginny zoomed in as close as she could get. She could see the snake easily enough, but the resolution wasn't good enough to be sure it was Dupree.

If Dupree was onstage in Shreveport at ten p.m., she wasn't in Dallas at midnight. But, maybe she wasn't the woman on that stage. Ginny considered the possibility.

ICU nurses were interchangeable. They covered for one another all the time. What did Dupree do if she was sick? A voodoo priestess might be harder to find, but it would be better than cancelling the show. And Dupree *had* been sick! She'd eaten haggis and suffered from it. What if—and this was the crux of the issue—what if someone else had taken Dupree's place onstage?

Dupree could still have been there, of course, backstage or in a hotel room. But the alibi wouldn't hold up if there was no way to prove it. Credit card receipts on the road between Dallas and Shreveport would support her story, but a camera would have to be found that recorded Dupree pumping gas, or behind the wheel at a toll booth. Had Detective Tran looked?

The question brought Ginny right back to where she started. There was no reasonable suspicion to allow the police to investigate. Ginny's suspicions had been classified as "unreasonable." Tran was being polite, but there was circumstantial evidence that implicated Caroline and no evidence at all to link Dupree.

Which just meant she'd been very, very careful.

Ginny got up from the computer and started pacing the floor. She had the biometrics which suggested Costas (whose DNA they found on the body even though she hadn't been there) had a twin (whose DNA they did NOT find on the body). Three photos in all. And photographs can lie. Images can be manipulated, or be too vague to be used as evidence.

She had evidence Dupree had been in Dallas: the haggis, her own eyes and ears, and dozens of witnesses and camera images. She had Alan's assertion that Dupree had mailed in her DNA sample, no doubt through secured police channels, but mailed nonetheless. A chance for a mix-up, or worse.

She had no firm evidence Dupree was actually in Shreveport at the time Jamieson fell over the railing. She only had a video of someone who looked like Dupree performing on stage from nine oh-seven to nine fifty-three p.m., which (with costume changes, autographs, and packing up) probably meant she could not have left Shreveport earlier than ten p.m. She had no evidence (security camera footage, witnesses, or DNA) showing Dupree on the Games grounds after the time she was supposed to have left for Louisiana. She had no evidence Dupree had ever touched Jamieson.

Ginny stopped pacing. How hard would it be to keep all one's skin and hair cells from drifting across two feet or so of a small dining table set up in the Skybox to afford a truly spectacular view of the Games grounds? Tran had said they found transfer DNA on Jamieson and asked Dupree for a sample for exclusion purposes. But they'd had dinner together, eaten haggis together, drunk scotch together.

The cup, plate, and utensils were all long gone. They would have been disposable and burned with the other refuse. The Skybox would have been cleaned, but not disinfected. It might be possible to pick up DNA from the seat Dupree used, but there would be no exemplar to compare it to. Such a sample could belong to anyone.

No, the more interesting question was why there had been no incidental DNA transfer during that meal. Did they not shake hands when they met? Share a bottle of scotch? Exchange contact information? It was unthinkable that no DNA managed to get off of Dupree and onto Jamieson that evening.

And what was with the business card that had been treated to make sure it didn't collect DNA or fingerprints? Ginny sucked in a breath, shut down her computer, and headed for her bedroom.

There were only two credible possibilities. The first was that DNA transfer occurred, but the sample supplied by Dupree was—somehow—not a match to the DNA on her hands. The second was that Dupree—somehow—managed to keep her DNA to herself. Both possibilities argued a level of sophistication bordering on fanaticism.

Which made perfect sense. If you were planning to commit a murder, the difference between a happy retirement on a South Seas island and a fatal rendezvous with the criminal justice system might be the presence or absence of a healthy dose of paranoia. Josephine Dupree wasn't bulletproof after all.

* * *

Chapter 33

Wednesday Evening
Laird's Residence, Brochaber

Jim was pacing back and forth in his grandfather's living room. He had squeezed this interview into the space between two shifts and was anxious to get it over with.

If truth were told, he was glad his grandfather had invited Dr. Gordon to come for dinner. Gordon had combined a professional conference with the wedding, spending his days at meetings in Ft. Worth, and his evenings with his old friend, Angus Mackenzie. Which gave Jim a chance to air some of the things that were troubling him about Ginny's behavior. He had, however, expected a more sympathetic listener.

"Best learn tae pick yer battles, lad. Tha's a fight ye canna win."

Jim bristled. "All I want is for her to listen to me, to stay out of things that are none of her business."

"Her business is th' people aroond her, as is yers. You'll find she canna easily say no tae a cry fer help."

Jim frowned harder. "It sounds like a moth drawn to a flame, something that will kill her if she gets too close."

"Perhaps, but mayhap she'll find better things tae do wi' her time after th' wedding."

Jim picked up the scotch bottle and brought it over, refilling Gordon's glass, then settled down on the couch, facing the psychiatrist.

"That's something else I want to ask you about." Jim caught his lower lip between his teeth, then took a breath. "She may not go through with it, the wedding. She's pulling away from me. Is there anything I can do to fix that?"

"Tell me, all o' it."

Jim recounted everything he could think of, starting with Ginny's reaction to the dead woman on the field. "Which I can understand because, you know, her father died that way."

Gordon nodded. "And she probably hadnae visualized tha' death so clearly."

"No, I don't think she had. She tried to distance herself from that corpse, until Caroline was accused, then she was nose down to the trail, no matter what I said."

"They were in school together?"

Jim nodded. "Best friends. More like sisters."

"Ahm. Go on."

Jim hesitated, then confessed to Gordon about the trust fund. "I should have told her at once. I see that now, but I thought I was protecting her. Then I couldn't find the right time to bring it up."

Gordon's bushy white eyebrows rose over twinkling blue eyes. "And th' lass took yer kindness amiss?"

Jim nodded. "She wouldn't let me kiss her goodnight. Then she stopped taking my calls." Jim was having trouble confessing how much this had hurt him. "Is she just mad at me? Or having second thoughts? Or what?" Jim rose and went back to his pacing. He was grasping at straws, and he knew it, but—

"Could she be getting cold feet? Could it be that simple? I mean, this is an awfully public affair. I could understand if she's nervous about making promises with so many eyes watching."

Dr. Gordon shook his head. "It's no' weddin' jitters, at least no' th' way ye usually think o' them."

"Then what's going on?"

"Look at th' evidence, lad. Ye keep tryin' tae talk sense inta her, aye?"

Jim nodded.

"And she's resistin' ye."

"Right."

"Has she done that afore?"

Jim thought for a moment. "Yes. When we were in Albany."

The psychiatrist nodded. "Can ye recall tha' conversation?"

"Vividly. I was trying to explain to her that I couldn't protect her if she wouldn't follow my instructions." Jim looked over at Dr. Gordon. "But that was before you and I had our little chat."

"Aye. Now, wha' was her argument?"

Jim shook his head. "She didn't argue, she just left." He felt his heart contract at the memory.

Dr. Gordon nodded. "Let me tell ye a bit about tha' lass o' yours. She's no' good at confrontations. She'll jouk and let the jaw gae by."

"She can fight. I've seen her."

"Aye, but no' wi' you."

Jim's brow furrowed heavily. That had been part of the issue last time, that she hadn't confronted him. He could have handled a direct challenge, but not the stricken whiteness of her face.

"I thought we'd gotten past that."

"'Tis a big step, as ye say, and complicated by th' predicament her friend is in. But tha's no' th' problem."

Jim found himself losing patience. "Then what is?"

"Can ye no' guess?"

"She's running from responsibility?"

"It's you she's runnin' frae, lad."

Jim caught his breath. "Me?"

"Aye, only she disnae know it. 'Tis unconscious."

Jim stared at the other man. "Why would she run from *me*? I adore her."

Gordon nodded. "Her conscious mind knows tha' and she'll gi'e lip service tae bein' ready tae go forward wi' th' marriage. But her subconscious is fightin' her. It's tellin' her she's no' safe."

"Why?"

"Think, lad, think back tae when ye first met."

Understanding hit him like a blow. Jim felt his gorge rise. "I'm not Hal."

"And she knows it, but her subconscious is tryin' tae protect her."

"How do I get past *that*?" Jim heard the catch in his voice and hoped the older man would forgive the emotion.

"Afore we can answer tha', I must ask ye, Jim. Do ye love her enough tae put her needs ahead o' yer ain?"

Jim collapsed into the other chair and put his head in his hands. He'd been telling himself she was the most important thing in his life, but was it really true? He could hear his voice telling her how he wanted their lives to be, after the wedding, after the children started to arrive, after he became laird. Had he even once asked her to share *her* vision of their future? Had he included her in his planning? Had he considered the adjustments she would have to make, the parts of her life she would have to give up? Gordon's voice penetrated the fog of uncertainty and guilt.

"It's been six months. If she were a patient o' yours, would ye consider tha' enough time tae get over th' emotional trauma?"

Jim lifted his head and looked at the psychiatrist. "No."

"Then why are ye surprised she's draggin' her heels?"

Jim's gaze turned inward. "She said it was behind her, and I wanted to believe it." He gave himself a little shake. "Okay. I was wrong. What do I do about it?"

"I'll ha'e a talk wi' her tomorrow. In th' meantime, ye can be a wee bit more supportive o' her friend. Wha' matters tae her should matter tae th' both o' ye."

"It does, just not as much as she matters to me."

"I understand, lad. Just keep remindin' yerself o' why ye want her tae wife. Then ask yerself if the prize is worth th' price."

Jim nodded, thanked Dr. Gordon, and headed for the car, going over the discussion in his mind.

He wanted Ginny because he could no longer imagine life without her. If putting his plans on the back burner until she could share in them was what it would take, it was a price he was willing to pay.

It was true he hadn't been sympathetic enough toward Caroline's plight. He'd have to make that up to Ginny tomorrow. He would wait until after Dr. Gordon had a chance to talk to her, then take her out to dinner, just the two of them. Somewhere quiet. Somewhere he could ask her some of those hard questions he'd come up with this afternoon, and listen to her answers.

But for right now, he'd better hustle or he was going to be late for work.

* * *

Chapter 34

Thursday Morning
Cameron Residence

Caroline stood on Ginny's left side, a makeshift bouquet in her hands.

"When am I supposed to pull off this stunt?"

"As soon as the rings have been exchanged, Jim will turn to Alex, and Alex will pass him the Mackenzie sash. That's how much time you have to get the train detached and out of the way."

The unusual design was a concession to the Scottish Country Dancing Ginny would be doing at the reception. She could not have a heavy train dragging her down during the reels.

Caroline tried several methods of undoing the hooks that anchored the train to the shoulders of the gown, while juggling the flowers. "I give up!" She thrust the bouquet at Alan. "Here, hold this!"

Ginny started laughing. "It looks as if I need another bridesmaid. Is it too late to recruit someone?"

Caroline removed the heavy fabric from the gown and draped it over her arm, then took back the bouquet. "I'm going to need someone to hand the train off to as well. I can't recess down the aisle with anything this bulky over my arm."

Ginny looked at the admittedly voluminous garment and nodded. "Would your mother be willing to help out?"

Caroline nodded. "I'm sure she would, and if she can't we'll find someone else. Let's practice the sash bit."

"That's Jim's job," Alan said.

"You're going to stand in for him." Caroline was already handing him the tartan sash she had pulled out of her closet to practice with. "I don't have a pin. What's Jim going to use?"

"That penannular Angus gave me for a Christmas present, but it will already be attached. What we need is a way to use the loop on that shoulder as an anchor point." Ginny reached up and touched it with her finger. "Let me think for a minute."

The usual way of anchoring a sash—and what she would have to do before trying to dance in it—was to use safety pins, but that required turning the fabric of the dress inside out and could not be done in public. If she had access to the sash ahead of time, she could sew a hook in place, or a snap. Her eyes narrowed.

"Does your mother have any hook and loop fasteners?"

Ginny was unable to join in the search, being weighed down by a firm injunction not to move. She could hear Caroline and Alan calling to one another and laughing as they dismantled closets and drawers. Laughing, as if they didn't have a murder charge hanging over their heads.

"Here!" Alan's triumphant voice soared over an ominous crashing sound in the kitchen. It was followed by hushed giggling, then the reappearance of the other two in the living room where Ginny stood, waiting.

"Okay. Now what?"

"Make a loop of the soft part and put it through the fabric loop on the shoulder." Ginny tried to help, but just got in the way. She repressed her growing impatience and waited with as much grace as she could muster.

"Okay. I've got a loop of it in place and pinned so it can't escape." Caroline pushed her hair back from her face.

"Now make a tab of the other part, the hook half, and pin it to the underside of the sash."

That was easily accomplished, but it was clear Ginny would have to oversee the positioning on the Mackenzie sash or the result would be neither graceful nor becoming. Something else to have to deal with.

"I like it," Caroline stood back, admiring their work. "I may adopt that method of attaching my sash from now on."

Ginny tugged gently at the Cameron sash and found it resisting her efforts to dislodge it. "It feels fine. Now, let's make sure the fastener doesn't get in the way of the train."

Caroline obligingly removed the tartan sash and reapplied the train. "It's a bit tight. How does it feel?"

"Feels the same to me. How does it look?"

Caroline studied the subject from several angles, asking Ginny to walk so they could make sure the train wouldn't pop off. "I think it will work fine. But you're going to need to set the hooked tape on the Mackenzie sash ahead of time. And you'll need help. We'd better plan another dress rehearsal."

"Friday would work for me. Saturday is going to be too busy. Can you squeeze me in?"

Caroline nodded, her smile fading. "I haven't been allowed to go back to work since they found out about that package from Redmond. I'm afraid they think I'll try to destroy evidence or something."

Ginny turned toward her friend and held out her arms for a hug, but Caroline backed away, shaking her head.

"Let's get you out of the gown first, then we can talk."

They banished Alan until Ginny had been stripped out of her wedding finery, re-dressed in casual pants and top, and the dress carefully put away in its bag. Once that was done, the three of them moved into the kitchen.

Caroline set a glass of juice down in front of Ginny, then took a seat at the table. "Now that we've got that behind us, tell us where we are in the investigation."

Ginny sighed. "I haven't spoken to Tran in days."

"I don't mean the police investigation. I mean *your* investigation."

Ginny looked up in surprise. "Mine?"

"Yes, yours. And don't bother to pretend you don't know what I mean. This is your fourth corpse."

Ginny squirmed. "It's not like I go looking for the things."

Caroline leaned across the table, and tapped her finger in front of Ginny. "That is exactly what you do."

Ginny opened her mouth to protest, but Caroline interrupted her.

"They've always been there. The bodies, I mean. Do you remember Marsha Gillett?"

"The one who got sent to a foster home?"

"Yes. We knew all about those bruises, but no one thought to ask *us*. Then there was Morgan Appleton."

Ginny screwed up her face in an effort to remember. "He drowned."

Caroline nodded emphatically. "At the age of nine, with six years of swimming lessons under his belt and those long legs and arms that let him win every race he ever entered. Drowned."

"Why did that happen? Did we ever find out?"

Alan shook his head. "He was in my scout troop. The adults made a short announcement saying he would be missed, and there was a moment of silence, then we went back to working on our badges."

"And then, there was Camilla."

Ginny had a sudden vision of a dark beauty with huge eyes. Camilla had been very much sought after in the public high school. Not the regular one the Homestead students attended. The Dallas ISD campus they used for extension courses. She had committed suicide.

"That was such a tragedy."

"Did you ever find out who it was, the guy who raped and beat her so violently they said she would never be able to have children?"

"No, of course not. It was none of my business."

Caroline nodded. "Hardly a day goes by when we don't hear of some horrible crime on the TV. Dallas is a very big city and there are a lot of people in it."

"And a certain percentage of them will commit crimes, I get it. What's your point?"

"My point is that the bodies have been there all along. It's only in the last year that you've started taking the investigations on yourself."

Ginny squirmed. "You make me sound like a voyeur."

"What you are is a very successful solver of people puzzles."

Alan laughed. "People puzzles?"

Caroline nodded at him. "Who did what to whom and why." She looked over at Ginny. "Most of us are content to read or watch stories about crime, and leave the actual detection to the police."

Ginny protested. "This is *not* fair. I got pushed into it."

Caroline held up her hand. "You don't need to tell me. I was there. My point is, it's my turn. I'm the one knee-deep in circumstantial evidence, with no alibi, and no way to prove I'm not lying. So come on, Sherlock, where do we stand in this investigation?"

Ginny raised her hands in surrender. "All right, I admit it. I want you cleared of all suspicion before the wedding." She took a breath, then outlined what she had come up with so far.

Alan looked thoughtful. "You think she had a stand-in."

"I think there's a fifty-fifty chance, based on the fact that she ate haggis – a lot of it, by the way, Nessie said she had three helpings—and the fact that, according to the DNA under Jamieson's nails, we're looking for a black female. And they aren't thick on the ground at our Highland Games, no matter how diverse the attendees may be."

Caroline shook her head. "One of the things Detective Tran told me was that the skin under Jamieson's nails might be from earlier in the day, or the day before or—as you know—planted there by someone else. She kindly allowed the possibility that it wasn't me!"

"Decent of her," Alan said, "considering."

"I know," Ginny said. "But there are also the biometrics. The algorithm on the computer pulled up Dupree's image when I was looking for Costas. I didn't come up with that on my own. And when I *did* consider the possibility, there it was. Ears don't lie."

"Images can be faked." Caroline frowned into her orange juice.

"Harder with video," Alan volunteered.

"Also harder to be sure who you're looking at," Ginny said. "Besides, with the costume and face paint and headdress, all I've got to go on is a general resemblance. But—"

The other two looked up as she paused. "But?"

"Alan said it last night. Only a guilty person needs an alibi. So the fact that she had one—two, actually, if you count Costas—is suspicious."

"The show in Louisiana was a prior commitment," Caroline pointed out.

Ginny nodded. "According to the flyers, she'd been planning that gig for months. So why did she *have to* come to Dallas on that particular weekend?"

"To make money?" Alan ventured.

Ginny lifted an eyebrow. "You two have worked the Games as long as I have. When a new tent shows up, what do you see in the way of equipment?"

They exchanged glances, then shrugged. "Rented stuff. Hand-me-downs. The bare minimum to get the job done."

Ginny nodded. "That's for the clans, and the societies. What about the pros?"

Alan's eyes were fixed on hers. "Depending on how big they are, how long they've been in the business, and how far they have to come, trailers filled with stuff, and a whole lot of gear, for every conceivable disaster."

Ginny nodded. "I saw a mix of that at Dupree's booth. Some of her stuff looked old and well worn. Some of it was still in the plastic."

Caroline nodded. "So?"

"She overlooked something in particular, and we've all made this mistake, which is why I noticed. She had no way for visitors to add their names to a mailing list."

Caroline's eyebrows rose. "You're right. That's a beginner's mistake."

"Once I realized what I had seen, I went looking for Mama Dupree on the Internet Games Calendar. She wasn't listed, not even on ours."

"Okay, so what? We all have to start somewhere."

"So we do, but would you chose to try to do *two* weekend long events on the same weekend if you've never done one of them before and have no idea what you'll be up against?"

Alan's brow was furrowed. "Probably not, but common sense may not have been a factor."

"She was a last minute add-on."

Caroline sat up straighter. "How much last minute?"

"Four days."

"And they let her in?"

"We had an opening in the row. The committee thought it sounded like fun. Something different."

"You spoke to them?"

Ginny shook her head. "I got that from Himself."

Alan was leaning back in his chair, his eyes alert. "Two alibis, a double booking, with the Games as the last minute change of plans, ears that match one of the alibis, a haggis-induced incapacity, and a fuzzy image of some woman on a stage. If you have that much on Dupree, why haven't the police brought her in for questioning?"

"It's not enough for probable cause, which is what Tran needs before she can search Dupree's house, or van, or bank account. We have nothing that ties her to Jamieson."

Alan's brow furrowed. "What does that mean, exactly, 'probable cause'?"

"Something that would lead a reasonable person to believe Dupree killed Jamieson."

"Are you telling me Tran needs to be able to *prove* Dupree's guilty before she can go looking for evidence? That doesn't seem reasonable to me."

Ginny shrugged. "It's a strict legal standard, but it keeps us honest. And it's what I'm relying on to get our prime suspect here out of trouble." She nudged Caroline's foot with her own.

Alan nodded. "Okay. So what do we need to establish probable cause?"

"Some sort of forensic evidence that can't be refuted in court."

"Like what?"

"Well, how about a canceled check made out to Dupree with a handwritten note on it that says, 'Paid in full for the murder of Judge Jamieson.'"

Caroline laughed. "That would be nice, wouldn't it?"

Ginny nodded. "But I doubt we'll find anything like that. Next best would be a fresh sample of Dupree's DNA, just to make sure she doesn't match those skin cells. But to get another DNA sample, especially if Dupree has switched the first one on us, would require a warrant."

Alan's brow furrowed. "On the TV, they get the suspect to drink something, then use the saliva sample as a source for DNA. I think I've seen them rummage through trash for the same reason."

Ginny nodded. "I thought of that, too, and did a bit of research. Once you throw something away, it's considered abandoned property, and anyone can take it. Trash that's been put out for collection would be fair game. There's no telling what we might find, of course. Lots of DNA, but no guarantee any of it would be hers."

Caroline was leaning forward again, her eyes alight. "True, but there might be other evidence to corroborate the DNA, fingerprints on a toothpaste tube, for instance."

Alan was smiling at her. "I can have Terri ready in an hour."

"Who?" Ginny stared at Alan.

"That's the name of my little Cessna. Tír na nÓg, Terri for short."

Ginny couldn't help smiling. Tír na nÓg was the Celtic version of Heaven, the land in the mythic west, where everyone wanted to go. An excellent name for an airplane. "Are you suggesting now?"

"I can fly to New Orleans, get a rent car, collect the trash, and be home in time for dinner." He grabbed his cell phone and started scrolling. "I just need a weather report."

Ginny watched his smile fade as he studied the information.

"There's a front moving in from New Mexico. They're considering grounding all light aircraft." He sighed. "Well, it was a good idea while it lasted."

Ginny's brow furrowed. If she was going to solve this mystery before the wedding, today was her last chance. Once the guests started to arrive, she would be trapped.

"Explain, please."

Alan shrugged. "We've been thinking we can grab a trash bag sitting on the curb, but there might not be one. It might not be pickup day."

"She has an address," Caroline said. "There must be a door handle or gate latch we can swab, something she has to touch to get inside."

Alan nodded. "But the storm will wash away any trace of DNA." He sighed. "And, if this front is moving as fast as they say it is, I won't have time to swab anything."

Ginny was thinking hard. "How much time would you need?"

He turned his eyes on her. "The issue is the turnaround. Flight time each way is about two hours. Once the front arrives, they'll shut down the airport."

"What if you had help?"

Alan's brow furrowed. "If I stayed with the plane—got it refueled and pre-flighted while someone else went to go collect the garbage—we could beat that front. We'd have to hurry, though."

Ginny glanced at the clock. Jim was asleep. Her mother and a crew of clanswomen were hard at work on the cooking, baking, and decorating. No telling what Angus was up to, but undoubtedly he had preparations to make as well. She would not be missed for a few hours. As long as she was back before dark, no one need ever know she was gone.

"I'll come with you."

Caroline started up. "No, you won't."

Ginny felt a stab of temper. This might be her last chance to do what *she* wanted before settling down to married life. "And why not?" Ginny could feel the frustration building.

"Jim will skin you alive if you run off just before the wedding."

Ginny's eyes narrowed, the irritation boiling over. "If I hear that man's name one more time," she hissed, "I'm going to scream!"

The shocked silence lasted for a dozen heart beats, then Caroline asked, "Have you two had a fight?"

"No!" Ginny turned away, taking her glass to the sink, rinsing it out and setting it down, to give herself time to think. Her hands were shaking. She turned to face the other two, then lifted her chin.

"I'm allowed to make my own decisions, at least for a few more days."

She looked at Alan. "I need to go home first, to pick up my talisman."

Caroline's frown deepened. "Ginny, you're not being reasonable."

"Wanting to take my lucky charm with me on a trip that will certainly need all the luck we can get?"

"It's just superstition. That thing won't protect you if something goes wrong."

"Maybe not, but I'm not going to take that chance." She tuned to face Alan. "When do we leave?"

Alan looked from Ginny to Caroline, then back to Ginny. "I'll pick you up in front of your house in twenty minutes."

Ginny nodded. "I'll be there." She collected her things and headed for the door. Caroline got there first.

"Ginny, I'm sorry! I asked for your help and I'm grateful, really. Just be careful."

Ginny threw her arms around her friend. "I told you I wasn't going to let him come between us!"

* * *

CHAPTER 35

Thursday Morning
Airborne toward New Orleans, LA

Ginny had never been in a single engine prop plane before. From the outside, it looked small. From the inside, it felt like a closet with windows. Big windows. And no grab bars.

She climbed into the right hand seat, buckled up, and put on her headphones, then watched Alan go through the pre-flight check lists. She knew he was a good swordsman, and he had his own architectural firm (though she suspected Angus might be a silent partner in it), and he had proposed to Caroline—all good things. What she hadn't expected was the calm efficiency with which he set about flying the two of them to Louisiana. Any hesitation she might have had about trusting her life to his skills vanished as she watched.

Alan kept his little Cessna in a hanger at one of the small private airfields on the northeast side of Dallas. The field had only one runway, angled NNW/SSE, painted "15" and "33" on opposite ends of the tarmac, indicating the compass headings a plane would be facing if taking off at that end. The windsock indicated a thirteen knot breeze from the southeast, an inflow pattern off the Gulf of Mexico that (according to the weather forecaster) would intercept the front headed their way. This would add moisture to the rotation caused by the afternoon heating common in this part of Texas at this time of year.

Planes (and pilots) prefer to take off into the wind, to take advantage of the extra lift the moving air provides, so they would be taking off south-southeast, then turning sharply east to avoid flying over downtown Dallas, and Love Field. The air space over the Metroplex handled an average of one thousand commercial planes a day, and that didn't count the military aircraft, police and news helicopters, and private pilots. Ginny hadn't known any of this before the flight, but Alan must have decided that the best way to put her at ease was to teach her how to fly. He had kept up a running commentary as they approached takeoff. When they got clearance, he taxied onto the runway, increased the rpms, and released the brakes.

Ginny found the ascent easy. It took her a minute to realize she was looking down, rather than ahead as she tried to make out the scenery. She'd seen some of the same sights before, from the tops of the downtown skyscrapers and the Oil Derrick at Six Flags. Then the scenery below became too distant to make out details and began to blur into a vast patchwork of squares, the still active farms to the east of DFW, peppered with urban intersections. She could make out the interstate and some of the lakes, then those, too, faded into the distance. They were climbing.

Alan looked over at her and smiled. "It's safe to talk now."

Ginny laughed. "I didn't want to distract you, but I do have a question or two."

"Fire away."

"Is it my imagination or are there more clouds than you expected between Dallas and New Orleans?"

Alan's lips twitched. "You noticed that, did you?"

"It's kind of hard to miss. Besides, I've been watching the radar. It looks as if there's something brewing."

Alan nodded. "The forecast called for another line of storms between Houston and New Orleans, but not until late this afternoon. It seems to be forming ahead of schedule."

"Can we fly above it?"

"No. This plane can go up to 18,000 feet, but the cabin is unpressurized so you'd notice the difference, and it's not necessary, at least, not yet. We'll stay on Visual Flight Rules as long as we can."

"Visual Flight Rules?"

"I have to keep enough clear air space around us so I can see an obstacle coming, in time to avoid hitting it. We also have to stay out of the commercial airliners' way, and at least 1000 feet over the tallest object on the ground."

Ginny's appreciation of Alan's expertise rose another notch. "Where are we going to land?"

"New Orleans Lakefront Airport. It's about the same size as the Addison airport, just older and set right on the edge of Lake Pontchartrain. I expect they'll make me circle around and come in from the water side. That's another reason I'd like to get home before the storm reaches Fort Worth. I don't want my baby girl swept into the lake by the wind. I'd rather she was safely in her hanger before then."

Ginny smiled at his use of the feminine pronoun. "Does Caroline know you have a girl on the side?"

Alan grinned. "She does, and we may have some interesting discussions in our future, but I'm hoping she'll fall in love with flying. It's a big part of who I am." He looked over at Ginny. "When she marries me, she marries the sky."

Ginny looked out at the vast emptiness, pale blue in the noonday sun, except for the clouds. Not very many, and not very close, but growing as she watched, building towers of dazzling white. As promised, Alan was steering between them.

Ginny usually flew commercial, and those planes invariably climbed above the clouds before settling down for a smooth ride to wherever they were going. Each time she saw that brilliant carpet of white, opaque and lovely and mysterious, she was tempted to try her foot upon it, to see if it would hold her weight. Tempted, even if it meant her death.

Ginny felt a sudden tightness in the region of her gut. From what she had heard, and read, and seen, marriage was like that cloud—a pretty fantasy, but in reality cold, wet, and potentially dangerous. She swallowed hard and tried to turn her mind to another subject. It didn't work.

An image of Jim rose before her eyes. He was so much bigger than she. Those arms and shoulders she admired so much could do real damage. If he wanted to hurt her, there would be nothing short of her Glock to prevent it.

Her hand came up unconsciously, trying to find the scar over her left ear, a souvenir from the fall, but the headset was in the way. She scowled, then scolded herself. He wasn't the same man, she told herself. *No*, said the little voice in her head, *but he's a man, and after Sunday there will be no turning back.*

"Ginny?" Alan's voice came to her through the speakers. "Look over there. It's the Gulf."

Ginny shoved the memory of violence away, and looked where Alan was pointing. She could see the sun reflected off a great sheet of water, but no details. They were too high to see the shipping, or even the oil rigs. "Are we getting close?"

"Another twenty minutes, then the approach. How are you holding up?"

The corner of Ginny's mouth twitched. "I'm ready to stretch my legs anytime now."

Alan laughed. "Yeah, me, too. Two hours in the cockpit is just about my limit. Look! There's New Orleans."

Ginny held her tongue while he contacted the New Orleans air traffic controller and followed the instructions to get them down, then over to the refueling station. She climbed stiffly out of her seat when Alan indicated it was safe do so.

"You'll need to hike over to the terminal, I'm afraid."

Ginny nodded. The rent car would be in the parking lot beyond the main entrance. But there should be restrooms and maybe some fast food as well.

"Stay in touch. I'll make sure we're ready to go as soon as you get back. Have you got the address?"

"Yes, Mother. And the maps, and the cash to pay off any policeman who might get too nosey."

Alan grinned. "All right. I'll stop. But I'd appreciate it if you didn't linger. I really do want to beat that storm home." He paused for a split second, then threw his arms around her and gave her a hug. "Thank you for helping Caroline! I won't forget it."

Ginny returned the hug, then set off across the airport as quickly as her stiff legs would allow. She had no trouble finding her way to the terminal, addressing her bodily needs, and collecting the paperwork on the rent car, along with better directions on how to get to the shop.

"Mama Dupree?"

Ginny was startled to find the girl behind the counter recognized the address. "Yes. Do you know her?"

"We all does. But she's not theah today. They've got a big shindig planned for the night. She'll be out getting ready, I shouldn't wonder."

Ginny thanked her informant, got in the car and headed south, toward Hwy 90 and New Orleans. Not there today! That was a stroke of luck. It would make it easier to slip in and out without arousing suspicion. She settled down to navigating the numerous "you can't get there from here" access points familiar to anyone who has ever lived near the mouth of a river.

The shop, she had been told, could be found in a cul-de-sac on the eastern side of the fairgrounds, away from the tourists and the so-called Voodoo Museum of the French Quarter. A much more appropriate location for Mama Dupree, considering.

"Considering what?" Ginny had asked.

"Considering she don't sell to tourists."

Ginny had no trouble finding the address. She paused on the edge of the cul-de-sac and examined her surroundings. The shop was in an old house, flanked by other old houses, none of them in pristine condition. The blinds were down on Mama Dupree's windows, and a sign on the door announced the owner had, "Gone Crawfishin'."

Ginny put her car in gear and drove around back, only to find that New Orleans did not believe in alleys. The yards were miniscule and bled into one another where the chain link fence had fallen down. There wasn't even a walkway between the properties. She finished circling the block and parked in front.

The scene looked deserted, not even a cat dozing in the afternoon sun. There was one small blue sedan, very old, parked on the grass. No sign of the van.

There was just one trash can, much battered, marked with the house number in red paint. Ginny got out of the rent car and approached the receptacle on foot. She peeked inside and found it empty, so she put the lid back in place, and looked around for something else to sample.

Her nerves were playing tricks on her. With each passing moment, her unease grew. Why had the girl said Mama Dupree didn't sell to tourists? She'd driven to Dallas, to the Games, and done just that. Different rules for different situations?

There would be DNA aplenty inside the shop, but Ginny knew anything seized without a warrant would be excluded in the courtroom. What she needed was something that could be sacrificed for the cause. She moved cautiously up to the window and peered in through a chink in the shades. Darkness, silence, not even dust moving.

She turned her back on the shop and looked around again, her eye falling on the ancient blue sedan. Most people left strands of hair on the headrest. She peered through the window of the car. No telling if Dupree had ever been in this car, of course, but the strands were there. What's more, it wasn't locked. Ginny put her hand on the latch and pulled the door open. The air inside was musty with age and dust, she sneezed, then fished a baggie out of her pocket and reached for the hair on the headrest. In the same instant she heard a whoosh, then felt a sting on the side of her neck.

She caught her breath in surprise and turned to find Dupree in the doorway of the shop. In her hands was a long wooden tube. Ginny reached for her neck, her fingers closing on a metal shaft, decorated with feathers. She pulled it out and looked at it. A dart of some sort. She dropped it on the pavement, and turned toward her car, but it was already too late. Her legs weren't cooperating. She staggered and dropped to her knees. Pushing herself up, she rose and stumbled forward a few more steps, then fell and lay still. Her last conscious thought was a muddled feeling of regret. Alan's pretty little plane wouldn't be making it home tonight. Not in time to beat the storm.

* * *

Chapter 36

Thursday Afternoon
Laird's Residence, Brochaber

Jim stretched luxuriously, awake but still abed, reveling in the thought that he didn't have to go back to work for ten days. This was Thursday. Two more days. Two more days alone in his bed, then—well, then he wouldn't be alone any more. He smiled at the thought. On Sunday, the two of them would start their married life in the new house. The lease on his apartment wouldn't be up for another three months so he had plenty of time to finish moving. She, of course, would be leaving her childhood home.

The thought sobered him. He sat up, ran his hands through his hair, and looked at the clock—four p.m. Ginny's brother, Alex and his wife and their three boys were due to arrive at the airport at five, drop their bags at the Homestead guest house reserved for them, then report to the Forbes residence for dinner. They would be coming from Atlanta and would gain an hour, but, for the boys in particular, it would be a long day.

Jim was invited to be on hand to help with the luggage and transportation, and he was glad to do it. He and Alex didn't know one another well, but in default of brothers of his own, Jim was hoping they would become friends.

He rose and showered, then slid into comfortable slacks and

shirt. The mild April evening would not require a jacket, but he wanted to look reasonably respectable. He smiled at the tag painted on his thigh even as he covered it. Tomorrow, maybe, he would ask Reggie if he'd learned anything from the data he was collecting.

Jim grabbed his keys and headed out, noticing a rising wind and clouds billowing overhead. He found a weather report on the car radio and listened with half an ear. He must have slept through the first round of storms. They had pushed through Dallas leaving debris on the roadways, stop lights out, and traffic snarled. Typical for spring in Texas. Gone as quickly as it came. This front was big, however and – also typical for the area in the springtime – points south and east of him were getting hammered.

It took Jim twenty minutes to reach Love Field, then another fifteen to park, go inside, and locate the Forbes family. He strode up to his soon-to-be brother-in-law and held out his hand.

"Alex! Welcome to Dallas. I hope your flight wasn't too bad."

The other man took his hand and smiled. "No problem. Bumpy getting in, and they threatened to divert us to Kansas City, but we were able to come in between the squall lines. You remember my wife, Wendy?"

Jim smiled at her. "Of course, from Christmas."

She ignored his hand, and pulled him into a hug. "Welcome to the family, Jim. I'm so glad Ginny found you!"

"We found each other."

"That's the best way."

Jim took command of one of the baggage carts, and the small boy riding on the suitcases, and headed off to the parking lot. He managed to squeeze the luggage and five in-laws into his car, then drove the whole party to the Homestead and the cottage that would be theirs for the duration.

The Matron met them at the door and helped them get inside, explaining they would have the use of a Homestead car as well as the cottage, then plucked Jim's sleeve. She lowered her voice.

"Angus asked me to send you to Brochaber, as soon as you got here."

"Everyone?"

"He didn't specify. It was you he was looking for."

"I'll follow you," Alex said, "as soon as we get turned around."

"You know the way?"

"I'll see he doesn't get lost." The Matron put a hand in the middle of Jim's back and pushed him toward his car. "Go."

Jim did as told. This close to the wedding, there was no telling what Angus wanted. Perhaps Mrs. Forbes needed help getting supper on the table. He tossed a mean salad, and he was practically family, would *be* family, in just under seventy-two hours.

He'd gotten lucky in his mother-in-law. He liked Sinia immensely, and was pretty sure the feeling was mutual. A good thing, too, since she was hand-in-glove with his grandfather. He drove around the top of the lake, turned the corner, and pulled up in front of the Forbes' residence.

Her daughter, too. He hoped she wasn't still mad at him. If Gordon was right, and he probably was, it might take some time to convince Ginny to trust him again.

He strode up the walk, lifting his nose to the freshening breeze. Jim raised his hand to ring the bell, but the door opened before his finger reached it.

"Jim!" It was Sinia Forbes, her usually calm demeanor gone. "Come in." She stepped aside to let him enter.

Jim frowned at her. "What's wrong?"

She didn't answer, just turned away and motioned for him to follow her. "Come into the kitchen."

In the kitchen Jim found his grandfather, Detective Tran, and, to his surprise, Caroline Cameron seated around the table. He looked at the troubled faces, his stomach churning. "What's happened?"

His grandfather gestured at an empty chair. "Sit, lad."

Jim ignored him. "Where's Ginny?"

"That's the trouble. We don't know—" Sinia started, but Angus waved her to silence. He looked over at Caroline. "Tell him wha' ye told us."

Jim turned to face Caroline. "What's going on?"

She swallowed, then took a deep breath and began.

"Alan called, around four, to ask if any of us had heard from her."

Jim pulled his phone out and glanced at it. Finding nothing, he put it away again. "Why would Alan care if Ginny called one of us?"

"They flew to New Orleans this morning—"

Jim interrupted. "New Orleans?"

Caroline nodded. "To get evidence Detective Tran needed to clear me. They were supposed to be back by dinner time."

Jim put a hand out to steady himself, then decided he would sit down after all.

"Alan was going to go alone. Ginny volunteered to go with him, because of the storm." As if to punctuate her explanation, there was a rumble of thunder in the middle distance.

Caroline took another breath. "Alan planned to stay with the plane, get it gassed up and ready to go as soon as Ginny got back with the evidence. They could save almost two hours that way. But she didn't show up."

Jim felt his jaw clench, then his fist. Dupree was in New Orleans. "I told her not to do anything stupid!"

"I'm sorry, Jim. It's my fault. She did it for me, to save me." Caroline put her face down in her hands and wept.

Angus looked a warning. "Another time, lad."

Jim swallowed bile. "What's being done?"

Detective Tran answered him. "The New Orleans police visited the address on file for Ms. Dupree. There was no answer."

"They didn't go in?"

"They had no warrant and no probable cause to believe a crime has been committed."

Jim was in no mood for legal niceties. He turned back to Caroline. "Did she tell you what her plan was?"

Caroline nodded. "She needed Dupree's DNA. She said it was legal to take someone's trash after they put it out on the street. She was going to grab the bag, drive back to the airport, and fly home."

Jim sucked in a deep breath. "Dupree must have caught her at it."

Detective Tran nodded. "The last person to see Miss Forbes, so far as we have been able to tell, was the clerk at the rental car counter. She told Miss Forbes that Ms. Dupree was preparing for a party and was not expected to be at home. They found Miss Forbes' rent car parked in front of Ms. Dupree's shop."

"So it's a kidnapping! That gives you probable cause, doesn't it?"

"There was no evidence of force or coercion. She could have gone willingly."

Jim controlled himself with difficulty. "I assure you, Ginny would not have gone anywhere with that woman, not voluntarily. She was convinced Dupree killed Jamieson. Even if she was mistaken, she wouldn't have let Dupree separate her from the rent car. She's not that stupid."

"Her personal effects were not in the car."

"So Dupree took them as well. Has anybody tried to trace her phone?"

Tran nodded. "The phone is out of service."

"Dupree must have taken the battery out." Jim had learned about staying off the grid on their trip to Nova Scotia.

"Or she is in an area with poor cell reception."

There was another clap of thunder, louder, followed by the sound of hard rain on the roof. Jim jumped to his feet.

"Why are we wasting our time sitting here talking?"

"Easy, lad." Angus's voice cut through the fear in Jim's mind. "No time's been wasted. I've got th' Burnside Homestead workin' on it, wi' Detective Tran actin' as liaison tae th' New Orleans police. They've got Ginny's photograph, and as much information as we could gi'e them."

Detective Tran interjected. "I have thought of someone else who may be able to help. You recall there was an investigation of the fire at Professor Craig's house. The officer who conducted that investigation, Pierre Michel, is from Louisiana. I would like to ask him if he could offer any suggestions."

Angus nodded. "'Tis a guid thought."

Detective Tran picked up the phone and dialed a number. When a voice answered, she identified herself and explained the situation. The others listened to her end of the conversation. "Yes, New Orleans, around two p.m. today. No, nothing disturbed. You know the woman? By reputation. I see." Tran nodded. "Yes, I understand. That would be most helpful. We will wait for your call." She hung up and reported to the group. "He wants to talk to someone in New Orleans. He will call me back after he has done so."

Angus sighed. "Then we mus' wait. In th' meantime, has anyone anythin' else tae suggest?"

Jim felt his eyes widen. "Yes! I need to talk to Reggie."

Angus picked up his phone and made the connection. "Reggie? My grandson would like a word wi' ye." He handed the phone over.

"What's up?"

"Ginny's missing." Jim wasted no time on small talk.

"Missing? As in nowhere to be found? And her with a tag on her back?"

"That's what I want to talk about. Were you tracking her today?" The rest of the people around the table looked mystified, but Angus nodded.

"Both of you, yes, but I wasn't looking at the data. It's just being dumped into the computer databases. We'll do analysis once we have some time under our belts. You've only had the tags on for four days."

"I know that. What I need is your tracker. Is it portable? Can you take it with you?"

"Oh, yes. Car, train, boat, plane, whatever you need."

"Were you able to increase the range?"

"Not yet, the signal's weak and the connection isn't stable I've had to baby it along every time we've taken it out for a test run. Even one mile is stretching it and the signal degrades if there's electrical interference and there's no way to attach it to a cell tower yet, which is a pity because if we had that app we'd be able to cover a much larger area, but it's not ready. I need another month."

"But you've got one tracker that will work if we get close enough?"

"Right and if we point it in the right direction, just like I told you. What did you have in mind? And do you want me to go with you?"

"Can I run the thing?"

There was a hesitation on the other end of the line. "No offense, but probably not. It's not you—it's the device. It will probably need calibrating more than once and it will just be faster if I do it myself. No hard feelings?"

"None. How soon can you be ready?"

"How far are we going?"

"New Orleans."

"Half an hour. Where are you?"

"Brochaber."

"Meet you there." There was a click as Reggie broke the connection.

Jim looked at his grandfather. "Now all I need is a way to get to New Orleans." He crossed the kitchen and looked out at the storm. Through the flashes of lightning he could see sheets of rain, and small branches torn from their parent trees flying across the yard, and hear the high-pitched whine as the wind forced its way through the eaves of the house. "We can't fly in this. How long is it supposed to last?"

Angus picked up his phone again, selected a number from his contact list, and hit the *call* button. He spoke to someone, asking about weather conditions and flight possibilities. When he was through, he thanked his contact, and hung up. "He says th' storm hae grounded everything until midnight at least."

Jim turned and started pacing. "There has to be some way to get to New Orleans!"

Detective Tran raised a finger. "Excuse me, Dr. Mackenzie. What did you and Mr. Macdonald mean by a 'tag' and 'tracking her'?"

Jim turned to the detective. "It's an experiment. Reggie put RFID tags on each of us and has been collecting information about our movements."

"RFID? The same thing they use to identify items available for purchase in the store?"

"Yes. These are new technology, much smaller and—as of right now—they don't use cell towers or satellites. They use that device Reggie invented. Which means that device has to go to New Orleans so we can use it to find Ginny. It will take all night if we have to drive in this rain. We need transportation." Jim quashed the thought that it might already be too late.

"Gie me a minute," Angus said. He picked up the phone and placed another call. Jim listed to his end of the conversation.

"Aye, Dallas tae New Orleans. . . Naught flying oot o' here . . . 'Twill take a wee bit o' convincing . . . Aye, we can do tha'. . . Can ye meet them on th' other end? . . . Aye, an' I thank ye fer it!" Angus put away the phone and looked at Jim.

"Yer tae go tae th' Homestead and meet a Seahawk frae th' old Carswell Naval Air Station. They'll tak ye tae Galveston where ye must pick up a Coast Guard Search and Rescue helicopter. Ye need tae be on the Games grounds in fifty-eight minutes."

"They'll fly in this weather?"

"Aye, they will. 'Tis a training run fer them."

The doorbell announced Reggie's arrival, along with the Atlanta branch of the Forbes family. Sinia rose to deal with the out-of-town guests while Reggie joined the others in the kitchen.

Detective Tran's phone had gone off during this exchange and she had taken the call in the living room. She reentered the kitchen with news in her face.

"Officer Michel has spoken to his sister in New Orleans. She tells us Lachlan Russell has already persuaded the New Orleans police to treat this as a woman-in-jeopardy situation. They will give us whatever we need."

"Lachlan Russell?" Jim asked.

"Th' Laird o' the Burnside Homestead. 'Tis aboot thirty minutes south o' Baton Rouge."

"I'm guessing the Navy helicopter is his doing, too," Reggie inserted. Angus nodded.

"Aye. Th' Coast Guard, too. He's ex-Navy and still hae lots o' contacts."

"We'll need a car when we get there."

"Leave th' logistics tae Lachlan. He'll see all done richt. And eat. Y'ell no get anither chance this nicht." Jim nodded, then took Reggie by the arm and steered him up the stairs and into the room his grandfather kept ready for him.

Reggie eyed the bed. "I don't suppose there will be any chance to catch a few winks on the flight, but then, you slept all day so it won't hurt you to be up all night. We're going to be airborne for, what? Two hours, from Galveston to New Orleans? That will give me time to calibrate on your tag, which we'll need to do to make sure I can tell you apart, especially as you get closer."

"You think this is going to work?" Jim kept his voice down.

"No reason to think not. The tag will do its job whatever the circumstances." Reggie hesitated. "I mean, there's no reason to think we can't find the tag, I mean, her." He looked helplessly at Jim.

Jim laid a hand on his arm. "I understand and she's all right, for the moment."

"How do you know?"

Jim turned away. "Gut feeling."

He was acutely aware that he had no clear impression of Ginny's condition. Not like last time. That cut both ways. He was praying it meant she wasn't in danger, but his nerves were on high alert, and he wasn't completely sure he wasn't getting the first twinges of uneasiness from her, rather than from himself.

If it was true, the uneasiness was coming from her, it meant she was still alive. If it was coming from him, it meant nothing, except that he needed to keep a grip on his emotions or dissolve into a gibbering idiot and be best left home while real men went to do his work for him. And this line of thought was getting him nowhere. Second Sight or not, he was a minimum of four hours away from where he wanted to be.

There was a tap on the door, followed by Alex's head.

"May I come in?"

Jim opened the door and let him in, then watched as Alex closed it behind him. He turned to face Jim and spoke without preamble.

"My sister got all the brains in the family." Jim started to protest, but Alex stopped him. "What's more, she's lucky. Not just normally lucky. She was always managing to get herself out of scrapes we both got into. I'd be left stuck, and she'd have to pull me out after her. I used to think that was normal."

Jim wondered where this was going.

Alex continued. "Part of it is her insatiable curiosity. She reads constantly, and remembers what she reads. Part of it is a razor-sharp intellect that can analyze problems and identify consequences when no one else can. We used to think she could see into the future." The corner of his mouth twitched. "Don't play chess with her if you don't want to lose."

He took a breath, then lifted his chin and looked Jim square in the eye. "Here's my point. If there's a way to survive this, she'll find it."

* * *

CHAPTER 37

Thursday Evening
Paradis, LA

Ginny woke slowly, unhappily aware of her stomach and a tendency for her head to spin if she moved. Like being drunk. Must have been some party. She had no recollection of it.

She was lying on something hard and there was an odor lingering in the vicinity. One she might have smelled before. The zoo, maybe? Yes, that was it. It reminded her of the zoo.

If she got up, she could move away from the odor. That would be a good idea because the odor was getting stronger and her stomach definitely did not like it. Ginny pulled her eyes open.

At first she couldn't make out anything. She had no point of reference, no familiar thing to link the data to. There was a breeze, a small one. It wasn't cool, but it was moving.

She pushed herself up to a semi-sitting position and tried to look around. The whole scene was still fuzzy. Moiré rather, as if there were a screen of watery zig-zags between her and whatever she looked at. Ginny squinted at the brightest bit of color and decided it must be a tree. Green on the top, brown below, and a breeze. She was outside. Somewhere.

It took several more minutes, but eventually Ginny was able to look around and make out shapes. She was sitting in one. It was a box with a concrete floor and sides made of chain link, so she could see out, and the breeze could get in. Her box joined others, more boxes made of chain link, on either side of her, the whole series bolted to a concrete base. Cages, for animals.

There was a padlock on the door. The roof was metal. It shut out the sky and did nothing to make the breeze cooler. What's more, the sun was going down. It was in her eyes. If she tried to look in that direction, all she saw was dazzle.

She lay down again, put her head on her arms, and tried to remember. What was the last thing she had seen? Dupree. Smiling at her. Laughing, actually.

The breeze was freshening. Ginny turned her nose into it and smelled rain. Good. Rain would cool her box off, and she might be able to drink some of it. Her mouth felt dry, and tasted brassy.

Ginny lay in her box and looked at the world on the other side of the chain link. She watched as the sun dipped behind a bank of clouds. Not the white, fluffy cumulonimbus she had seen from Alan's plane. These were dark and heavy and menacing.

Alan!

Ginny sat up suddenly and hit her head. "Ow!" The box was not tall enough for her to sit comfortably. A semi-recline was the best she could do. But she had remembered something.

Alan had been with her. Alan had flown her from Dallas to New Orleans, to do something. Something important. Ginny shook her head, trying to clear it. Where was Alan? Not in her box. In a box of his own?

Ginny reached for her pocket and found it missing. So were her clothes. She wasn't naked, but the white cotton sheath she was wearing was not hers, and it had no pockets. No cellphone. No wallet. Not even tissues. She took a moment to make sure the underclothes were hers, then sank back into the box to try to make sense of it all.

Whoever it was, and Dupree seemed the likely suspect, had taken her talisman, and her hair clip and rubber band. She had undone Ginny's braid and let her hair fall loose. There was a leather thong, very short, holding back the sides. Her shoes were gone, and her socks. That was bad news. Even if she got out, she'd have trouble running away.

Ginny was beginning to feel better. Her vision had cleared and she could move without nausea. Bits of memory were floating into her brain, as yet meaningless, but that would come. She wasn't dead—yet—but she was a prisoner.

Ginny scooted around in her cage, examining her surroundings. To the west, where the sun had disappeared behind the clouds, was the storm and trees and a series of low concrete walls. Between her and those walls were two empty cages, an open space, and a long, spare building. The whole area was surrounded by chain link fence.

To the south, out the back of the line of cages, Ginny could see more concrete and chain link fence, with the glitter of water broken by Cypress trees beyond. Lots of water. To the east was open field, inhabited by cows, all moving away from her, headed for a distant barn and dinner.

In front, on the door side of the cages, was a cleared area, set up for picnickers. Tables and chairs faced away from the water, toward something that looked for all the world like a stage. It was a primitive affair, made of wood, and raised off the ground about three feet. No curtains or sound equipment or footlights. Two metal barrels, large enough for a man to hide in, sat on the ground in front, one at each corner. They were black and charred and looked as if they might have been burned at some point.

Here, at last, was a possible explanation. Dupree's van was parked behind and to the (stage) right of the platform, nose in to a modern building with arrows indicating food, restrooms, and a museum shop. The doors of the van were open and Dupree herself was unloading something with the help of a younger woman. Both were in costume.

There was no question of calling out to them, even if they had been close enough. Better if they thought she was still unconscious. She might need that element of surprise.

Ginny watched as they dragged a heavy wooden frame up onto the stage. They fitted it into a stand of some sort and hauled it upright. It was a rough cross, heavy enough, and large enough, to give the impression of Calvary on the edge of the bayou.

Ginny had been to a number of unorthodox religious ceremonies, but none in which the clergy looked like this. Both women were black and both wore white fabric wound around their waists and falling to their bare feet. The younger one wore white flowers in her hair, artistically positioned to accentuate her elaborate coiffure. Dupree wore a twisted white headdress that made her taller and indicated her greater status. The skin of their arms and chests bore paint in longitudinal white streaks from shoulder to waist, and their faces were drawn in black and white, to resemble bleached skulls. Both wore bands of multicolored beads wrapped around their upper arms and wrists and ankles, and strung around their necks were masses of the same, the beads and paint obscuring their naked breasts. In other circumstances, Ginny might have laughed at the getup. As it was, she began to be just a little bit uneasy.

Beyond the van was more open field and a dirt road. Ginny could see dust rising in the distance, making its way toward them. She watched as dozens of people, many in similar attire, parked along the road, then trudged the rest of the way, taking up positions in the space between the picnic tables and the platform.

The light was fading fast, and Ginny could hear rumbles of thunder in the distance. The sky in her immediate area was still clear, but she was pretty sure she was going to get wet before the night was out. She watched as two men lit the contents of the oil drums and fanned them into flames.

The assembled crowd began to move. At first it was a slow sway, accompanied by vocalizations, and punctuated by setting the feet down firmly, precisely, as if in some primitive dance. Someone brought out a steel drum, tapping out a beat. Others joined with variants of wood and metal percussion instruments. No animal hides, Ginny noticed. There were no kettle drums in the collection.

The pace of the drumming and clacking accelerated, as did the movements of the dancers, the scene lit only by the fires and by the fading light. Several dancers broke ranks and leaped into the center of the circle. The crowd encouraged them, chanting, clapping in unison, still swaying from side to side, moving their feet, moving their bodies. Those in the middle of the space took energy from the crowd and transformed it into thinly-veiled demonstrations of procreation.

Ginny knew just enough about the origin of religion to know there had been a time when people believed they had to show their deities what they wanted—crops or animals or children— and that they were willing to pay for these blessings, sometimes in blood. She also knew that, in Louisiana, Roman Catholicism had been incorporated into the older beliefs of the African immigrants, not replacing them, intertwining with them. Ginny watched in fascination as members of the crowd sent up shrieks and fell to the ground.

Dupree appeared on the stage and the crowd roared. Ginny had not seen where she came from and her sudden appearance had the same effect as that of a magician appearing in a puff of smoke. Dupree danced on stage, in a manner similar to that of her flock, then reached into an earthenware jar, and brought out a brush with white paint on it. Turning to the wooden cross, she painted strange symbols on it, accompanied by what could only be incantations.

The younger woman Ginny had seen helping to set up, now mounted the stage, carrying a large snake draped across her shoulders and wrapped around one arm. She paced to the end of the stage, showing the boa constrictor to the crowd, kissing it, twining it around her arm and waist. The animal was a pale gray, with ovals of darker pigment, outlined first in light yellow, then in black. Ginny could see its tongue flicking in and out, tasting the air. It added to the exotic flavor of the show, for a show it certainly was. It might be that some of the worshippers genuinely believed in the power of spirits, but the Dupree Ginny had met in Dallas did not.

There was a pitcher circulating among the worshippers, with a ceremonial fluid in it. Ginny could see it run down some of their chins, making a dark stain on the white robes. Wine, probably. Drugged, too, almost certainly.

In one way, it was exciting to watch the spectacle. The storm was getting closer, adding to the drama. Ginny gave a passing thought to her situation, trapped in a metal cage with an electrical storm approaching, and hoped the same physics that protected airplanes would work for her. She wondered for a brief moment if Faraday cages had to have all six sides made out of metal and if concrete was a good conductor of electricity, then decided she wasn't going to find out. Someone was coming.

* * *

CHAPTER 38

Thursday Evening
Airborne toward Galveston, TX

Jim was not happy. Not only were they flying south to Galveston, rather than east, toward New Orleans, but he was beginning to get flashes in his mind of a place he was sure he had never seen. They weren't clear images, not like a movie, just bits and pieces, and the glimpses seemed skewed, as if the camera had been dropped on its side.

He had struggled with a hastily packed meal and declined the offer of scotch, wanting a clear head for whatever he might have to face this night. He told himself—again—that traditional Second Sight didn't happen in real time and wasn't a window into Ginny's mind and usually foretold a death. Which didn't help. What's more, he couldn't tell if the images in his mind were his—something he'd seen in a movie—or hers, something seen through her eyes. There was lightning, or was it flames? And rain, just like the rain here. And a sense of foreboding.

His cellphone went off and he took it out to look at the text message. They would be unable to talk while in the helicopters, but the phones should still work. The helos were equipped with Internet access.

Where are you? Angus asking.

Slightly more than halfway to Galveston. Why?

Coast Guard says the weather is looking bad and they may have to cancel.

Jim felt his chest constrict. *When will they decide?*

After you get there. I'll keep you informed.

Thanks.

Jim put the phone away, then buried his head in his hands. The helmet prevented reaching his throbbing temples. Aspirin, maybe, as soon as they landed.

* * *

Thursday Evening
Paradis, LA

The two men who hauled Ginny out of the cage marched her up onto the platform. They forced her to stand with her back to the wooden cross, facing the dancers, and bound her hands with leather strips, one to each limb of the crossbar. They then retired, rejoining the watchers on the ground below, leaving Ginny to try to wriggle out of the trap.

Two things in particular caught her attention. The first was that the younger woman was arguing with Dupree. Ginny could hear part of the conversation. The younger was complaining that it was her role to be the woman tied to the cross. She had earned that right, and she didn't appreciate being replaced, especially not without warning. Ginny turned her head in time to see the girl reach for the dagger Dupree was holding. What Dupree said, Ginny could not hear, but she saw what happened when the dagger came down, cutting a long gash in the younger woman's arm. She screamed, then disappeared, leaving Ginny with a strong impression that bleeding hadn't been part of the script.

The second thing she noticed was the thunder, much closer

and louder. She knew thunder meant lightning and that she was now standing on an elevated stage in an open field. The last gleams of the setting sun, pouring through the gap between earth and sky, stabbed across the field showing her the faces of the watchers, some of them caught up in the throes of the dance, some motionless, some glancing uneasily at the approaching storm.

Ginny turned her attention to the cords securing her wrists. She knew leather could be stretched, wet leather more easily than dry, and both could be made to yield, sometimes torn. She concentrated on moving one of the tethers toward the end of the crossbar, then pulling down to try to give her thumb room to slip inside the loop. But the knots held. She took a breath and tried to think.

Dupree was circling her, muttering, then crying out in a language Ginny could not identify. The knife was in her right hand, a thick staff in the other. Dupree raised the staff to the sky, then brought it down and planted it in front of the cross. Ginny found herself eye to eye with the heavily carved image on the head of the cane. It was worth looking at.

At the top of the image was a tall, cylindrical hat that reminded Ginny of a fez without the tassel. It was about three inches in diameter, six or seven inches high, painted bright red, and decorated with embroidered bands. It sat on the head of an elongated, stylized skull, painted white, except for the eyes and nostrils, which were hollow pools of pitch. The cheeks and chin were rounded, covering the entire circumference of the staff. Between the nostrils and the chin was a full set of skeletal teeth, discolored with age, the lower jaw ever so slightly parted from the upper. The skull had an excess of personality, and Ginny would not have been surprised if it had spoken to her.

Dupree whirled, turning her back on Ginny, and facing the audience. She raised her arms again and delivered a demand to the ether. A sudden wind crossed the stage, whipping at Ginny's hair, and it was tempting to believe Dupree had conjured it. The faces on the watchers seemed to confirm their belief in an unseen power, whatever its source.

Ginny looked around, searching for a way to escape. She might be able to trip Dupree, but she could see no advantage in it. Better if she could strike at the woman's face, which she could do if she could lift her pillory from its mooring.

The pole to which she was tied had been inserted into a groove cut in the stage, buttressed by a heavy block of wood to keep it from swaying. Ginny lifted first one, then the other of her feet onto the block. This resulted in an uncomfortable crouch, but allowed her to shift her back into position. She bent her knees, and tried to lift the cross up out of its casing. It proved immovable, far too heavy for her, even with the additional leverage.

Dupree seemed to be working up to a climax. She shrieked at the gathering clouds, then turned to face Ginny and said, this time in English, "Curiosity killed the cat, my dear. Mustn't poke your nose in where it's not wanted." She gave tongue in fierce ululation, thrusting the voodoo staff toward the sky, the knife flashing in the firelight as she raised her hand.

Ginny cringed, curling into as much of a fetal position as she could manage, trying to protect her heart and other vital organs. In the split second before the blow fell, Ginny scolded herself. This was it. She was going to die and Jim was going to be furious. She felt a wave of remorse. If only she had realized what she was risking! If only there were some way to escape, to get a second chance. She'd be the wife he wanted. She'd be docile and biddable and give up anything to please him. If only—

The lightning seared her eyes even through the closed lids. She opened them to see Dupree, a hideous rictus on her face, falling backward off the stage as the thunder arrived, so loud it hurt. She could see the worshippers' eyes, huge and terrified, and their open mouths, but could not hear their screams through the ringing in her ears.

The audience was running, scattering. It was almost an anticlimax when the heavens opened up and buckets of water fell from the sky. The crowd ran from the picnic area, past the stage, headed for their cars. No one came to release her.

Ginny was soaked to the skin in seconds. Another bolt of lightning, far too near for safety, galvanized her. She struggled with every ounce of her being, forcing the wetted leather to soften and yield. She managed to pull her right hand free, then her left, then jumped down off the wooden block.

Ginny knew about lightning safety. With Dupree and her voodoo stick lying dead on the ground, the tallest object in the area was now that cross. If it got hit, the stage and anyone hiding under it would be fried. Ginny hurried down the steps and turned right.

She was impressed and, if truth be told, alarmed by the ferocity of the storm. She could hardly see her hand in front of her face. The two fire drums had gone out. The only light still remaining was provided by the electrical storm. When the flashes came, they showed a world in chaos, rain falling sideways, debris flying through the air.

Dupree's van was parked just behind the stage. If Ginny could get into it, she would be safe. She slithered toward the dim white shape, found it, felt her way forward to the door handles, and tried them all. Locked tight. The key would be on Dupree and, in this modern age, the remote would be electrical, which meant shorted out. There might be an old-fashioned metal key, but that would mean searching Dupree's body. She could do that later, after the storm passed. Ginny sucked in a breath, and went to Plan B.

The visitor's center, too, was locked up tight. Ginny looked for a way to break down a door or smash in a window. There were trees surrounding the visitor's center, no doubt for the aesthetic effect. Some had already lost limbs to the violent wind. Others swayed dramatically, creaking, then splintering, sending a hail of leaves and debris to the ground. Ginny picked up a stout limb and began pounding at the glass door. She almost didn't hear the crack, but instinct saved her. Ginny looked up in time to see a tall tree, backlit by the sky, leaning toward her, growing larger. She dropped her stick and ran sideways, just missing being pinned under the tree as it smashed through the roof of the visitor's center, bringing down the electrical wires with it.

The wrecked visitors' center no longer offered shelter from either the rain or the wind, and the wires sparked and hissed. Ginny knew better than to get close enough to be caught in the electrical circuit. She looked for another refuge.

The building she'd seen earlier, across the field to the west, had gutters and wires on the outside, maybe plumbing as well, and no trees near enough to pose a danger. It would be grounded, and a safe place to wait out the storm. She headed toward it, fighting her way into the wind. The rain stung like fire ants.

Ginny had never been outside during a storm of this magnitude before. The lightning fell around her in nerve-shattering proximity. One bolt hit the trees behind the picnic tables, splitting an old magnolia into three pieces which crashed to the ground in flames. Another hit the chain link fence in front of her, forcing her to hide her eyes. When Ginny felt the hair on her arms rise, she crouched down, heels up, legs pressed together, in the hope that the lightning would find a better target. In between, she ran, head down, bent double. It was inevitable that she would stumble and fall.

What tripped her was the chain link fence, now lying on the ground. That was good. It meant she didn't have to climb it. She rose and drove onward only to fall again, this time into a pit or gulley of some sort.

Ginny picked herself up and, in the next flash of light, examined the wall down which she had tumbled. It was made of concrete, sloped, and rose two feet above her head. There were no handholds and sheets of water were flowing down it. She could not climb out that way.

Her position, at the bottom of this trench, meant she was momentarily out of the wind. It howled over her head and gusts invaded the space, to remind her of its power, but still, it was a comfort not to be fighting for every step.

She turned her back to the wall, and waited for the next flash of lightning. When it came, it showed her a half dozen alligators, each as long as she was tall, twenty feet from where she stood.

Ginny's throat closed. She was not given to panic, but it seemed appropriate at the moment. Those were man eaters. Apex predators. Known to kill and eat humans. And she was trespassing on their turf.

Ginny felt her head swim, but decided she needed to hold still more than she needed to sit down. It was wet down there, anyway, and the water was rising. Ginny blinked. A pen for reptiles would need a drain as well as a constant source of fresh water. If she could block the drain, the rain might fill the pit. She could float on the rising tide and, when she got high enough, she could climb out.

Moving slowly, her eyes on the gators, she stripped off the sodden white shift and followed the flow of water to the shortest (and steepest) wall. The drain was there, too small for her to fit through and covered with a steel grille, covered also with debris—leaves and small branches, and human trash the wind had brought in. She threaded her shift through the bars of the grille, mostly by touch, damming the outlet further, then leaned back against the wall and waited.

The gators had not moved. Perhaps that was how they dealt with storms, just waited them out. She kept an eye on the other end of the pen as the water rose.

It came up quickly, reaching her waist in less than fifteen minutes. She was floating in another ten. She needed to be very still, she knew. She had read somewhere that hands and feet treading water would look like fish. She could lose one that way.

In the intermittent light, Ginny had trouble keeping track of the animals. She found herself clinging to the edge of the pit, then trying to hoist herself out, then struggling for a foot hold. To her horror, her bare foot came down on scales. She scrambled out, using the alligator as a step stool, rolled over in the grass, thrust herself to her feet, and ran. Alligators can run, too, faster than the average woman. She hoped this one wasn't hungry.

Ginny made it to the building on the western perimeter of the complex without further incident, and searched for a way in. As she rounded the back edge, she found it was really just a long shed, one whole side open. She slipped around the corner, out of the rain for the first time since the storm had broken.

She stood for a few minutes, shivering in the cold wind, her wet hair plastered to her skin, and reminded herself that her troubles weren't over yet. She still had to find a way back to New Orleans. But with Dupree dead, the lightning no longer a problem, and the rain on the roof instead of her head, she took heart. Someone must have been listening. She'd gotten her second chance.

* * *

Chapter 39

Thursday Evening
New Orleans, LA

It was one for the record books. The storm front arrived packing winds of up to 70 mph, just under Category One hurricane level. It was not, however, circulating. These were straight line winds, as damaging as a hurricane, but without the associated storm surge.

The New Orleans Lakefront Airport was ready. They had all the necessary protocols in place to shelter small aircraft caught by violent weather. Alan paid the rental on hanger space, stowed his Cessna, and hurried into the terminal just as the front began to lick the edges of Lake Pontchartrain. He grabbed a burger on his way to the Ground Transportation kiosk. Several minutes of negotiation with the agent assured him that nothing would be running—air, rail, or ground—until the brunt of the storm had passed. After which, he would be able to get a taxi to the police station and see what they were doing to find Ginny. He retired with his meal, ate it, then called home.

"Alan? Alan! Are you all right?" Caroline's voice had a quaver in it.

"I'm fine. I'm in the airport terminal waiting for the storm to lift."

"I let your parents know where you are. You should

˜ 325 ˜

probably call your mom."

Alan sighed, then nodded. "I'll do that. What else is going on?"

"Jim and Reggie are flying to New Orleans. They've got some kind of tracking device they think they can use to locate Ginny."

"Tracking device? Are they there? Can I talk to them?"

"They left over an hour ago."

"Oh. Well, all right, I don't need the details. Just tell me what they're planning."

Alan heard Caroline take a breath. "Okay. I was listening, but I'm not sure I understood everything. Reggie put some kind of tag on Ginny earlier this week. It works like a price tag at the store. You can scan it and it will give you information about the item it's attached to."

Alan nodded into the phone. "Okay. They want to scan for the tag. Got that much."

"The problem is the tag doesn't have much range. I think I heard Reggie say five miles, but I could be wrong. In any case, they have to get close before they can look for the tag."

Alan frowned. "That sounds like you need to know where to look before you can find something."

"Well, that's how it works at the store. You pick something up off the shelf and get it scanned with one of those handheld things, or at the counter, or as you exit, and the machine does all the work."

"But no good for searching half the state of Louisiana."

"I'm afraid not."

"Did they say how they were going to decide where to look?"

"Not a word. They just took off."

Alan hesitated. "Was Jim mad?"

Caroline's voice sounded small. "Yes, and scared."

Alan's brow furrowed. So was he. "Listen, sweetheart. It's going to be all right. We're going to find her and I'm going to get that DNA sample and we're going to put Dupree behind bars. Is Himself there? Can I speak to him?"

Alan heard the phone being passed to the laird.

"Aye, lad? Are ye all right?"

"Yes, sir, but I have a favor to ask."

"Wha' is it?"

"Is there a way I can talk to Jim directly? I think I may be able to help, but we need to coordinate our efforts."

"Text messages are gettin' through. Ye can try that."

"Thank you."

"Ye'll let me know wha' yer planning, aye?"

"Yes sir."

"All right, here's yer girl."

Caroline's voice. "Me, too, please. I want to know what's going on."

Alan smiled into the phone. "Only if you promise not to hop a plane to New Orleans."

"You're a hard man to please, but all right."

"I'll call you again as soon as there's news. Bye."

Alan hung up and considered the task before him. He was a stranger to the area, but surrounded by people who were not. It wouldn't hurt to ask questions while he waited. He tossed his trash in the receptacle, put on a smile, and went to go interrogate the local vendors.

A dozen conversations later, he had a list of places the locals associated with Mama Dupree. He had no idea whether he'd be able to use any of this information, but it had been better than sitting alone, fretting.

He was standing at the door, watching the rain cascade off the roof, when he was approached by an old man.

"Buy me a coffee?" he asked. Alan looked him over, noting

his torn cloths and lack of dental hygiene, then nodded. He added a sandwich and a second coffee, then paid the bill, intending to go back to the taxi stand to wait for the weather to break.

"Sit wi' me."

Alan looked at the unabated storm, then shrugged to himself and sat.

"Good coffee. Thank ye."

"You're welcome."

"I hear'd you were lookin' fer Mama Dupree," the man said.

Alan nodded.

"Whatchu want from her?" The old man stuffed half the sandwich in his mouth and chewed industriously.

Alan took a moment to decide what to say. "I'm looking for a friend who might be with her."

"She in town for th' show?" The old man finished the sandwich, then picked up the coffee, slurping, and smacking his lips over the meal.

"Maybe." Alan smiled at his new friend. "Would you like some more?"

"Chips would be mighty nice right now."

Alan fetched a bag of potato chips and watched the old man tear into the package. He paused between bites. "'Cause if she's in town for th' show, she ortter be getting' home 'bout now." He gestured toward the door with his head. "'Cause o' th' rain."

Alan folded his arms casually on the table, and smiled. "Tell me about the show."

"Might be th' storm missed 'em. I wouldn't know."

"Is the show a regular feature, on a schedule?"

"Heck, yeah. For th' tourists. They lov' that woman and her snake." He broke into a cackle. "When ye go to New Orleens, you gots to see Mama Dupree and her snake."

Alan took a careful breath. "Where would I go to see the show?"

"Ye gots to go to Paradis."

At first Alan thought he'd misheard the man, then, possibly, that you had to die to see Mama Dupree, but it turned out there was a town south and west of New Orleans, about forty-five minutes away, called Paradis.

"Thas whe' th gator farm is."

Alan drew in a cautious breath. "Mama Dupree gives shows at the gator farm?"

"Yep."

"And she had a show scheduled for tonight?"

"Yep. Private show, I hear'd. Sometimes, ye have to be from New Orleens. But you gotta see it 'for ye leave town."

Alan nodded. "I'll do that." He slipped a couple of dollars across the table. "For dessert, when you're ready."

Alan plied the old man with a third cup of coffee, but didn't learn anything more. He made his call home to his parents, to let them know he was safe, then went back to his vigil, watching the rain slow, then taper off. The minute it let up, Alan took the first taxi he could grab and headed for the New Orleans Police District Three Station, which covered the fairgrounds, and the area where Dupree's shop was located. The normally ten minute ride took thirty.

There was debris on the road, large enough to force the driver to stop and move it out of the way. Some sections were flooded. Traffic and street lights were out. They encountered two fender-benders, but no one was hurt and those involved had already notified the police.

Alan paid off the cab, tipped the driver handsomely, and hurried into the police building. He was stopped at the reception desk.

"I'd like to speak to someone about a missing person."

"Name?"

"Ginny Forbes."

The woman behind the counter looked up, then lifted an eyebrow. "That's your name?"

Alan shook his head impatiently. "No, that's the name of the person who's missing."

The woman looked back down at her form. "Your name?"

Alan took a breath, carefully pronounced it, then spelled his name for her.

"Alan Christie." The woman put down her pen and reached for a stack of notes. She thumbed through them slowly, then nodded. "You're to report to Detective Leroux. I'll let him know you've arrived."

Alan blinked. "Detective Leroux? Are you sure? I haven't filled in the missing person report yet." He hadn't even been able to get through on the telephone.

She looked up at him, clearly not amused. "I'm sure."

A door opened, with the sound of a lock releasing, then snapping back into place.

"Mr. Christie?"

Alan turned to look at the man who had emerged from the back of the station.

"Yes."

"I'm Giles Leroux. I've been expecting you." He held out his hand and Alan took it.

"I'm sorry. I'm a bit confused. What's going on?"

Detective Leroux gestured toward the door through which he had come, now open again to admit the pair of them. "You're looking for Miss Forbes, right?"

Alan nodded.

"I had orders to wait until you got here, then pop you in a car, and take you to the Voodoo shop."

Alan followed him down a long hall flanked by small offices

into a large open area filled with desks. Leroux went to one, opened a drawer, retrieved his weapon, holstered it, grabbed a jacket off the back of his chair, and indicated they were leaving. "Lochlan Russell called. You know him?"

Alan shook his head.

"I thought all you Scots stuck together."

"We do. I'm from Dallas."

"Oh. Well, Russell, he's someone who doesn't take 'no' for an answer. He suggested we go look at the Voodoo shop and he suggested we take you along. Said you'd be here as soon as the rain let up. And he was right."

Leroux held the passenger side door of an unmarked car open. Once both of them were in place, seatbelts on and the car in motion, he looked over at Alan. "Now, suppose you tell me why I'm taking you along on what is officially an investigation into a missing woman."

"Because I'm the reason she's missing."

Leroux glanced at Alan, then back at the roadway. They were having the same problems the cab driver had had, plus downed power lines. "You want to share?"

Alan took a breath, then told the detective everything he knew about the dead woman in Dallas, the connection to New Orleans, and the failed attempt to provide the Dallas police with evidence enough to obtain a search warrant. At the end of it Leroux nodded.

"Nothing wrong with the plan."

"Except she didn't come back."

"Yeah, except for that. You stay in the car until I tell you to come in." Leroux did not wait for Alan's promise, just put the car in park, and slid out from behind the wheel.

There were police squad cars already on the scene. Leroux consulted with them, then knocked, rang the bell, and called to the occupant, with no response. Two men stepped up to the door, carrying something heavy. Leroux nodded and they proceeded to break into the shop.

Alan watched as the police entered, moving in darkness, using flashlights. They were inside for only five minutes before the interior lights sprang on and Leroux appeared in the doorway, motioning to Alan to come in. Alan lost no time.

"We've found something." Leroux motioned for Alan to follow him. "Can you identify these?"

Alan looked at the clothes Ginny had worn in the airplane, at her jewelry in a neat pile on top of the garments, at her purse, and her cellphone, laid out by the police to show to him. He nodded. "All of these belong to Ginny Forbes." He felt his throat tighten. Was it *belong* or *belonged*?

Leroux nodded. "Thank you."

"May I look around?" Alan asked.

Leroux hesitated for a moment, then nodded. "Just don't touch anything."

Alan slipped away from the police, making his way through the shop, then up a back stairs to the living quarters. Here he found what he was looking for. The first was a tiny kitchen, the shelves complete with the plastic bags everyone uses for transporting food from place to place. He helped himself to one. The second stop was the bathroom where he found one toothbrush in a cup.

Alan inverted the baggie over his hand and grasped the toothbrush, then turned the bag right side out and sealed it. He'd seen that done on some cop show somewhere along the line and hoped it had protected the DNA. He stowed his prize in an inner pocket of his jacket, and made his way back downstairs, trying to look innocent.

"Where've you been?" Leroux asked him.

"Upstairs. She must live above the shop."

Leroux nodded. "We've got enough evidence to presume a

kidnapping. Even if she changed clothes for some reason, no woman I know would voluntarily leave her purse *and* her cellphone behind. No innocent woman. Let's get back to the station."

Alan followed him out to the car, thinking hard. Now that he had the evidence he'd come for, he could turn his full attention to Ginny. Was there anything he could do to help in the search?

The storm appeared to be over, except for some lingering light rain. It was time he checked on his little Cessna and called Dallas, something he didn't want to do within earshot of the police.

"Can you drop me at the airfield?"

Leroux glanced over at him.

Alan shrugged. "If my plane is undamaged, I can take it up and look around. I might be able to spot something from the air."

Leroux nodded. "That's not a bad idea. I can send someone with you, someone familiar with the territory."

Alan saw the sense in that and nodded. He'd have to stow his stolen evidence in the plane before the policeman got in, but he could do that. He felt the blood rise in his cheeks and was glad the night was dark. He was unaccustomed to being on the wrong side of the law.

"Have him meet me at the Lakefront terminal as soon as he can get here. I may need his help to talk them into letting me go up again."

Leroux nodded. "I'll make some calls."

* * *

<h1 style="text-align:center">Chapter 40</h1>

Thursday Night
Laird's Residence, Brochaber

Angus Mackenzie watched as Detective Tran put down her phone. Their eyes met over the debris littering the kitchen table.

They were the only people left at Brochaber. Sinia Forbes had taken her son and his family home to her house to be fed and soothed. Caroline had gone to stay with her parents for the night, though she was unlikely to get much sleep. The rest were scattered over the Louisiana countryside.

"There is news, of a sort," Detective Tran said.

"Oh, aye?" Angus knew how to read people, even this inscrutable Asian woman. The news was not all bad, not yet.

"She has not been admitted to any hospital or clinic within a one hundred and fifty mile radius of New Orleans. Nor have any of the Parishes reported a Jane Doe of her description either alive or dead."

Angus nodded. Good to know.

"The weather has disrupted power and communications for half the residents in that same geographic area. The repairmen are already working on restoring those services, but the streets are almost impassable because of debris and flooding. The New Orleans police assure us they will do what they can, but they have other emergencies to address in addition to ours."

She had her notebook out on the table in front of her and consulted it now. "There was a possible sighting."

Angus perked up his ears.

"A woman, a known associate of Ms. Dupree's, was treated in the University Medical Center emergency department this evening, for a knife wound."

Angus's brows furrowed. *Knives, was it?* Tran lifted her eyes to his and held his gaze as she spoke.

"Officer Michel, our contact here, has a sister who is employed in the New Orleans Police force. She is not a detective herself, but she is acquainted with some of them. She relayed his request to the detective assigned to Ms. Dupree. That woman, Angelique Bourgeois, who has been undercover for a year and a half, lives in the apartment next door to the known associate." Tran's eyes narrowed.

"Ms. Dupree has a long history of shady practices, but has managed to evade prosecution, so far. Detective Bourgeois is of the opinion that money may be changing hands under the table. In addition, Ms. Dupree is a source of revenue for the city. She is well known for her voodoo performances and is considered a tourist attraction. Her business records appear to be in order."

"And Ginny?" Angus asked.

Detective Tran nodded. "Ms. Dupree had a show scheduled for this evening. The known associate, her assistant and protégé, Tasia Greer, was present during the set up. She was injured and left the location to seek help."

"A remote location was it?"

"Remote enough to require her to leave it to reach competent medical care."

Angus's eyebrows twitched. "Wha' is it yer no telling me?"

Detective Tran smiled at him. "She did not seek medical

help immediately. She went home."

"Did she noo?"

According to the report, she encountered difficulty on the roadways. She gave up and went to her apartment, which was without power, but not under water."

Angus nodded. "Go on."

"When Detective Bourgeois heard the apartment door next to hers open and shut, she decided to investigate. It is her testimony that she was unaware of the event planned for this evening. She reports that some are described as private and she had not received an invitation. She had arrived at her apartment this afternoon to find Ms. Greer was not at home. This is not unusual and was no cause for immediate alarm. Given the excuse of the power outage, however, she proceeded to visit her neighbor and offer help."

"Ah-um."

"She found Ms. Greer shivering in the bathroom, bleeding from the knife wound, and trying to put a bandage on it herself. She assisted in staunching the bleeding, examined the wound with a flashlight, and pronounced Ms. Greer in need of stitches. Under protest, she bundled the young woman into the car and drove her to the hospital." Tran paused for a moment and consulted her notes again.

"Ms. Greer was unable to account for her injury satisfactorily. She changed her story twice, saying first she had been working in a friend's yard and caught her arm on a torn metal fence, then that she had fallen on a piece of broken glass. Neither explanation aligned with the actual injury. After being confronted with the facts, she admitted to having been involved with a drug deal that had gone bad when the storm hit. She had tried to grab her bag and run, but had been persuaded to abandon both the drugs and the money and escape with her life."

Detective Tran sighed. "That story fit with the evidence, but it is still not the truth."

"How do ye ken?"

"Ms. Greer was still wearing traces of the performance makeup and she had dropped her costume onto the floor of the bathroom. Detective Bourgeois was able to slip into the apartment while Ms. Greer was being questioned by the drug interdiction team. Detective Bourgeois found a single long red hair on the costume."

Angus caught his breath. "Did she say aught aboot th' lass wi' th' long red hair?"

Tran shook her head. "Ms. Greer denied any knowledge and clammed up when confronted with the evidence. She is currently being detained, awaiting her lawyer, and no doubt cooking up a story to cover the facts."

Angus sat back in his chair, thinking furiously. It was possible there were other women with long red hair in the New Orleans area, but the behavior of the witness implied this was the one they were looking for.

"The woman mus' tell us where she got th' wound and under wha' conditions she encountered Ginny."

Detective Tran nodded. "I agree. I have relayed that request to the New Orleans authorities." She took a deep breath. "I am afraid, however, that they do not attach the same amount of urgency to the request as we do."

Angus nodded, then leaned forward and picked up his phone.

"Weel, e'en if they do not, I ken someone who will."

* * *

Thursday Night
Airborne toward New Orleans, LA

Jim was suffering. They'd been allowed to board the Coast Guard Search and Rescue helicopter and were flying east at a steady 140 nautical miles per hour. They had been airborne for an hour and each passing moment Jim's hopes fell further.

He'd been seeing mostly darkness in his mind's eye, with flashes of light that might have been lightning, or might indicate a detached retina. In addition to the darkness, and contrary to his experience with the Austin incident, he'd felt his skin grow cold and wet. There was fear, too, though less of that than a focus on escape.

He had conjured up a dozen images of things Ginny might need to escape from, none more disturbing than a skeletal, knife-wielding fiend. But whether the images were visions, or his own imagination, he could not tell.

After the Austin trip, he'd spent some time researching remote viewing and other instances of parapsychic ability. There was a lot of anecdotal information, much of it linked to the Second Sight. All had failed the close scrutiny of properly designed double-blind experimentation.

He tried to remember what his grandmother had told him about the Sight and failed. He'd been very young, and not interested in spooky things. Also, he had maintained a skepticism that matched his opinion of himself as a scientist. Hubris, as it turned out. He should have listened better.

Reggie had been trying to distract him, with semaphore instructions to follow while he calibrated the tracking device against the tag on Jim's leg. They were chasing the storm, coming in along its southern and trailing edge, and that, apparently, was not really the best scenario for Reggie's machine. There was a fair amount of turbulence. When they actually reached their destination, the device might not work at all.

And where were they heading, anyway? How were they to find Ginny? How to know even where to look? His phone went off and he glanced down at the text message from his grandfather. He read it and almost jumped out of his harness.

Ginny may have been seen earlier this evening by a woman now in police custody. She is being questioned.

The New Orleans police had located a suspect. Jim's fingers flew across the screen.

Was it Dupree?

The reply was almost immediate.

Her assistant.

Jim's brow furrowed. Dupree had an assistant?

The police are trying to get a warrant to find out where her car was this evening.

How long will that take?

They have to find and convince a judge, then take the GPS out of the car and analyze it. Two hours, maybe more.

Tell them to hurry.

I will, lad.

Jim closed the phone and tried to connect the existence of an assistant to what he knew of Dupree. If she was a con artist, an assistant could work both ways. Someone, like a magician's assistant, who knew all the tricks, could stand in, if one was sick. That same someone could turn state's evidence, if the game became too dangerous. But if Dupree was a murderer, an assistant might be too dangerous a luxury.

Jim checked his watch. Forty-five minutes out, and nothing to do but worry. He settled down to make a good job of it.

* * *

CHAPTER 41

Thursday Night
Paradis, LA

The rain was still hammering the earth, the wind threatening to rip the metal roof off the shed, the lightning slashing the sky and striking, first here, then there, but the intervals were beginning to lengthen between the lighting and the thunder, and the darkness was less intense. The storm was moving off.

Ginny suddenly realized she was thirsty. *Water, water, everywhere, and not a drop to drink.* Brains are funny things. The line floated up to her unbidden. And it wasn't even true. Unlike the *Ancient Mariner*, Ginny had pure, fresh, clean water to drink. All she had to do was collect some.

She turned her back on the storm and waited for illumination. In the next flash of lightning, she saw what she wanted, a metal bucket sitting on the floor of her shelter. She felt her way over to it, lifted it, turned it over, knocked it against the wall to remove anything that might be lurking inside, explored the bottom to see if it had holes, rinsed it in the water pouring off the roof, then set it outside. The bucket was half full in a matter of minutes. Ginny put it to her lips, closed her mind to the infection risk and drank deeply.

That done (and it took her several minutes to quench her thirst), Ginny realized she had other issues. For one, she was cold. The air was saturated, which meant the wind could do nothing more than suck the heat from her body. It could not dry her off. She explored further and found several pairs of rubber boots, one small enough to fit her, but nothing to wrap up in, not even a horse blanket. She emptied the boots the way she had the bucket (not wanting to share the space with insects or other wildlife), then put them on. At least her feet would be warm.

She sat down on the floor, out of the direct wind, and pulled her legs up, trying to conserve as much heat as possible. She would have to wait. That was the bad news. The good news was that none of these spring storms ever lasted very long. She would be able to try for the road again in an hour. In the meantime, she could think.

Dupree hadn't confessed to murdering Jamieson. She had implied she had secrets. Okay. Privacy was supposed to be a basic freedom in the U.S.

But Dupree had decided to kill Ginny, to protect her privacy. That was *not* considered an appropriate response to a snoop. One was supposed to call the police.

So Dupree's secrets were such that she didn't want the police involved. That still covered a whole lot of less-than-lethal ground. Cheating on taxes, illegal immigrants, forgery even. The natural conclusion was that whatever Dupree had been mixed up in, it killed people.

Drugs sprang to mind, and Dupree dabbled in potions, so maybe that was it. Ginny frowned, trying to remember exactly what Dupree had told her when she visited the woman's tent at the Games. She was selling witchcraft on that occasion, but "natural" remedies as well. She was a professional toxicologist—that was it! That meant she understood drugs, which explained how she could dart Ginny with a tranquilizer that lasted just long enough to get her here (wherever here was) from her shop in New Orleans, without killing her.

Ginny sucked in a deep breath. Without killing her outright, because Dupree's plan was to kill her, onstage, in front of witnesses. That knife had been no joke.

Ginny's brow wrinkled. The younger woman, the assistant, hadn't expected that. She had reached for the knife, trying to take it away from Dupree, and been cut, and it had shocked and terrified her. So she hadn't known Dupree's plan. Nor had the watchers. Some of them had looked confused, some uneasy at the change in the ceremony.

Ginny ran her hands up and down her bare arms and shivered, and not from the cold. Why had none of the witnesses come to her aid? Not one of them had tried to free her. Nor, she was pretty sure, had they taken Dupree away with them. Guilty consciences notwithstanding, surely one of them had enough humanity to check on their fallen leader? Perhaps they were too afraid of her. That might explain it.

Or—and here was a thought—perhaps they were afraid they'd be struck by lightning, too. If you had taken part in a questionable assembly and you knew yourself to be on shaky ground, you wouldn't *have* to believe in Divine Retribution. It was an electrical storm, after all. But you might want to play it safe, and not chance any further bolts from the heavens.

Whether they believed or not, the insiders would keep their mouths shut. Dupree was dead and Ginny was an outsider. Better if the weather and the alligators removed the evidence. There would probably be more candles than usual lit in Roman Catholic churches this week.

Ginny had a clear understanding of human nature. She worked in an industry where every stranger she came into contact with was frightened or in pain or worried sick, sometimes all three. It was a lot to ask of them to behave in a civilized manner under those circumstances. The Good

Samaritan was an enduring story specifically because it wasn't the norm.

Which meant it was unlikely that any of the people present at tonight's event would run to the authorities. She couldn't just sit tight and wait to be rescued. She would have to see what she could do about rescuing herself.

* * *

Thursday Night
Lakefront Airport, New Orleans, LA

The storm had blown through New Orleans, most of it, and was headed east. There were still pockets of rain and occasional gusts, but there were also places where Alan could see stars between the clouds. He'd gotten clearance to fly recognizance using Instrument Flight Rules and with the restriction of having a police spotter in the plane with him, so he could concentrate on the flying. He was working his way through the pre-flight checklist.

He'd paid for twenty-four hours of hangar protection and intended to bring Terri back to this airport before setting off for Dallas in the morning, so that was all right. The attendant had topped off his fuel and Alan had checked the gauges, all correct. He had gotten the GPS coordinates for Paradis from the MSY Tower computer, with additional warnings about restricted and congested airspace. And weather, of course. He looked up as a man approached from the terminal side.

"They said I would find you here."

"Detective Leroux!" Alan tried not to look at the bag that held Dupree's toothbrush. "Just finishing up here. What can I do for you?"

"I'm going with you."

Alan blinked, then smiled. "Glad to have you. You won't mind if I concentrate on getting the rest of this done?" He reached in and tossed the bag into the back. "You can sit up front, with me."

"Don't let me interrupt you."

Detective Leroux spent the fifteen minutes it took Alan to finish his prep inspecting the plane inside and out, running a hand over the skin, peering at the instrument panel, and making Alan wish the toothbrush was back in its cup at the voodoo shop.

When all was ready, Alan taxied out to the beginning of runway 27, headed due west and into the remaining wind, communicating with both the ground control at Lakefront and the Air Traffic Control Tower at Louis Armstrong International airport. This flight would be entirely Instrument Rules. No sightseeing this time.

"You ready?" he asked Detective Leroux.

Leroux took a firm grip on the seat harness and nodded. "Let's go."

It took them twenty more minutes to get airborne, then fifteen to circle clear of the incoming traffic, Alan talking to the tower the whole time.

Leroux was looking out the window. "Good thing we've got GPS. The lights are out all over the city. Can't tell a thing." He looked over at Alan. "Where are we headed?"

"We're playing a hunch." Alan explained about the old man he'd talked to.

Leroux nodded. "I know the spot. Take my boy scout troop out there every year." His cellphone pinged and he glanced at it. "Well, what do you know? Your hunch seems to be right on the money."

Alan looked over. "Oh?"

Leroux nodded. "The girl with the knife wound. Her car was at the farm this evening." He met Alan's gaze. "You knew about her?"

Alan nodded. When he'd checked in an hour ago, he'd spoken first to Caroline, then to Himself, then to Jim. They were all converging on Paradis on the basis of that one strand of red hair.

Leroux studied him for a moment. "I'm not going to ask you how Lachlan Russell managed to get that warrant bumped to the head of the line, or how he got the analysis done with the power out. What I am going to ask you is, if this turns out to be a crime scene, are you going to be able to hold it together?"

Alan turned back to his instrument panel and thought about it. From a thousand feet up, it was unlikely he would see anything disturbing, but if they found Ginny's body, he was going to feel awfully bad about it.

"I can fly you over the site and fly you back to New Orleans and I won't make any mistakes because of what you may find. Will that do?"

"Good enough." Leroux reached into the bag he'd brought and pulled out a large pair of binoculars. "You just stay on course. I'll let you know if there's anything we need to get closer to."

Alan did exactly that, following the north-south groove with u-turns at the bottom and top of the search pattern as they got closer to the town of Paradis. Here, too, the lights were out.

Alan peered out his window. He could see small spots of light that looked as if they were moving.

Leroux nodded. "Boats on the canal." He had his eyes to the binoculars.

"Turning north," Alan said. He frowned. "What is that?"

Leroux turned his binoculars in the other direction. "Smoke."

"Hell!" Alan contacted the tower and reported the smoke cloud, getting permission to drop below it (but no lower than 800 feet), to climb above it (but no higher than 15,000 feet), or to fly through it, which he did not want to do because of the potential for engine damage.

He negotiated a modified search pattern and dropped below the obstruction.

"I see the problem now," Leroux said. "The swamp is burning."

Alan looked over at him, puzzled. "How can a swamp burn?"

"The rotting vegetable matter lays down a layer of what amounts to peat. Lightning strikes and it starts a fire. Happens all the time. We usually just let them burn themselves out. It's good for the soil and good for the underbrush."

Alan turned his eyes back to the window. "What's that?" He pointed.

Leroux leaned forward, his eyes to the binoculars. "That is what we came to see. The farm."

"Well," Alan said, "I can make two passes over it before I have to turn to stay out of the smoke."

"Just don't hit anything," Leroux replied.

Alan had reduced his airspeed with the other modifications to his search pattern, to bring him closer to the ground. Terri was no crop duster and he had no wish to lose his license, but he wanted to see the farm, if he could.

"Got it!" Leroux said. He continued to study the ground with the binoculars.

Alan could see nothing and kept a nervous eye on his gauges. "Got what?"

"The visitor's center is burning." He swung his binoculars to the west. "So is the woods." He set down the binoculars and picked up his phone. "Leroux here. We've got a wildfire on our hands. Activate the sirens and evacuate the area. This is going to be a big one."

* * *

Chapter 42

Thursday Night
Paradis, LA

Ginny poked her head around the corner of the shed and noticed patches of night sky appearing on the western horizon. Good. The wind would blow the clouds away and she might get some moonlight. There was another source of light on the horizon though, and the faint, familiar scent of camp fires. The Loch Lonach Homesteaders had a bonfire every year at midsummer, and there was the Up Helly Aa, of course, and Yule logs. Ginny smiled at the memories, then blinked, and looked again.

The light flickered, gold and red and orange, mirrored on the scudding clouds. It stretched from the edge of the shed on her right to a point beyond her vision on the left. And there was a faint noise on the wind, also familiar. Ginny strained to hear, then identified the memory. Wildfire!

She climbed to her feet and studied the line of trees beyond the perimeter fence. Was it her imagination, or was the fire coming closer? It would run before the wind, like a sailing ship, the embers riding the currents of air, falling and igniting where they fell, starting more fires. But didn't a wildfire need dry wood? And hadn't the storm just saturated all the vegetation for miles? What was feeding this fire?

Ginny suddenly came to herself. It didn't matter what was fueling the blaze. It was headed toward her and she needed to escape. A metal building would become an oven when the flames arrived. She turned again to look at her refuge. Along the open side there was enough light to see where to put her feet. She headed in that direction, peering into the gloom, and discovered that side of the shed lined with more concrete pits, about half of them occupied.

A penny dropped in Ginny's mind. They raised alligators here. It was an alligator farm. She looked down into the first few enclosures, seeing starlight reflected off the backs of the animals in the pens. They were bigger than the ones she'd gone swimming with. And a lot more alert. Several tried to climb the walls as she passed.

She moved carefully, putting her feet down only when she was sure she would not trip again, but made no effort to be silent. The alligators weren't silent, either.

Ginny had never spent any time in close proximity to alligators. All she knew of them she'd learned from reading or watching videos. South Texas had them, in the bayous around Houston. If the waters rose, as they did after each major hurricane, the gators would be flooded out of their homes, and could end up in backyards and driveways, or swimming down flooded streets. Officials told residents to leave them alone, but there were always some four-legged pets that went missing at about the same time. Alligators, she had heard, will eat anything, including each other.

Crocodylia have existed essentially unchanged for one hundred and fifty million years, and they have no natural enemies. They are ambush predators. They have excellent eyesight, a keen sense of smell, and a habit of hunting when prey presents itself, then stashing the carcass to eat later. Their jaws are capable of exerting more than two thousand pounds of pressure per square inch, and some gators have been photographed climbing fences. They prefer prey that won't fight back. So, according to the experts, the thing to do if a gator is chasing you is to run, and, if you get caught, kick and punch and gouge its eyes out. Ginny hoped it wouldn't come to that.

As she passed the edge of one of the pits, the animal in it hissed, it's mouth open. (She could see the gleam of its teeth in the pale light.) Ginny backed off a step and the animal lunged. Like the others, it was in a concrete pit without fences. The depth of the trough had been considered sufficient protection for the handlers. This one, however, managed to get all the way to the edge of the enclosure before gravity dragged him back down to the bottom of his prison. Ginny found her heart pounding.

She moved carefully to the next pen. This one was empty, but she noticed a sound coming from the one beyond, a voice. In another few steps she could hear a woman, talking to the animal.

"That's right! Just like that, my lovely. I know you're hungry. Don't worry, you'll be fed before the night is over. I promise."

Ginny froze, but the woman must have heard her approach.

"I see you found your way to the processing barn."

Ginny's skin crawled. Dupree!

"I thought you were dead."

"It takes more than lightning to kill someone like me."

Ginny heard a scrape and saw a movement in the darkness. She backed away, but Dupree was still speaking.

"My car remote wouldn't work. I had to use the key." It was said matter-of-factly, as if the two were chatting about reasons to call the Automobile Association. "And the Visitor's Center was crushed. So I knew you had to be in here."

The sound of the storm was dying, the pounding on the

metal roof giving way to the echo of water running down the gutters, hitting the concrete and the pools of water in the alligator pens.

"You may have already guessed. I use this place for certain—purposes. What you may not have realized is that it is mine. Oh, not in my name, of course. That would be unwise. But I have found it useful. Did you know that alligators will eat human flesh?"

Ginny backed off another step and saw Dupree's shadow follow her. The moon appeared from behind a fleeing cloud, and hung just above their shelter, the light pouring in the open side of the shed. Dupree moved into it, then turned to face Ginny.

As she did, Ginny saw the reason for the scraping. Dupree was dragging her left foot behind her. Her left arm, too, hung limp. Ginny caught her breath.

"You're hurt. Let me help you get to a hospital."

Dupree's laughter was short and cold. "You won't be helping anyone." Ginny could see the woman pretty well. There was no knife in her hand this time.

"Lightning injuries can be treated. We just need to let someone know to come get us."

Dupree hissed, sounding eerily like the alligator. "Do you really think I can go back to living my life, as if nothing has happened?"

"None of us can do that. We have to find a way to move forward." It was not the first time Ginny'd had to talk to someone with devastating injuries. "We can help you recover, teach you how to cope, support you." She took a step toward Dupree. "We'll find a phone, and call an ambulance."

The light had been getting brighter, in hues of orange and gold, as if the sun was rising, but that couldn't be true. Ginny realized with a shock that she could see Dupree's face.

"We need to move away from this shed. There's a fire headed our way." She took another step toward Dupree, intent on turning her, and leading her out of danger.

Dupree ignored her, turning instead to a rope that hung from the ceiling. She pulled on it, and Ginny saw a metal mesh curtain descending, just like the kind used to protect storefronts in sketchier parts of town. The bottom edge hit the concrete, but it didn't stop coming until there was a two foot pile right on the edge of the alligator pit.

Dupree put her good hand on the pile and pushed. With a crash, it fell into the pen. Ginny's eyes followed the motion, watching the animal react. He must have seen this before. He put a claw out and began to climb the side of the pen, using the metal mesh for traction.

Ginny's eyes grew wide. Not only was the beast trained to climb fences, Dupree had been promising to feed it.

"Come on! We have to go!" She grabbed Dupree's arm and started to haul her toward the other end of the shed, but Dupree reached out with her good hand, grabbed something hanging from one of the supports, and swung it at Ginny.

What saved Ginny from the blow was the rubber boots. She had tried to run, had tried to pull Dupree with her, had put her foot down on something slick, and lost her footing. The shovel glanced off her shoulder.

She threw her arms up to protect herself from another blow, and found Dupree advancing upon her, coldly, almost dispassionately, trying to kill her. Ginny scrambled to her feet, and ran. Behind her she heard the sound of more metal fences being lowered into more alligator pens.

* * *

Thursday Night
Airborne toward Paradis

The inside of the Search & Rescue helicopter reminded Jim of an ambulance. The ceiling and walls had been painted white, the floor blue. Along one side was a series of jump seats upholstered in a color-coordinated faux leather that undoubtedly allowed them to be disinfected easily. They sprang up, out of the way when not in use, just as theater seats did in an auditorium.

Along the other wall was a platform supporting a basket designed to be lowered into the water or onto the deck of a ship, into which one could put an injured passenger. Resuscitation equipment was mounted on the wall above.

The cabin was lit only by the LEDs on communication and control panels, by the red and green running lights on the fuselage, and by the glowing studs on the floor that marked the emergency exit route. Outside the windows, the storm enveloped them in raindrops and sheet lightning that exploded behind banks of clouds all rolling east in front of them.

Jim was unable to see the surface of the Gulf below, or tell when they crossed over to Louisiana bayou. Nor was his headset on the correct frequency to hear what the pilot was saying. He had to rely on an intermediary, one of the medics, for news. The man approached him now, moving with practiced grace, head lowered, hands on stanchions and grips and loops embedded in the fabric of the helicopter. He made an adjustment to his headset, then spoke into the microphone.

"We've got new orders. We're headed inland, to a town called Paradis. Ten minutes."

Jim nodded, then texted that detail to his grandfather and got back the information that they were headed for an alligator farm.

Reggie touched his helmet to Jim's and shouted over the background noise. "Somehow I didn't expect to find Paradise in Louisiana."

Reggie's assessment seemed borne out by the sudden change in aspect. Both men found themselves on their backs, their feet rising into the air as the chopper changed course.

The captain must have decided his passengers needed to hear what was going on for there was now a running stream of comments, albeit one-sided, to which they were privy.

"How big is it?"

"And we're flying into that thing?"

"Has anyone made visual contact, yet?"

The medic glanced back at Jim and Reggie. "Tucked in tight, Captain." He nodded, then passed on the instruction.

"Hang on, boys. It's gonna get bumpy."

* * *

<h1 style="text-align:center">CHAPTER 43</h1>

Dupree was calling to her. "These gators are a bit unusual. They like to chase prey. If you stay still, they might ignore you, but I doubt it." The voice followed her out of the building, into the night. "You see, I've made pets of them. I give them something that makes them feel strong, and very, very hungry."

Ginny glanced back over her shoulder to see four enormous alligators emerging from the barn, Dupree behind them, making herding motions with her arms. Ginny turned toward the road and put on a burst of speed.

The rubber boots didn't help. Well, they did provide some protection when she hit the gravel, but otherwise they slowed her down. Her feet slid within them, destroying both balance and traction. She curved up the road, following the direction the fleeing worshippers had taken, and sprinted hard.

She glanced back over her shoulder. The gators were closer, terrifyingly close, and moving as if everything she'd ever heard about them being water animals was a lie. Ginny was in reasonably good physical condition for a woman her age, what with the dancing and the skating, but the drug Dupree had used appeared to be still in her system. She found herself short of breath, panting, her legs cramping.

There were no more buildings along her route. The forest had been allowed to close in, providing what must be a pleasant, tree-lined avenue in daylight. The fire was louder, now, and still coming toward her, but Ginny decided she would rather take her chances in the trees than on the road. She ran to a live oak with limbs low enough for her to grasp, hauled herself up, and began to climb, her hands slipping on the wet Spanish moss. When she was ten feet in the air, she turned and looked down.

The moonlight shone on the expanse of mud that had been the access road, and in it she could clearly see the four gators, with Dupree following along behind, dragging her left leg. She called to Ginny again.

"Don't you want to know why these animals want to rip your flesh from your bones while you're still alive? I taught them to, that's why. First, I taught them to respond to a dinner bell. Just like Pavlov." Ginny heard Dupree laugh.

"Then I read in one of the toxicology journals about a boa constrictor rescued from a meth house. It was addicted. They had trouble handling it, it was *much* more aggressive than usual. That gave me an idea. What a good way to dispose of bodies. No flesh, no bones, not a trace."

The methamphetamine-enhanced gators had gathered below Ginny's tree. To her horror, one of them put his forelegs on a limb that dragged the ground. The beast mounted the limb and began to move toward her. Ginny scrambled higher.

"They can climb trees, you know, if the limbs are close enough together. And these are, I think." Dupree laughed. "They just have to be sufficiently motivated."

From her perch about half way up the tree Ginny could see the leading edge of the fire. It was definitely coming toward them. So much for her second chance. She wondered if she would asphyxiate before the flames reached her. Probably not.

The alternative was to try to get past those animals. If she rested here for a few minutes, to catch her breath, maybe she could get enough of a head start to put something nonflammable between herself and the beasts.

Dupree was still addressing her, bragging about her accomplishments. Ginny wondered if a lightning strike could affect a person's mental acuity. And common sense.

"After that, I decided to give my pets a taste for human flesh. Street people. The kind no one notices if they go missing. Worked like a charm." Dupree laughed again. "Shall I tell you why you have to die?"

Ginny was pretty sure she already knew the answer to that one. "Why did you kill Jamieson?"

Dupree shrugged. "Someone wanted her dead."

"Who wanted her dead? Why?"

Ginny didn't know whether she would get an answer, or the chance to pass it on, but maybe she could satisfy her curiosity.

Dupree laughed. "I don't know and I don't care, as long as the money's good." Dupree had been moving closer, peering up through the leaves at her intended victim.

"You don't need the money. You've got your regular job and your voodoo sideshow. Why take the risk?" Ginny could see Dupree's face. Their eyes met and Dupree smiled.

"For the intellectual challenge. Each mark is different. There's a lot of planning and preparation and when everything goes right, you wouldn't believe the rush."

Dupree looked over at the approaching flames. "I will be gone when the fire gets here, but I expect it will help cover my tracks. Rather fortuitous, don't you think?" She took out her cellphone and started scrolling through the apps. "Luckily I left this in the van. Otherwise it would have been destroyed. Let's see now—"

At her touch, Dupree's cellphone loaded the stored

messages, and an alarm went off. It was the emergency tone used by local authorities to get the public's attention so it could announce a kidnapping or weather alert. Dupree seemed surprised. "What?" She frowned, then her eyes widened. She dropped the phone, addressing the alligator that had turned to look at her. "No! Wait! Not me, you stupid brute!"

Ginny heard a scrambling noise, then a hiss, then something she was sure she really didn't want to hear, a high pitched scream that didn't seem to stop, in spite of the crunching noises. Ginny shut her eyes and clapped her hands over her ears. When the screaming faded, Ginny leaned over a branch, and was promptly sick.

After that, the sounds changed. There was more hissing, the slap of something heavy against the mud, and the snap of jaws closing. Ginny peeked through the branches, and found two of the gators fighting over the carcass. They were rolling over and over, flipping one another, not letting go. A third seemed to have avoided the fight. Ginny could see it moving off, dragging one of Dupree's legs with it. The fourth gator was still climbing.

* * *

Thursday Night
Paradis, LA

Jim had to twist around in his seat to see out the window. This required loosening his harness a bit, which was taking a chance. The medic had been right. The helicopter was bouncing around like a toy boat in a bathtub.

"Wow!" He could see the wildfire easily, approaching from the left, and see vortices rising from the flames. The heated air made it harder for the helicopter to stay aloft, and the convection buffeted them. The helicopter slewed around, showing Jim the ground beneath them, then righting itself, then plowing forward parallel to the inferno.

Reggie had his device on his lap, hanging on, and trying to aim it toward the ground. "This is not going to work," he muttered.

"What do you need?" Jim asked.

"Spot for me. Are we over the farm, yet?"

Jim peered out the window. "Yes. I can see buildings and fences."

"Okay. Help me turn this around."

Between the two of them, they managed to get the sensor pointed in the right direction.

"Are we close enough?" Jim asked.

Reggie nodded. "If she's there."

The medic came back to talk to them. "Gentlemen, I need to ask you to resume your seats."

Jim shook his head. "This is what we came for. This device can tell us if Ginny is anywhere on that property."

"I'm sorry. The captain has decided it's too dangerous. The fire is too close. We have to go back."

Jim released the catches on his harness and grabbed the medic's arm. "Take me to him."

"I'm sorry, sir."

"TAKE ME TO HIM!"

The medic shrugged and led Jim toward the cockpit. The Captain turned to face Jim, switching the comm link over so they could hear one another.

"The conditions do not allow us to stay in the area."

"All we need is a few minutes. Either she's there, or she's not."

"I thought there was no GPS signal."

"She's wearing an RFID tag."

"RFID? Like they tag books with?"

"Yes."

"Never heard of such a thing."

"It's experimental."

"This vessel isn't built—" They were interrupted by Reggie's whoop.

"Got her!"

"Where?" the Captain asked.

Jim moved out of the way, letting the medic relay Reggie's instructions to the Captain.

He clung to a metal bar set into the wall next to the doorframe and a polyester strap dangling from the ceiling, and peered at the latches used to attach people to the hoist cable. He'd seen pictures of course, but never done it himself. It looked easy, but these highly trained professionals might disagree. He listened in on their comments.

"Can't see her, yet."

"Are those alligators? Yikes!"

"Can we set down beyond them?"

"If we set down, we'll never get airborne again."

"There she is!"

"Where?"

"Over to the left. In that tree!"

"Is that an *alligator* in the tree?"

"Can this get any worse?"

"That fire's closing awfully fast. If we want to be gone when it arrives, someone will have to go get her."

"The way those branches are whipping around, you could get knocked cold."

Jim caught the arm of the last speaker. "I'll go. She's my responsibility. If I die, or she does, it won't be your fault."

There was silence among the crew, then the Captain nodded. "Hook him up."

The next five minutes had Jim climbing into a special harness designed for two, being told to hang on while they opened the door, then being attached to a massive hook. He tightened his helmet and made sure the goggles were in place.

Then they were hovering over the tree. Jim sat on the edge of the door and dangled his feet out over the space, his gut churning. He was given last minute instructions, then eased out the door and into the air.

* * *

Thursday Night
Paradis, LA

The fire had reached the perimeter fence, bringing with it the first waves of heat. Ginny could hear the fire breathe, a sucking sound, followed by whistling. The woods cracked and splattered and roared. Huge limbs split with a shriek and fell, landing with a muted thud, cushioned by the flames.

There was movement in the grass beneath her. She saw a raccoon run past, joined on the road by rodents and other small animals. In the trees, birds were taking flight. Squirrels chittered as they jumped from limb to limb. Somewhere nearby she heard horses whinnying.

Ginny had read somewhere that wildfires average a forward speed of between six and ten miles per hour. If the alligators decided to make a run for it, maybe she could jump down, and run with them. Ginny wondered which was worse, being burned or eaten—alive in either case. She could still hear Dupree's screams in her ears, along with something else. She contemplated the new noise, assigned it to a probable category, and prepared to cooperate.

Peering up between the branches, she could see a helicopter over on the far side of the picnic area. It moved across the expanse of the farm, disappearing, then reappearing, a spotlight sweeping the ground. She watched it search, crisscrossing the road, pausing to investigate areas of special interest, the stage, an alligator or two, Dupree's van.

Then it stopped, the light fixed on the bloody mess at the foot of her tree. The copter moved in, hovering as the searchlight climbed the tree, and came to rest on her.

The rotor wash whipped at the leaves and small branches, forcing her to cover her face with her arms. Ginny kept her mouth shut, knowing she could not be heard over the noise the machine was making, and tried to see what was happening. The copter was hovering. Someone was coming out, on a cable.

If they meant to lift her out of the tree, she should move closer to the top. She shook off the boots and climbed barefoot, slipping on the Spanish moss, her hands grabbing at branches too small to hold her weight, branches that broke and fell to the ground when she let go of them. She was as high as the tree allowed. She shielded her eyes and looked up.

The man was closer, was just above her head. He was dangling something. A harness. She grabbed it and he came down beside her, the tree lashing the pair of them. He helped her scramble into the webbing, attaching her harness to his, pulling her to him, chest to chest, then signaling to someone to pull them up. She buried her face on his shoulder and closed her eyes.

She was thrust inside, and someone grabbed her, stripping the harness off, lifting her, laying her on something lined with blankets, covering her with another. He wrapped a blood pressure cuff around her arm, then attached an oxygen probe.

There was a different man leaning over her. He braced his arms on the walls as they veered off toward New Orleans, then slipped a headset over her ears and turned it on.

"Are you hurt?" Jim's voice.

"Jim!"

"Yes. Are you hurt?" He slid the goggles up so she could see his face.

Ginny swallowed the tears that had sprung into her eyes. "I don't think so. Not much, anyway."

"We'll get you checked out."

"How—?"

"The paint tags."

Ginny felt her lower lip tremble. He had come for her, had come all the way from Dallas to find her. The tears spilled over.

"Don't cry," his voice sounded strained. "Not yet. I can't do anything about it yet. Hold on, just a little while longer." Someone was pushing him back into his seat, strapping him in, then making sure she was strapped in as well.

She did her best, sucking in huge lungfuls of clean air, her eyes on him as they flew to the Naval Air Station. What was he going to say to her, when they could talk in private? What could she say to him? He might have been a stranger in the night, one of the strangers who had risked their lives to rescue her. He sat there, out of reach, as alien as if he had dropped from heaven, and for the first time that night, Ginny was afraid.

* * *

Chapter 44

Friday, Early Morning
Burnside Homestead

It was two o'clock on Friday morning. Jim sat in the room assigned to Ginny at the Burnside Homestead, trying to tell himself the danger was over. She was safe. She was alive. They both were.

The helicopter had set them down on the field at the Naval Air Station and they'd been taken directly to the base hospital where Ginny had been examined. Jim had stayed with her, watching all but the part where they checked for signs of sexual assault, mercifully absent. He'd also been in the room at the police station when she gave her statement. No one had tried to stop him. No one had asked Ginny if she wanted him there. It had been assumed. She was his fiancée.

He'd had a dog when he was eight. A puppy, really. Named for the Monongahela River, but everyone called him Mongrel. A large, loud, exuberant bundle of fur. Untameable. Ungovernable at that age. Jim felt his throat close. If Mongrel had listened to him, had come to his call— He hadn't replaced his pet.

He watched as Ginny moved under the covers, restlessly, as if in pain, and scolded himself. She wasn't a dog. She was a woman, a strong-willed, capable, professional woman. She'd been telling him so almost from the start. And he'd listened, in an amused, superior sort of way. As if all he had to do was marry her and she would come to heel.

She'd promised him she'd be careful. And he'd believed her. Because he wanted to. Because he hadn't wanted to face the alternative. That there might still be something in her life more important than he was. Selfish, self-centered, arrogant. Him, not her. A better man would have tried to help. If he'd been more sympathetic, she might have felt it safe to ask him for help.

"Jim?"

He rose and came over, perching on the edge of her bed. "I'm here."

She sat up, pulling her knees to her chin and wrapping her arms around them. There was a lamp on in the corner, so they could see one another. She looked exhausted, haunted.

"You came after me."

"Did you think I wouldn't?"

"I didn't know. I thought you might be angry."

He reached out and took one of her hands, twining his fingers with hers. "Terrified. I was terrified."

She frowned. "It's not fair to expect you to haul me out of whatever trouble I get into. You have better things to do with your life."

Jim felt his throat close, but tried to keep it light. "Not at the moment. Maybe next week." He smiled at her. "This is going to make a great story to tell our children."

She took a breath. "You still want that?"

"Yes."

"You can back out. No one would blame you." There was a catch in her voice.

Jim shook with the force of the emotions in his breast. There had been a moment during the ride from Dallas to

Galveston when something one of the crew had said, casually, carelessly, had stabbed him to the heart. "A lot of trouble for just one woman," he had said, and Jim had almost tossed him out the door of the helicopter.

Just one woman was the lynchpin of a good man's life, his reason for being alive. How many men had placed themselves in harm's way for the fun of it, then found it was no fun after all, and had to find a reason to keep going? How many had understood, sooner or later, that the reason to fight, the reason to survive was the girl he'd left behind? How many had known peace in their hearts because they had a helpmeet at home, taking care of things while he took care of business? How many were lonely and did not take solace where offered because he didn't want a substitute? How many understood the link between a man and a woman made for one another?

"Because you're trouble?"

She nodded.

Jim smiled. "Well, you warned me, so I have no right to complain if I choose to marry you anyway." He sucked in a deep breath and asked the question. "What about you? Do you still want me?"

She was trembling, and Jim tried to read her answer in her face, but couldn't, not this time. What good was having the Sight if it didn't work in moments like this?

She swallowed hard, then nodded. "But I'm scared, Jim. I don't know who I am anymore." She sucked in a deep breath. "Part of me wants to be taken care of. Part of me is nauseated at the very idea. I've spent years learning to be the woman who can cope with anything. But I can't. I can't." She brought her hand up to hide her face from him.

Jim shook his head at her, his heart aching. "You don't have to. And whatever they told you at school, you're not supposed to have to. We're supposed to help one another, support one another. Life is hard enough without having to live it alone." He brushed her cheek with his fingers. "I will always be there for you, Ginny. No matter how much trouble you get into."

Her face twisted. "It should have been easy—just grab the trash and toss it in the car and high-tail it back to Texas."

"So, what went wrong?"

"I didn't know I was dealing with a professional assassin."

"You suspected she'd killed Jamieson, though."

Ginny nodded.

"So you suspected she was dangerous."

A single tear escaped, running down her cheek. He brushed it away.

"I'm sorry, Jim! I wanted to prove myself to you."

Alan had been at the police station. He'd filled Jim in on what had happened at the Cameron's that morning, including Ginny's explosion.

"Because you were mad at me?"

She dropped her eyes to the bedclothes. "Because you didn't trust me to make decisions about myself, my life." She looked up. "I wanted to prove it to myself, too." Her shoulders sagged. "And look what a mess I made of it."

Jim stood up and moved to the head of the bed. "Scoot over." He stretched out on her bed, his back to the headboard, and pulled her into his arms.

"I was listening when you told the police what happened. If I understood you, and correct me if I'm wrong, you managed to wriggle out of restraints tied around your wrists." She nodded. "Then, you avoided being crushed by a falling tree." He felt her shiver and tightened his grip. "Then, faced with a pen full of overgrown lizards, you kept your wits about you, controlled the storm water, used it to float to the top of the pit, and escaped by standing on the snout of one of the animals. After which you were confronted with a woman you thought was dead. But, instead of thinking she was a ghost, you tried to nurse her, to help her." Ginny sighed and Jim gave her a squeeze. "And, when it became clear she wanted no help, you made the very sensible decision to leave, to get away from her by climbing a tree, high enough so that the hoist cable could reach you." Jim kissed her head. "If we hadn't come along, you could have dropped out of the tree and run. You weren't even out of options. There was still Dupree's van and I won't be surprised to find out you know how to hotwire an engine."

Ginny rolled over and buried her face in his shoulder. "But you came for me," she mumbled into his shoulder.

"Well, I didn't realize you had it all under control."

She laughed and Jim's heart swelled at the sound.

"You, Ginny Forbes, are a woman worth having and I wasn't going to let you go so easily." He sucked in a breath "Why didn't you ask for my help in the first place?"

"You had already told me you would object, and I didn't want to fight with you."

Jim shook his head. "I'm sorry I put you in that position. Can you forgive me?"

She looked up at him and nodded. "If you can forgive me for trying to sneak one past you."

Jim smiled weakly. "Please don't shut me out of your life. I can handle anything but that."

She sighed, her brows drawing closer. "This is going to be hard."

"What is?"

"Getting used to being half of a whole."

Jim smiled. "It's going to be a great adventure, and neither one of us knows what may come, but I promise you this, my love, whatever you and I were before we met, we're better, stronger as a team. We can face anything, as long as we're together."

She said no more, just closed her eyes, and relaxed into his embrace. Jim lay awake for the better part of an hour, holding her as she drifted into sleep.

He'd dodged a bullet this time. Against all odds, she was alive, and in his arms. He hadn't told her, of course, but his grandfather had taken him aside before the chopper left Dallas. "Bring her back," he had said. "Bring her body back, if ye canna do better." His grandfather had frowned heavily, studying Jim. "I'll no tell ye how tae live yer life," he had continued, "but, if ye break with the lass o'er this, yer the daftest man that e'er lived."

Jim hadn't bothered to answer, but he had agreed. For better, for worse, for whatever came, he had found the woman who made him whole. Besides, having tracked her down and snatched her from the jaws of a man-eating beast made him feel a tad heroic. He didn't want to repeat the experience, mind you, but he could look back on it with satisfaction. He had escaped the dragon and rescued the fair maiden and they were now free to live happily ever after. That's how it always was in the fairy tales. A fairy tale wedding, a fairy tale life. It could work, as long as they were together—and still believed in fairy tales.

* * *

Friday Afternoon
Airborne toward Dallas

Ginny sat in the right hand seat of Alan's little Cessna, in the back this time, with Jim beside her. Reggie was up front, with Alan. From this position she could not see the earth, just the sky. Blue sky, white clouds.

Ginny was wearing a headset, but she had the sound turned off. From the moment they had landed at the Naval Air Station, there had been voices: conversation, questions, commands. Jim had been silent for most of it, letting everyone else do the talking. She'd never seen him so patient.

She shifted in her seat, trying to ease the general discomfort. There were bruises from the falls, and on her shoulder where Dupree's blow had landed, and around her wrists from being bound. The bottoms of her feet were miraculously free from any crippling injury, but her legs ached from the running and climbing and fighting. She'd been chilled to the bone, and Jim had worried about her catching a cold. He'd plied her with zinc and hot soup, but her chest felt tight. He reached over and took her hand, and she smiled at him in response.

He still wanted her, even this miserable, fallible, guilty version of her. Ginny flushed at the thought of what she'd put him through. Hard on its heels came the memory of what she had felt when she realized he'd come for her, and when he promised never to abandon her, no matter how stupid she had been.

Humbled. She had taunted him with his need to learn humility and here she was, forced to admit he wasn't the only one.

There was another source of humility waiting for her. Dupree had said she'd been paid by someone who wanted Jamieson dead, but hadn't told her who. There would be no resolution before Sunday. No closure.

At least Caroline would be cleared. Not that Dupree's confession could be accepted as genuine. No one other than Ginny had heard it, and she was heavily biased, and might have fabricated a lie, to help her friend. But Alan had found the DNA evidence. Sort of.

Ginny's mouth twitched at the memory of the conversations that had taken place over breakfast. As it turned out, the Laird of Burnside was a formidable presence, with as much clout as Angus Mackenzie, maybe more. Once he heard the story, he issued a request for DNA confirmation of identity, using the remains recovered from the alligator farm and materials found at Dupree's residence.

The police had puzzled over the lack of a toothbrush. Alan had blushed and stammered and confessed to tampering with a crime scene. He had been forced to hand over his prize. After a fairly stern warning from the local authorities, he had been released, with orders to make a full statement to Detective Tran.

Ginny closed her eyes and leaned back in her seat. It would take some time for the police in both states to wade through the evidence. There was Dupree's assistant, testifying in the hope of a reduced sentence. There was Ginny's testimony, which she would have to repeat in its entirety to Detective Tran. There was the shop, and no telling what might come to light from a thorough search there.

The crime lab would be all over the alligator farm today. Animal control, too. All taking photographs and notes. Unless the rain had washed it away, or the fire consumed it, Ginny's DNA would be on the leather straps she had left still tied to the wooden cross. Perhaps on the white shift she had worn. It would certainly be in the back of Dupree's van.

Jim touched her knee and pointed. Ginny sat forward, looking out the window at the eastern edge of the Dallas/Fort Worth metroplex. When Jim tapped his headphone, Ginny reached up and turned on her set.

Alan was talking to the tower, being given instructions on which way to approach the field.

"We're almost there. Grandfather is going to meet us." Jim smiled at her.

Ginny watched the remainder of the approach with interest. It felt rather like landing a car. In a commercial jetliner all she ever saw was out the side windows, never forward. Here, in full sunlight, she could see the sprawling city, then the runway and the tarmac rising to meet them.

Alan followed the tower's instructions to taxi to the hanger. He brought the plane to a stop, announced their arrival, climbed down from his seat, and helped everyone to descend to the ground safely.

"I'll see y'all later," he said. "I've got paperwork and maintenance to do."

Ginny caught him by the arm before he could hurry off, and hugged him tightly. "Thank you, Alan, for everything."

He grinned, and hugged her back. "We did it, Ginny!" He paused, his brow wrinkling. "Do me a favor? Let me tell Caroline."

Ginny smiled. "She may already know, but I promise not to say anything to her until you let me."

"Good enough." He climbed back into his plane, and reached for the logs.

"Come on," Jim slid an arm around her waist, and steered her toward the terminal, Reggie in their wake. Inside, they were greeted with cheers and hugs all around. Angus had made a party of it. Sinia Forbes was present, with Alex and Wendy. Reggie's wife, Pauline, had come, and brought his youngest son. Caroline sent her greetings, and a bottle of scotch.

They piled into the cars, and made their way back to Brochaber where they opened Caroline's scotch and passed around wee drams to everyone assembled.

"Slàinte." Angus raised his glass. "And may good fortune always favor fools."

"Amen!" Ginny couldn't help blushing. More humility. She swallowed it gamely. She deserved the rebuke.

"We've a day and a half afore th' wedding," Angus said. "Sinia ha' prepared a timetable and assignments. "'Tis tae be hoped all of ye will fall in wi' her plans." He turned a stern eye on the bride and groom. "I'll brook nae further disaster."

"Aye Mackenzie!"

The words had been spoken reflexively, but had come out in unison. Jim and Ginny grinned at one another, then took their leave of the company and departed to their respective tasks, Ginny regretfully shelving the question of who had paid to have Jamieson killed. The answer, if it could be found, would have to wait.

* * *

CHAPTER 45

Ginny sat where told to sit and stood when told to stand and in every particular obeyed the commands given. She'd had three hours to get cleaned up and dressed and get her shopping done and get back to the church for the rehearsal, followed by the rehearsal dinner. She and Jim and Caroline and Alex and Father Amos and her mother and Himself and a couple of extras to make sure nothing got overlooked spent an hour and a half going over the ceremony.

The dinner was wedding party only, plus spouses, so she only had to deal with the restrained interrogations of those who had been on scene yesterday. That helped. She hadn't gotten to the point where she could speak freely about her experience, and Angus had brought them all back to the issue at hand (the wedding) if they strayed too far afield. For which she'd been grateful.

Jim seemed calm enough. His eyes drifted toward her every few minutes, but that could just be the anticipation of their change in status, not the brushes with death the two had endured. He hadn't actually told her about his adventures. Reggie had spilled the beans, explaining to her, quietly, but emphatically, how Jim had ended up on the end of that cable, rather than one of the Coast Guard crew. Ginny had listened in rapt silence. She'd never been more impressed with Jim than she was this evening, after hearing that recital. How was she ever to live up to his example?

Jim had let her off the hook this morning, casually mentioning at breakfast that they were even now, since she'd rescued him from the wolf and he her from the alligators. Nice of him. He was a nice man. A gallant man. A gentle man.

"Ginny!"

Ginny snapped out of her reverie and attended to Alex's demand to pass the salt. She smiled at him and at Wendy, seated beyond him. Jim had also told her, over breakfast, what Alex had said to him, about her being lucky. She had nodded emphatically. That lightning bolt had been pure luck. But it didn't do to count on it. She'd rather not have to be that lucky again.

Angus raised his glass in a toast.

"To the bride and groom."

"Here, here!"

Ginny smiled her thanks.

The party broke up, but only to reconvene at the Cooperative Hall. This was Friday night and everyone went to the weekly ceilidhs, no matter how many alligators they'd had to fight off the night before. There would be many out-of-town guests present tonight as well, to swell the sets and occupy the chairs.

Ginny looked over at Jim and found his eyes on her. She smiled at him, a small secret smile. His eyes warmed in response.

"Ginny!" Alex again. "Come on! We're going to be late for the ceilidh!"

* * *

Friday Night
Cooperative Hall

Ginny stood across the set from Jim and watched him breathe. She was breathing, too, forcing her bruised ribs to expand and let in the cool, clean scent of the Cooperative Hall air conditioning system. There was a tang to it. Nothing to do with citrus, everything to do with refrigeration. Her nostrils flared, hungry for proof of life, that she was still alive.

They were at the bottom of the set, in fourth couple's place, waiting out a rotation and in danger of forgetting to pay attention to the dance in the intensity of paying attention to one another. His eyes burned.

Her ribs weren't the only things that hurt. She had run barefoot across turf and gravel and barked her shins on the bark of the Live Oak tree that had saved her life. She had bruised knuckles and torn nails and the manicurist at the shop would have her work cut out for her tomorrow to make them presentable for the wedding. She had managed to avoid broken bones and would be able to make it up the long aisle (and back) on Sunday, so long as she had a strong arm to lean on. Tonight she would walk the dances, and might have to sit some of them out, but that was all right. They were well-beloved favorites that everyone knew.

This one was a strathspey, slow and dignified and graceful. One was supposed to gaze into one's partner's eyes during the turns. Ginny stepped in and gave Jim her hands. He had wrapped them for her after dinner, to cushion the abrasions and prevent further damage. She felt him touch the gauze and recoil, then take a soft, firm grip, to lead her through the dance. Their silence held off the noise in the room, except for the music. The strathspey surged, the notes swelling like waves on the bank of the loch, then ebbing, then swelling again, like a heartbeat, only slower.

She stepped carefully, rising with the music, as she should, and finding it no more painful than full sole on the wooden floor. No toe pointing tonight, though. Maybe Sunday.

All the chosen dances required twisting. That was the worst. Ginny grit her teeth and smiled, letting no one, not even Jim, see the penance she was paying for her folly. The pain instructed, and reassured, and chastened her. And Jim seemed to know. He held her gently, supporting her through the turns, lending her his strength. She smiled at him, only for him, then relinquished him to the next round of dances.

In the exchange of partners between dances, Ginny shuffled across the floor, heading for the punch bowl. She hadn't quite made it when she became aware of a young woman, a girl really, waiting for her. Ginny turned to face the girl, thinking she looked vaguely familiar, but so did they all.

"Miss Forbes?"

Ginny nodded, smiling at the girl, and trying not to look at the phalanx of determined faces behind her.

"I have something I need to tell you."

"*We* need to tell you." A young man had stepped up beside the girl, putting his arm around her shoulders, and straightening his back, even as he dropped his eyes to the floor. Ginny waited in silence for them to begin.

The girl took a breath, then met Ginny's eyes. "We were there. We saw something. And we didn't tell you. We didn't tell anyone." She glanced swiftly over her right shoulder, then turned back to Ginny.

"What we saw." The boy spoke this time. "Was a woman, dressed in black. Well, more than that. We saw the fall."

Ginny caught her breath, then started as Jim slid an arm around her waist. She hadn't heard him come up behind her.

"Jamieson?" he asked. The young couple nodded.

"We didn't know who it was, at the time," the girl said. "We were—occupied—and I had my back to the stadium."

The young man explained. "I heard a scuffle up in the stands, and voices. I put my hand over Irene's mouth and pulled her back into the shadows. I didn't want anyone to know we were there."

"If you were under the stands, how could you see the fall?" Jim asked.

"We didn't. Not the fall, but the landing, and that was bad enough."

The girl nodded. "Ben made a sort of gagging sound, and I looked around and there she was, draped over the seats."

Ginny could imagine what sort of impression that experience had made on these two young people. "Did you recognize who it was? You're a Highland dancer, aren't you?"

"Yes, ma'am, and no, I didn't. It was too dark."

"Okay, what did you do?"

The boy answered. "We just stood there, in shock, I think, afraid to move. Then the other woman showed up."

"Another woman?" Jim asked.

The young man nodded. "Yes, sir. She came down the ramp at a pretty fast clip, messed with the body, then slipped away."

Ginny took a breath. "Would you recognize her if you saw her again?"

Both of the youngsters shook their heads. "Not for sure," Ben said. "I got a pretty good look at her when she stood up, but she was just a silhouette."

"About how big was this silhouette? Tall? Short? Thin? Fat?" Jim asked.

"As tall as I am?" Ginny asked.

The boy shook his head. "Taller than you, and fat." He held his hand up almost to scalp level. "I'm guessing about this tall."

Since he was already almost fully grown, this made the estimate about five-foot-eight.

"And fat?" Anything over rail thin would be fat to this youth.

"Yes ma'am."

Ginny looked around the room, searching for someone, and found her. She gestured Caroline over, then positioned her with her back to Ben. She and Caroline were about the same height, but Caroline had a fuller figure.

"Was this what you saw?" she asked.

Ben shook his head firmly. "No. She was taller and thicker. Dressed all in black. I couldn't even see her face. It was like it wasn't there."

Ginny grabbed a pen and napkin from the table, took down the two witnesses names, thanked them for coming forward, warned them Detective Tran would want statements, and let them go. She made eye contact with the two sets of parents hovering in the background and smiled. No doubt that young couple would be cautioned strongly against sneaking off together in the future. No need to mention it to them here.

When the witnesses were gone, she looked at Caroline, her mind assimilating the new data.

"All dressed in black, and not your shape."

Caroline frowned. "I could NOT get in and out of an airsaid in the available time, no matter what the police think."

"What they will suggest," Jim said, "is that you had the black outfit on under your airsaid and simply stripped in the bathroom."

"Well they can suggest all they like. If they want to test the theory, I can loan Detective Tran my costume and let her time herself getting into and out of it."

Ginny laughed. "You don't have to convince me. What do you suppose Dupree wanted with the body?"

"To see if Jamieson was really dead, of course." Caroline looked smug.

"That won't work," Jim corrected. "If she had touched her, or listened to her heart, she would have realized Jamieson was *not* dead, and had to do something about it."

"Okay, she was stealing her wallet."

"Nope," Ginny said. "It was on her when they did the inventory the next day. Nothing stolen, as far as they could tell."

"Removing evidence?" Caroline suggested.

Ginny jerked straight up. "Oh!" She turned, scanned the room, found the young couple again and hurried over. "One more question, please. Can you tell me if the woman in black did something to Judge Jamieson's hands? Did you see?"

The young man, Ben, nodded. "Yes, she lifted first one hand, then the other, then let them drop."

"Could you see what she was doing?"

"No, I'm sorry."

"Is there anything else you can tell me?"

"Yes." Irene's expression sharpened. "I've just remembered. She picked up Judge Jamieson's purse and opened it and took something out and slipped it into her pocket."

Ginny thanked them again and hurried back.

"Dupree did touch Judge Jamieson's hands and she did take something out of her purse and took it away with her."

"Well," Jim sighed, "we can't ask her what it was. Maybe the New Orleans police can figure it out."

"Maybe," Ginny said, "but I know someone else who might be able to tell us what happened." She looked at the clock. "Too late to call tonight. I'll have to catch up with him in the morning."

Jim took her by the shoulders and turned her to face him. Ginny froze, expecting a lecture on how busy she was going to be on the day before the wedding.

"I can't stop you," he said. "And I've always been told if you can't lick 'em, join 'em, so, I'm in. Just tell me when and where and what you want me to do."

Ginny threw her arms around him and hugged him tightly. A united front, the two of them, working in concert toward the same goal. It was a good omen for the future.

"Thank you!"

With eyewitness statements putting Dupree at the scene, however disguised, Tran would be able to exonerate Caroline. It would be better if they could figure out who paid for the "hit," of course, but that might not be possible. And something else might surface, even at this late date. You never knew what tomorrow might bring.

* * *

CHAPTER 46

Saturday Morning
Loch Lonach Homestead

On Saturday morning Ginny rose late. She climbed out of bed wondering if she'd been wise to go dancing the night before. A hot shower and clean clothes eased some of the stiffness, and she was able to brush her hair and braid it as usual with only a few pauses to let her muscles rest.

The trip had not been a success. She was lucky she hadn't ended up in the hospital, or the morgue. And all for nothing. Neither she nor Alan had been able to obtain a sample of Dupree's DNA.

She stood in front of her mirror, putting on her everyday jewelry, and breathed thanks that she'd left it home when she flew off to New Orleans. The pieces would have been a great temptation to anyone with sticky fingers.

There was a necklace of twisted gold, just the right length for the pendants she added on special occasions, a scrollwork band she wore on her right hand that had belonged to her grandmother Stewart, and a pair of earrings. The earrings were hollow tubes, decorated with etched leaves and raised vines soldered onto the gold loops. She had pierced ears so the earrings had hinges and catches, and curved posts, to hold them securely in place. They were well made and almost never got caught in her clothing. Ginny's fingers deftly manipulated the closure, sliding along the bars, avoiding the clasps, brushing the edges of the decorations. She froze, staring at the position of her fingers on the second earring.

Dupree had undressed her while she lay drugged. That included her hair clip and talisman, all she'd been wearing that day. They'd been found in Dupree's shop. The New Orleans police had taken them away, but Dupree was dead, so they didn't need the evidence to use in court. The clothes and other items had been returned to Ginny

Her eyes narrowed. Had Dupree remembered to wear gloves?

The hair clip had been cleaned, soaked in disinfectant before being put back into service. But the talisman was too delicate for anything of the sort.

It hung on a chain of sterling silver almost as old as the wood itself, the links forged and formed and soldered, but worn for many generations and over many years. Some of the joins, she knew had been pulled apart, leaving tiny imperfections that could catch in a sweater.

The bale and image—the Celtic Tree of Life—were carved from a single piece of the rowan wood. The front and back had been worn smooth by countless encounters with human hands. But the interior carving, the limbs and branches of the tree, had been protected from wear by their position within the design. There was a spot, Ginny knew, where the grain of the wood had pulled away from the original shape and left a splinter for the unwary to find. It had been known to bite.

Ginny leaped into action. She hurried down stairs and grabbed a plastic bag from the storage supply. Not sterile, but presumably free of extraneous DNA. She retrieved her clothes from the laundry basket and stuffed them in the bag. Grabbing coffee and calling her intentions to her mother, she headed for the garage.

Reggie was in. He looked up and smiled.

"The bride to be. Safe and sound."

"Thanks to you and those paint tags."

Reggie nodded. "That worked out pretty well. There are a lot of things I'd like to modify of course since we learned what the tags would and wouldn't do but nothing we can't figure out and fix and Jon has already gotten some ideas of his down on paper which I'm sure will work because you know he's good at that sort of thing."

"Reggie!" Ginny interrupted. "I have a favor to ask, a big one." She held out the bag of clothing. "Can you pull DNA from these?"

He put on a pair of gloves and examined the clothing, frowning. "Maybe. Are we looking for body fluids?"

"Probably not." She explained about Dupree stripping her before dressing her in the white shift.

Reggie shook his head. "Maybe, but it would be easier if we had a zipper or something else that was likely to scrape a bit as she pulled them off."

She nodded. "Do you have a magnifying glass?"

He opened a drawer and pulled one out, handing it to her in silence. Ginny showed him the talisman.

"Look, can you see that?"

Reggie peered through the glass and nodded. "Looks like blood."

"I've jammed my finger on that sharp point in the past so it might have my DNA on it, but it might also have Dupree's. And if that doesn't work, here, on this bit of silver where the link has separated. Look there. Or the clasp. She would have to have handled that to get it off. The chain's not long enough to pull off over my head."

Reggie's eyes lit up. "Now that's more like it! Blood would

be best, but we can work with skin cells. You just give me a couple of hours and I'll have an answer for you."

"How will you know whose DNA is whose?"

"We have yours on file. We'll just ask the computer to subtract your markers from the result and anything left will be hers, or someone else's. No telling what we might find, especially on something so old. Hmmm."

Ginny left him to it, knowing she would be a distraction. Besides, she had appointments she couldn't miss. She hurried home to a belated breakfast and considered how she could spend her day most profitably.

Any guest not already here would be coming in today, but Ginny was not expected to pick them up at the airport or greet them until tonight. They would be settled into their accommodations and left to rest, then get ready for the banquet. She, too, was expected to nap, so she could be gracious and animated as she greeted old friends and new acquaintances. She had a role to play this evening, but the afternoon was hers.

She badly wanted to solve Judge Jamieson's murder before the wedding. She had turned the young lovers over to Detective Tran and, presumably, their testimony would help, but there was someone she hadn't spoken to about that night. Someone who'd been present and left his fingerprints on the railing. Ginny grabbed her files and looked up Gary Feldman's telephone number. A man's voice answered.

"Mr. Feldman? I'm Ginny Forbes, Caroline's friend."

"I know who you are. She told me about you." He sounded wary. "What can I do for you Ms. Forbes?"

Ginny took a breath. "I don't know if you've been following the murder investigation so you may not be aware that the actual murderer has been identified and is dead."

"Dead?" He sounded startled. He hadn't known about

Dupree.

"Yes, on Thursday evening."

"That's very good news. I'm sure Caroline is relieved."

"Not completely. That's why I'm calling you. I would like to know if you saw the murderer."

There was a silence on the other end of the line, then a cautiously indrawn breath. "What makes you think I might have?"

"We found a pair of witnesses who were there when Jamieson landed on the stadium seating. They saw a woman dressed in black examine the body. Did you see a woman in black?"

Again, there was a silence on the other end of the line. Ginny got the impression Gary Feldman was weighing the pros and cons of admitting to anything having to do with Judge Jamieson's death.

"You are not under suspicion. The evidence points to a woman and she confessed to me before she died. I just want to know if you saw her."

He sighed. "Yes, I did."

"Tell me about it, please."

"I was waiting to talk to Jamieson again, to try to get her to relent, and working up the courage to face her." He hesitated.

"I know about your alibi. Don't worry about that."

"Okay. So you know I heard the scream and you know I went down to the rail and looked over."

"Yes."

"Well, what I didn't tell the police was that I saw a figure in black, hardly more than a shadow, making its way down the steps and off into the darkness. I didn't see which way it went and I wasn't able to tell whether it was a man or a woman."

"You know Caroline Cameron well, I believe?"

"Yes. We work together."

"Did the figure in black remind you of Caroline, in the way she moved, or general size and shape, anything like that?"

"No, not even close."

"Can you think of anything else that could help us identify this person?"

Ginny could hear the shrug on the other end of the line.

"The only thing I can add is that whoever it was needed to work out more. She paused at one point, clutching the railing and breathing hard. I could hear her from where I stood."

Ginny frowned. "Breathing hard, as if she'd been running?"

"Yeah, and then a kind of low moan, then she moved on and I didn't hear any more."

"Thank you Mr. Feldman. You've been very helpful."

"I'm not sorry, you know. We need someone with more compassion in her place."

Ginny hesitated for a split second, then made up her mind. "Would it surprise you to hear Judge Jamieson was already dying of a particularly nasty disease that made every day of her life a living hell?"

This time the silence was thicker. "I'm sorry to hear of any soul in torment, but she shouldn't have taken it out on us."

"For what it's worth, Mr. Feldman, I agree with you. Thank you again."

Ginny hung up the phone thinking it had been worth the effort. He'd given her a new detail to chew on. She glanced at the clock, grabbed her purse and headed out again.

The beauty shop was terra incognita to Ginny. She was not a devotee and had been inside only once before, to pick up a package that had been left for her by someone who was. Her nostrils twitched at the acrid fumes rising from a dozen styling stations. If Caroline had not appeared between her and the door, she might have retreated and gone home to file her own nails.

"There you are! I tried calling earlier, but your phone went straight to voicemail."

"You must have caught me when I was talking to Gary."

"Feldman?"

"Yes."

"You can tell me all about it while the girls work." Caroline grabbed her arm and pulled her deeper into the shop. "Let's get started."

Over the course of the next hour Ginny suffered the indignity of having her finger and toe nails smoothed and shaped, her skin examined minutely, and her hair washed, accompanied by a series of 'tsk tsk' noises. Apparently there were a lot of areas with room for improvement. She allowed the addition of clear nail polish and a hair rinse designed to soften and smooth her thick curls, but refused highlights, skin care treatments, and waxing. Caroline, in the next chair over, laughed at her naiveté and teased her about the reclusive life she would no longer be leading. Ginny found the interruption of her phone ringing an excellent excuse for not responding. It was Jim.

"May I take you to lunch?"

"Please! But you'll have to wait until I can escape this torture chamber."

He sounded instantly concerned. "What are you talking about?"

Ginny explained. "I'll meet you at my house in thirty minutes."

"Okay. See you there."

The beauty treatments were Caroline's gift to the bride and the two parted at the door, giving Ginny a chance to be gracious without having to admit to the headache the process had given her. She rolled down the windows in her car and drew in the (relatively) clean April air in an attempt to remove the poisons from her system. She regretted, for a moment, the loss of a honeymoon. A camping trip, heavy on the woods and water, would have suited her right about now.

It was just as well, though. She couldn't leave town with the murder still unsolved. She wouldn't have been able to leave it behind, even with Jim as a distraction.

* * *

Saturday Noon
Loch Lonach Homestead

Jim leaned against the door of his car and watched Ginny approach. She parked behind him, got out and came to him, a defiant look in her eye. He sniffed the air. "What am I smelling?"

"The female equivalent of bear bait."

Jim burst out laughing. "It doesn't smell that bad."

Ginny lifted an eyebrow. "Good thing, since we're stuck with it."

Jim was still laughing. "Come on. I have something I want to show you before we go eat."

He took her to the Loch and parked, then took her up a small hill covered in bluebonnets. He settled the two of them on the ground in the shade of an ancient oak and wrapped his arms around her.

"This is one of my favorite spots." He gazed out over the lake. From this position he could see almost a third of Loch Lonach as it swept north towards its source. The breeze lifted his hair and brushed away the early afternoon heat. It didn't get much better than this in spring in Texas. He smiled down at Ginny, thanking all the various gods of earth and heaven that tomorrow would see a wedding, not a funeral.

"You're frowning. Is it something I should know about?"

She stirred. "Am I? Sorry. It's Jamieson's murder. We still don't know who hired Dupree or what the motive was."

Jim's brows drew together. He was remembering Gordon's admonition, that what mattered to her should matter to both of them, but he wanted to put this behind them.

"You've told Tran everything, right?"

She nodded.

"So you can turn it over to the police and let them take it from here."

"Yes."

"But?"

She stirred in his arms. "It's like an itch that won't go away. I have this feeling I know something. That *tip-of-the-tongue* phenomenon. It's there, just out of reach." She shook her head. "Well, it will either come back to me, or it won't. In the meantime—"

She sat up, reached into a pocket, and handed him a small package wrapped in tissue paper and tied with a bow. "This is the bride's present to the groom."

Jim tore the paper off, his eyes widening. He stared at the carved figurine of a medieval knight, a miniature work of art in cast marble, and wondered if the Second Sight was contagious. "When did you get this?"

"Yesterday." She touched it with her fingertip. "It seemed appropriate. I know you had help, but without you and Reggie and the paint tags, I'd be dead. Eaten by the meth gators, or burned up in the wildfire. You rescued me." She smiled up at him. "You're my knight in shining armor, and always will be."

Jim blinked back a sudden dampness threatening his vision. He reached into the backpack he had brought with him, and handed her his gift.

She peeled back the wrapping, took out the heavily illustrated book of fairy tales, and caught her breath. "Oh, Jim!" She opened the cover and carefully turned the pages. "It's beautiful!" He saw her swallow. "When did you get this?"

"Yesterday. It's for you, to read to our children."

"Yesterday."

Their eyes met and he nodded.

"You are my fairy princess, rescued from the tower."

She started to laugh. "This is ridiculous."

He brushed her cheek with his hand. "No. It just proves you and I were made for each other. We were meant to be together."

She caught her breath. "That's what Charlie said."

"Well, he was right." He took her hand and lifted it to his lips, kissing the knuckles. "My lady."

She blinked rapidly, then the corner of her mouth twitched. "My lord."

Jim fell his heart swell. He drew his bride to him and kissed her. "Tell me you love me."

"I love you, Jim Mackenzie."

"And I you, soon-to-be Mrs. Mackenzie."

She laughed, leaning against him, then lifted her head and looked up at him. "I have a sudden craving for pizza."

"A craving? Already?"

She drew back and swatted his arm. "Not that kind of craving. I just want to do something normal. No fairy tales, no murder, just pizza."

"Okay," he said. They rose and headed for the car. "And after that we can track down Reggie and see about getting these paint tags removed. It seems indelicate to be wearing them on our wedding night."

Ginny pulled him to a stop, blushing.

"What is it, my love?"

"Well, it's just that everyone already knows where we'll be, and what we'll be doing tomorrow night, so it's not really a secret."

"True, my heart. And?"

"Well, you've heard the rhyme, 'Something old and something new, something borrowed, something blue?' It's superstition, I know, but it's supposed to ensure good luck in the marriage if a bride wears one of each on her wedding day."

Jim nodded. "I've heard of it."

"Well, it's just this. I'd like to keep my tag until after the wedding. It's something blue, and it has certainly brought me good luck." She looked at him anxiously. "If you don't mind?"

A smile spread across his face as he looked down at his bride. "I don't mind. You shall have your wish, but mine comes off. It turns out it catches a bit and I don't want anything distracting me tomorrow night. I have a duty to perform and a lady to please."

She dropped her eyes, her color rising, but her face serene. "Oh, I don't think you need to worry about that. If I remember the stories correctly, they all end with, 'And they lived happily ever after.'"

* * *

<h1 style="text-align:center">Chapter 47</h1>

Saturday Afternoon
Forbes Residence

After lunch, Ginny and Jim returned to her house to put up their feet and relax for a little while. Ginny went straight to her computer and printed out the matrix she had created for the investigation. She laid the pieces of paper out on the kitchen table and ticked off the elements with a colored marker.

"Means. Throwing the victim off a high place and hoping she will land badly. It almost worked."

"It did work," Mrs. Forbes pointed out.

"Not immediately," Jim said. "And it wouldn't be the method I would choose. There are cases on record of people whose parachutes didn't open who survived the impact."

"Ugh."

Ginny nodded. "Add to that the woman in black who didn't check Jamieson's pulse. How do we explain that?"

"She didn't know how?" Mrs. Forbes suggested.

Jim laughed. "Who hasn't seen someone pretend to check a pulse on TV?"

"Okay, something came up that prevented her," Mrs. Forbes said.

"She was interrupted?" Jim suggested.

"Not by a person." Ginny added a note to one of the boxes.

Jim reached for his coffee. "Explain yourself, woman!"

Ginny smiled at him. "Gary said she behaved as if she was out of breath. He saw her hanging onto a rail, and heard her groan."

"Did he?"

"Yes. So, here's a suggestion. Maybe she was feeling ill, really ill, the way you might if you'd had three helpings of tainted haggis."

Jim's brow furrowed. "It's still awfully early in the time line."

"She was seen eating haggis at around five-fifteen. The murder occurred around midnight. That's almost seven hours."

"Still early."

"But possible, right?"

Jim nodded. "Sure. Patients vary in their response to toxins and she had a lot of exposure."

"Okay, she goes down to see if her victim is dead and does two things that we know of. She takes something away with her and she tries to clean under Jamieson's nails."

The other two nodded.

"The skin under the nails we know about." Ginny slid a printout across the table to Jim. "Here is the DNA comparison."

Jim picked it up and examined it. "These two samples match. What does this prove?"

"The first thing it proves is that Dupree cheated. The DNA she sent the Dallas police was not hers."

Jim studied the printouts. "Did the New Orleans police send this?"

"No. Reggie did the analysis."

He looked over at her. "Alan had to give up the toothbrush. Where did you get a sample of Dupree's DNA?"

"Off my talisman." Ginny explained about her hunch and enlisting Reggie's help.

"More coffee?" Mrs. Forbes fetched the pot and Jim held out his cup.

Ginny refused a refill. "Look at what else Reggie found. There was a third DNA sample, other than mine and Dupree's, on that talisman. A man's. An ancestor, from the markers, presumably a Forbes."

"Wow!"

"We should be able to add it to the database and identify who else might have handled that talisman."

Jim smiled at her. "You should see your face right now!"

"As the family genealogist, this is pure gold!"

"We should have thought of doing that sooner," Sinia said.

"But wait! There's more!" Ginny grinned. She slid another sheet across the table at Jim. "Take a look at those blowups."

Jim squinted at the images, then took a red pen and put tick marks at several points on the report. "These *don't* match."

"Correct! The epigenetic markers are different."

Jim put the paper down on the table and looked at her. "Which means Costas and Dupree were twins. They shared identical DNA to start with."

Ginny nodded. "And still do, but their lives went in separate directions and the DNA methylation allows us to prove these are two women, not one."

"The what?" Mrs. Forbes looked baffled.

Jim explained. "Methylation refers to the addition of a methyl group to part of the DNA molecule, which prevents genes from being expressed. DNA controls *how* and *when* as well as *what* and epigenetics allows us to see how environment affects who we become."

"And the DNA that ended up under Jamieson's fingernails matches Dupree, right down to the last detail."

"So she was here and her Shreveport alibi is broken," Mrs. Forbes said.

Ginny smiled at her mother. "Yes."

"And you've told Detective Tran what you found?"

"I asked Reggie to do it, so she could quiz him on how and why he came to that conclusion."

Jim nodded. "Good thought. Okay. It was Dupree and she was suffering from salmonella poisoning, which is why she did a poor job of making sure her victim was actually dead. What did she take out of Jamieson's purse?"

Ginny added cream and sugar to her coffee. "I've been giving that quite a lot of thought and here's what I suspect. Dupree told me she was a professional, an assassin for hire."

Jim nodded and Mrs. Forbes shuddered.

"If I had to kill someone," Ginny continued, "and I was setting up an alibi that required I leave the area, in front of witnesses, I'd want to be able to locate my mark when I got back. I think it was a tracking device of some sort, and I think Dupree knew the police would recognize it when they went through Jamieson's belongings. So she took it back."

"Makes sense." Jim nodded. "Jamieson must have scratched her during the struggle. That's why she was trying to remove the DNA evidence, but she was too ill to do a good job of it."

"I'm surprised she even tried," Mrs. Forbes said. "If I understand you correctly, she had a twin who could establish a second alibi for her."

"Yes, but it wasn't perfect. The Dallas police excluded Costas, but could not exclude the evidence. It was a loose thread. A real pro would want that DNA gone before she left the scene. I expect, if we could ask her, Dupree would tell us she had some of the solvent Reggie uses to clean his equipment, all ready to wash away the trace evidence. What went wrong with her plan was the haggis."

Mrs. Forbes smiled. "Clever girl!"

"Me, or Dupree?"

"Both of you. Have you told Detective Tran?"

"I didn't need to. She'd already come up with that much on her own."

"That makes three clever girls." Mrs. Forbes' eyes twinkled at Jim. "You'd better watch your step, young man!"

"I intend to," Jim smiled.

"Do we tell Nessie she helped catch a cold-blooded killer?" Ginny asked.

"It would be a kindness," Mrs. Forbes added.

Jim shook his head. "I think not. We have to be able to trust the haggis."

Ginny snorted. "I may never touch the stuff again."

"Suits me," Jim smiled.

"Well, I would miss it," Mrs. Forbes said.

Ginny reached for another page of her notes. "Moving on. We've pretty much covered opportunity. Dupree was here. Her skin was found under Jamieson's fingernails. She must have hired someone to take her place on stage in Shreveport and the New Orleans police will be able to identify who that was. Her alibi is broken. What's more, we've located three witnesses who saw the woman in black, all of whom will testify that it wasn't Caroline. Gary knew Caroline well. The teenagers were confronted with her and agreed they must have seen someone else."

"Okay, that leaves motive," Jim said.

Ginny sighed. "Dupree was hired to kill Jamieson. She said as much. But I can't find anyone who would be willing to pay to have her killed. Not the Highland dance community. That official I talked to seemed sorry to lose an experienced judge. Nessie crossed the line in her attempt to manipulate the outcome of a competition and Douglas said feelings run high every single time, but no one suggested she should die for her sins." Ginny's brow furrowed.

"She left bad feelings everywhere she went. Those angry fathers all blamed her for their problems. But when I checked, they were all found guilty—in other courts—of the crimes that lost them their parental rights. Jamieson didn't hand down *those* convictions. Besides, those men had no money. How were they supposed to pay for an assassination?" She made a brushing motion with her hand.

"Caroline's motive is nonsense, of course. TI wouldn't knuckle under to bullying from an enraged Family Courts Law judge. They would have to see a civil lawsuit looming even to listen to the charges. And Caroline is a valuable asset. They would want to hold onto her if there was any way they could. Wally and the caber were nothing more than an accident." Ginny sighed.

"It's possible I missed someone, of course. A woman like that, who went out of her way to make enemies, might still have secrets."

"The important thing is you've cleared Caroline," Mrs. Forbes said. "You proved who did the actual killing, and that's what matters."

Ginny nodded. "You're right. I guess I shouldn't get greedy."

"Now you can turn your whole attention to the wedding. Do you realize you have fifty more thank you notes to write?"

"Oh, no!" Ginny sprang to her feet and ran into the dining room to discover her mother was not exaggerating. "So much for my nap."

Jim had followed her in. "Can I help?"

Ginny turned on him. "You'd better or we'll neither one of us make it to the banquet on time."

* * *

Ginny closed the door on Jim and climbed the stairs, heading for her bedroom. She knew she should be happy, but she was still fretting about the motive for Jamieson's murder. That little something in the back of her mind was driving her nuts.

She bathed and did her hair and makeup, trying not to think about failure. It would place a damper on the evening and might show. She would be cheerful, upbeat, positive. She had done her part and could close her files and put them away.

Ginny felt her mind snap. Close the file! That was it!

She ran into the office and looked up a number, then grabbed her phone.

"I need to speak to the laird, please."

"I'm sorry miss, but he's in Dallas for a wedding."

"Oh!" Of course. "Then may I have his cell phone number, please?"

"I don't know, miss. Can you tell me what this is about?"

"Would it help to tell you I'm the bride?"

"Oh!"

Ginny had no further trouble reaching Lachlan Russell. She asked her favor and had an answer before she finished dressing.

"Thank you!"

Ginny felt her heart soar. She had no proof, but she had the answer. More than one answer. She was bursting to tell someone, but refrained until she could get everyone together at the Cooperative Hall.

"What on earth has gotten into you?" her mother demanded.

"Just wait a few minutes more."

Ginny flew around the room, making excuses to the early arrivals and rounding up her investigation team. She gathered them in one of the anterooms.

"What's this about?" Jim asked.

"I know, I *think* I know, what happened."

"Weel, lass, tell us."

"Yes, sir." Ginny took a breath. "Jamieson had an offshore bank account. She made one payment, then she closed it, and the bank wouldn't tell us who the payment went to, but we do know the amount." Angus nodded.

"Jamieson also had a life insurance policy in an obscene amount, the beneficiary of which was the research foundation." This time, everyone nodded.

"I asked Lochlan Russell for help. His people were able to access Dupree's bank account. And I'm not supposed to tell anyone that happened, or how they managed it."

Jim lifted an eyebrow. "I think I know where this is headed."

Ginny nodded. "The amounts match and so does the timing. I think she paid for it herself."

There were gasps among the listeners and a protest from her mother. "Even if you're right about the money, why would anyone pay to have themselves murdered?"

"Two reasons. One, to escape what she knew was coming, a horrible and humiliating death. And two, to benefit the research foundation. There was a double indemnity clause."

"But," Caroline's face registered dismay, "to not know when a stranger would suddenly appear, and what form of death you would have to suffer! I can't even imagine it. If I were in her position, I'd ask someone I trusted to help me die peacefully, painlessly." She turned to Jim.

Jim shook his head. "Assisted suicide is illegal in Texas. She'd have trouble finding a physician willing to help her."

"What about other states?" Alan asked.

Jim shrugged. "It might be possible, but it would be hard."

"And it couldn't be done anonymously," Ginny added.

"Why care aboot th' secrecy?" Angus asked.

"Because," Jim answered, "the life insurance wouldn't

payout if you committed suicide."

Ginny nodded. "And they won't pay when they find out she contracted to have herself killed."

"Oh." Caroline took a step closer to Alan, who slipped an arm around her waist. "How sad!"

"And how futile!" Mrs. Forbes looked angry.

Ginny smiled and turned to Jim. "Not completely. Blair Jamieson has given me a way to solve one of my problems." She saw Jim's smile and knew they were reading each other's minds, again. "I'm going to turn that trust fund over to the Huntington Research Foundation."

He nodded. "Perfect."

"Wha' gied ye th' idea, lass?"

"About the murder?"

"Aye."

Ginny sighed. "I've had Huntington patients." She looked at Jim. "They don't come through the emergency room, but they do need nursing care, and counseling, lots of counseling. Jamieson was enrolled in support groups from the time of her initial diagnosis. She must have known decades worth of people caught in the same trap, all trying to make some sense out of it, to manage their fate in some small way. I think one of them must have suggested what Caroline did, euthanasia, probably pointing out that we're willing to put our pets out of their misery, but not our people." Ginny took a breath.

"I think, eventually, someone suggested an assassin, probably as a joke, and Jamieson saw the possibilities. You remember her physician said how determined she was to stay in control. Well, she found a way."

Jim's smile was as warm as human heart can make it. "And you've found a way to honor her wish and her memory."

Himself nodded. "'Tis a worthy cause. We'll see tae th' paperwork next week." He planted a kiss on Ginny's cheek.

"I'm proud o' ye, lass. And now, ye've other work tae do."

Ginny grinned at him, then dropped her eyelashes and a curtsey. "Aye, Mackenzie."

Jim stepped up and took possession of his bride, preparatory to leading her in to dinner. "Wish I could get her to do that."

"All in guid time, lad. All in guid time."

* * *

CHAPTER 48

Sunday, Beltane
Loch Lonach Homestead

Ginny stretched, then opened her eyes. Eight o'clock. She was supposed to be sleeping, resting for the big day, but it hadn't worked. She was too excited. This was her wedding day!

She sat up on the side of the bed, her bed. It was the last time she would sleep in that bed as a member of the household. After today, she would be a guest.

She was alone at the moment. Her mother had gone to divine service with everyone else, except Jim. Neither bride nor groom would attend the early service this Sunday. They would make their communion later, as man and wife.

Man and wife! Ginny bounced out of bed, threw on sweats and went down to find something to eat. There was a lot of food in the house and she helped herself. She wouldn't get another chance until the reception.

She looked over the timetable again as she ate. She needed to bathe before the dressers arrived, the crew of women who would do her hair and makeup and get her into her wedding gown and make sure everything was perfect.

She lingered over breakfast, indulging in a second cup of coffee, then made a tour of the house, feeling sentimental and nostalgic. But she wasn't allowed to brood for long. Caroline was early.

"Ginny!" Caroline threw herself into Ginny's arms. "It's done! It's over! Detective Tran says I'm free! Thanks to you!"

"Thanks be to God!"

"Him, too. And Alan. And Detective Tran, but mostly to you. I owe you one."

Ginny nodded. "I'll make a note. Come in."

Caroline had brought her Maid of Honor dress with her and the two girls hung it carefully on the bathroom door.

The rest of the support crew arrived in rapid succession, Mrs. Cameron exclaiming over the length of the sermon.

"Auch! And why he chose to go on at such length today of all days I cannot think, unless the size of the congregation went to his head!" She set her gear down and surveyed the premises. "We'll work in the den, I think. It's got good lighting."

For the next two hours, Ginny had no say in what happened to her. There were dozens of details to attend to, adjustments to be made, rituals to perform, and emergency runs to fetch forgotten tools. This included adding the hook and loop arrangement to the Dress Mackenzie tartan Jim would use during the ceremony.

Her hair took the longest. On this occasion, the braid started on top of her head, and was arranged in a crown, the remainder cascading down her back to mid-scapula. Once the hair was secured in place, the ornaments had to be applied. This was serious business because there would be no time for her to change between the wedding and the dancing. The heavy braid had to stay up throughout the demands of the evening, and the ornaments were not allowed to fly off and hit someone in the face.

Mrs. Cameron was keeping an eye on the clock. "One hour. Caroline, go put your dress on."

Caroline, too, had to have her hair pinned into place and make-up applied, then the finished product inspected. By the time that was done, it was time to put Ginny into her wedding gown.

The crew of seamstresses had done a masterful job. The gold satin shone with an elegant patina that did nothing to diminish the luster of Ginny's skin. The side zipper closed easily, allowing the princess lines to fall to the floor unobstructed. The train would stay in place until Caroline released it, taking it aside and handing it off to a designated helper waiting in the wings on the bride's side. The modest neckline provided a smooth backdrop for the moment when the tartan sash would mark Ginny's transformation from a Forbes to a Mackenzie.

"Shoes!" Caroline looked stricken.

"On the chair in my bedroom."

Caroline ran up to get them, then helped Ginny don the elegant little slippers she had chosen to wear in church. "You didn't want heels? Not even for today? Jim's going to tower over you."

"I'm not used to heels. I'd just fall off. And he already does, so it won't make any difference." Ginny smiled at her reflection in the mirror.

"Here, darling." Her mother came up behind her and fastened a string of pearls in place. "I wore those at my wedding. That's something borrowed. Once the Mackenzie brooch is in place, you'll be all set." Ginny had already had to confess why the paint tag was still on her back. The gown covered it, but her entourage had seen it when she took her robe off. Caroline, in particular, had approved. "I like to see a level-headed thinker like you go all mushy over some sentimental rubbish." Ginny had kept her mouth shut, but smiled to herself. Jim had promised to take a picture of her back before Reggie removed the tag.

The doorbell rang. "Time to go!" Mrs. Forbes called. She opened the door and admitted Angus.

When Ginny saw him, she almost forgot the occasion. He always looked distinguished, even in casual kilt and shirt, but today he was dressed to impress. His Prince Charlie jacket and vest were custom made, his kilt and plaide perfectly pressed and draped, his shoes gleamed. Every detail, from the top of his head to the bottom of his shoes proclaimed him Laird.

"Will I do, lass?" He smiled at her and Ginny was forced to remember her makeup.

"Dad would approve," she said, and gave him her hand.

It took three cars to get the whole group from the Forbes residence to the church. Caroline scouted the entrance, to make sure Jim was out of sight while they smuggled Ginny into the Bride's room. Then it was a waiting game.

Ginny's wedding attire did not include a watch. She found herself pacing, glancing at the clock on the wall every few minutes. What if something had gone wrong? What if Jim wasn't there? She'd heard of being left at the altar. It had happened. What if he'd changed his mind? What if he'd come to his senses, and realized she wasn't going to work out, that she wasn't what he thought she was? What if—? She lifted her head to catch the first faint notes. The bagpiper had started.

The first stage of the ceremony was four hundred years old. A lone piper stood on the steps of the church, and played a tune that was not a tune. Not a melody in the traditional sense. A call to the clan. It was pibroch, pipe music, consisting of a theme and variations. Each clan had at least one. Each clan also had a designated hillock, a high place, where the piper stood to play, calling the clan to come together. The Mackenzie's

Tulloch Ard, had started, and any stragglers were advised to get to their seats promptly.

It was happening. Ginny put her hand on her chest, struggling for breath, telling herself it was ridiculous to panic, that she wasn't the kind to give in to fear. She swayed, feeling weak in the knees, and dropped onto one of the velvet stools provided in the cushioned retreat, so she wouldn't fall over. Her ears were buzzing. Hypoxia. Not enough oxygen in her body. Not enough oxygen in the room. What if Jim hadn't come? What would she do then?

"Ginny." It was her mother, crouching before her, taking her hands, and holding them tightly. "Take a breath, then answer my question."

Ginny looked into her mother's face.

"Last chance. Do you want to marry Jim? To give up your freedom, and accept the responsibilities that go with him? Tell the truth."

Ginny almost laughed out loud. "Yes! I'm just afraid he's decided he doesn't want *me*."

Her mother relaxed. "No fear of that." She looked over at the other two women. Caroline was in her own mother's arms, looking very young and frightened. "You can relax now."

Ginny lifted an eyebrow at her best friend. "Your turn's coming."

Caroline smiled and nodded. "Soon, I hope."

There was a knock at the door. Sinia Forbes opened to Angus Mackenzie, and let him come in.

"Are ye ready, lass?"

Ginny nodded, then rose, glad to be able to lean on a strong arm as she made her way to the door, then through it, and into the vestibule.

They waited there, listening as the call ended, the sound fading into the distance. The piper entered, and Ginny saw it was a friend, someone she knew, and somehow that helped. He smiled at her, took his place in front of the wedding party, and waited for the signal.

"Here." Caroline handed her the bouquet, then bent to make sure the train was properly spread out behind her.

"Good luck, darling!" Her mother kissed her then allowed herself to be led to her place in the pews. The congregation rose.

The piper kicked in the drones, and launched into a cheerful rendition of *Highland Wedding*. Both doors were opened wide, and the procession began, the piper first, followed by Caroline, then Ginny on the Laird's arm.

As they passed row after row of honored guests, there was a sigh that followed them, a murmur of delight, and smiles everywhere she looked. Halfway up the aisle Jim suddenly came into focus. He was here, Alex at his side. He hadn't deserted her.

Once she had found him, Ginny couldn't take her eyes off him. If Angus had been impressive, Jim was gorgeous. He waited for her, his eyes on her, a smile on his lips, and it was all Ginny could do to remember her part.

"Dearly beloved—" The service had started.

"Who giveth this woman to be wedded to this man?"

"I do." Angus kissed her cheek, then retired to his seat.

Her hand was in Jim's, his voice in her ears, making promises.

"I do."

Her own voice, trembling. "I do."

Rings, those glorious gold bands she had seen three weeks earlier, on her hand and on his.

Jim, slipping the Mackenzie tartan over her head, and attaching it on her shoulder.

The two of them, kneeling before the altar, solemnizing their vows with the Eucharist.

The blessing, the adjurement. (Those whom God has joined together let no man put asunder.)

Jim raising her to her feet, then bending down to kiss her. Applause, then cheering, then the piper again, leading the newly wedded couple down the aisle to the tune of *Glendaurel Highlanders*, followed by Caroline and Alex, then Angus and Sinia, then all of the visiting lairds and their spouses, then all of the lesser lights of the assembled host.

As the piper emerged from the sanctuary, he was joined by the rest of the band, thirty strong, swelling the sound until it filled the street from end to end. They marched down the steps, turning in a practiced wheel, pausing to wait on the young Mackenzies. Jim lifted Ginny into the open carriage and helped her get settled, then sat down beside her, taking her hand in his. The driver signaled the horse, and they set off down the avenue, the carriage following the band, the guests following the carriage.

It was a two mile stretch from the church to the Cooperative Hall. The infirm drove, the healthy walked the route. And all along the way, both sides of the street were filled with those unable to get into the church to see the young laird married. They cheered and called blessings and celebrated. Indeed, it was clear they had been celebrating for quite some time already.

It took Ginny's breath away. If it hadn't been for the warmth of Jim's hand in hers, she might have thought the whole thing an illusion. But he was real. He was here, beside her, having promised, in front of a multitude the likes of which hadn't been seen in Loch Lonach for over a century, to love and cherish her.

Everyone was invited to the reception. The Loch Lonach Pipes and Drums ranged themselves along the walkway, still playing. The carriage rolled up to the doors, opened wide to admit the crowd, and Jim lifted her down. They entered to more cheers, this time from those who had missed the wedding to make sure the reception was ready. Angus was there before them. He stood on the stage and motioned for them to join him. It took less than ten minutes for the hall to fill to overflowing, each guest with a glass in his or her hand.

Angus raised his hands for silence, then stepped to the edge of the stage.

"Honored guests, clansmen, friends. Thank ye for joining us on this great day tae celebrate th' marriage o' my grandson to this daughter of Caledonia." He turned to face Jim and Ginny. "A long and healthy life tae ye, and may ye know th' blessing o' a happy home." He turned back to the crowd and lifted his glass. "Clansmen, I gi'e ye Dr. and Mrs. Angus James Mackenzie."

The rest of the evening was a blur to Ginny. There were hundreds of guests to greet, a snatched meal, then the Matrimonial Ball, at which she and Jim were required to lead off with a waltz.

The sets of dancers filled the room, everyone wanting to join in the festivities. Ginny found herself partnered with strangers who claimed a kiss, then passed her on to the next. Jim kept showing up and being denied permission to dance with his wife, he being a public possession for the evening.

As soon as the sun was down, the fireworks began. Ginny found herself swept outside, to the edge of the loch, to "ooo" and "aahh" with the rest, then back inside for more dancing.

As the night wore on and the older guests retired to their beds, Ginny took a moment to listen to the musicians, a fiddler and piper and bodhrán ensemble. They were among the best she'd ever heard, and she was wondering where Angus had found them when she felt an arm curve around her waist. Jim drew her to him, and bent down to be heard over the music.

"How are you holding up?"

Ginny leaned against him, admitting to herself that she was beginning to fade. "What time is it?"

"Does it matter? This party will go on all night."

"True." She looked up into her husband's face. "Shall we go?"

Jim nodded. "They're waiting for us."

"That's silly. We're only going to the other side of the lake."

"They want their fun, and who are we to deny them?"

Ginny smiled, and nodded. "All right. I'll collect my things, and meet you at the door."

She didn't have much, just lipstick and tissue in a hidden pocket in her gown, and her dancing shoes. No purse, no car, no coat. Not that she needed one. The night was mild and dry. Caroline had brought the train to the Hall and hung it on the coat rack. Ginny picked it up, threw it around her shoulders, and looked for Jim.

He was there, fishing his car keys out of his sporran.

"Okay, I'm ready." Ginny reached up and kissed him, for luck, then the two of them opened the door and stepped out.

"There they are! Hooray! Hip, hip hooray!"

They hurried toward the car, being pelted with a combination of rice and bird seed. Ginny endured it good-naturedly. It was going to take hours to brush it out of her hair, but, as Jim had said, who was she to spoil the fun? She waved as Jim took her away from the laughing crowd.

Neither of them spoke as Jim drove around the lake. Ginny had the window down, watching the houses slip past, listening to the night birds, and the slap of the water against the pier. It had been quite a day, but she—they—had gotten through it.

She hoped Angus was pleased. There would be out-of-town guests staying for several days. And more parties, though not like this one. Luckily, she and Jim were excused from attending, though she would probably make time for her brother and his family. Other than that, they would have a few precious days to themselves.

Jim drove up in front of the new house, parked the car, and got out. Ginny looked at him in surprise. "Aren't you going to use the garage?"

He opened her door, and shook his head. "Later. Maybe." He held out his hand and she put hers into it, allowing him to help her climb out of the car. Which help, if truth be told, she needed. A wedding dress *cum* ballgown, even shorn of its train, was still a handful.

A breeze ruffled the loose tendrils of hair at her temples, and she turned to face the loch, breathing in the night air. There were fireworks still going off over the water. Jim slipped his arm around her waist and stood watching them with her.

"Aren't they lovely!" she said.

"Not as lovely as you."

The house was three lots down from the corner, the streetlight far enough away that it didn't shine into their windows. His face was in shadow, but his voice was smiling.

Ginny leaned against him, wrapping her arms around his waist. "Are you happy, Jim?"

He drew her close. "Yes. Are you?"

"Yes."

He unwound her arms from his torso, and offered her his arm. "May I?"

She smiled. "Indeed you may, sir."

He escorted her up to the front door, then pulled out his keys, unlocked it, and pushed it open. Ginny started to go inside, thinking that a hot shower was going to feel mighty good tonight, but he caught her arm.

"Oh, no you don't!"

"What?"

"Have you forgotten?" He scooped her up, and carried her over the threshold, then set her down, closed the door behind them, and drew her into his arms. In darkness broken only by the fireworks shining through the front window, he kissed her.

"Welcome home, darling!"

THE END

GLOSSARY

Airsaid (pronounced "air-i-sayed") – full length wool, fleece or silk cloak that goes from the neck to the heels, fastened with a metal brooch at the breast, belted at the waist. Frequently white or a pale colored tartan with blue or red stripes.

Ain – own

Ane - one

Aye – yes

Bairn(s) – child / children

BFF – Best Friends Forever

Bonnie – handsome

Caber – tree trunk used in Scottish Heavy Athletics as a test of strength and accuracy

Canna – cannot

Ceilidh – party

Coo - cow

Dinna – did not / do not

Doesnae – does not

Eucharist – another name for Holy Communion

Ghillies – flexible, lace-up dancing shoes, akin to ballet slippers

Gied – gave

Gloaming – the time of day immediately following sunset

Guid – good

Hielan(d) – Highland, of or from the Highlands of Scotland

Jouk and let the jaw gae by – duck to avoid an oncoming wave

Ken – know

Kith and kin – friends and relatives

Mony - many

Nae – none

Nay – no

Nicht – night

No – not

Noo – now
Oot - out
Sae – so
Slàinte – ("slahn - shu") – Good health
Tae – to
Topo – topographic, a map that shows the surface features of a region, indicating their relative positions and elevations
Uisge-beatha – "water of life", aka "whisky"
Wee – small
Wee dram – an indeterminate amount of whisky

THE LOCH LONACH COLLECTION

The Loch Lonach Mysteries
- *The Arms of Death:* Loch Lonach Mysteries, Book One
- *The Swick and the Dead:* Loch Lonach Mysteries, Book Two
- *Viking Vengeance:* Loch Lonach Mysteries, Book Three
- *Final Fling*: Loch Lonach Mysteries, Book Four

Loch Lonach Short Stories
- *Dead Easy*
- *Duncan Died Dunkin'*
- *The Aviemore Cabin Boy*
- *Fifteen Minutes*
- *Out on a Limb*

Loch Lonach Histories
- *Loch Lonach, Its History and Inhabitants*

Award winning and addictive, every book is a five-star read!

To find out more about Ginny, Jim, and the Loch Lonach Mystery Series visit www.lochlonach.com

About the Author

MAGGIE FOSTER is a seventh-generation Texan of Scottish descent. In addition to being steeped in Scottish traditions and culture, she has spent a lifetime in healthcare as a nurse, lawyer, educator, and redhead. Her interests include history, genealogy, music, dancing, travel, dark chocolate, good whisky, and men in kilts, not necessarily in that order.

You can contact her at:
maggiesmysteries@gmail.com or
Maggie@maggiesmysteries.com

Website – www.lochlonach.com
GoodReads – www.goodreads.com/maggiefoster
Facebook – www.facebook.com/lochlonach/
Twitter – www.Twitter.com/maggiefoster55
Instagram – www.instagram.com/scottishsleuthsofdallas/
LinkedIn – www.linkedin.com/in/maggie-foster-lochlonach

Six Virtual Ways to
Support Your
Favorite Author

Buy their books
Write reviews
Recommend on Goodreads
Request at your library
Post pictures holding their books
Sign up for the e-mail list